i

S T U N G

A Techno-Thriller

by

Cullen Scott

STUNG: A Techno-Thriller

Cullen Scott

Paperback ISBN: 978-1-915221-13-1
e-Book ISBN: 978-1-915221-14-8

Papillon du Père Publishing

Dedication

This book is brought to you by my wife, Nancy. I had always wanted to write a book—until I started writing one. Without Nancy staying up late at night with me, listening to me read a chapter for the fourth time, and simply telling me I can't quit, this exercise would have been short lived. Day in and day out, Nancy keeps my life happily motoring along.

Also, special thanks to my sons, Joshua and Tyler, for being such wonderful young men and letting me borrow from their days growing up in a small town.

Finally, let me share my deep gratitude for Brad Kava and Jeanne Howard, who signed on to edit Stung and then delivered so much more. I especially appreciate their relentless efforts to kill off my bad ideas and to keep the story moving forward.

Contents

Chapter One

Shadow

April 17, 2047 - 2:54 a.m.

It felt wrong … the roof access door sat wide open, a clear invitation to enter.

Shadow's night-vision glasses barely illuminated the concrete staircase. He descended cautiously, straining to make out each step. He stopped when he reached the landing and a plain metal door labeled "4th Floor." He leaned over the metal rail, trying to peer into the shadows that devoured the flights below. Assuming the alarm had already been triggered, he had ten minutes to be in and out.

Yet he hesitated. He did not trust easily.

With precious seconds ticking away, he forced himself to continue downward, suspiciously eyeing every dark recess and corner on his way down. Desperately wanting out of the pitch-black stairwell, he fought back his anxiety and approached the industrial-looking door. Pulling the handle to peek inside, he was greeted by flashing red lights lining the hallway ceilings, blaring his presence.

He had to stop his trembling hands from slamming the door closed as he struggled with the thought of entering the heart of the government program from which he fled years ago. The handler who encouraged him to take on this assignment had received assurances Shadow's chip was off limits, and that he couldn't be identified. Shadow wished he'd had more time to check out the source because the cost of being identified would be paid with death. All Shadow knew was that the assurances had come from a government employee immersed in a government program—a thought that left him grabbing the doorframe to steady his fraying nerves.

Not wanting to let his handler down, he gathered his strength and slid through the doorway. The pulsing lights forced him to remove his night-vision glasses. No harm. He stalked down the hallway, squinting through his stretched black head covering, matching doorways and signs to the descriptions he'd been given. He peered around the corner at the end of the hall, only to find another windowless corridor with pulsing lights trailing off into the distance. Easing into the passageway, he reminded himself he only needed to make it as far as the third door on the left.

Every footfall echoed off the tile floor until fading into the dark depths left untouched by the flashing lights. He could feel the hair on the back of his neck rise as his senses waited for some answering sound. He shook his head to clear the nonsense and continued forward.

The first door he passed had no window or sign. Most likely a janitors' closet or an equipment room. The next door was marked with what appeared to be a showerhead. Despite the jitters—or perhaps because of them—he chuckled to himself, suppressing the urge to sidetrack the mission to indulge in the luxury within. He hadn't taken a shower in years. A plunge into a lake or stream was the best he had managed. The thought of the freezing waters in which he bathed gave him chills and returned his focus to the equally chilling gloom ahead. One more door.

A few cautious steps had him passing a large interior window. Had he been told about the window? He vaguely recalled he had. Catching a glimpse of metal tech benches and scattered chairs, he knew this was the right room. Using each flash of light, he scanned the nearby table until his eyes locked on the prize. This was easy.

Too easy?

Maybe. He had never had inside help before.

Shadow continued past the long window to the adjacent door. Pulling on the handle, the unlocked door yielded.

Way too easy!

With a bad feeling riding him, he quickly walked to the nearest bench, grabbed the only object resting there, and rushed back to the hallway.

He pushed into the corridor, only to be jolted by a blast of sirens. His head swiveled up and down the hall, anticipating threats materializing from places he could not see, which were everywhere, allowing the terror to amplify in his mind.

He dashed for the exit, realizing the object now tucked away in his black fatigues had sent out a warning. Not good. It meant the chip readers were active, bringing doubts about the safety of his ID.

He ran down the passageways, pushing caution aside, fearing the building could be locked down at any moment, his ID might be captured, and security was likely closing in. Reaching the stairway entry, he gave the door a big shove and to his relief—and alarm—it banged open. No longer able to contain his goblins, he scrambled up the unlit stairway, relying on his lean, agile body to compensate for the treacherous footing on the darkened stairs. Reaching the last flight, he bounded up three steps at a time until he crashed through the roof access and out into the starlit night. His heart fluttered as two silhouettes heaved themselves up and over the lip of the roof, not more than twenty yards away.

Adrenaline surged through his body as he shot off in the opposite direction. Bounding over vent pipes and skylights, he dashed madly to the end of the roof, his breathing ragged, hardly slowing as he flung himself over the edge, reaching out with both hands to snag the zip line harness. The zip line's pulley released, launching him forward along the metal cable. Pulling himself up with one arm to secure his other hand, he followed the sight line of his descent, only to see disaster parked at the end.

A dark SUV was parked right below the cable.

He heard a shout from behind. "Jake! It's Shadow! Coming your way!"

Shadow was halfway down the glide path and picking up speed. His mind flashed between dropping before the vehicle or trying to clear it. Indecision left him raising his legs in front of him, desperately seeking separation from the fast-approaching rooftop. His feet cleared, but his butt slapped down hard, skipping him forward over the other side of the SUV and past a figure diving out of the way. Shadow tumbled across the ground before making it to his feet. He then hobbled forward and around an expansive redwood tree, where he located his mountain bike. He wrenched it up off the ground and hopped on in one motion.

Shadow's only hope was to reach the shelter of the nearby forested mountains.

Heading into an open field, Shadow glanced over his shoulder to see the officer he had buzzed racing back to his SUV.

Unable to locate a path across the field, even though he had staked it out earlier, he trudged forward through the soft soil that had been tilled up by an army of gophers and moles. It didn't take long before a swarm of lights entered the playing field all around him, each vehicle racing to cut him off from his maddeningly slow grind toward the trees.

This was not how he imagined spending his nineteenth birthday.

He briefly wondered what would happen if the chase didn't go his way, then quickly batted the thought aside, realizing that anyone with the nickname Shadow who had just broken into the high-security data center at UC Santa Cruz had nothing to gain by asking himself that question.

Focus!

He was standing up, thrusting hard against his pedals, shifting his weight side to side. Craning his neck, he picked out multiple sets of lights, all moving much faster than he was. He managed to slip on his night-vision glasses while churning forward. He made out the worn earth off to his left and slightly altered course to merge with the trail. He surveyed his pursuers again. They were closing fast, but having made the trail, his lead was good.

Shadow knew his mere existence had to jeopardize the officers' careers. His activities had gone unchecked under their watch, and he was about to pull off another escape for the ages. The best opportunity left to them was to take a shot.

It was also their best way to die. No one would take that chance.

With immense redwoods rising up to engulf him, the chase was coming to a swift end. He hopped his bike over a log and hit the trail leading into the murky forest.

Shadow smiled to himself when the lights ground to a halt behind him. Then to his amazement, a single headlight continued forward. Judging by the lack of sound, it had to be an electric motorcycle. OK—motorbike versus mountain bike. Game on.

He flipped down the night-vision lenses and hunted for an alternate path. The trail's lack of technical difficulty played into the motorcycle's ability to outpace him. And he had an idea of who was on that bike. Relentless.

The path began winding up the hill, with the incline slowing his advance and the tight turns working against his pursuer. Frustratingly, with every turn, he could tell his adversary was doing an excellent job navigating the terrain. The encroaching headlight was soon splashing the trail and bordering shrubs with light, threatening to knock out his vision with blinding fireworks displays.

The search for side trails was nearly impossible without visibility. Panic crept back in. What did he have? Four, maybe five, turns before he fell prey? But after a few turns up the hill, Shadow realized the hunter had begun to track him without closing in. This brought no joy. What was the point? Was the rider playing with him?

Fueled by thoughts of surrender and his lungs heaving, rage drove him forward. The trail was now bathed completely in light, searing his eyes and adding pain to his hopeless search. Rounding what he accepted was his last turn, he took a chance. Glimpsing an opening off to his right, he crashed through a slight break in the tangled branches and shrubs. He spilled out onto a deer trail that skirted the side of the hill he had been so futilely climbing. Even better, the narrow trail offered limbs to clear and bushes to navigate, swinging the technical difficulty in his favor.

Shadow pushed on with the last of his energy seeping away. Soon he hit the edge of a familiar ravine and followed it downhill until he found a felled redwood tree that spanned the waters below.

He vaulted his bike over the knots and through branches that clawed at his clothing until he was deposited on the other side. He slowed his pace upon re-entering the trees. Looking back to make sure he was right, he was soon rewarded when he saw the solitary light stop its advance. He was thrilled to have escaped, but confused over what had taken place. Then through the blinding beam, he thought he made out a raised hand in what looked like a half-hearted wave.

Resuming his journey up the Santa Cruz Mountains, Shadow reflected on the irony of the pursuit. In the eyes of the Chip Integration Division—the CID, now the most powerful department in the government—this heist or any other criminal activity would never compare to the atrocity he committed almost three years ago. His choice to live with fugitives and forego a life within the network could never be forgiven by the CID.

Or by society in general.

Chapter Two

Talon

April 17 – 3:17 p.m.

Talon decided to walk home from school, giving him thirty minutes to clear his head. He was tempted to count the concrete squares that passed underneath as he made his way along the sidewalk that bordered Ridge Crest Drive. Counting could be soothing for Talon, but not today. He looked over his shoulder, certain some form of trouble was headed his way. It always was.

He returned his sights to the walk before him, where a relatively quiet, two-lane road snaked its way through redwood-forested hills. Looking at the beauty before him, he reminded himself that life was not all bad as he began his process of overcoming anxieties; he would start with the adversity he could face and lead himself to the fears he dared not look upon.

School he could handle. He didn't enjoy much about being a sophomore in high school. He could do without the taunts and occasional punches thrown to remind him he didn't belong. He knew he didn't fit in. He was tall, gangly, with 'old man' bushy eyebrows. He'd had them since he could remember, and the demeanor to match. Perhaps as a result of the blows life had dealt him, he was overly analytical with a tendency to put caution into every move he made. This approach came off as awkward, which combined with his unusual features, made him easy entertainment for his peers.

Still, he reasoned that school would be over soon. His sophomore year was coming to a close—just a few months— and then it was on to his senior year. He would not be one of the few that returned for a fourth. Those few, called Super Seniors, were made up of students who legitimately couldn't get through the curriculum in three years and the jocks that sought one more year of athletic glory. He was grateful not to fall into either category.

As he approached the single-lane road that transitioned into oak-lined corridors leading back into his neighborhood, thoughts of his programming day seeped into his mind. This was a special day for most. It had come to signal passage into adulthood, with adult privileges and responsibilities that came with being connected to the government network. The privileges tempted Talon, sure—he was human. The responsibilities were a different matter. It wasn't that he didn't understand that growing up meant more obligations and sacrifices. The problem for his analytical mind was that the sacrifices were too great.

His thinking led to the monster that stood outside his door. Three years ago, his brother wrestled with the same anxieties. Deciding not to be networked, Wilder headed for the depths of the surrounding mountains, where it ended badly. Talon was supposed to be able to acknowledge this. That Wilder starved to death. Starving was one of the many self-inflicted consequences awaiting those that fled. Through many counseling sessions, Talon came to understand Wilder had made bad choices. The problem was, with Talon's 'special day' drawing near, he couldn't guarantee to himself he would choose differently.

These morbid thoughts trailed him all the way to his driveway, where he stopped and stared up at the large two-story brick house. He peered through the foliage of the ancient oaks that gave life to their virtual lawns and gardens, trying to catch a glimpse of any life inside. He knew his dad had finished up his police work early and would be waiting within. His sister, too. She would have rushed home from classes at UC Santa Cruz for what she called family night. Well, what was left of their family. His mom had passed when he was four from a hard-fought battle with cancer. With Wilder gone too, 'family' felt like an exaggeration. His sister felt differently, insisting they had more reason than ever to hang together. It was them against a hostile world.

Talon plodded up the driveway, then veered off to the left onto the springy, porous material that projected the green glow of grass onto his similarly colored shoes. He crossed in front of the living room window. His view through the window was computer generated, designed to block out any prying eyes. The scene was quite life-like, capturing in detail what lay beyond with one big exception—the depicted setting was from a time as far back as he could remember, not refreshed since his mom had passed.

Knowing anyone from within could still see out, Talon scampered past the window and up the porch steps. Looking at the dark-cherry door standing before him, he gathered himself, then commanded the door to open. It slowly swung inward, exposing the vacant foyer. Talon stood in the doorway until he picked up the back and forth of pleading voices desperately crying out for understanding. The conversation drifted to him from the living room, where he could make out his sister saying, "Dad, that's why I moved back home. I want to be here for you. For my family. You need to talk to me."

Sage's words brought a lump to Talon's throat. She had given up so much for her family. At the age of nine, with their mom's death, Sage grew up in mere hours. She not only played a major part in raising Wilder and Talon, but almost single-handedly pulled their father out of his funk, continually reminding him she couldn't run the family alone. By the time Talon reached thirteen, he was fairly self-sufficient and Sage, five years older, was ready to fly. She practically ripped the hinges off their front door as she bolted for the campus life. Then Wilder disappeared and Sage's freshman year abruptly ended, with her returning home to once again piece together what was left of the family.

Talon only wished he could be as strong as Sage, but he wasn't.

He knew he wanted nothing to do with their conversation. He eyed the kitchen entry directly in front of him, tempted by the prospect of food, but the sure escape was up the stairs to the left, where the sanctuary of his bedroom lay. He crossed the foyer and slowly climbed the steps, ears straining for any tell of detection. Halfway up his ascent, he jumped at the sound of his father's deep voice, only to realize his dad was finally answering Sage, "I'm sorry. You know I have a hard time talking about Shadow."

That name! Talon stopped mid-step, as his father continued. "He reminds me too much of Wilder. Might even be the same age."

Talon absorbed the sting of these last words, striving to concentrate on what had caught his interest. Any mention of Shadow was big news to Talon and his friends. Shadow was legendary. His mere existence went against everything their small community of almost nine thousand had come to expect.

The town's official name was Ridge Crest, but most high schoolers, and even some parents, called it Cop's Rest. Crime was nearly nonexistent in their tight-knit community. It wasn't uncommon for garage doors to be left open all night. Cars, bikes, and scooters would still be there in the morning. If something did go amiss, a call to the station would bring a swarm of officers in less than five minutes. Even a lost dog or an unmanned school crossing could warrant help from the local police.

The one anomaly was Shadow. He had made his presence known a few years back when he successfully robbed the local grocery store, Shopper's Corner. Someone stole a cartload of groceries without their chip registering. The thief was in and out in less than two minutes. This astonishing act was followed by the theft of a top-of-the-line Santa Cruz mountain bike, camping gear from Outdoor World, and, audaciously, more food from Shopper's Corner.

The police were embarrassed and angry. They took pride in tracking down any criminal dumb enough to try their luck in Ridge Crest. The small town was bisected by the mountain highway that connected Silicon Valley to the Pacific Ocean at Santa Cruz. From time to time, transients would jump off the highway, make a heist, and race off, certain they had made a clean getaway. They were dead wrong.

Smart and getting a kick out of solving crimes, Ridge Crest's officers worked relentlessly with neighboring police forces and departments throughout the state to hunt down suspects. Very few got away. The news of the officers' feats spread, and criminals largely learned to steer clear of the mountain town.

Shadow's exploits, though, were making a mockery of Ridge Crest CID's cherished reputation. His jobs were well thought out, with escape routes known to be his strength. The police had been lucky enough to track him to the woods outside of town a few times, only to have him vanish. Which was why Talon's dad started calling him Shadow, and the name stuck.

The descriptions of Shadow were vague, with his height ranging 5'6' to well over 6', his weight falling anywhere between 150 and 250 pounds. Witnesses generally agreed Shadow was male. Everything else about him was well guarded: his head and face were always covered, and he either went to great lengths to avoid chip readers or his chip had not been connected to the network.

Shadow soon expanded his craft to neighboring towns. He even started going after high-risk targets. If there was a careless guard or a vent that led where he wanted to go, Shadow was destined to pull off another daring caper.

Most of his exploits were swept under the rug. Until he broke into the Santa Cruz CID and lifted a pair of night-vision glasses. Burglarizing the Santa Cruz CID, the larger police department located in the town next to Ridge Crest, was too much to be covered up. Shadow's actions demanded attention—attention from Drake Russit.

Most teens questioned everything about their parents, and Talon was no different, but he had never questioned his dad's intelligence. Drake Russit was the person everyone sought when cases got tough.

So, naturally, Ridge Crest CID assigned Drake to work across the county and throughout the state to silence this menace. The CID was done playing nice: Drake would capture this clown.

Except, more than six months had passed since Drake had taken over and Shadow was still out there.

Talon's attention drifted back, hearing his father trying to come to grips with his demons. "We had him. My team was *on campus* when a mysterious figure was reported sleuthing around the university. We knew it was Shadow and my team was prepared. Everything went according to plan, too, until I was faced with the reality of catching him. Then I just couldn't. We suspect he's not networked ..." He trailed off before finally adding, "Sage, I might not be the best person for this job."

This admission left Talon feeling sad. He raced upstairs, fully aware of the torture his father was reliving. When his brother disappeared, his dad had nearly destroyed himself. He had initially woken up every day certain he would find Wilder by nightfall. Runaways always had limited options: without a chip or authorization from a guardian, purchasing food, clothing, or other supplies became virtually impossible. Wilder had to surface. With days slipping into weeks and even months, Drake redoubled his efforts, siphoning off time from eating and sleeping.

Then eighteen months ago, a photo was left on their front porch, with a letter of regret. Talon found his sister kneeling outside the front door, shaking and crying. Talon turned fifteen before his dad let him see that picture. He wished he never had. With every bone on display, there was no mistaking the fact that Wilder had starved to death.

And now the pursuit of Shadow was digging up Wilder's grave. The comparisons between the two were unavoidable. Talon's father was most certainly trapped, forced to continually ask himself the same question: had Wilder lived, would his life have been any different from that of the fugitive he was now chasing?

His dad was definitely not the one for the job.

Chapter Three

Sofia

April 17 - 3:55 p.m.

"**D**ad, aren't there laws against holding your daughter captive?" Sofia sat alone in the Mini-transport. "One would think you'd worry about such things as head of the CID."

Gabriel Abreo's baritone voice flooded into her space. "Darling, when did visiting your dear old dad at work become such a hardship?"

Sofia cringed, hardly thrilled at heading to the Ridge Crest station, where she would be dropped off in a matter of minutes if she couldn't make an escape. She pushed on the door release panel one more time, confirming she was still trapped.

"You know, Dad, in three months I'll turn sixteen. Isn't it time you let me get networked? Then I could get my own rides, maybe even get a job after school, or choose to skip softball practice and hang out at the beach." That was exactly where she was headed when she was intercepted. Sofia and her best friend, Arissa, had decided an eighty-degree day in late April was too hot for playing ball and had talked Arissa's mom into authorizing a Mini to take them to the Boardwalk, where they planned to meet up with some classmates— mostly boys. Plans had gone wrong when Arissa's mom checked with Sofia's parents to make sure they were on board. They were not. The girls' ride was met by a second Mini at the edge of town. Embarrassingly, the voice of Arissa's mother had erupted over the sound system, instructing Sofia to get out.

Sofia was left seething by the side of the road, watching her friend's ride merge onto the freeway, headed toward the beach. She deliberated over the vehicle sitting patiently before her, with its single gull-wing door retracted over its roof.

The driverless car reminded her of those horse-drawn buggies she had seen in history class. The seats faced each other from opposite sides of the otherwise empty cabin. Passengers didn't need to worry about the road. The vehicle was fully equipped to handle the driving.

Defiance burned through Sofia. She turned from the vehicle and marched toward town, only to hear her ride slowly rolling behind her. She spun back toward the vehicle. It stopped. Holding her hand up to signal the car to stay put, she slowly backed away from the Mini. The Mini crept forward. Sofia shot off like the sprinter that she was. The vehicle easily kept pace, making it clear she was also an idiot. Sofia stopped and hung her head. The idea of being trailed the whole way into town was too embarrassing. Angry and defeated, she allowed herself to be imprisoned in the vehicle.

"Sofie? Did you hear me?" asked her dad. "That's exactly what I want to talk about—your independence. Mom is going to meet us for an early dinner, and we'll discuss the responsibilities that go with programming."

Sofia held back a groan. She regularly endured talks about the stark realities of programming. She was repeatedly warned that defending one's home or even life would no longer be possible. This responsibility would be surrendered to the Program. If she took a life, even in self-defense, she would be exterminated.

Sofia didn't buy into her father's disturbing warnings. She had grown up with the Program. She trusted it. She certainly wasn't planning to defend her home with the help of a gun anytime soon. Who even owned a gun? Did her dad? She knew about guns, but they were part of history, like the buggies.

Sofia loved her father, but she wanted to live in today's world. She was excited to expand her universe and, above all else, to attain the perks of her upper-classmates. Any concerns about the Program were washed away by thoughts of popping into a virtual reality center or catching an air transport to San Francisco.

"Before your stunt today," Sofia's father continued, "we were planning to let you participate in the May programming clinic. Now you need to convince us that we *shouldn't* wait."

Oh, hell no! Sofia knew what her dad was threatening. While everyone was all but mandated to be networked before their sixteenth birthday, her birthday was several months off. Clinics were held every couple of weeks, giving her father the option of pushing her glorious day well into July.

That was *not* going to happen.

With a lifetime of experience negotiating with her dad, Sofia was already mentally reciting her merits: straight-A student, starting pitcher on the varsity softball team, and participant in countless school charity drives. She was more than his blue-eyed little girl. Was her father ready for her? Sofia smiled to herself, knowing he had no chance.

Chapter Four

Drake

April 18 - 10:11 a.m.

Drake knocked on his boss's open door and walked in. Gabriel was lost in thought, gazing out the window at the parking lot. He picked up on Gabriel's reflection, realizing that the dimmer image of him in the glass accurately captured his diminished presence. Tall, lean, and muscular, Gabriel had once been larger than life. The red-laced blue eyes, accompanied by a few days of beard growth, heralded the arrival of a new persona.

Gabriel and Drake, while respecting one another's positions, had always been good friends. Hell, they had been in the same department for almost ten years. Their children had even gone to the same schools and were currently tenth graders together.

Studying Gabriel's worried expression, Drake had a good idea of why he had been called into the office, but he decided to tackle that later. "How did your talk go with Sofia last night?" he began.

Gabriel spun around, sizing up Drake before forcing a smile. "Sorry, I'm a bit preoccupied. Sofie's great. As you probably guessed, she's still doing the May clinic. Her mother keeps telling me to stop issuing idle threats if I plan to cave every time. For the record, I never plan to cave," he added with a genuine smile. "How about you? Have you had second thoughts about Talon doing the clinic?"

Drake knew the minute Gabriel asked the question, he regretted it. After Wilder's death, Drake questioned everything about the Program.

The Program got its start when Neuro-Activated Chips (NACs) were invented nearly twenty-five years ago, making a nearly seamless integration of human thought and machine processing. The breakthrough came at a time when fear and unrest dominated every waking hour for most Americans. An extremely divisive president had come into office proclaiming he could fix all the world's problems. Unfortunately, his definition of problems was women, minorities, immigrants, and members of most religions.

Yet, it took less than a year for the president's hate to reverberate throughout the U.S. and outward to the rest of the world. Ceaseless domestic and foreign terrorism became the new reality. A day rarely passed without a massacre carried out in the name of religion, nationalism, or simply hate. Then in an ironic twist, one well-placed bomb wiped out half the House of Representatives—and the visiting president.

The vice president survived and sent out a plea for the nation to alter its course before the world ripped itself apart. Along with this call for self-reflection, the new president humbly solicited ideas from all corners of the Earth to help build a new path forward. Naya Jordan, a brilliant neuro-engineer pursuing her Ph.D. at Stanford University, heard the request and felt uniquely positioned to answer the president's call to action.

In an odd turn of fate, Naya had been stung by a bee while sitting next to a swimming pool. She watched its life drain away, feeling vindicated for the pain the bee had inflicted—when an idea hit her. Why not create a stinger—an NAC—that would be triggered if its host killed someone? If properly engineered and located, the NAC could self-destruct, taking its host with it. Naya was convinced this would be a great deterrent to terrorism and murder.

The idea crawled its way through the many layers of government, initially condemned at every level. The president vigorously rejected the idea as well. The development of the technology would require human testing that no sane society would embrace. Despite this, within two years, Naya and the

NSA had what they believed was a working system, and a solution to the thorny issue of human testing was proposed: immigrants.

By 2024, the U.S. had completely shut down immigration. Most people feared anyone that didn't talk and walk like themselves, which was everybody else. Strangely enough, the U.S. was still sought after by many people in foreign lands. Perhaps, as some claimed, this was because the U.S. had effectively spread fear and hate throughout the rest of the world, making one country no better than the rest when it came to persecution.

With the pent-up demand to enter the U.S., the NSA convinced Congress and the president to allow ten thousand immigrants into the country under the condition that they have chips inserted at the base of their skulls. With this ethical hurdle out of the way, the Program, codenamed Bee Sting, was launched.

Two years passed before a member of this new immigrant population was the first victim of bee-sting justice. The killer's chip had exploded as designed, destroying the portion of the medulla oblongata regulating the heart and lungs.

The Program then picked up momentum as U.S. citizens began requesting chip insertions, forming exclusive enclaves in rural parts of Nevada and Arizona. If you were not networked, you were not welcome.

Shortly after, the Program went mainstream. Requests to participate in the Bee Sting Program poured in from all over the U.S., as people recognized that they could get a job and be welcome almost anywhere if they could prove they were networked.

Twenty years later, the Program was pervasive. "Bee Sting," the unofficial name for the government-branded Life Protection System, echoed across the world.

Chip insertion and programming had become routine. Chips were typically embedded within twenty-four hours of birth, with programming delayed until the age of fifteen but completed before age sixteen. The Program was widely recognized as an unparalleled success, having reduced murders by more than ninety-five percent.

Drake was an anomaly in the law enforcement community, refusing to shout the Program's praises from the highest mountaintop. He knew the Program had some glaring side effects, some proving nastier than others. Wilder's death was the nastiest. And it stemmed from his decision to live off network.

When the Bee Sting Program started to gain acceptance across the globe, those choosing to be networked woke up to an even more threatening world. They were left feeling defenseless against people living off network. Disconnects, as those off network became known, were left to play by a different set of rules: killing was not a fatal act for them. Alarmed by this realization, the call to ostracize disconnects went out ... and was well received.

Those who were networked turned on those who were not, forcing their conversions and allowing the Program to spread across the world like a zombie plague. In the end, chip readers were installed to protect against the remaining few nonconformists. Whether it was work, transportation, or grocery shopping, everyone was funneled through portals, ensuring all were networked.

While society still pretended that everyone exercised free will in deciding whether to be networked, in the U.S. disconnects had two choices: join what amounted to a government labor camp, or run like hell in an effort to stay one step ahead of the CID.

The Chip Integration Division was the largest enforcement agency in the United States and had become such an integral part of keeping the peace that it had taken over most local policing agencies.

When their police department became Ridge Crest CID, Drake refused to acknowledge the name, still dismayed that his department's years of passive resistance had finally collapsed, allowing their tiny outpost to be absorbed. Drake placed the blame for that collapse on Gabriel and Jesse Taylor, a fellow detective. Gabriel's desire to be part of a bigger organization, with greater resources and possibly more lucrative management salaries, was somewhat understandable. Jesse's near-religious effort to bring co-workers into the glorious light of the Program was not.

Drake wasn't blind to the calm the Program had brought to the world, but he was disenchanted by the ruthless nature in which that calm was enforced, especially when it cost him his son. Thinking of Wilder reminded him of why he was standing in his boss's office.

"Gabriel, we should probably talk about why you called me in here."

Gabriel, visibly uncomfortable, cleared his throat. "I'm not going to dance around. People throughout the community, including our very own department, are questioning how Shadow is still free. Some are even spreading crazy theories about a half-assed pursuit the other night." He paused, offering Drake a chance to protest. Drake merely crossed his arms, patiently waiting for some point to be made. Gabriel let out a sigh and continued, "Look, I'm doing my best to have your back, but any further failure is going to force me to shake up your team, including its leadership. Understood?"

Drake knew the response Gabriel expected. He wanted Drake to confirm he would move heaven and earth to get the job done. He hated to disappoint his boss and good friend, but he was not willing to lie. "Loud and clear, boss," he replied before slipping out the office door.

Chapter Five

General Stafford

April 18 - 10:30 a.m.

The window extended the length of the fourth-floor conference room. The view was expansive, taking in the rolling hills and quaint city below before giving way to the sandy shoreline and unending blue ocean waters. The general sat in the conference room, wondering how anyone could possibly be productive here. It had been a long overnight trip from D.C. to Santa Cruz. He was exhausted and wondered if he was getting too old for the pace of his work. The view that lay before him was tempting. Someday soon he needed to be satisfied with what he had done for his country and find a place to be an ordinary citizen and soak in the world around him.

Bringing his attention back to the person sitting across from him at the table, he knew today was not that day. Dr. Naya Jordan, now in her early fifties, adjusted her black wire-rimmed glasses and fiddled with the collar on her buttoned-up white shirt. She seemed full of nervous energy for a woman so run down.

And make no mistake, Dr. Jordan looked tremendously worn, as if she had lived the general's sixty-two years and had been the one to catch last night's red-eye. She appeared sickly thin with hunched shoulders, unkempt gray hair, and puffy brown eyes.

The contrast with the youthful doctor he had come to know over twenty years ago was unnerving. The young doctor had radiated enthusiasm and practically flaunted her unwavering conviction that she would save the world. The general, or a colonel as he was at the time, attended one meeting in which the doctor laid out her plans for launching her NAC-based Program and he was sold.

He remembered pushing hard to gain oversight of efforts to recruit and chip immigrants. He would have chipped the entire armed forces if his superiors had let him. He knew a good idea when he heard one and he could tell Dr. Jordan was just getting started.

Having spent the next twenty years nudging the doctor's visions toward reality, he had been granted a first-row seat to an unparalleled evolution of humankind.

The embedded NACs were initially designed to deter people from directly murdering others. In essence, "you intentionally kill, you die." With early success, the NAC software was quickly upgraded to target the masterminds behind murder, especially terrorists who recruited disadvantaged people for bombings and other suicide missions. If "you have someone killed, you die." Finally, the software capabilities were soon expanded to discourage torture, targeting any intended harm that resulted in death. If "the recipient of your intended harm dies, you die." With each software enhancement, the world took another step back from annihilation.

For all practical purposes, Bee Sting had attained the same stature as gravity, with the Program becoming another force responsible for preventing the world from ripping itself apart. Yet, unlike gravity, all man-made things—societies, businesses, governments—had to evolve or fail. While Bee Sting had spent the last twenty years expanding to every corner of the earth, the underlying technology, including the NAC software, had remained virtually the same, which left the masses with a sense that major change was overdue. The general could feel the tension building across the population, and judging by the doctor's appearance, he was certain the tension was greatest right here. He suspected Dr. Jordan was feeling the enormity of what she had unleashed on humankind and perhaps found herself overwhelmed with the prospect of moving forward.

The general recommitted to himself that if the doctor were to stumble, he would be there to catch her.

"Doctor, I'm here to help, but you have to tell me what was stolen," he finally said.

He had flown out after being notified of a break-in at Dr. Jordan's covert development center. The building they sat in was nestled on the University of California, Santa Cruz campus, far from Washington D.C. It had been the perfect place to keep a low profile while the development team churned out the next phase of the Program. Bee Sting had its detractors, but all those responsible for the Program's evolution had been smug in their sense of security. Until now.

"I simply don't know," Jordan said. "Everything looks in order. My people have scoured the building. Nothing missing has been identified."

"Anything on the intruder? Did the readers pick up an ID? Did we capture images? Anything at all?"

Dr. Jordan shook her head throughout the series of questions. "Nothing. We know someone entered through the roof access and triggered the primary alarm. That's about it. Of course, if we're looking at an inside job, then records could have been erased, alarms disabled, readers turned off, and so much more."

"Inside job, really?"

"My job is to assume the worst, even if my people are insulted by the prospect."

"Understood. Any guess as to what our culprit was after?"

The doctor surprised him by breaking into laughter. "Sorry. I know everyone assumes Bee Sting is so wonderful that it would be the rare soul that would want to do it harm. But we need to remind ourselves the Program was put in place because we have absolutely no clue what might motivate someone to kill their neighbors or set out to destroy an entire village. I could spend days drafting a list of potential culprits and their possible motives."

The general nodded to assure the doctor he understood. "Humor me. Share a few thoughts that come to mind."

"Alright. The most obvious choice would be someone who wants to steal our development plans and release them to the public in the hopes of setting off panic and a possible uprising against the Program."

The general let a smile reach his face. "OK, being on the board, you know that possibility was exactly why I was sent here." The doctor was one of thirteen members that made up the National CID Board that oversaw the Program. The general, in charge of Program security, reported directly to the board. Several members were quite worried about anything that could lead to unrest surrounding Bee Sting and wanted the general to personally investigate this matter.

He wasn't going to be blown off by some canned answer. He wanted to know what the doctor was really thinking, so he decided to push. "Come now, Doctor. I know you can do better. How about a more creative theory?"

Dr. Jordan hesitated for a moment, then leaned forward with her eyes coming alive. "You want creative? How about you got tired of waiting for that software module you've been bugging me about forever? You know, the one that could turn the army you've been amassing into an unstoppable force?"

The general stiffened before forcing himself to relax. Their long journey together had been full of sacrifices and grueling decisions, leaving them with little patience for dancing around matters. He shook his head. "We both know that module is important. I'm going to need a highly effective force to discourage extremists if we want any hope of rolling out the next phase of your program. In fact—"

"Please, don't call it *my* program," Dr. Jordan interrupted. "Obviously, I'm not in control. If it were my program, we would be having candid national discussions about what we're doing. Look, we've probably done more to stop killing than capital punishment ever could. Maybe even saved the world. But at what cost?"

The general held his hands out in front of him, signaling her to stop. "I get it. While I might argue there were no right answers, we did force people to make sacrifices."

"'Sacrifices'? That's what you're calling it? That sounds so tame. People were killed. Freedoms wiped out."

The general heard the rage coming at him, but also something more. "So new theory. The Program's founder and visionary, overcome with guilt, plots to have the next-generation software stolen and released to the public, in the delusional belief that the masses would somehow strike the right balance between safety and freedom."

Crinkles at the edge of her eyes and upturned lips betrayed the smile the doctor held back. "I think the correct military term would be 'touché.' No, a widespread release of the NAC code would be too dangerous, especially considering your prototype module's ability to bypass all security."

"Too dangerous? Perhaps you're forgetting the kill switch? The board can terminate anyone that has this next-gen software."

"Right. The kill switch. Did you know that code hasn't been inserted into your new module yet?"

"So, we could have a big problem on our hands," the general stated.

"Close. I was supposed to integrate your module with the primary software routine yesterday. It was to be distributed internally for testing but was delayed a day."

"And if someone had been counting on you hitting your deadline, then we caught a break."

"Exactly."

Chapter Six

Shadow

April 19 – 12:37 a.m.

Shadow returned to the grounds the same way he came, easily disappearing into the trees. The operation had been a near disaster! Despite this, he did take comfort in knowing he had achieved his primary objective: he had successfully broken into the Ridge Crest *CID*.

After breaking into the Santa Cruz CID, he assumed it would be insane, if not impossible, to break into Ridge Crest. His fears were doubled when he scoped out the building's security. Every door and window was alarmed. At least one officer was stationed at all hours in the front lobby, while others worked in the back office, which was the focal point of the mission.

His big break had come when he noticed Cal's Roofing trucks parked outside the building two days earlier. Upon climbing one of the many oak trees surrounding the building, he found the setup was better than he could have imagined. Two of the air conditioning units had been removed, with plywood left behind to cover the openings.

On the night of the operation, Shadow used one of the construction ladders to reach the roof. Then sliding back the plywood, he was pleased to find even the ductwork had been removed, giving him a straight descent into his target area. Sliding leg first into the hole, he clung to the wood framing, only to have it crumble apart in his hands. He crashed to the floor with a clear understanding of why the AC units had been removed. Surprisingly, the dull thud attracted no attention. Even better, it resulted in no broken bones. He completed the mission, and relying solely on his rope, made his way back out into the starry night.

Retreating deeper into the heavily wooded forest, Shadow knew he had just kicked over a hornets' nest. He also knew the resulting chaos and confusion were necessary to shroud his true intent.

Chapter Seven

Talon

April 19 – 7:09 a.m.

Disturbed by a banging noise, Talon's eyes flew open. Turning to the enhanced window, he could see it was 7:09 a.m. and sunny. He really needed to change the overlay to some chill sports scene, like surfing or snowboarding. The current image of the sun rising over a forest canopy was pretty much what he had outside his window anyway. His thoughts were interrupted by the banging that had woken him in the first place. "I'm awake! You know I can handle waking myself up for school. I'm in high school, remember?"

The response was his sister's laughter trailing off down the hallway.

"Turn off the alarm, Morty," Talon grumbled to his control system.

"No alarm has been set. Did you wish to set an alarm?" came the computer-generated reply.

Stomping across the room to his closet, he rummaged through a stack of clothes he had yet to put away. Grabbing jeans and a shirt, Talon turned to the window and called out. "Morty, mirror." The sunny day was quickly replaced by Talon's image looking back at him. His thick, dark-brown hair was pushing off his head in every direction. He patted it down and brushed it off his forehead, revealing his intense green eyes and bushy eyebrows. As he pulled his jeans up over his boxers, he acknowledged how skinny he was, having grown four inches in six months to stand at nearly six feet. Unfortunately, the rapid growth had left him at a gangly 150 pounds. He tried to find comfort in the fact that his father was six feet three and a muscular two hundred-plus pounds, but

Talon was a long way off from filling out like his dad. Sadly, *potential* was doing nothing to help him with the girls.

Food was a priority as he headed downstairs. Barely noticing his dad and sister sitting at the kitchen table, he went straight for the fridge.

"Hold up. Breakfast's already on the table," Sage pointed out.

There sat a plate of bacon and eggs. He plopped down and dug in. It wasn't until his plate was halfway cleared that he looked up. "Who made this?"

Across from him, his father sat with his hand on Sage's shoulder as if holding her back. "Stay back, honey. I don't want you to get devoured by that eating machine." The comment was lame, but it was nice to have his dad kidding around.

"Hey, I see you working your way to fatness. I'm just trying to keep up," Talon shot back.

"I remember those days when food was more important than breathing," his dad chuckled. "Which, by the way, you can't do when you're stuffing food down so fast."

"I'll survive, Dad. So, anything big going on today?"

"You might have a longer commute today," Sage answered.

"More than my usual three minutes?"

"We've got a stiff," Drake said.

"A dead person?"

"No. A driver that parks their car in the middle of the road. They freeze up with the sudden fear that they could cause an accident and that if someone dies they'll be stung out," his dad explained.

"Two stiffs," Sage corrected. "A driver going around the other stiff lost it as well."

This was crazy to Talon, "I don't get this. If these drivers are so afraid, why don't they just take a Mini?"

"No doubt we'd all relax if they did, but a lot of old folks don't think that way. And by 'old folks' I'm not talking about people my age, Talon," Drake added, stopping Talon before he could pop off. "The older generations aren't about to trust some 'brainless driving contraption.' You know how you complain about going forty on the freeways? You probably wouldn't believe it, but before people were networked, everyone pretty much drove seventy-five or eighty. It's the fear of being stung out that clogs up the freeways."

"I thought someone couldn't be stung out if they killed someone without intending to harm anyone or do anything violent. Unless they're out there trying to run people over, then they're OK, right?" Talon asked.

"Right. It's an irrational fear, common though. You know why we've hardly had any new driverless cars introduced in the last five years? Automotive engineers are afraid to introduce a car with any possibility of a defect. They figure any resulting death could be their demise."

Talon's mind went back to where it always went when he thought about being networked. Was this a good thing? He had heard the stories about the wars and terrorism that had been all but eliminated. He knew that life was a lot safer than when his dad was his age. He simply wasn't sure he agreed with the ever-increasing cost of the bargain. Would he live in fear of being stung out? Would he abandon his dreams? He was a bit of a techie and had visions of being a big-time inventor. Now he wondered if he too would lose his nerve for fear of bringing harm. Or for fear of his inventions being rejected by a population that increasingly spurned anything new. Life seemed to be getting 'safer,' but at what cost?

He returned to the present, only to realize his dad was staring at him. The terror he felt every time he thought about being networked must have leaked out across his face. Ugh! He didn't want to torment his family. He was certain Wilder had struggled with the same fears and chose to run. Talon had no intention of making them endure that pain again.

"Sorry, I forgot I have a quiz in chemistry today," he lied. "I'm not ready, and I've got maybe five minutes to get off to school." He rose and hurried upstairs to make his getaway.

Chapter Eight

Drake

April 19 – 8:28 a.m.

The stiffs were long gone when Drake made his five-minute commute to the south end of Ridge Crest Drive. His colleagues Ari and Rani were working the front desk when he entered the office lobby. He said good morning as he passed by, but they were in too intense of a discussion to give him more than a nod. Making his way through the halls, he passed several others engaged in animated discussions. He slipped into his private office only to find Jesse Taylor resting on the edge of the desk. He sat in his chair, motioning for Jesse to get off his desk.

"Well? What's everyone so excited about?"

"You don' know?" Jesse said, no effort to hide his anger. "A note was left in the boss's office last night and he went out of his way to give everybody a copy."

Drake sighed as he accepted the note. This was not how he wanted to start his Friday. Seeing the signature, his heart sank. Shadow! The note simply read, "Just checking in."

"Where'd he leave it?"

"Boss's desk."

"What'd he take?"

"No idea. If the chief knows, he ain't sharin'."

"Came in through the roof?"

"Yep."

"And you're angry because ...?" Drake said, getting to the real point of Jesse's visit.

"You gotta ask? You know it's all of our jobs to catch this guy. That freak is makin' us look bad. I get that you've caught a tough break with your son, but—"

Drake's head snapped up. He didn't see losing his son as merely a 'tough break.'

Jesse backtracked. "'OK, OK. Sorry to go there. Sorry. I got no kids and can't begin to comprehend. Point is you've been through some hard times. Now them hard times seem to have come back with a vengeance when it comes to this Shadow character. 'Kay, so your head's not in the game. 'S obvious."

"So I've heard," Drake muttered to himself, reflecting on his prior discussion with Gabriel.

"Man, you're probably the best detective in this department, maybe even the entire county. But right now, buddy, you're worthless. Wake up or you're goin' to get all of us freakin' fired!" He rose to his feet. He stood there glaring down at Drake, then stormed out, slamming the door.

Drake sat back in his chair and stared at his desk. He knew there was a lot of truth in what Jesse said. Drake could even convince himself he had it coming.

Yet, something was ... off. He couldn't buy into the idea that Jesse was worried about losing his job. Maybe he was becoming obsessed with Bee Sting and getting the bad guys who weren't programmed?

He sat back in his chair. He would worry about Jesse's motives later. The real question was what was Shadow up to? He had taken a big risk with this stunt. The heat was already turned up on him, but he had decided something was worth turning it up higher. Gabriel had to know something. No way Shadow dropped in only to taunt the CID.

Chapter Nine

Sofia

April 22 – 1:12 a.m.

cared shitless! That's what her dad would be calling her right now. No, if her dad knew what she was up to, he would be calling her 'dead'. Sofia knew she was psyching herself out, but couldn't shut her fears down. She was sitting behind bushes outside the CID Programming Center in the middle of the night.

This was dumb. Really dumb. It was also her idea. When your dad's the chief, you spend your life convincing classmates you're not some toxic troll just waiting to ruin the fun.

Whap! Something hit her in the back, and she barely held back a scream. She turned to see her friends Arissa and Liz giggling. A tennis ball was at her feet.

"You should have seen your face!" Arissa said.

"Never seen your eyes so big," Liz squeezed out between giggles.

"You know if we get caught, we won't be getting any freedoms in our lifetimes." Sofia couldn't believe they weren't freaked out about this stunt.

"It's your plan. Things go bad, we'll just let you go down for it," Arissa said, smiling.

Sofia started to relax. One thing she loved about Ridge Crest, most of the time, was that she had grown up with over half the sophomore class. She had been seated between Arissa and Liz the first day of kindergarten and they had been inseparable ever since. Sofia knew they had her back. Sofia dreamed up most of their adventures, but they would *never* let her go down alone if they were caught.

"So where are the guys? Did they get the goods?" Liz asked in her best conspiratorial voice.

"Got the goods, sista," Sofia mimicked back at Liz. "We'll get those bitches!" She wasn't joking about the last part. Girls could be quite mean to each other, and the senior girls had generally been anything but nice to the sophomore girls.

A particularly nasty pair of them were young for their class and were finally about to turn sixteen. Sofia knew they hadn't been networked due to disciplinary problems at school. With programming sessions only being scheduled every few weeks, Sofia figured these bitches had run out of time. They had to make the session on Monday, which was why Sofia had arranged this late Sunday night excursion: they were going to make tomorrow memorable for the girls who had spent all year raining on their sophomore experience.

As if on cue, the boys could be heard laughing and crashing through the bushes as they approached the rendezvous.

"We can hear you!" Sofia called out in a whisper. Geoff and Ronnie came into view, both holding bulging plastic trash bags. "Where's Talon?" she asked, trying to hide her concern.

She didn't take Talon's presence for granted. In fact, she knew she was in a bitter fight to hang on to his friendship, a friendship that went all the way back to first grade. Well, technically kindergarten, when she thought about it.

Talon, whose family was new in town, was introduced to her class with a month left in the school year. Sofia didn't pay him much attention, but after weeks of watching him sit on the swings at recess and mouth words to himself, her curiosity got the best of her. Sofia approached Talon

"Whatcha doin'?"

"Counting. Most days I count to a thousand."

Sofia didn't even try to make sense of this. "Wanna play?" She pointed to the girls and boys chasing each other and spinning circles until they could no longer stand.

"Not sure 'bout that."

"Is there something you wanna do?" Sofia never gave up easily.

"Count bees. Do you know how many bees are in a hive?" Talon asked.

"No. How many?" Sofia asked, even though she was not the least bit curious.

"I don't know either." Talon looked sad that he didn't know.

Sofia had no idea what to do with this strange boy. She eventually turned and walked away, deciding it was best to give him space.

A swarm of bees moving into her backyard over the summer changed everything. She could barely contain her excitement as she hunted Talon down on the first day of school. A play date was quickly arranged, and they both found themselves staring fifteen feet up, where the nest hung from the branch of an old oak tree.

"Go ahead, Talon. Count the bees!"

Talon continued to look up until a discouraged look overcame him. "I can't. They're all in their nest."

Not one to be discouraged and ever the problem solver, Sofia grabbed the hose, with the sprayer conveniently attached, and the rest was history. Their friendship was cemented and, yes, they were stung repeatedly. This established the pattern of their deep friendship. Talon most often would come up with an odd idea, such as sneaking up on a skunk or catching leeches, then Sofia would throw together a plan and lead them into action.

Invariably, they both suffered.

Now here she was with a scheme she had cooked up, one she didn't dare think of carrying through without Talon. She had tried being patient with him when his brother died, but when a year passed with Talon growing more reclusive every day, she barged back into his life, demanding he spend time with her. They then entered a dance, where he hid from her at school and at home, while she sought him out, learning every one of his hiding places. While the dance still wasn't over, she was confident she was breaking through. Most days, he seemed happy to see her. Not all days. She still had to hang in there on those days when he barely uttered a word. She knew being present on his worst days was more important than basking in those when he had a smile or maybe even a laugh to share.

Despite the many setbacks she had suffered as she tried to draw Talon out, she would be crushed if Talon didn't show. He had promised he would come, and Talon knew his promises were important. He simply didn't break a promise. Not one made to Sofia.

She could hear herself exhale when Ronnie finally said, "He's coming. He's going around the bushes. No idea why. There's not much around here. A vet's office on one side and a couple of homes with lights out on the other. What's he worried about?"

"How about cameras?" Talon said as he quietly appeared out of nowhere. Almost as one, the group peered through the bushes to the building, horrified. "Luckily, Cop's Rest must be considered low risk," he added. "The cameras are mounted in plain sight and not one appeared to track your movements. Just the same, let's not be stupid and get caught."

"Why would anyone worry about protecting the Programming Center?" Geoff asked, striving to regain his composure. "Everyone knows they download the program from ... well, from somewhere. They don't have much more than a chip-programming station in there. What's to steal?"

"Nice shoes, Talon," Sofia said as she looked down at a green pair of sneakers. "We talked about wearing all black."

"Right. Best I could do." Then making a point that she wasn't perfect, he moved forward and tucked a strand of long auburn hair back under her black beanie.

"Do you have the skunk juice?" Sofia asked.

"Got a gallon of it. We brought the gravity feeds you wanted, too," Talon said as Geoff and Ronny unveiled the contents of their bags. They each held buckets with quarter-inch tubing extending out the bottom. "We were thinking we can use good old double-sided tape to attach the buckets to the wall."

"Primitive, but it should work. Alright, let me have the smelly stuff."

Talon handed it to her as if he couldn't get rid of it quickly enough. "Don't get it on you. It's concentrated. You won't stop smelling for weeks. Can we really fit the tubes under the doors?"

"Oh yeah. Masks on. Let's make our daddies proud," Sofia said, winking at Talon.

Talon groaned. They both knew what it was like to have a cop as a dad. They had been getting into trouble together as far back as either could remember. At some point, they started saying to each other, "Let's make our daddies proud," before doing something completely stupid.

Everyone pulled on masks and headed to the building. There wasn't much to the structure: it was rectangular with metal doors at each end, while the walls were perhaps sixteen feet high with the windows eight feet off the ground. Programming was a private affair.

Sofia took Geoff and Arissa with her and went to the farthest set of doors. She glanced back to see the rest of the crew head around the corner to the other doors. A quick glance at the cameras and it was clear they still weren't tracking their movements.

Reaching the doors, Geoff started to crack up and Arissa nudged him to be quiet. "This is going to be easy," he whispered. "These doors must have a half-inch gap under them." He got down on his knees and began threading the tubing under the door. "The tubing is fifteen feet, so what do you say we shove all but five feet in there? Are you attaching the bucket?" Geoff tended to talk when he was nervous.

Meanwhile, Arissa and Sofia were almost finished attaching the bucket, leaving it dangling a few feet off the ground.

"Geoff, go check on the others. I'll start pouring this shit in. Arissa, you might want to take a step back." Sofia opened the lid to the gallon container.

The smell was ... *shocking.*

Arissa stepped farther back, and Sofia did all she could not to throw up. She turned her head and held the container as far away as she could, still starting to gag.

Talon came up to her and snatched the container. He calmly poured about half into the bucket and set it on the ground. He then rushed away and took in a few gasping breaths.

"Saved your butt. Hold your breath and put the cap back on. Then let's get the stuff to the other side. We're ready."

Sofia was all too happy to put the cap back on. As they headed to the other side, she wasn't sure, but she thought she caught the smell already creeping out from under the doors. This just might work!

Arriving at the other doors, Sofia held the juice out to Talon. Now wasn't the time for her to worry about learning a new skill. Talon took a deep breath and unscrewed the lid. Everyone backed away as he poured the last of it into the bucket. He must have lost his air more quickly this time as he tossed the container aside and gasped for breath.

Almost as if the container hitting the ground was some type of trigger, all hell broke loose. Lights and sirens sprang to life in the nearby parking lot. Everyone froze, trying to see into the lights of what must have been three cop cars. As the pranksters were just making out officers piling out of the cars, they heard a loud metal bang on the other side of the building. The far door on the building had sprung open, and out streaked a cloaked figure, sprinting for the creek below. The officers hardly took notice of the teens as they ran right through the group of students in hot pursuit of the escapee. The last cop yelled at them, "Stay there!" as she sprinted to catch up with her fellow officers.

The teens stood blinking at each other until Sofia screamed, "Run!" and took off.

A moment later, the rest of them had found their legs and shot after her as she headed for the bushes. She looked back to see Talon lagging. It was so like him to have second thoughts about fleeing the scene.

"Decision's been made, Talon. Let's go!" she yelled. That seemed to snap him out of it, and he picked up the pace. They ran until they must have been a half-mile up the hill on the other side of Ridge Crest Drive. By the time they settled into a cluster of trees, they could hear sirens echoing through the valley below.

The whole group had made it out. She turned to Talon, who she couldn't help notice had tracked her throughout the flight to safety. Right now, he stood staring at her as if he was unsure what to do with this crazy person. "I see how you're looking at me," she said.

Talon continued to stare, then finally said, "Sorry. I was just trying to think which was dumber—my signing up for this stunt or putting myself in a position where I was forced to flee the scene with you."

This stung Sofia. She wanted to clap back at Talon, but all she could do was watch as Talon walked off, fading into the trees.

Chapter Ten

Talon

April 22 - 7:07 a.m.

Talon had a first-period algebra test, but he was running late and had to stop by his locker to get his math book. In his panic to get to class, he blanked on the location of his locker. He couldn't remember for the life of him where it was. As he ran down the halls, he heard a steady banging. He ran toward the sound, with a feeling that his locker was trying to signal him. Then the sound stopped. Then it started again, but louder. More urgent. He raced forward, only to have it stop again. Then the banging came again at a furious pace. Talon! The locker was even now yelling his name?!

Bang! Bang! Bang! Talon! Wake up!!

His eyes popped open. "Oh, Sage! I–I ... I'm awake."

A few minutes later, Talon was creeping down the stairs, hoping his dad was already off to work. Most mornings, he was eager to check in with his family; he guessed he needed to reassure himself they were alive and breathing, but he wasn't feeling such a need this morning. Did his father see him last night? Would he have recognized his son? After all, Talon was pretty well covered up. And he didn't know if his father had even been there. He had almost talked himself down from being a nervous wreck when his dad came into view.

Damn! OK, play it cool. "Morning, Dad."

Drake looked up from his plate and studied him for what seemed like an hour. Just as he was about to confess, Drake gripped his coffee and greeted him with, "Morning." Whew! Time to step smoothly to the fridge. "You look really tired," Drake added.

"Me? Oh, getting up this early is never easy."

"You're going to have a lot of unhappy classmates at school today."

"Wha ... what do you mean?" He caught his breath.

"Seems like some kids stunk up the Programming Center. Probably kids pranking their fellow classmates. They got the job done, too. Anyone walking in that place is going to come out smelling like a skunk."

Wait! Oh, god. What was that smell? Oh no! It was coming from his dad. "So you ...?"

"Oh yeah, I had to go in there, too. A lot of officers are smelling just like me right now."

Talon was dying, but had to ask, "Why would you think you had to go into a place like that?"

"The desk fielded a couple of calls about strange noises around the Programming Center. Half the force went down to check it out, only to realize it was a group of kids. Imagine that," his dad said, glancing over at him. "Just as we were about to give them the lesson of a lifetime, something came screaming out of the building, and we gave chase."

"So, the group kind of stunk him out of there?" Talon said hopefully, trying to paint them as heroes.

"Sure," his dad returned. "Know any of them? We'd love to have a chance to thank them personally."

Was his dad grinning? Why didn't he just come out and say he knew Talon was there? He had to be toying with him. "Did you catch him?"

The last trace of a smile left his dad's face. "No. He simply disappeared across the creek. Like a shadow."

Talon's eyes went wide. "And was it?"

"Shadow? We went into the building to see what the person had been after. As far as we can tell, though, nothing was missing."

"Perhaps the thief was scared off before he could grab anything?"

"Not if it was Shadow. He broke into UCSC and our CID Headquarters—not a thing left out of place. This job fits his profile. Again, the intruder doesn't take a thing and shakes us in the woods. It was Shadow."

"Seems like a lot to go through just to make a name for himself."

"Exactly! He's up to something."

Talon's thoughts returned to the situation at hand. His dad would have already torn into him if he had ID'd him, right? Shadow's presence at the building may have actually saved him.

"I would appreciate it if you asked around school to see what your classmates have heard about the break-in," Drake said.

"Sure thing," Talon replied as he prepared for his exit.

"Thanks, Tal. Oh, and just a bit of fashion advice ..." His dad looked him up and down. "Green shoes don't look as good during the daytime."

Talon didn't dare say a word as he rushed for the door.

Chapter Eleven

General Stafford

April 22 - 7:39 a.m.

"You caught me swimming a few laps," General Stafford said, continuing his backstrokes across the Olympic-sized pool.

"Sorry to interrupt. Call you back later?"

"No, Mr. Abreo. I'm always ready to get an update."

"You must be in good shape. I can't hear you gasping for breath," Gabriel replied.

"I'm dying here. Fortunately, I'm trying out a new audio system that filters out everything but my words. What've you got? Any discoveries on the break-in at your station?"

"Nothing. No one has any idea what Shadow was after. He broke into the local CID Programming Center last night as well."

"And?"

"And nothing missing or out of place."

"Damn. What's this guy up to?" The general reached the edge of the pool and hoisted himself onto the pool deck with ease. He could have put in a few more laps, but there were quite a few others getting their workouts in at the Officer's Club. It was good to see people keeping in shape, but he needed some privacy and wanted to find an empty poolside steam room. "Has your detective reached out to our former operative?"

"He sent the word through a few fringe players, like you suggested. No response."

"That's fine. Mr. Haris will surface if we offer him a mission he believes in. I'll try to think of something. If we get him hooked, he'll know everything about the fugitive community, including Shadow. You can count on it. The important part for now is that he knows you're looking to make contact."

"How do we know if he's even gotten word?" Gabriel asked.

"He'll hear. Who are you using to make contact? Not Mr. Russit, I hope."

"Jesse Taylor. Another one of my officers. Don't worry about him being conflicted, though. His first commitment is to the CID. He's a big advocate for the Program. Sometimes I worry he's too big of an advocate." Gabriel added, clearly looking to solicit the general's thoughts on Taylor.

"Is he good?"

"Next to Russit, he's probably the best."

"Does he follow orders?"

"Religiously."

"We're good, then," the general concluded. "Sounds like he'd make a good soldier. There's always room in my army for those who believe in our cause."

"Understood. Then, should we sideline Russit?"

"No. As long as he doesn't impede our efforts, it probably isn't wise to get his nose out of joint. Do keep me informed on his effort, though."

"I hear you, general. We'll work with you to get this closed. You can trust the Ridge Crest CID."

Chapter Twelve

Sofia

April 23 - 7:44 a.m.

Sofia sat in the passenger seat, determined not to say a word. She arrived at school with her mom, who had pretended to drive. Her mom's real motive for 'driving' her to school had been to pry information out of her about the 'skunk stunt,' as she kept calling it. Most people looked at her mom and didn't give a thought to her intelligence. She had blonde hair and blue eyes, with a body that completed the stereotypical blonde fantasy, but Sofia had a lifetime of learning that her mother was sharp. And right now, her mother was on to her, knowing this prank was a good fit for a stunt she would pull.

Sofia had no defense. As her mother sat staring at her, waiting for her to crack, it turned into a test of wills. She stared back and occasionally glanced at the door release, which was prominently displayed on the control panel.

Her mother was having none of it, so Sofia decided enough was enough. She rolled her eyes and fixed them on the release icon, implying that in a blonde moment her mother needed to be reminded how to open the car door.

Her mom struggled to contain the smile creeping over her face before quickly losing it and beginning to shake with laughter. She then reached over and touched the icon, granting Sofia her freedom. Sofia loved her mom's humor, but wasn't taking any chances. She gave her a kiss on the cheek and darted out the door.

She had been dropped off at the lower parking lot, which was the farthest lot from the school. A short walk across the lot brought her to a retaining wall below the upper lot. Following the wall would discreetly deposit her on the main sidewalk leading to the school entrance, with no one the wiser that she had not been allowed to drive herself to school. Halfway along her trek to the sidewalk, she noticed a small gathering up ahead. Just her luck. She recognized her ex-boyfriend, Devlin Calvano, who had broken from the group and was heading her way.

Devlin walked deliberately toward her, doing his best to flex every muscle with each movement. Sofia had to acknowledge he was quite the specimen. As a senior, he was the starting quarterback on the football team. He could have had almost any girl in the school, but he chose her. She watched his muscular frame glide her way, remembering what had attracted her to him. It had taken half the school year to realize he was never going to develop a personality beyond that of self-centered jerk.

Sofia decided she would change course and veer around him. Now only twenty feet away, Devlin merely altered his course to intercept her. Why? She thought he had finally resigned himself to leaving her alone. He wasn't getting her back. Ever. She had almost forgotten he could speak when he called.

"Sofie! Hey, wait up. What're you up to?"

"Trying to get to class, Devlin. What are you and your homies doing over there?" Sofia noticed that half of the football team was huddled near the wall, apparently trying to stay out of sight.

"Nothing you want to know about," Devlin replied a little too quickly. He approached and walked alongside Sofia. She began to understand he had no interest in saying 'hi'. He was intent on steering her away from the gathering. Which was fine with her. She wasn't part of that crowd and certainly didn't want to be caught up in anything stupid. She allowed him to escort her past the group until she heard someone gasp in pain. She looked back and caught the group pushing and shoving someone trapped in the middle.

Instantly, she reversed direction and slipped around Devlin. He tried to grab her arm, but she jerked it away and ran toward the group.

"Sofie! Don't!" Devlin yelled but didn't dare to chase her down.

Sofia had a horrible feeling as she squeezed past the wall of players into the middle of the ring. "Idiots!" she screamed, jostling to get to the body lying on the ground.

Talon rolled to his back and groaned. With scrapes, bumps, and gashes covering his exposed arms and face, he looked like he had been pushed and beaten down to the pavement a dozen times. Seeing Sofia, he started to rise.

"*Stay down*, Talon!" she hissed. Talon and his skinny frame were noticeably overmatched against the hulking figures around him.

Still, somewhat unsteady, Talon rose and began to move toward his antagonists. Sofia moved beside him, grabbing his arm to keep him standing.

"Move back, cowards!" she snapped before realizing words had escaped her mouth.

A few players visibly winced, but no one made any effort to move. Talon was not backing down. He veered toward a couple of the larger senior players and began pushing his way past them. He was rewarded with an elbow to the ribs, though he managed to stay on his feet and push on through. He probably would have received a nice jab in the back had Sofia not been trailing right behind. Emerging from the circle of bodies, Sofia turned to get a good look at the creature that had delivered the elbow to Talon. Todd Blakely, the team captain and super senior, sneered at her.

Sofia lost it. Her knee connected full on with Todd's groin, and he went down hard. She silently thanked her father for all the self-defense training while she watched Todd squirm on the ground. She hurried after Talon, knowing she had pushed her luck. Catching up to him, she looked over her shoulder to see Todd, on his side, staring her down. Todd wasn't getting up soon, but he was able to yell, "I'll get you back, bitch! And your little girlfriend, too!"

"Just remember who stayed down, you gutless wonder!" Sofia yelled back.

Seeing Devlin emerge from the angry crowd and scramble to reach her, Sofia greeted him coldly. "Are you going to try a sucker punch as well?"

"Me? No! But you don't want to make enemies with the football team. You might want to go back and apologize."

Slap! Sofia heard the sound of her hand connecting with Devlin's face. "Go back to your spineless homies! Thanks for reminding me why I broke up with you."

Hurrying to catch up to Talon, who had continued to stumble along, she couldn't help thinking she had made a big mess. She made some enemies, but she knew the person that was going to pay dearly was Talon. Since he was a guy, the football crowd would feel free to mercilessly stalk him around the campus.

Chapter Thirteen

Talon

April 23 - 7:57 a.m.

He was hurting. No doubt about it, but he was on his feet and intent on getting anywhere else. He needed to find a place where he could breathe and assess the damage, and he needed to escape his embarrassment. The last thing he wanted was for Sofia to see him destroyed.

"Let's get you to the hospital," Sofia broke in on Talon's thoughts as she forced his arm over her shoulder. "I'm calling my dad and getting us a ride."

"No! I'm fine. I'm hanging out until the bell rings and then getting to a bathroom." Talon was *not* retreating to a hospital. He didn't think anything was broken; perhaps his pride. He pulled his arm back from her shoulder. "Get to class, Sofia. Thank you for coming to my rescue, but I've got this now."

"What? No! You need to see a doctor."

"Not happening. Just let me be."

"I'm not leaving. You know that. What happened?"

Talon stopped stumbling along. He turned toward Sofia. She had tears in her eyes.

"I'm not leaving," she repeated slowly.

"OK. Your boyfriend knew about our prank. Turns out the girls who got networked yesterday happen to have boyfriends on the football team. They evidently wanted to let me know that they didn't get the joke."

"Ex-boyfriend."

"What?"

"Devlin is my ex-boyfriend. You realize no one told him anything. He just knows me enough to realize I might do this.

And if I was in on it, so were you. Did you ever think to deny it?"

"Well, no." Great. He could add stupidity to the day's list of problems. Talon heard the bell and figured it was time to go find that bathroom, but Sofia continued to trail him. He stepped through the entrance and into the hallway. Thankfully, no one was around. Halfway down the hall, he entered the men's bathroom. Alone at last.

"So is it all clear in there?" Sofia called as she pushed through the door. "Let's get you cleaned up."

"Sofia, I'm embarrassed enough. Let me die in peace." He wanted to cry, but was not about to achieve a new low in front of her.

Sofia held his head with both hands and made him look at her. "I've never been more impressed. They ganged up to beat you down. You could have curled up and surrendered. I sure wanted you to. Talon, no one else I know would have gotten up."

Looking into those intense blue eyes, she had Talon rethinking everything. "Really?"

"Oh, and you were incredibly stupid. Don't do that again."

She wetted some paper towels and dabbed his arms and face. The pain brought him back to reality. "I decided I'm getting networked," he said.

"OK, where did that come from? I mean, that's great! You have to know the last thing I want is for you to run off, like— your brother. I'm ... I'm trying to say it's the right decision, but how did you all of a sudden make up your mind?"

"I think the decision got beat into me." Talon's attempt at a smile turned into a painful grimace. "Look, I'm still not certain the whole Program is a good idea. When I hear about people freezing up in traffic, or I read about a doctor retiring rather than taking the chance of screwing up an operation, I'm more convinced the Program wasn't completely thought out.

"But running away isn't the answer. At some point, while I was getting destroyed a moment ago, I realized I was in for the pain. They were wrong and I wasn't going to run and make it easy on them to be f-ing bullies."

"I'm not sure they got your lesson, Talon."

"Too true," Talon said, suddenly feeling foolish. "So, I'm droning on here."

"No! You got me wrong," Sofia said. "I was just making a dumb joke. I want to understand your decision. I mean, I'm pretty excited. I can't wait to hail my own car and have the freedom to go places without checking in. But I probably take it all for granted. I like how you think about everything that goes with what the programming gives us. I really want to know why you're now good with it when you're obviously not as excited as I am."

Talon studied her, confirming she was sincere. He appreciated the way she could enjoy simply living in the moment but then change pace and have a serious discussion.

"Alright, I agree my lesson was probably lost on the football trolls. And if Bee Sting has flaws, most likely no one's going to listen if I point them out. But you never know. I've decided that if something scares me, I'd rather face it and try to do something about it because the other option is to run away, guaranteeing I can't do anything."

Sofia studied him. "You know, that was a life-changing decision you just made. Pretty profound. My dad always says men do their best thinking in the bathroom—or something like that. And now here I am amongst the toilets, getting a behind-the-scenes look at how that thinking gets done! Fascinating." She gave him a light jab on the arm and walked out.

Chapter Fourteen

Drake

May 6—10:38 a.m.

Talon was running late. Nothing new. So why was Drake so nervous? He needed to face it: thoughts of Wilder were weighing on him. Leading up to Wilder's chip-programming day, Wilder and Drake constantly argued about being networked. The arguments pretty much always went the same way. Wilder said programming wasn't for him; Drake asked what alternatives he had. When Wilder didn't answer, Drake assumed the argument was over and Wilder would simply deal with the inevitable.

Little did he know that the night before Wilder's programming appointment, he would disappear. Dinner was a normal family event with a few good laughs at the "old man's" expense. The rest of the evening had seen everyone hanging out at home, not an angry word spoken. Finally, Wilder said goodnight to everyone, including his brother.

The next morning Wilder was gone.

Drake was still beating himself up over that one. The evening was too normal.

He'd had a lot of days since the disappearance to think about how he should have taken Wilder's concerns more seriously, especially knowing Wilder had every reason to fear being networked. Wilder's best friend growing up had been J.T. Novak. JT's parents started him in school late, so he was a year older than Wilder and most of their classmates. He was an exceptional athlete, the best in his class. Wilder loved sports and relished the competition. Initially, they were rivals more than anything else. This changed when JT was the first on their baseball team to warmly welcome a new young batboy who was very nervous about being accepted by the older boys. It didn't hurt that the boy turned out to be Talon. JT and Wilder grew close and took turns over the years to watch over Talon. JT had a huge influence on both of Drake's boys.

Everything began to go sideways when JT was networked. At first, his dad thought he was foundering because he was the only one in his class who was networked, but soon, JT refused to go anywhere that had a reader, including school. He developed anxiety over being watched. JT's mother had died several years earlier, so his father took leave from work in order to provide the support needed to make this adjustment. JT didn't improve. And then, one day, JT and his father ... vanished. Rumor had it that they went off to live in the Santa Cruz Mountains, among the disconnects and other fugitives looking to escape the Program and its suffocating network.

Wilder lived this whole episode with JT, spending time with him nearly every day until he disappeared. Then, a few months later, Wilder went to Drake about a rumor making the rounds at school. Supposedly JT's dad had died, leaving JT out there on his own. Drake's only assurance was advising Wilder not to put too much stock in rumors. He was a fool for not doing more. Maybe he should have tracked JT and his father down.

Why hadn't he? He still wondered where they were and, admittedly, if JT's father was alive. Talon worried about them as well. Drake should have gotten answers. Now that he was beating himself up, he realized he had failed his boys. He sure wished he'd run off with Wilder. And why hadn't he discussed the possibility of running with Talon?

Then it hit him: Talon wasn't showing up to the Programming Center. At this very moment, he was on the run! Talon's excuse for not riding with him was lame. He supposedly wanted to embrace his upcoming independence. Sage begged off as well. Some of her mom's relatives were immigrants, sacrificed in the name of advancing the Program.

He thought nothing of Sage claiming she couldn't witness the programming. So, with five minutes to go until Talon's 11:00 a.m. appointment, everything started to fall into place. Sage and Talon had decided to do what Drake never thought to offer. They were running without him!

"Drive home!" he snapped at the vehicle, just as he spotted Talon pulling into the parking lot.

He tried to clear away his fear as Talon's ride pulled up next to his car. Talon got out, gave him a quick wave, and hurried off to his appointment. Fortunately, Talon hadn't taken a moment to notice how worked up Drake was. The last thing he wanted to do was spoil Talon's big day. Drake lost track of time as he watched Talon stand outside the entry door, waiting to be let in. For a period that seemed to drag on forever, he continually reminded himself to breathe in and out, in and out. It struck him as funny that he could stay dead calm when dealing with the dangers of his job, but could hardly contain his fears when it came to parenting.

A knock on his window brought him back to the moment. Talon was standing at his door. "Hey, Dad. They won't let me in. They asked if a guardian was nearby, then told me to get you."

"They didn't give you any hint at what's going on?"

"Nope."

"Your friends ever had this happen?"

"No idea."

Drake stepped up to the building door and pulled. It was locked.

"Just one moment please," said a voice from a speaker mounted over the door. A few seconds later, the voice said, "Please enter."

From the middle of the room a slender man in a lab coat approached them. "You must be Drake and Talon. I'm Rich Wilcox. Sorry about the confusion. Follow me and we'll get this straightened out."

As Drake and Talon followed Rich, Drake had to ask, "Is that skunk smell real or is it my imagination?"

"I'm pretty sure the smell is still lingering," Rich chuckled. "I can't pick it up anymore, but several people who've come in the last few days ask about it. My daughter keeps complaining that I'm stinking up the house. That was quite the stunt those kids pulled off." Rich motioned toward a woman standing at one of the workstations. "This is my co-worker, Dreama Chan. We're pretty much the entire staff during the week."

Dreama came over and shook their hands. "Yes, the skunk smell is real. I met you a couple weeks ago, right?" Dreama said to Drake. "You were helping to solve this whole prank. Any luck?"

Drake couldn't help but look at Talon, who seemed to be staring unusually hard down at his shoes. "We did meet, and no, sorry, no luck yet. Is everything else back to normal here?"

"All good," Rich replied. Sensing the anxiety in the room, he motioned for everyone to be seated at a conference table near the workstations. "Programming is normally somewhat boring. We identify each person coming into the Center by their chip ID. Every chip, whether programmed or not, has a unique ID. The ID gets confirmed in a national database and ..." Rich got to his feet and walked to one of the stations, then returned with a device that he set on the table. "This handheld gets loaded with the latest program and the associated ID. At that point, we hold the handheld a few inches from the back of the recipient's neck, press the trigger, and in less than sixty seconds, you're good to go. The chip is programmed, and another young person has been given a new life."

"Anyway, Talon," Dreama cut in, "your situation is unique. Your ID couldn't be confirmed in the database. This is why we asked you to get your dad. Technically, we can't let a minor in here without a confirmed ID, unless accompanied by a guardian."

Drake was trying to be patient, but the questions in his mind were stacking up. "So how could Talon's ID not be in the national database?"

"I have no idea. So, you know, this is the first time anyone has tried to access Talon's ID. Legally, IDs can't be accessed prior to an individual's programming day. My understanding is that when the Program was launched, administrators agreed IDs were off limits unless someone willingly signed up to be networked. The idea was to protect the privacy of juveniles and those who chose to live off network."

"So what do we do now?" Drake asked.

"Sorry, we understand this is disturbing," Rich said. "Neither Dreama nor I have ever been confronted with this. However, we think it can be resolved. We have a backup handheld that contains the Program. Though we never had to use it, its purpose is to overcome a situation in which the primary handheld fails for whatever reason. Our understanding is that we need to confirm that the software version put in the handheld has not changed since it was last serviced, which was about three months ago."

"This should merely be a formality," Dreama said. "We happen to know the Program hasn't changed in over six months."

"We also need to confirm that Talon's ID wasn't flagged or removed from the national database for some reason. Assuming that's not the case, then we should receive the green light to program Talon's chip. Later we'll get the paperwork straightened out so that Talon is properly registered in the database."

"So when can I get this program?" Talon asked.

"Oh, well, how about coming back at 12:30? Couldn't we squeeze Talon in over lunch?" Dreama asked Rich.

"Sure. Does 12:30 work?"

"12:30 sounds good. Dad?"

"I'll make it work," Drake said with relief. "That easy?"

"Should be," Dreama agreed. "But as Talon's guardian, I need your signature, acknowledging the programming will be done without a link to the national database. The other option is to get Talon's ID into the national database, then follow the standard programming process. This could take several weeks, and then you're bumping up against Talon's sixteenth birthday."

"I'm good to sign," Drake replied quickly.

Exiting the Center, Drake was in good spirits. He felt they had dodged a bullet. "Want to get some food? We have some time to kill."

"Sofia's appointment is at 11:30. Mind if I hang out and see how it goes for her?"

"Of course. Wish her luck for me. I'll see you back here at 12:30?"

"You got it."

Chapter Fifteen

Drake

May 6 - 12:32 p.m.

Waiting for Talon the second time around wasn't as nerve-wracking. It was after 12:30, but Drake hadn't expected his son to be on time. Kids! Sure enough, Talon showed up at 12:35. Drake greeted him, "How'd it go for Sofia?"

"Great. Just like they said. Routine. Done in fifteen minutes. Her parents grabbed her for a quick celebration, but she's going to meet me later this afternoon."

"Good to hear. Are you good on your own? Or do you want me to join you?"

"I'm good. Be back in a bit," Talon said as he jogged off to the Center.

Drake watched Talon at the front door for a few seconds before he was let inside. Much better. Funny how his worries could change. Drake was no longer concerned about the programming being done. He wondered how he had overlooked making plans for a celebration. Sage too. She used to live for the slightest excuse to celebrate a family accomplishment.

He sighed, unable to help but blame himself and question, for the thousandth time, whether he was a good father. Parenting wasn't for the faint of heart.

Time passed while Drake beat himself up. Twenty minutes later, Talon walked through the door. Drake went to meet Talon, thinking furiously as to how they might put together an impromptu celebration. "So?" Drake called.

"Not good."

"What?" Drake took Talon by the shoulders so he could look him in the eyes. No humor there.

"It didn't take. They said my chip won't program."

"What does that mean? The backup handheld wouldn't work? Do we try again later?"

"No. They say it won't program. Ever."

"Let's go back in there and talk this over," Drake said as he began guiding them toward the entrance. "We need to explore our options."

Drake walked to the entrance and pulled the door open. They were inside before Drake realized the door hadn't been locked.

Rich and Dreama looked up in surprise. "How'd you get in?" Rich asked, rising to meet them.

"Good question." Drake's investigative mind couldn't help but wonder if the faulty door was connected to Shadow's illegal entry, but the distraction lasted a split second as the present anxiety rushed back in. "I hope you have a moment to talk. You can imagine we have a few questions." He was trying to take a calm approach for Talon's sake, but he wasn't going to be turned away. He imagined that Dreama and Rich could read the strain painted across his face, but they didn't seem alarmed or put off.

Rich was first to speak up. "Of course. I'm so sorry about this. You must have questions." He led them to the conference table, and Dreama joined them as they seated themselves.

"So, tell me what happened."

Rich looked at Dreama to make sure she was good with him taking the lead. "We were able to get approval from Central Programming to proceed with Talon. We also confirmed the program held in the backup handheld didn't require an update. All systems were go, so Dreama proceeded to program Talon's chip."

"I hit the trigger," Dreama said. "After about a minute, the handheld LED went green, indicating the program was successful. Then we started the basic tests to confirm a successful download. It's odd, but there's nothing in the chip.

We can't read the program version. Nothing. The chip doesn't come back with anything."

"Can't you just program it again?" Drake asked.

"No. Bee Sting relies on what are called 'one-time programmable chips.' The idea is to prevent hackers from being able to reprogram them. The negative is that a bad download can't be corrected. We get one shot."

"That's ridiculous! Does this happen a lot?"

"Yes and no. It does with people over the age of sixteen. Almost one in a hundred can't be downloaded. You would think this bug would be fixed by now, but the workaround is to program everyone before age sixteen. Talon's problem is extremely rare. Only about one in a hundred thousand have faulty downloads at his age," Dreama explained. "I know you're looking to us for a solution, and I wish—"

"There are no other experts we might turn to?" Drake interrupted, not wanting to hear it was hopeless. "Is there a central tech service that deals with such problems?"

Dreama looked at Drake with a frown. "I'm sorry. Someone from CID will be in touch. I believe you'll need to work on setting up a guardianship ... Talon," Dreama said, shifting the discussion to the true victim, "do you know what that is?"

"Seriously?" Talon cried out. "I won't do that!"

Drake knew Talon was well aware of the guardianship program. Every kid on the playground teased each other about becoming one of Peter Pan's Lost Boys—stuck with a guardian forever, never being allowed to grow up. He remembered Talon taking it hard when his friends told him he would end up "a toddler for life."

"Let's go, Tal. We'll figure this out," Drake said, not wanting to explore their options further in front of CID officials.

Chapter Sixteen

Sofia

May 6 - 1:20 p.m.

"Effy's Salon—no! Ridge Crest High School," Sofia commanded her ride. She was officially on her way to pick out a new dress in preparation for tonight's family-and-friends celebration, but for now, she wanted to drift through campus to share her news and perhaps taunt a few of her mates who had to attend school today. It was 1:20 p.m., so she would arrive during the break, just before the last period. Later, she would hit the salon, pick up her dress, and meet Talon at 3:30 at the LCC.

The LCC, the Life Creation Center, was a virtual reality entertainment center where you could venture through your own realities and which you could enhance from visit to visit. A person had to be programmed to enter, so Sofia only knew as much as her upper-classmates were willing to share. There was a tradition of secrecy, leaving Sofia and Talon fairly clueless, but this type of adventure appealed to Talon's techy-nerdy side, and he couldn't wait to go. He had made Sofia promise they would go together the moment they both could.

She was so lost in thoughts about her day of freedom that she barely realized her ride had reached its destination. She instructed the Mini to stop at the school entrance. "Photo driver ... Photo building left ... Zap Liz Isles and Arissa Friedland."

A mechanical voice responded, "Contacts could not be found."

A jolt of panic hit Sofia. She quickly searched her pockets—nothing. She rummaged through her utility bag until she found what she was looking for. Relieved, she pulled out a two-inch-square silver device that was a quarter-inch thick.

She knew not to lose her "Cube." The device contained all her information—contacts, personal details, crypto balance. By syncing it to a car, gym locker, or even an exercise machine, the linked device would be customized for her use.

Now that she was networked, Sofia could choose to put most of her information on the CID network itself and rely on her chip to handle the device syncing. While many of her friends were rushing to ditch their Cubes, Sofia wasn't too excited yet. She wasn't sure she fully trusted the network. Besides, the Cube acted as a phone in case you weren't near a networked screen, car, or other device.

She put her Cube in her pocket and commanded, "information on."

A moment later, the Mini's mechanical voice confirmed, "Zap complete."

She started seeing activity at the school as her mates were let out of classes. A minute or two later, Liz and Arissa came running out to meet her. Arissa was beaming, "I'm so excited for you! I nearly yelled in class when I got your pictures!"

"I did yell! Or maybe it was a squeal," Liz said. "So, what do we do for a celebration? Break into another building?"

They broke out laughing. "I think criminal life is behind me. I'm all grown up now!" Sofia half screamed, barely containing her excitement. Not a second later, the Mini shut down.

"What just happened?" she asked, bewildered. As they looked at each other confused, the Mini came back to life. "Alright, so screeching reboots the rides? Not sure what happened, but ..."

She didn't get to finish her thought, as she spotted Espar Crashan walking their way. While Espar's dark features were strikingly beautiful and her six-foot height was impressive, Sofia locked onto her because she was also one of the senior bitches they had targeted with their prank. And her long, purposeful strides, screamed that she was coming for them.

Sofia would have sped off had she not worried about her friends. Instead, she watched with dread as Espar squeezed between Liz and Arissa until she could peer into the carriage.

"Thought that was you. I'm surprised you're here. I thought you'd be comforting Talon—you being his protector and all." Espar must have caught her confused look. "Oh, you don't know? It's tough being a tenth grader. So dumb. It's going around that Talon's chip failed. You know what that means, right?"

Sofia was rocked, but did she believe Espar ...? Yes. Unless she was an incredible actress, Espar wasn't pranking her. She was enjoying this moment way too much for it to be anything but true.

Espar smiled sweetly. "Your boy is going to be hanging with Peter Pan."

Chapter Seventeen

Shadow

May 7 - 12:52 a.m.

He stood in the shadows of the giant redwoods, looking down the hill at the long-abandoned limekilns. The rock archways stood as a reminder of a thriving lime industry back in the late 1800s.

Shadow first visited this site when he was ten-years-old. Back then, his biggest concern was whether he would be allowed to pee on one of the big trees. He was almost overwhelmed by how much life had changed.

Now he scoured the flat land surrounding the kilns with his night-vision glasses, making sure no one was waiting to apprehend fugitives.

Shadow was one of thousands hiding out in the Santa Cruz Mountains, trying to survive outside the accepted communities. It seemed like every other day someone died in this wilderness so near town. The most common death was starvation, but there were so many other possibilities when visiting a hospital wasn't an option.

He dreamed of bringing this miserable way of living to an end. Not just for himself and disconnects like him, but for all the fugitives. He knew most of the fugitive ranks were made up of disconnects, but a surprising number simply couldn't buy into the Program. They had struggled to conform and had been run off for minor infractions. While a few were a bit unsavory, most didn't deserve to be treated as such. This was the reason he found himself hanging out in a remote location, well after midnight.

His contact, Dajani Haris, had arranged the time and meeting place. Haris was cautious, especially when dealing with Shadow. It wasn't that Haris didn't trust him. In fact, he was his mentor and perhaps, at forty-five years of age, even a father figure. Haris was merely looking out for both of them. After all, Shadow was sought after. The CID had a cold dark cell awaiting to entomb him. The fugitive community, according to Haris, had a warm embrace.

This last part was bullshit, but Shadow appreciated Haris's attempt to lift his spirits. In reality, fugitives did all they could to keep low profiles. It was better not to even know those around you. Then if your neighbor happened to get captured by the CID, you had less chance of being given up.

Shadow's notoriety with the CID did little to endear him with his fellow outlaws. In fact, Shadow mused that if his identity were discovered, he might get his wish in uniting his community, with the masses gathering to drown him in the nearest puddle of water.

Before his thoughts could further unnerve him, a dark figure separated itself from the deep shadows of the trees below. The person stood in the limited light, knowing he was being watched. Haris was signaling that it was him and it was safe.

Shadow did one last scan of the hazy darkness below before heading down to the limekilns. He moved cautiously, sticking to the shadows and making sure not to step on any dead branches. He worked his way down to the flatlands and within fifteen yards of Haris before Haris locked onto his location.

"Impressive," Haris said.

"I can do better. I scoured the entire flatlands and never picked you up until you wanted to be seen."

Haris greeted Shadow with a strong handshake, then stood before him, taking stock of his condition. "You're too hard on yourself. Only two years ago I doubt you could have gotten within a hundred yards of me."

"Just proves you've aged a lot in two years," Shadow teased. He really liked Haris. He felt safe around him. For reasons unknown to him, Haris had taken it upon himself to train him for his new life. They spent almost two years together, with Haris teaching him how to survive, then teaching him how to strike back against those that threatened his survival.

While Haris didn't talk much about himself, he did drop a few hints about his past. As best as he could piece together, Haris played a key role in shutting down the drug cartels in Central and South America. He led teams to extract key cartel members, who were then networked and set free. In the beginning, most of these cartel members proceeded to get stung out. In time, a few major players realized that life in the cartels was no longer possible. Not being able to defend themselves, they were easy targets. Even their most loyal employees were tempted by their easy demise. And if these drug lords chose to run, the cartels would track them down. The only means to survive was to get the competing drug lords and their teams networked as well, leaving the new inductees equally powerless. It wasn't long before Bee Sting took hold of the cartels like a drug addiction. Then with the members being networked and stung out by the thousands, the cartels quickly collapsed.

With the drug syndicates mopped up, Haris's field expertise was no longer needed. His superiors decided that Haris's time had come. His NAC was scheduled for programming. What they didn't consider was that Haris might not be excited about being networked, having seen countless people stung out. He understood that these were bad people, of course. It just struck him as chilling that given a choice between giving up their free will or dying, so many had chosen death. Haris drew upon his field operations experience and disappeared.

"... and that's all you need to do."

Haris's voice snapped Shadow back to the present. "Wait. What?"

Haris laughed. "Messing with you. I saw your mind drift off somewhere. Alright, let me lay out our request." He paused and looked at him to be certain he was focused. "Within the next week or two, we may need to extract someone from a bad situation. If so, we want you to be part of the operation."

"Extract? As in help escape?" Shadow asked, now paying full attention.

"Close enough. We can't exactly get this person's permission, so we're kind of betting our target will be happy with the intervention."

"So more like an abduction." This sent Shadow's mind reeling. He had pulled off some pretty high-risk thefts, but stealing a person—that's what he was being asked to do, right? He had previously been satisfied with the belief that his missions targeted those who threatened his freedom, if not his very existence, but the magnitude of this mission was beyond anything he had been asked to do before. Wasn't it time to learn more about the big picture? What was the end game of all these efforts, and who was behind them?

"No," Haris cut in on his thoughts. "You aren't going to be given all the answers if you accept this assignment. If it helps, we're part of a resistance. Not a mighty one. The CID could snuff us out if they cared to. I can share who we're up against and maybe some thoughts on what we're doing and why, but you aren't going to learn who's on our side. To be honest, I'm mostly in the dark myself. So if I'm asking too much—"

"I'm in," Shadow said. Who was he kidding? He would take what information he could get from Haris and keep doing his part. Being part of a resistance, no matter how overmatched, was better than no hope at all. And he wasn't giving up his dream of sparking that same passion for freedom and having it spread throughout his fugitive community.

Chapter Eighteen

General Stafford

May 7 - 11:00 a.m.

The general stood in his field office, overlooking forces of a thousand strong in their training exercises. He would join them soon. It was important for him to spend time with his recruits, building loyalty through participating in drills. He strongly believed in only asking his soldiers to do things he was willing to do. For now, though, he resigned himself to being a mere observer while he waited for an important call.

The call would be low-tech. No visual. Just one of the many precautions taken to mask the facility's existence from the rest of the world. The world wasn't ready to know that a facility located in Modoc County, a sparsely populated region in Northeastern California, was home to an army of disconnects. The fact that these disconnects would soon be networked, and go on to play a crucial role in protecting the Program and society as a whole, would not matter.

Disconnects everywhere were feared. It made no difference whether they were contained in a training facility or roaming the mountains of Santa Cruz. The general understood this fear and did not try to impose a different way of thinking. He was content to keep a low profile and do everything possible to avoid fanning the flames.

A subtle vibration from the transparent collar he wore around his neck alerted him to an incoming call. While the collar was not his first choice of wearables, he did appreciate the added security of tuning out all sound except his words. "Identify caller," he commanded.

"Gabriel Abreo," came the synthesized reply.

"Good to hear from you, Chief Abreo," the general said, triggering the call to engage.

"Thank you for taking my call, General."

"Sorry to hear about your detective's son, Talon Russit."

"You heard about him?" Gabriel's voice conveyed his surprise.

"One of my primary responsibilities is Bee Sting security, so I get a daily report on all disconnects—or, sorry, I should say programming complications. You might understand that with Shadow's ongoing activities, I'm currently quite tuned into activities in your area," the general stated, trying to make his knowledge sound more a matter of routine security operations.

"Right. I guess I should have expected this. Thank you for your concern."

"You have a report for me?"

"Yes. Your former operative, Dajani Haris, reached out to Detective Taylor. He was vague about his intentions, but he was quite interested in the latest situation with Talon."

"Talon Russit? What does he know about Russit?"

"A lot. He said he thought Talon might be in trouble after his programming snafu and he wanted Jesse to know he was there if needed."

"Interesting. What does he expect to go wrong?"

"He wouldn't give up anything more."

"Did Detective Taylor get a chance to probe his knowledge of Shadow?"

"No. Dajani wasn't too talkative. You can bet he wouldn't have contacted Jesse at all if not for him being Drake's fellow officer."

"Agreed. He bet on the strong bond that exists between most fellow officers. We're fortunate Detective Taylor's loyalties lie with the Program. I commend your selection."

"Thank you, sir. Other than waiting Dajani out, is there anything we should be doing?"

"No. In fact, let's sit on what we know. No need to share it with Drake. I'm pretty sure Mr. Haris will be reaching out again soon. Until then, no sense in getting anyone worked up about this."

Chapter Nineteen

Sofia

May 7 - 4:01 p.m.

Sofia's Cube notified her that someone was at the front door. Good. Talon had come. She had worked hard all day at school to get Talon to commit. His world was shrinking again, and she was determined to draw him back out.

She sat listening in her room as her mom got the door. "Hi, Mrs. Abreo,"

"Talon, you make me feel old. It's time you called me Avan. Are you here to study?"

"Biology. First final for both of us next week. OK to come in?"

"Of course. Sofia's upstairs," Talon headed straight for the stairs as Avan yelled after him. "Remember, Sofia, the door stays open!"

"Mom, it's Talon!" Sofia yelled back.

Talon's bright-red cheeks soon appeared through the door. Sofia realized she must have embarrassed him by declaring he was no threat to try anything. Sometimes she wondered what she would do if he did. Now she was blushing. "Hi. Shut the door," Sofia teased.

"Not happening. You scare me!" Talon shot back.

Sofia was lying on the carpet with a screen in front of her. She watched Talon look at the desk and then at the bed, realizing the floor was the only option. The bed was covered with clothes. Some, she had tried on and rejected. Others were folded, waiting to be put away. The desk—well, Sofia could never sit at a desk. Besides, it was covered with trophies, a few hairbrushes, a jewelry case, and more clutter that rendered it worthless for studying.

"OK, the usual setup," Talon said as he plopped down on the floor with his screen.

Sofia sat up, crossed her legs, and faced Talon. She gripped both of Talon's hands in hers. She waited for Talon to look her in the eyes, needing him to know it was time to be real with his forever friend. "Tell me how you're holding up. Nothing but the truth."

Talon hesitated briefly, then surrendered. "I don't know. But I don't think I can stay in this town."

"Why? Where would you go?"

"I don't know. Just not here. When word gets out that I'm a disconnect, the town's going to start treating me differently. Having people I grew up with pity me or even shy away from me ... I'd rather get that treatment around strangers than friends."

Sofia squeezed Talon's hands. "Listen, you may lose a few friends. Not your real ones, though. And your family's all here. This is where you need to be right now." Peering into the deep green eyes before her, Sofia could see the doubt lingering. "Ok then. What are your options?"

"Not sure. I've heard I can choose to join one of the disconnect work communities, where I wouldn't have a guardian. Maybe I'd sign up for the Fabrication Center."

"Seriously? The Center? You don't join the Center! If you're an outcast, you get sent there. Never to be heard from again."

"You don't know that," Talon said. "Besides, that's where they make all the Bee Sting devices. Kind of appeals to my inner geek."

"Inner and outer. You're full-on geek. And I love that," Sofia added. "Why not the Tech Lab then? People don't disappear there."

"I'd love to. If you're going to pick a career, why not be where all the products get designed? One small problem—they don't send disconnects there. People have to earn their way in. It's not a place where people like me land when they're cast aside."

This reality hit Sofia hard. "This is wrong. You haven't done anything. You didn't screw up your chip. The people who came up with this system are to blame." Sofia couldn't stop her anger from building. "Those are the people who should be punished! They should be sent away!" Talon laughed, and Sofia did too, realizing she must once again sound like a raving lunatic. "Alright, I'm probably not doing a great job of helping you get your thoughts together."

"No, you're the distraction I need. Really. I like you being real."

"How is this for real then? What if you run? If you don't want to stay here, then head for the mountains! I'll go with you."

"Wait—what are you talking about? I ... I haven't even thought about that."

Sofia quickly realized her offer was absurd. Maybe before the world had collapsed on Talon, the offer wouldn't have been so crazy. They had helped each other grow over the years. Talon had made her look at life differently. She no longer feared being out of step with everyone else. Sofia, for her part, had infected Talon with a desire to explore the forests, the streams, and all the outdoors had to offer, but now Talon was running from the world. The more she thought about it, Talon wasn't leaving town anytime soon. Joining a disconnect community was all just talk, even if Talon didn't realize it yet. Despite all her efforts to drag Talon back out into the world, his safe haven was still his home. She waited to see if he would acknowledge this reality.

Talon latched onto another truth instead. "I couldn't run. When my brother ran, it nearly destroyed my dad. Forget what it did to me. I couldn't do that to him. Or my sister. I couldn't let you do it to your parents either." Then he quickly added,

"Hey, you good with listening to a little music while we study?"

"Oh, sure," Sofia said, understanding the topic had been closed.

"Great. How about you link my screen to your system? I have some stuff I want you to check out. Ever hear of Felice Suthers?"

"No. Luscious, connect Talon's screen," Sofia said.

"Access denied," the control system responded.

"Excuse me?"

"Your identity is unknown."

"Perhaps getting programmed altered your connection?" Talon suggested.

"How? Being programmed shouldn't change my identity."

"Maybe your mom or dad did something?"

"Maybe."

"Did you hear about Espar Crashan?" Talon asked. "She was denied access to the school grounds this morning. Rumor has it that her chip is defective and her network connection is spotty. Looks like I'm not the only Lost Boy."

Horror suddenly filled Sofia.

"What? I thought you hated Espar," Talon said.

"Talon, this is the second time my access has failed. My ride went down yesterday. I thought it was some random thing, but now I'm not sure."

"That's weird. Not unheard of, though. Things break all the time."

"But twice in the last couple of days?"

"Think of everything you've accessed in the last few days, including school today. You should probably check with your mom about your system before freaking out."

"Yeah, sorry. Having this happen to you and Espar, I shouldn't be making this about me. And I don't wish this problem on Espar, no matter the size of her inner bitch."

Chapter Twenty

Drake

May 8 – 9:26 a.m.

Drake stood outside of Gabriel's office, trying to keep his fears under control. Bottom line, he was feeling the CID was stalking his family. Every time he went anywhere near the network, he was getting visual and audio prompts, urgently requesting he contact some guy concerning Talon. He wasn't interested in talking to some stranger about his son's future, but now the messages had turned threatening, suggesting Drake may be deemed an unfit parent if he didn't check in with this CID goon.

He knew he couldn't avoid this guy forever, but he needed to get a little background before responding. For all he knew, this was some deranged individual getting some sadistic thrill out of his family's misfortune.

Since his department had been swallowed up by the CID and Gabriel was in the middle of that whole change, Drake figured his boss would know damn well what the CID's interest in Talon was.

Giving up on gathering any composure, Drake knocked on the door and entered.

"I guess I should say 'Enter,'" Gabriel said.

"Sorry, boss. You got a moment for me?" Drake asked as he closed the door behind him.

"Looks like I do. Have a seat," Gabriel said as he spun his chair to face Drake.

"So you've heard about Talon?"

"Of course. I'm really sorry about this. I can't imagine what your family is going through."

"Thanks. I'm not going to pretend it isn't rough. After Wilder, this feels like lightning striking twice. Look, some CID guy, let's call him Christopher Robin, seems to have some fetish for Talon ..."

"Christopher Rombern," Gabriel clarified.

"So you know about him?"

"Of course. Isn't that why you're here?"

"Yeah, you know, we find out about Talon's shitty situation two days ago and some CID thug is already hounding us. Talon's completely unnerved. He doesn't know what to think. I'm trying to offer to continue as his guardian for as long as he'll have me, but Talon's having none of it. He's not even sixteen and people are expecting him to nail down the rest of his life. This is complete crap!"

"Hey, slow down," Gabriel said. "I'm not disagreeing with you. How can I help?"

"Right. Sorry. I don't mean to be taking this out on you. So, tell me, assuming I can get Talon to go along, how do I get this guardian situation worked out? Do I really need to work with some Winnie the Pooh character?"

"No, but things have changed. Rombern has been trying to inform you that a CID panel has been set up to handle these matters. Any request for guardianship must be submitted to the panel."

"You can't be serious. Who's on this panel?"

"I am, for one. The rest are out-of-towners. There's five total."

"Interesting. Not sure what to make of that. At least you're involved. That's good," Drake said, trying to absorb this news. "So how does this work then? Can I submit a request through you?"

"Actually, this is pretty new. The panel hasn't even met yet. I think Talon will have to handle any requests, though. He's almost sixteen and it's his future."

"Seriously? Are you listening to yourself? Talon's fifteen. Did you have your crap together at that age? I know I was well into my twenties before I started figuring things out."

"These are different times, Drake. We've all had to grow up. Get more serious. We almost wiped ourselves off the face of the earth. It's the way it is now. Sixteen is what society considers to be an adult."

"You're going to have to explain that one to me. The same people that you admit almost annihilated humankind, who clearly didn't grow up enough to make good choices, are going to make a better world by asking the succeeding generations to rush to adulthood? I'm sorry if I can't buy in, but I think I'll still be there for my boy. I'm betting you wouldn't be preaching this shit if Sofia was in Talon's place."

"Again, I'm here to help," Gabriel said, trying to diffuse the rising tension. "Let me investigate what needs to be done. I'm sure we can get this worked out."

Drake looked at his boss and friend of fifteen years. He was being silly. Drake knew Gabriel was on his side. "You're right. Sorry. Again. I can't help wondering if I'm cut out to be a parent. Every challenge seems to be beyond me."

Chapter Twenty-One

Sofia

May 8 – 7:36 p.m.

"Dad, did you make any changes to the access system?" Sofia had been waiting to get her father alone. They had finished dinner and it was her mother's night to do the dishes.

Her dad thought for a moment. "No, honey, why?"

"I have a big problem."

"What do you mean?"

"My chip ... it's defective." Sofia fought to hold back tears. Saying it out loud made reality sink in. She no longer had any doubt her chip was flawed.

"Sofie, why do you think that?" He tried to sound concerned, but Sofia could tell he didn't believe her. Sofia knew her father thought she had a problem because Talon had one. Her dad always said that if someone in the family had a sore throat, then Sofia would be certain she was coming down with pneumonia.

"Daddy, I'm serious. I lost access to a Mini three days ago. Then yesterday I couldn't access our control system. The system couldn't read my—"

"Welcome to technology. Things go wrong. I'm sorry you had these problems. And I know Talon's situation is hard on you. But you're coping by making his problem your own. You know that, right?"

"Dad, listen to me. You heard about Espar Crashan?"

"Of course. Very sad. Is that weighing on you as well?"

"I had the same problem today. I couldn't access the school buildings."

"How's that? I would have been notified."

Sofia could tell her dad was having a hard time letting go of his doubts. "On my way into the school, the alarm went off. I froze, knowing I was the next Espar Crashan. It turns out Talon had gone in seconds before me, and when he heard the alarm, he made the connection. He ran back, grabbed me, and told me to leave. He stayed and took the blame for setting off the alarm."

"Then how did you go to school today?"

"I–I ... I didn't." Sofia's voice trembled. "I called in sick."

Gabriel got up and walked around the table to stand before Sofia. She stood up and fell into his arms, crying.

"I got you, Sofie," he said. "It's going to be OK. I'm going to get this worked out. Count on it."

Chapter Twenty-Two

Talon

May 9 – 4:22 p.m.

"We got here, right? If we can't get access to a ride going back, my dad's on standby to authorize one for us."

Talon was just happy to make it to Costanoa, a small camping destination thirty minutes north of Santa Cruz in the heart of a fifty-mile stretch known as the Slow Coast. Sofia, on the other hand, had found no joy in their drama-free journey. The minute they arrived, Talon could tell she worried about whether her chip would glitch again, leaving them scrambling to find a way home.

It had been his idea to get away to Costanoa. The Slow Coast was a sparsely populated mix of farms and open space where you could search for a roadside diner, an artisan shop, or a trailhead leading you to the ocean or inland to the redwood forests. Best of all, you didn't have to compete with countless people to enjoy your destination spot. Most people who visited the area were amazed that such a scenic area was only a stone's throw from Silicon Valley. Most also realized it couldn't last much longer.

While Costanoa had every type of glamping—tents, cabins, and even a boutique hotel—Talon hadn't actually brought Sofia to enjoy the campgrounds. The site was bordered by trails that climbed into the coastal hills. The vistas from on top of those hills offered unobstructed, panoramic views of the coastline. Talon was aware that most people thought Sofia had a wild side. It was true, but it wasn't the stunts that she pulled. Those were just Sofia rebelling against being labeled a cop's daughter. The outdoors appealed to Sofia's true wild side. Since the first grade, when their families began spending time together, Sofia would lure Talon over the backyard fence and out into the woods. If they were lucky, they would find a pond to catch pollywogs, but more often than not, they found a hornets' nest or a patch of poison oak. As they grew, they extended their trips up into the wooded mountains in search of vistas seen by few.

He hoped this area would call to Sofia and drown out the worries that had been riding her hard. So far, his plan wasn't working. They sat perched on a log at the base of the trailhead, and Talon had a hard time convincing Sofia to go any farther. Perhaps it was time to throw in the towel.

"Hey, sorry for dragging you out here."

"I know I'm being a toad," Sofia sighed. "I'm sitting here wetting all over your plans."

The laughter came spilling out of Talon. He had no idea where that description had come from, but that was Sofia. She always kept him off balance.

"Seriously," Sofia said, even though she laughed too, "I know you're trying to distract us from this whole mess. I'm doing a horrible job of going along. I can't seem to wrap my head around this. I feel like everyone is looking at me, knowing I'm defective. And if they don't know, I'm sure my chip will glitch in some way, making it obvious I've got problems. Even worse, I had no idea what you were going through. I was a lousy friend for thinking so little about your situation and maybe less of a friend now because I'm still selfishly thinking about myself. I'm a fraud on so many levels."

"Sofia, stop. Your chip isn't your doing. Neither is mine. You're an amazing friend who tried hard to understand my problem, and now that you fully understand it, you feel like you let me down. You've never let me down." Talon gave her hand a squeeze. "The fact that you're here right now says it all. Only yesterday, you discovered your chip is off. And let me tell you from personal experience, the natural reaction is to spend a few days locked up in your room, freaking out. Four days, if I'm being completely honest. Instead, here you are, day two, freaking *me* out." Sofia actually giggled a little, and Talon realized how much it meant to see her lighten up. "There's no getting around it. You need to talk about this. What's going through your head?"

"I don't know. I mean, maybe my mind will settle down once we go before the panel."

"We should learn when that is any day now."

They looked at the view surrounding them, Talon hoping they could both find some of its peace.

"At this point, it can't come quick enough," Sofia said.

Talon picked up a stone, feeling the cool, mossy earth in his hand, and casually tossed it. "Why? You already know you're opting for guardianship. Your mom, right?"

"Yeah, I keep telling myself that. You know me, though. Until that board seals our fate, my mind's open to any other offers."

"Remember JT?" Talon asked.

"I do, but I don't think of him often," Sofia admitted. "Why?"

"If he's still alive, I wonder what his life is like."

"And why'd this pop into your head right now?"

"Remember how I said I wouldn't run? I would now."

"You? Suggesting we run?"

"There's more at stake now," Talon said, no longer concerned about hiding his desire to protect Sofia.

"I ... I'm not sure how to react to that one," Sofia said, grabbing his hands. Talon knew this was Sofia's way of telling him to listen up. "That's an amazing offer, especially when I think of what you've been through. But you were right the other day. We can't run; our parents would never recover. We have to trust our town won't let us down. They'll accept us for who we've always been. Are you good with that?"

The irony didn't escape Talon. "So, I'm offering to run and you're trusting your life to others? No one would ever believe this!"

Sofia laughed. "I know. This goes against my better judgment."

"What judgment?"

"Good point. Seriously, you need to tell me if I'm letting you down."

"You never let me down. We both know you're the one who's been keeping me from sinking under. I'm pretty sure life is going to get a lot more difficult in this town, but I'm good facing it with you."

Sofia looked at Talon hard for a moment, then leaned in and kissed him on the cheek. "We should probably appreciate what we have right now. Let's take a walk," she said and led the journey toward the hills.

Talon stumbled after her in a daze. A kiss on the cheek shouldn't mean much, right? Only, it was new territory.

Chapter Twenty-Three

General Stafford

May 11 - 7:00 p.m.

"My understanding is you have another update for me," General Stafford said, finding it difficult to be anything but abrupt. He had concluded a long training session with his troops and wished he could wrap his day up on that positive note. His troops were dedicated, united, and eager to achieve. Alas, he had calls to take and then a late flight back to D.C., where he had congressional members, his board, and even the president waiting for him to assure them all would be OK. He hated this part of his job but reminded himself that this was only the beginning. The more the next phase of the Program came into focus, the more handholding would be required.

"Yes, I do," Gabriel replied.

"Please proceed then." Damn—he knew how this call would go and he wanted to get it over with. Yet, he knew the chief deserved more compassion.

"Alright. Dajani reached out to Taylor again. He was inquiring about Talon Russit, Espar Crashan, and my daughter."

"Right. I'm sorry to learn about your daughter and Miss Crashan. This must be quite difficult for you."

"Thank you, sir. It has been a difficult time for many in our community."

"No doubt. Did Mr. Haris mention the reason for his concern?"

"No, he merely mentioned he thought they might be in trouble."

"That's it?"

"Well, I'm not sure if it's significant, but before ending the call, Dajani said, 'Remember what I said about being here to help if Talon needs me.'"

"You're thinking it's important that he didn't clarify he was there for Miss Crashan and your daughter?" the general asked, knowing damn well it was.

"Possibly."

"Other than Mr. Haris's possible focus on Talon, do you have any further updates?" the general prompted, pushing the conversation where it was destined to go.

"Actually, I do. I'm on a five-member panel that determines the fate of my daughter as well as the others. I reached out to my fellow members to sort through the details, expecting the perpetual guardianship to be straightforward."

"And?" the general interjected, trying to speed matters up.

"They shut me out. I was told the first meeting would be as early as Tuesday and the second a week later. So, I asked why two meetings? I mean, the panel knows all the parents will be requesting guardianship. What needs to be decided?"

"What was their response?"

"The most any of them would tell me was that it was more complex than I thought. Something was off with one small town ending up with three disconnects. Of course, I pressed them since I'm on the panel and have every right to know what's going on. But they claimed my daughter puts my status on shaky ground. They suggested I recuse myself. They want me to step away from the panel while this is all sorted out."

"Anything else?"

"Just that our kids should come prepared to state their case at the first meeting and a decision will be made at the next. General, I'm going to tell you, as a parent, this makes me awfully nervous. Guardianship isn't looking like a sure thing."

The general did his best to exercise patience, waiting for the request to be made.

"I guess what I'm getting at is," Gabriel continued, "with your connections, do you think you could help?"

"I think I could. Is Miss McNealy chairing your panel?" he asked, already aware of the answer.

"Yes, sir."

"Good. We go way back. There are a few stories I can't share, but let's say we worked closely together." The general acknowledged to himself that Mr. Haris did as well, which was common in the early days of the Program. He made a note to investigate whether they had stayed in touch. "We left matters on good terms," he continued, "I'll see what we can work out regarding your daughter."

"And the other two?"

"Let's not overestimate my abilities. If tough choices have to be made, I'm guessing the priority is your daughter. Is that correct?"

"Well, yes, of course. Any parent looks after their children. But as a protector of Ridge Crest, I'm hoping for more."

"I'll see what can be done," the general said, promising nothing.

"I appreciate that, sir. Is there anything you need from me?"

The general gave credit to Gabriel for being sharp enough to realize this was an exchange. "I'd like to work directly with Detective Taylor to better understand Mr. Haris's interest here. I know Mr. Haris, so I'm best equipped to unravel this mystery. Does that work?"

After a brief hesitation, Gabriel responded. "Yes, sir. May I ask what involvement you envision for me personally?"

"None. You will need complete deniability should anyone question whether your daughter's predicament influenced any of the upcoming decisions. This means you will have to recuse yourself as the panel requested. You and I will, however, be in constant touch regarding your daughter."

He had just laid bare the terms of their agreement—he would handle all matters regarding the young disconnects and Dajani Haris; Gabriel would not participate in decisions, including any panel votes, when it came to the disconnects—and Gabriel's cooperation would determine his daughter's fate.

Gabriel resigned himself to the harsh reality. "Understood, sir."

The general didn't feel great about backing Gabriel into a corner. He simply knew it was his responsibility to make the tough decisions in an effort to try to navigate the best possible outcomes for all involved. Such had been his burden for as far back as he could remember.

Chapter Twenty-Four

Drake

May 13 – 8:45 a.m.

Drake waited outside the CID entrance, grappling with how to balance his mood swings from feeling furious to feeling guilty for being angry. He had tried to reach Gabriel all weekend long and left urgent messages on his Cube. He even left messages over the CID network, which would prompt Gabriel to listen anytime his NAC was detected near a networked device. Gabriel had either listened to his messages or commanded the network to ignore them. Either way, Gabriel knew Drake was desperate to reach him. Yet Gabriel chose to go silent.

This complete lack of response was infuriating until Drake reminded himself that Gabriel was probably in shock about the misfortune that had struck Sofia. He may very well have retreated to his family and shut down all communication with others as he struggled to grasp the change of events.

Of course, Gabriel should now be able to fully empathize with what Drake was going through. If Gabriel was dealing with his personal hell, then he must understand Drake was in no less pain. He could have taken a moment to connect. With the hearing before the panel quickly approaching, Drake spent most of Sunday restraining himself from storming over to Gabriel's house to confront him. He imagined Sofia and Avan were probably also reeling, and an emotionally unstable Drake was not going to help by showing up on the scene.

When the sun came up Monday morning, Drake was out of patience. The panel was scheduled to meet the next day, but he was no closer to protecting Talon. In fact, the situation had taken a turn for the worse. The panel scheduling two meetings felt wrong.

Gabriel had promised to investigate Talon's situation and get back to him. Considering Sofia was now in the same mess, Drake was confident his boss had already thoroughly investigated their predicament. With time running out, it was time he shared. Drake was determined to catch Gabriel at work or hunt him down if he failed to show.

It was 8:45 a.m. Drake had planted himself outside the entrance, knowing Gabriel almost always made it to the office no later than 9 a.m. As he made his vigil, many of his co-workers arrived to start their workday. Most took one look at Drake and scurried past him into the building. The few that did try to start a conversation were quickly defeated by single-word responses.

Jesse was the most difficult to brush off. Beyond simple inquiries about Drake's well-being, Jesse decided he had some right to grill him about everything concerning Talon's fate, wanting to know if Drake had found anyone to intervene on Talon's behalf and then going on to ask bizarre questions about whether Talon had been approached by any strangers. Drake finally asked what angle he was working and what he wanted. Jesse pretended to be hurt, responding with something about wanting to be sure Drake didn't do anything stupid. Trying to save his outbursts for Gabriel, Drake replied, "If something stupid offers a chance at sorting out this mess, then I'm all in. If you've got some stupid ideas, now would be a good time to share. If you've got nothing, then leave."

Jesse had stomped off.

With 9 a.m. approaching, Drake began to figure someone had warned Gabriel he was a wanted man. He was about to call for a ride when he spotted his boss approaching. Preferring to have a private conversation, Drake walked out to meet him.

"Gabriel!" Gabriel visibly flinched. As he drew near, Drake looked Gabriel over. "How's Sofie?"

After a long pause, Gabriel responded, "Sofie's world is a bit upside down at the moment. I imagine Talon has given you some updates on her. They've certainly been spending a lot of time together the last few days."

"I've noticed. They both seem to be trying to figure out what's next for them. I kind of thought you would have come through with the panel a little earlier. I have to admit this two-meeting thing has shaken me a bit. Something's off."

"Sorry, Sofia's issues came as quite the shock. No excuses. I should have reached out. I did contact my fellow panel members, yeah. Apparently the first meeting is designed to allow our children to make their requests and the second for the final decisions to be made. Did Talon decide what he wants to do?"

"Yes. He's going for guardianship," Drake replied, brushing aside Gabriel's effort to change the subject. "Why two meetings? Are the guardianships being questioned?"

"I hope not, but I wasn't able to find out. The other members wouldn't discuss much with me."

"Why not? You're on the panel. The least they could do was provide some assurance!"

"It doesn't work that way. Since you work for me, I'm biased toward you and your son. And my conflict over Sofia goes without saying. I wouldn't be objective in trying to look out for the overall welfare of the community. So I had to recuse myself. I don't have a voice in the matter."

"What? That's ... look, you know Talon and Sofia better than anyone else on the board. Espar, too. You can vouch for them being great kids, but you backed away? I mean, wh—"

"Don't get worked up. It's not that simple."

"*How* is it not that simple?" Drake shot back, laboring to slow his breathing. "These are our kids. You were able to help, and you decided to walk away instead?"

"If I didn't recuse myself, I would have been removed by the other board members anyway. There was no choice,"

Gabriel reasoned. "Look, if the first meeting doesn't leave both of us feeling everything is headed in the right direction, I promise to move heaven and earth to set things back on track. I'm sure you will too. Am I right?"

Drake didn't bother answering Gabriel. His mind had been at work for days probing possible outcomes and how to react. Gabriel wasn't telling him everything, but he believed him when he said he would be all in if something went wrong. Drake reminded himself to remain composed. He trusted in himself, and he trusted Gabriel.

Chapter Twenty-Five

Rani

May 13 - 2:17 p.m.

Three captives had been sitting in the conference room for over half the workday. No one had offered them water or even a bathroom break. They weren't exactly being tortured, but the treatment annoyed Rani Kaswell. She had the distinct aggravation of being across the hall in an office with a perfect view of the conference room door. The fact that there were no windows was the only thing that kept her from having to stare at the detainees all day. Still, she knew they were in there. Jesse had ushered them in the room and loudly threatened them to stay put before walking out.

Jesse was always capturing fugitives. To her young eyes, he was fanatical about the Program and eager to stomp out—or in this case, detain—all those that opposed it. He typically held his captured prizes in the conference room while he got the papers together to transfer them to county jail. In this case, however, he had left his captives and not returned.

Unable to switch her thoughts away from the captives, Rani pulled up the access database for their office. She did a quick search for all those entering the building with unprogrammed chips. Sure enough, their NACs told her she was right about their fugitive status. Or mostly right.

Rani was all too aware that messing with another officer's perps was frowned upon. Being twenty-four-years-old and having joined the force only six months ago, she knew her place at this point. She needed to keep her eyes down and tread lightly.

Or so she always told herself.

Feeling her only option was to clear her head, she decided a walk outside would do her good, before she was tempted to do anything rash. She got up, walked past the conference room, but then doubled back.

It occurred to her she could have this all wrong. She had left for lunch earlier. That's it. Jesse must have grabbed the perps while she was out.

Not hearing anything from within, she tried the door. Three Hispanic males, all less than age thirty, stared back at her. One had to be no older than twenty. "Shit. Didn't know you were still in here." A white lie, but so what? "While I'm here, anyone need to visit the bathroom?"

Three hands shot up. She motioned them toward the door. When she finished escorting them to the restroom, she couldn't stop herself from being human. "Water?" Three hands shot up again. She bit her tongue to stop herself from asking if they were hungry; she wasn't running a hotel here. Instead, she said, "I'll be right back with the waters." Shutting the door, she spotted Gabriel walking back toward his office. She yelled out, "Chief, a minute?"

Gabriel sighed and detoured down the hallway to join her. "What's up?"

Rani couldn't help but notice Gabriel looked worn around the edges, so she did her best to try to tread lightly. "Jesse put some fugitives in the conference room ... this morning. Maybe he got pulled off on something else?"

"Jesse did what?!" Gabriel exploded. "I told him to stop this crap! This Program superhero shit ain't getting us any closer to the one fugitive I want to see sitting in that conference room—Shadow! Get them out of here!"

"You got it, Chief." Rani knew she wasn't going to score any points with Jesse, but she wasn't going to question orders, especially an order she agreed with.

She stepped back into the room. "You're all free to go. Water is in the lobby."

They didn't need to hear more. All three filed out, the youngest being the last in line. Rani stopped him at the door.

"Hey! Can I ask you something? Or will it be trouble for you?" she asked, motioning to the others as they fled without looking back.

"Them? Talking to you won't change anything," he said. "They don't trust me already. Just part of the life we lead."

"That sucks, I know. Can you tell me how you got caught?"

"Why do you care? It was one of your kind. Don't you all want the same thing?"

"My ... *kind*? Really?" She shook her head. "Shit, I'll bite. What's *my kind* and what do *we* want?"

Pointing at his shoulder, where a barbed wire tattoo poked out of a brown t-shirt, he said, "Your kind—all the networked people—you wanna keep us out and if that's not enough, then caged."

Rani didn't know how to respond. The young man hadn't lashed out in anger. If anything, he had sounded disappointed. "So, the barbed wire represents how you've been fenced off from civilization? And even caged when it suits 'my kind'?" It hurt to watch him nod his head. She knew he was right. Still, she persisted. "Look at me. You think my kind are all the same?"

He shrugged.

"Is it alright if I still care what happened?"

The young man towered well over her, and his eyes bored into hers for the first time. She found herself holding her breath, waiting for him to cast his judgment.

"We came across your buddy drowning in one of our fishing holes," he finally said. "We dragged him out and he pulled a Taser on us. Faked the whole thing. Who does that? You can bet next time we won't be helping your people out."

Rani couldn't help but shake her head. "That isn't me, friend. Look, let me give you my number for when you or your campmates need help, OK?"

"Really? Wouldn't that get you in trouble? Actually, I couldn't even consider it. Even if you're serious, I don't have a

Cube to store it. No one living off-grid has one. Best case, they would be used to track us."

"Well, you sure make it hard on a girl trying to give you her number," she said, not minding flirting with him a bit. She had caught him glancing at her a few times. No question he thought he was more skilled than he was. With her dark hair, dark eyes, and curvy build, she knew she had it going on, and she got confirmation from his blush and the fact that his tongue was now frozen. "Why don't we do this the old-fashioned way," she added, handing him her card before he turned away, eager to retreat. "One more thing!" she called out. "Why is someone who is networked and with no criminal past living amongst fugitives?"

He turned back toward her. Now he was angry. "Of course, you know all about me. You knew the moment I walked in here, right?"

Rani felt herself flush with guilt, but she wasn't going to be intimidated. "You can't simply turn off your chip, Juan Tescano."

"It's JT," he muttered, once again setting out for the exit.

Chapter Twenty-Six

Sofia

May 14 - 6:23 p.m.

The hearing was held at the county courthouse since Ridge Crest didn't have a courthouse of its own. Sofia welcomed the obscure location because she was embarrassed by her perceived defect. Several of her friends had offered to go with her, but she brushed them off with promises of leaning on them for next week's big meeting.

With her parents at her side, she ascended the immense steps leading to a large glass wall that formed the facade of the ten-story building. The two glass doors at the entryway were illuminated with red light, indicating the three were not cleared to enter. Sofia's dad let them know it should only take a few seconds for their chips to be accessed and their IDs confirmed. On cue, their names were displayed across the glass panels, with the illuminated doors turning green and beginning to open inward. Sofia couldn't help noting the irony that her chip had been successfully identified.

She barely had time to register the cavernous marble lobby before two guards came forward to escort them further. Gabriel forfeited his Taser and other police hardware. The officers must have been brought in from outside the county as no greetings were exchanged. Once satisfied with their search, the guards led them across the deserted lobby.

The special hearing was scheduled for 6:30 p.m. when the building was otherwise vacated. The small group made its way to the back of the lobby and down the hall to room 1C. Not a word was spoken. Reaching their destination, the guards motioned for the Abreo family to back up to the wall opposite the courtroom doors. This formal and cautious approach was unnerving and insulting. They weren't dangerous criminals.

Once everyone gave the guards space, only then did one of them turn and push open the large wooden double doors.

The Carrara marble floors anchored a large room with high ceilings. Combined with the ornate wood ceiling and walls, the room seemed almost inviting. Almost. An aisle proceeded forward between pew-style seating, where Espar and Talon's family members were already settled in. Sage and Drake waved cheerfully, doing their best to stay positive. The aisle deadened at a glass partition that divided the room. Beyond the wall, four people sat behind a raised dais, with Espar and Talon occupying a low-top table at the base of the dais where they sat motionless, seemingly intimidated by the elders looming over them.

The guards motioned for Sofia's parents to be seated, making it clear that Sofia was on her own from this point forward. Her mother gave her a hug before allowing the guards to escort Sofia down the aisle.

The doors glowed red as Sofia waited to be identified. This made her wonder how Talon had made it through, knowing his chip didn't function. Before she could think further on this, the doors turned green and opened. She stepped inside and the doors shut behind her. Only then did she notice four guards lining the walls. They almost blended with the dark surface as they stood perfectly still. Their presence couldn't be a good sign, a total contingent of six guards providing security for a hearing of three high-school students.

Sofia stood inside the glass doors, surveying the scene before her, in no rush to join Talon and Sage at the foot of the mountainous dais. Seeing her hesitate, Talon stood to offer encouragement, prompting a guard to take a quick step forward. The guard glared at Talon for a moment, then merged back into the woodwork, having decided Talon didn't pose a threat. Sofia, doing her best to overcome her nerves, walked quickly into Talon's embrace.

Talon whispered, "Hi. Scary, huh? These people don't look very friendly."

Sofia didn't bother looking at Espar, who was on the other side of Talon and no doubt scowling at her. Instead, she took Talon's cue and faced the board members. The panel members consisted of two women and two men. She had hoped her father would be seated there as well, but he had explained that he had been sidelined for this proceeding. He assured Sofia that while the hearing would be formal and probably intimidating, she and her mates would be thoughtfully heard. He teased that she merely needed to apply the same persuasive powers she'd been using her entire life to manipulate him. His words had comforted her earlier, but she didn't find much assurance in the faces before her now. One woman was perhaps her father's age. The rest had to be in their fifties and sixties. All wore pained expressions that reminded her of the look her dad carried when suffering from heartburn.

A woman seated near the middle of the panel picked up a gavel and banged it down twice as if she needed to silence the room. Sofia took a closer look at the woman and realized she had to be closer to seventy. She was rail thin, with a hawkish nose and orange-dyed hair. The name on the plaque before her read "Nancy J. McNealy."

"Now that we have everyone present, let's bring this meeting to order," McNealy began, with a voice that was anything but frail. "I am Nancy McNealy, Chief CID Panelist. To the left and right of me are the other distinguished members that have been working to address your community's unfortunate situation."

"Excuse me. Excuse me." Sofia turned to see Espar's mom stretched to her full six feet, waving both arms. Having the whole room's attention, she asked, "Why are we locked back here? Shouldn't we be up there sharing our thoughts with you? After all, not only are we their parents," she said, pointing at her daughter, "but we're also established members of the community, making us valuable resources for working through any concerns you or our community might have."

Sofia turned her attention back to the panel members to see them shaking their heads in unison. McNealy sat up straighter, squaring her shoulders, giving her an aura of determination. "This is not a community outreach event. Espar Crashan, Sofia Abreo, and Talon Russit are here before the Santa Cruz County CID panel due to chip or programming defects. The panel has confirmed these defects with the assistance of a CID technician specializing in network connectivity. One of the responsibilities falling on us members is to protect the Santa Cruz County community when faced with disconnects. We take this responsibility quite seriously. This means we make the decisions that a community overwhelmed by the emotions of the situation cannot bring itself to consider."

Nancy paused, perhaps to let everyone understand where this was going. Sofia had no problem following. The panel members' discomfort and McNealy's grim outline of their situation was quite clear: they were all condemned before this charade had even begun. The hearing would be a farce.

"The panel has already met on this matter," McNealy resumed. "As I stated, we have confirmed the defects. We have also investigated the backgrounds of the youths before us and evaluated the capabilities of the community to function with disconnected members. While difficult to face, we have all concluded that housing three disconnects, especially with a community of disconnects and other hardened fugitives entrenched mere miles from the city's reach, would be inviting the resistance to make your community its home base. Regretfully, both the Program and your community cannot accept such an outcome. With this in mind, we have decided to forego any charade of considering requests for guardianship."

The courtroom collectively gasped. Sofia, in an "oh my god!" moment, realized there would be no hearing at all. Except for the rigid McNealy, the panel members sported downcast faces, refusing to make eye contact with the condemned before them. McNealy, with the stiff backbone, seemed determined to bring this to a close, no matter how distasteful. None of them wanted to continue the pretense of caring about their duties or the community before them. Sofia might be young, but she recognized puppets resigned to finishing the play in a manner directed by their unseen puppeteer.

As if on cue, McNealy continued, "Our decisions, which will be implemented immediately, are as follows: Talon Russit, you are assigned to the Fabrication Center." Sofia heard a groan from the back of the room that had to be Talon's sister. "Espar Crashan, you are assigned to the Fabrication Center."

"Outrageous!" came a cry that could only have been Espar's father.

"Sofia Abreo," the chairwoman continued undeterred, "you are assigned to the Technology Lab."

A commotion broke out all at once. The guards disengaged from the walls and formed a line between the teens' table and the dais. The board members could be seen rising from their seats and filing out a door at the back of the room, two guards following to escort them out.

Sofia's focus on this procession was interrupted by a large thud on the glass behind her. She turned as Espar's dad began screaming.

"Open the damn door! You aren't taking my daughter anywhere! You touch her, and I will hunt each and every one of you down! Open the door *now!*"

Mr. Crashan pounded on the glass doors with both fists. The guards on his side of the glass divide moved to contain him, easily tackling him to the ground. Seconds later, the entry door slammed shut as someone sped out of the room. Looking around, Sofia saw that Drake Russit was gone. Sage sat by herself, apparently too stunned to move.

One of the remaining two guards who stood in front of their table cleared his throat, catching their attention. He motioned to the back door. It was only then that Sofia realized the board members and their escorts had finished their mass exit. "Mr. Russit and Miss Crashan, please proceed out that door," the guard commanded. Sofia rose with Talon and Espar, but the guard quickly clarified, "Please stay seated, Miss Abreo."

Talon stood before her, his face dropping to his feet as he clearly struggled to find the right words. He finally looked back up, saying, "I hope to see you again."

It wasn't until that moment that Sofia realized how much she had come to count on the boy with the intense green eyes being part of her life.

"No, Talon," she said, grabbing his hands. "Hope isn't enough. You must promise me you will see me again. You must *promise* me you will do whatever it takes."

"I will try. You know I will," Talon replied, looking at the guard who was motioning for him to get moving.

"No!" Sofia lashed out, yanking on his hands to get his full attention. "Not good enough. *Promise* me."

Talon looked her face over, eyeing the tears she could no longer contain. Squeezing her hands, Talon said with more conviction than she could ever remember, "I *will* make it back to you. I promise."

Everything was moving too fast as Talon seemed to drift past her, followed by Espar, whose disdain for her glowed from her hate-filled eyes

Talon and Espar exited with an escort, leaving one guard standing before Sofia. The guard said nothing, waiting for her mates to clear out. Sofia looked at her parents. They were the only two remaining people on that side of the barrier. Mr. Crashan had been forcibly removed from the room with a sobbing Mrs. Crashan following behind. Sage must have slipped out just after Talon left.

Her dad gave her a nod as if to say everything would be alright. It wouldn't. Yes, Sofia had been assigned to the Technology Lab, which was one of the coveted destinations for young professionals—the brightest and most ambitious competed to get their foot in the door there. Sofia was a quick study and a solid student, but she knew she hadn't been assigned to the Lab based on merit. She had not strived as hard as Talon and countless other schoolmates when it came to academics. Her dad had pulled strings.

Sofia glared at him. Why hadn't he pulled those same strings for Talon, or even Espar? No wonder Espar departed with a look of hatred. Sofia deserved the same scorn from Talon, but he was too kind. At that moment, she desperately wished she had been assigned to the Fabrication Center. Her father had done her no favors. She stood and looked at her guard. "You need to take me out of here, now."

She walked toward the back door and didn't look back.

Chapter Twenty-Seven

Drake

May 14 – 6:57 p.m.

The courtroom door shut behind Drake and he headed for the courthouse lobby. He suspected the guards wouldn't have orders to stop him yet, though he wasn't about to let them if they tried. He didn't stop to collect his police hardware, simply marching across the lobby and out the main doors.

He exited the parking lot and drove toward the freeway, making sure he kept to the speed limit, knowing the County CID would monitor his vehicle. Five minutes later, he was exiting the freeway at Ridge Crest. He was a quarter of a mile from his home when the car shut down. Having anticipated this, he was immediately out the door, sprinting along Ridge Crest Drive and up Redwood Way to his house.

Drake had strapped his hunting rifle to his Zero motorcycle the night before. He seized his filet knife and crammed it into his boot before sliding a newly acquired Cube into a slot at the back of the bike's screen.

Waiting for the Cube to engage, he cursed himself for not testing it earlier. He had acquired it from a local he had previously busted for stolen merchandise. The guy was in his early twenties and was considered an electronics and programming guru. Selling merchandise to a CID officer wasn't at the top of the techie's wish list until Drake told him his story of losing one son and now possibly another. Without further discussion, the young man went to work on a Cube that would use an alias to access the CID network and then lock onto Talon's Cube.

His new friend wouldn't accept payment and even threw in some free advice. He told Drake that the Cube wouldn't prevent him from being identified. Chip readers had been installed along most highways and freeways throughout the country. They worked very much like the readers on toll bridges and toll roads, but instead of reading transponders on a Mini, they accessed everyone's chips. If county, state, or federal CID decided to track Drake, they would quickly detect his movements.

Drake appreciated the concern, all too familiar with CID surveillance, which was the reason for the motorcycle.

A bright-red dot snapped Drake to attention. He concentrated on the map that popped up on the bike's screen where the red dot moved south along Highway 1 away from Santa Cruz.

He accelerated out of his driveway, and when he hit Ridge Crest Drive, he rode north. Within a few miles, he would hit the mountain roads. Using these roads and the numerous farm roads, he would stay off the main highways as he made his way south. Drake anxiously checked his display and confirmed he could still locate Talon.

The pursuit was on.

Chapter Twenty-Eight

Talon

May 14 – 8:04 p.m.

Plexiglas barriers were getting old. Talon and Espar were seated three rows back in a police transport that had eight rows of seating. The driver had the traditional bus-driver seat at the front left of the vehicle, across from the entry door. A second guard sat in the first row, behind the steps. Talon looked to his right, across the aisle at Espar. She stared straight ahead, her anger seemingly intense enough to melt a hole through the Plexiglas in front of them. Talon *wished* she could melt a hole. The idea that the guards needed protection from him and Espar was insane. The fact that they were prisoners was even crazier.

The guards continually scanned the road and countryside around them. The vehicle was in autonomous-drive mode so that driving wasn't a distraction. Talon couldn't tell if the guards' wariness stemmed from their training or whether they were expecting some type of threat.

They had reached Highway 101, passing miles and miles of vineyards as they continued the journey south. The green vines looked striking against the rich brown soil of the rolling hills. The few hills that didn't have crops were studded with oak trees. The countryside was at once beautiful and boring to Talon. He couldn't help wondering how many miles of vineyards were enough.

The excited chatter of the guards broke Talon from his boredom. He followed their sightline behind the vehicle, only to see flashing lights fast approaching. The fading sunlight made it difficult to identify the vehicle, but by the time it closed within one hundred yards, Talon could tell it was a CID police sedan. The cruiser settled in behind them, about twenty-five yards back, with lights still flashing.

He could hear the guards questioning whether the officer expected them to pull over. They figured they hadn't violated any laws. Their captors were just about to call for support, when the vehicle pulled to the other lane and began to pass. Talon caught the insignia on the door and realized it was Ridge Crest CID! This couldn't be a coincidence. The windows were too tinted for Talon to make out the driver and the vehicle quickly sped past.

He glanced at the guards. They had also recognized the insignia. The driver decided to take some action. "Call dispatch," he commanded. Nothing. "Call dispatch," he repeated. Silence. The guard examined the display console to determine what had gone wrong.

"Justin!" The other guard called and pointed in front of them. The police car was pulling into their lane. Then it slowed until it was perhaps fifteen yards ahead. Justin grasped the wheel and jerked the steering to the left. The transport didn't react. He pumped the brake. No effect.

"Bastard! He jacked us, Charlie!" Justin exclaimed.

Espar perked up. She looked at Talon as if to ask what was up. Talon knew full well. He just didn't know one police vehicle could do this to another. Almost all police vehicles had the ability to connect with and override another vehicle's control system. The target vehicle had to be within approximately forty yards, allowing the connection to be made over shortwave communications, the preferred connection since satellite signals, the backbone of the CID network, weren't one-hundred-percent reliable. They were also more susceptible to being jammed.

This feature was relatively new. It had been incorporated into police cars within the last two to three years. The justification was that it allowed police to peacefully assume control of any fleeing car or any vehicle deemed an imminent threat. Once the target vehicle had been jacked, the police could remotely control the vehicle through its autonomous control system. They could also jam the network communications so that occupants couldn't call for support. This was especially effective when the target occupants were known to have gang or crime syndicate connections.

Whoever was in the police car was taking full control of the situation. They couldn't have traveled more than a mile before the car began exiting the highway with the transport in tow. Talon hadn't thought to catch the exit number and had no idea where they were. The back-and-forth between the guards had been background noise to Talon, but now he listened for any clues as to what might be going on.

"This can't be good. The officer's not talking and he's taking us up into the hills," Justin was saying.

"What if we try to shoot out the tires?" Charlie suggested.

"Can't. The windows have been locked."

"Do you think he plans to force us off a cliff or something?"

"No, he may have control, but he can't override safety features. The system isn't going to allow the vehicle to simply drive over a cliff," the driver said, lacking conviction.

They were now taking deserted farm roads to climb into the hills. With darkness closing around them, it was hard to identify where they were. Talon wasn't sure whether he would know where he was if it were broad daylight. The vehicles finally stopped in the middle of a stand of oak trees.

"Lockdown vehicle," Justin called out.

"What's that do for us? He already locked all the doors and windows. Why help him lock us in?" Charlie asked.

"Think of it this way. We don't know what that person wants," Justin said, pointing to the car. "What if the officer decides he wants inside. I'm guessing we may not want to let him near us until we know his intentions."

Their transport's lights hadn't been turned off and they flooded the car in front of them. Talon and Espar couldn't help but keep their eyes riveted on the car, waiting to see the mystery driver. Seconds led to minutes, but no one came out.

Espar finally decided to break her silence. "It has to be someone you know, right? Is it your dad? What's he waiting for? Isn't he here to rescue us?"

Talon had considered the possibility they were being rescued, but he knew it wasn't his dad. His dad had let him in on his plans if things went bad. His father would be tracking him on his Zero. Unfortunately, he also would have lost any signal when they exited the highway. When the vehicle communications were jammed, Talon's Cube was taken out as well. As he looked at Espar's hopeful eyes, he didn't see any point in dashing her hopes. Besides, whoever was in that car was a Ridge Crest officer and that couldn't be bad. "Let's be ready in case our rescuer needs help." Then he turned back to the car.

The suspense was interrupted when two men wearing masks appeared from the trees. One was thin and over six feet tall. The other was stocky and much shorter. The stocky man carried a box that wasn't much bigger than a packing box, but the way he cradled it from underneath, resting against his stomach, suggested it was heavy. He reached the car and immediately set the box down. A few seconds later, the driver's door opened. The officer stepped out and looked at his companions, then past them to the transport.

"That's Jesse! My dad's known him for years," Talon whispered excitedly to Espar, who had moved across the aisle to sit next to him.

The three men huddled together, talking and occasionally pointing at the transport. Eventually, the stocky man bent down to open the box while the thinner one headed toward the transport. Talon was watching Jesse intently, trying to figure out his plan, when Jesse pulled his Taser from his belt and fired, first at the man who knelt before him and then at the man walking away from him. He scored a direct hit with both, and they dropped to the ground, jerking violently and uncontrollably.

Talon knew how Tasers worked, just like he had learned from his dad how a car could be jacked. Tasers had moved beyond their original tethered probes. They could shoot multiple rounds, with each round shaped like a dart. Only, these darts were electrically charged and released a quick, devastating pulse upon impact. Most people were immobilized for ten to fifteen minutes. It was a horribly painful weapon that left ugly burns, but it was better than a bullet, although Talon wondered if the guys flopping on the ground felt that way now.

Everyone in the transport gasped or shouted when Jesse turned on his companions. It was now anyone's guess as to what he had planned. Jesse wasn't wasting time, though. He reached inside his car for something.

"He released the locks," Justin said quietly. "He must not know we're in lockdown mode."

Jesse reached into the box, pulled out a cylindrical disk, then moved to their front door. He pulled on the outside handle to no avail. He wasn't disturbed by this revelation. He simply took a step back, withdrew his Taser, and fired at the window. Everyone watched as the dart merely bounced off. Jesse nodded to himself as if confirming the glass was bulletproof, then holstered the Taser.

He held out the disk so the guards could see what he was holding.

"What's that?" Espar whispered to Talon.

"An IED—an Improvised Explosive Device."

The guards must have recognized it as well because they got up and moved as far away from the door as possible. Jesse motioned for them to open the door. They weren't budging.

Jesse nodded again, then stepped forward and positioned the device under the vehicle, below the door.

"I'm not going to like this Jesse guy if he blows us up," Espar whispered. "Are you sure he knows what he's doing?"

Talon looked at Espar with admiration. She was scared, but she had a smirk on her face.

Talon wasn't so sure Jesse had a great idea. The underside of the transport was most likely armored, but who knew how much damage the explosive might do? It certainly might do a lot more than blow the door off. The guards' raised voices interrupted Talon's thoughts.

"You can go out there and try your luck with the nut job, Charlie. I'm going to bet he doesn't want to blow up these kids," Justin said.

"Hey! What if we use those two as hostages? Even if he gets in, what's he going to do?" Charlie smiled. Justin seemed to be considering it when Charlie pointed at the front window and said, "What now?"

Jesse walked back to the car, reached through the driver's window and poked away at the control panel, overriding the transport's system.

"Not sure why, but we're locked again," Charlie said.

Jesse returned, grabbed the box, and set it by the transport door. He reached in and pulled out another IED, then walked to the back of the transport, sliding the device underneath. He returned to the box, only to grab another unit and carry it to the middle of the transport. He placed that underneath as well.

Espar wasn't smiling this time when she said, "This is turning out to be one lousy rescue."

Talon got that. "What are you doing?" he screamed at Jesse through the window. "Jesse, you're going to kill us!"

Jesse could hear Talon and glanced in through the window after sliding another device under the transport. "Sorry, kid, I didn't want this!" he yelled back. He then headed back to the box, reached in, and brought out a device that had to be the detonator.

Talon and Espar both screamed at the guards.

"Open up!"

"Let us out!"

Justin barreled up to the driver's seat and poked furiously at the screen. After a few moments, he turned back to everyone. "We're locked in." He turned to look at Talon. "Kid, isn't this guy on your side?"

Talon looked out at Jesse. He was busy with the device that Talon assumed was a detonator. Why didn't Jesse detonate the IED directly? He was going to be stung out anyway. Why did he want to trigger these devices remotely? Then it occurred to Talon. Jesse wasn't worried about remote detonation. He was going to be stung out alright, but he needed to sync all four explosives. Otherwise, he'd be dead before he got to the second one. Talon wondered how much time Jesse needed to sync these devices.

"Justin, let us out of here," he pleaded. "I'm good with these control systems. Give me a shot at the screen."

Justin looked nervously at Talon, perhaps wondering if this was a setup. Talon needed to get Justin to move.

"Does he look like he's on my side? Justin, pull your Taser. Train it on me and let me out? What do you have to lose?"

That did it. Justin and Charlie pulled their Tasers. Charlie stepped to the Plexiglas door and released the outside latch. Then he stepped into the aisle behind the driver's seat and motioned for Talon to come out.

Talon pulled open the door and hurried to the front. Justin stepped down the stairs and turned his back on the door as he made room for Talon to reach the screen. Charlie shut and latched the door before Espar could think to follow. Both Charlie and Justin trained their Tasers on Talon, not happy about the risk they were taking.

Talon could just glimpse Jesse's face outside. He seemed pleased with the progress he was making. Talon looked to see if there was any movement from the other two. The stocky guy was sprawled face down next to the car, occasionally twitching. The thinner man was on his back. He wasn't having spasms anymore, but he lay there gasping like a fish out of water. They weren't going to save anyone.

He sat down and scanned the display. He didn't bother to see if the display was locked. He assumed it was. This was the most basic move, but he reached behind the display until he felt the reset button. He pushed and waited for the power to cycle.

"That's stupid! I could have done that!" Justin complained. "Get out of that chair!"

At that moment, the display came back to life. The screen flashed "ACCESS GRANTED" then "CONTROL OVERRIDE?" A green and a red button appeared next to the question, and Talon tapped on green. The display had a series of controls, making it confusing to understand. He searched the display until he noticed "LOCKDOWN" in the lower right-hand corner. He hit it and saw the button disappear. He then searched for the option he'd seen earlier and pressed "DOOR." The door swung open behind Justin, catching everyone off guard.

Jesse looked up in surprise. Justin was slow to react and before he could turn toward the door, Jesse got off a shot with his Taser. Justin fell backward out of the transport and squirmed on the ground. Not wanting Charlie to take a shot at him, Jesse stepped to the left of the doorway. He dropped the Taser and grasped the controller with both hands, looking up at Talon with a wicked grin.

They were out of time!

Before Talon could flinch, a blur shot across his view, collided with Jesse, and knocked him to the front of the transport.

Talon charged down the steps. When his feet hit the ground outside, he saw Jesse lying on his back. Blood seeped out the front of his shirt with each heartbeat. His hand was stretching for the controller only inches away. Just past Jesse, a man started to rise.

"Dad!"

Drake staggered, then righted himself. He looked around as if trying to take it all in. He finally managed to say, "I love you," before collapsing to the ground.

Talon looked at Jesse, whose eyes stared out at nothing, and he knew. Talon heard his own terrifying scream as he took off toward his father, only to make it mere steps before he felt a heart-stopping jolt. He then collided with the ground, where he became a prisoner to his body as it flailed in all directions. He continued to scream inside his head—not for the pain, but for his father ... until everything went black.

Chapter Twenty-Nine

The Warden

May 15 - 1:23 p.m.

"They'll kill 'em, boss."

The fifty-something-year-old man stood in the administration-building lobby watching the transport pull into the yard. He wore khaki pants and a khaki button-up shirt that blended with the desert sand outside and the lobby furniture within. He prided himself on not standing out. Next to him stood the muscle-bound chief of security.

"That's possible." The warden was easily annoyed by statements of the obvious.

"It's more than possible. Do my guys really deserve to be tortured and killed at the hands of the disconnects?" the security chief questioned.

"So you're looking to protect your men? Would you be willing to serve out their punishment for them?" the warden replied, irritated by the challenge to his authority.

"No, sir. If you say life sentence, I'll carry it out, but I'm pretty sure if you throw my guys in with the disconnects, they won't last a week."

The irony of their conversation was not lost on the warden. The fact that he called the shots while ex-jocks, such as his security chief, begged him for favors was a complete role reversal from his younger days.

When Alfred was growing up, he wanted to shine like everyone else. He just wasn't built for it. Always a bit overweight and a little slow, when it was time to pick teams for any sporting activity, he could count on being picked last, even behind the girls. It hurt.

Recognizing that he was never going to be a jock and was too lazy to be a high-achieving nerd, he made do with what he had. Girls loved his baby face, as if he was their favorite pet. He put aside his pride and went with it because it played well with his fellow mates. The other boys, with a little effort on his part, quickly learned that as his ally, they had an in with the girls.

He soon came to feel blessed by his station in life, like the jackal in a spy novel he had read. He was a predator that didn't have to win through strength. While others were preoccupied with stupid sports, he was concerned with sizing up social scenes and manipulating them to his advantage.

He learned to hang with those that would protect him, adore him, or even use him for an introduction. He didn't mind being used or even doing hours of homework for the popular kids. He knew they might one day return the favor.

The first time he decided to collect on his favors was in his early twenties, after he had washed out of the police academy. Well, washed out was not the right term. He had miscalculated his training instructor's appreciation for loyalty. Having the good fortune of discovering a fellow trainee was an immigrant, who just happened to be plagued by a few documentation errors, he seized on the opportunity to score a few points with his instructor and reported his mate's violations.

To his surprise, his instructor was not impressed. Or appreciative. The instructor reluctantly dismissed his classmate from the academy and promptly escorted Alfred out the door as well.

Fate soon presented another opportunity.

Within days, Brad O'Brien, his housemate of four years and best friend since fifth grade, asked him to help with an errand. O'Brien had learned about an opening at the CID Technology Complex for a security officer. He asked his housemate to drop off a resume for him since Alfred was often out that way. Jackpot.

For years, O'Brien had worked Alfred for introductions to girls. Alfred had sucked it up and accepted the role of frustrated wingman more times than he could count, but this was his opportunity to cash in! He knew his roommate had absolutely no background in law enforcement and had made no previous efforts to seek a job in the field. Alfred, on the other hand, had made it quite far in the academy before being so unfairly dumped. He weighed the fact that his housemate had no chance of getting the job while he himself at least had a remote chance.

He soon found himself dropping off his own resume without bothering to include his friend's. A tough decision that led to him getting the job while losing a longtime friend. A fair trade.

Cashing in on favors became a lot easier after that, enabling him to climb the ranks and establish his own kingdom. He now lived in two worlds. He dressed in stealth to make sure he never forgot the importance of working behind the scenes to manipulate those around him. He also relished his moments to shine as the absolute ruler under his self-titled position of 'warden.'

He had it all.

"They didn't know what they were thinking. They won't file the report," the chief continued to plead, interrupting his thoughts.

The warden's attention returned to the transport. Only two new workers were being delivered to his complex today. He was not here for them. He never made it a practice to meet new workers. What was the point? They would be thrown in with the thousands of other disconnects that would never be leaving here.

No, he was here to intercept the two escorting officers, Charlie Clemens and Justin Play. They reportedly had quite the ordeal the previous night and felt compelled to file an official report. This did not sit well with him. He always went out of his way to protect his kingdom from the scrutiny of outsiders. Even *thinking* of filing a report without his permission was a slight!

"Very well. One week living amongst the disconnects. I'm curious to see if your prediction is right."

The transport doors swung open, catching the warden's attention. A tall, young girl was the first to emerge from the transport and step onto the sweltering desert sand. The midday temperature was well over 110 degrees, and she grimaced as she extracted her first breaths from the oppressive heat waves. The girl looked defiant and angry. Good for her. He loved how the savage desert environment tested the resolve of every living thing. He didn't think of himself as a cruel man, oh no. It pained him tremendously to watch the workers' vitality and spirit quickly evaporate under the unforgiving conditions. This young lady seemed to have the will to fight back, which would hopefully slow the inevitable.

The girl was followed by a lanky, awkward-looking teenager, seemingly prepackaged with downcast, hunched shoulders and shocked, unblinking eyes. As he came to rest next to the girl, he looked down at his green tennis shoes and began lifting one and then the other. Yes, those thin soles would soon be melting away, just like this one's spirit. The warden regretfully knew with every ounce of his well-honed perceptive skills that this poor boy wouldn't make it more than a couple of days.

Chapter Thirty

General Stafford

May 20 - 1:58 p.m.

He looked at his reflection in his office window in Modoc, making sure the man he observed was prepared to lead and take action when others might hesitate.

His six-foot-five stature and muscular frame offered a good start to perfecting his image. The circular bullet-hole scar above his right eye was an accessory straight out of the movies. Combined with a navy-blue military uniform and salt-and-pepper hair buzzed short, he knew he looked every part the rugged officer, but the characteristic that fueled his confidence was the relentless determination shining back at him from his Caribbean-blue eyes.

General Stafford had plenty of opportunities during his career to test his determination. He had passed every test, including the early days of the Bee Sting Program, when he had stared down death and decided it would not defeat him. He hadn't literally stared down death, of course, but he did accept the loss of others' lives and, worse, faced the possible destruction of his career.

When he was given command of Bee Sting's chipping effort, no one had anticipated that embedding ten thousand immigrants with chips would result in more than twice that number of mortalities. With the initial surgeries yielding five deaths for every immigrant survivor, it would have been easy to bring these results to the attention of his superiors. He was, after all, only a lowly colonel at the time. This would have been the safest move for his career. It would also have been the complete demise of the Program. He knew full well his superiors would not have had the fortitude to carry on.

Fortunately for the U.S., and for the world at large, he was willing to risk a demotion and even the possibility of being expelled from the military. He covered up results and ran through near-countless lives in order to chip immigrants and perfect the experimental surgery.

He had no illusion about keeping the mounting immigrant deaths a secret; he was merely racing against time to achieve positive results that would offset the regrettable losses. He won the race. By the time investigative journalists pieced together the loss of life and published heartbreaking stories that his superiors didn't have the strength to endure, the Program had already been launched upon the citizenry of the U.S. Sure, a few of his superiors were outraged and tried to have him removed—even Naya Jordan called for his removal—before succumbing to the reality that he was the reason for the Program's continued existence.

Simply, he was a hero. One who had since received many promotions to ensure he continued to play that role quietly.

The general contemplated his mesmerizing blue eyes. He saw the steely conviction that all great leaders require, but he also noted something he felt many others missed: a hint of compassion. He had made a lot of difficult choices in his career that resulted in lost lives. Fortunately, this had not hardened him to the point that he no longer had concern for others. This compassion often served him well, as it would need to serve him now.

His thoughts returned to the two officers who had triggered his trip down memory lane, Jesse Taylor and Drake Russit. He knew the officers had served with Chief Abreo for many years. In such a small town as Ridge Crest, where you couldn't help but run into people outside of work, he imagined the chief had grown close to his fallen men. The general knew his responsibility was to get the chief past this loss and focused on the work ahead, knowing that a productive leader was what the community needed most right now.

One last look at his own image and he decided he was ready to take on the hardest role anyone could have to play in modern times—the role of General Stafford. "Call Chief Abreo," he commanded.

"General," Gabriel Abreo responded a few seconds later.

"Sorry to hear about your officers."

"Thank you. I appreciate you returning my calls."

"Of course," the general responded, letting go Abreo's reference to the many calls he had not returned. "I'm certain your tight-knit community will find the means to grieve and heal. Unfortunately, in my role, I have had to deal with such losses too many times. The one thing I have noticed is that smaller communities tend to band together and persevere in the face of such tragedies."

"Right, well, I will admit to not having the depth of experience. Nor do I hope to—ever. All I know is my community can't begin healing until they understand what happened. They need answers and the people you sent here aren't helping."

"Oh, but they are—"

"No, they're not," an increasingly aggravated Gabriel responded. "They are confiscating all crime-scene evidence and any associated communications. And while I'd welcome their involvement if they were using their expertise to reveal what happened, they seem more concerned with covering things up. There's no communication with me or with my people whatsoever."

"Chief, while I understand this situation is stressful, I do not appreciate your tone. You need to remain professional," he warned. "Understandably, no one is pleased with recent events and everyone wants answers. Let me make this clear: if there are answers to be found, my people will find them. Not your people. More than ever, you and your people need to keep a distance from this aftermath."

"But why is that? I'd say my involvement has been sorely missed. I'll give you the benefit of the doubt that the outcome wasn't anything you wanted, but I'm not giving you a pass on heading up this disaster. I think it's time you bring me up to speed on what you planned so we can better piece together what went wrong."

"You need to stop," the general said through gritted teeth. "There's plenty of blame to be shared by all. The fact that two of your officers went rogue doesn't say much about the culture in your department. But I'm not going to ask you to explain yourself. Nor am I about to explain myself to you. What I am going to do is remind you that not everything turned out tragically. Your daughter is safely tucked away at the Tech Lab."

"That's a good outcome? Her being shipped off? Are you serious?" Gabriel said, no longer trying to contain his anger.

The general lowered his voice further and responded slowly. "Listen closely ... the next words I want to hear from you are 'yes, sir.' Your daughter was supposed to be shipped off to the Center, along with her classmates. If you haven't heard, life expectancy is rather brief there. By the time the disconnects surrender to death, they're happy to have escaped hell. She just happens to be fortunate I have connections on your CID panel and at the Lab. In fact, not everyone was happy with her placement, and without my continued intervention, she could still easily find herself at the Fabrication Center," the general paused to let that sink in. The silence on the other end confirmed he had been understood. "The fact that I can even keep your daughter away from the Center I would call a good outcome. Wouldn't you?"

Barely above a whisper, Gabriel answered, "Yes, sir."

Realizing the chief's attitude had taken on the proper adjustment, he added, "Look, if I can get answers for your community without jeopardizing Program security, I will. Equally important, I may even be able to get your daughter home to you when everything cools down. You're going to have to trust that I have your interests in mind, just as I trust you to serve my interests. Are you good with that?"

"Yes, sir," Gabriel repeated softly.

"Good. I think we're really going to work well together," the general replied, pleased with himself for exercising such compassion.

Chapter Thirty-One

General Stafford

May 21 - 8:44 a.m.

"**G**eneral, I'm surprised to find you in my office," Dr. Jordan said. "Unless I'm more forgetful than I realize, we didn't have a meeting scheduled."

The general was seated on a worn brown leather couch. The couch was against the wall, well away from the bomb that apparently had gone off on the opposite side of the room, where paperwork was scattered across Dr. Jordan's desk and even the surrounding floor.

She didn't seem at all concerned with appearances or working conditions. While the office was rather large, the white walls were barren, not even interrupted by a single window. Dr. Jordan didn't have a single picture or decoration on her desk. The general wondered if this was a sign of shutting out the outside world and prioritizing the job. Or was it a lack of commitment to the Program and not wanting to put down roots?

"Sorry to barge in unannounced, Doctor," he said, knowing he could hardly remember a moment he was sorry about anything. "Any progress in positively identifying our intruder?"

"No. Nothing since yesterday's report. The primary suspect is still Shadow. Any luck bringing him in?"

"And still no idea what might have been taken?" the general asked, ignoring Dr. Jordan's question.

"Only guesses."

"Alright. Since we're guessing, is there any chance my module was stolen?"

"So that's why you're here. Should've known. It's always about your damn module," Dr. Jordan half muttered to herself. "I thought you were here to lobby for your latest request. Why do you want to be involved with the Fabrication Center Board anyway? Is it something to do with those Ridge Crest teens?"

The general didn't like the conversation's change in direction and thought about not answering again, but he reminded himself that the path to attaining influence over the Center's board went through the CID Board. It couldn't hurt to humor the doctor with a response. "You could say Mr. Russit and Miss Crashan's assignment there got me thinking more about the Center. The Center has a rather substantial disconnect population. As head of the Program's security, I should be paying more attention. That place seems a little too isolated. Maybe even a bit too secretive."

"Interesting. The last time we spoke, I voiced the same concern about the Program in general. You didn't seem too concerned."

"Sarcasm noted," the general said, deciding her vote was not worth the effort. "Could you answer my question about my module?"

"The module for your troops? Stolen from here? No." the doctor replied.

"So, no chance it's been leaked out into the public domain?"

"That's a different question. Are you asking me if it's possible your module is being downloaded into people's NACs, as we speak?"

"That's my concern, yes."

"Then you'll have to ask your people. Not mine."

"My people?"

"Come now. You know full well I was forced to farm your module out to the Tech Lab," the doctor said.

The general merely raised his eyebrows, inviting her to continue.

"You were in such a hurry to get your module into play that you couldn't wait for me to work it into my schedule. Plus, your connections with the Lab go way back. You probably trusted them with the module more than you trusted me," the doctor pointed out, adding, "You didn't think I was aware you orchestrated the whole thing?"

The general didn't bother arguing. He rose to leave, saying, "Sounds like my fears were overblown. It's clear the module wasn't part of the theft."

"That doesn't mean it wasn't the focus of the theft." the doctor said, stopping him cold.

"What's that supposed to mean?"

"It must have been frustrating for you to learn that farming out your module didn't give you control over its release."

He clamped his jaws, not liking her tone yet wanting to fully understand the accusation being made.

"Yes, you had to be upset when you learned your module couldn't be downloaded into your soldiers' NACs without first being integrated into the main routine. It makes me wonder how far your people would go to make you happy."

"I don't appreciate what you're implying," the general said. "If they had stolen the primary software on my behalf, why would I be asking you about my module?"

"Good question."

Chapter Thirty-Two

Sofia

July 2 - 11:09 a.m.

Lab rat.

Sofia stood in front of the glass door leading to the technicians' lab. Through the glass, she could see five technicians sitting at their benches, watching her. No one lifted a finger to help. They didn't even hide their amusement as she struggled to gain entry. She held her breath as she waited for a green LED. Nothing. Her chip didn't register. She stepped back from the door, waited a few seconds, and approached for the fifth time. Finally, the LED turned green and the door slid open. As she entered, the technicians began to clap.

"Assholes," she muttered.

"Hey! We've been told we can't help you when your chip glitches," one of the white coats said.

"And you listen so well. Can you roll over too? Don't give me that bull. You enjoyed watching me." She threw the package she was carrying at him, which he fumbled and let drop to the floor. She laughed and walked back out the door.

Once she was out of sight down the hall, she stopped, took a deep breath, and tried not to cry. She was tired of putting on a brave face. How could people be so cruel? Sofia had come to realize the deal her dad had reached with the Tech Lab. They needed a lab rat. Someone at the complex wanted to study the actual performance of her glitched chip as she made the rounds at the facilities.

Sofia was assigned to the mail department. Most deliveries throughout the complex were automated. A few weren't. Whether it was an odd-shaped package or a priority delivery that someone didn't want to trust to the autonomous bots,

Sofia's name would be called. She suspected that some delivery requests were excuses to get a good laugh at her inability to navigate the complex. It was rare when she could make her way through the numerous access points without failure. When access was denied, she was required to keep trying until she 'overcame', as her supervisor called it. She was pretty sure there was nothing in the package she had just delivered. The idiots felt bigger by dragging her down.

She took another deep breath, reminding herself that everything could be a lot worse. The Tech Lab was a sprawling campus in Seaside, California. The complex occupied a few square miles of the old Fort Ord army base, which had been well positioned to view the coastal sand dunes and beyond to the vast Monterey Bay.

The complex itself was secure, with restricted access in and out. In Sofia's case, she was told she could not leave the complex for the foreseeable future, but would soon be able to contact friends and family. She hoped for more, but was making the best of it for now.

The site was a mix of office buildings and technical labs. With almost all technology used in the Program originating from or passing through the Tech Lab, engineers, technicians, and accomplished professionals populated the buildings, coming together to further technological development.

The result was thousands of workers flooded into the complex each day. Sofia guessed there were more than twenty thousand employees. She had yet to meet others who were held captive like herself, but she found solace in the fact that hundreds lived on the campus full time. The former army base was one of many military base closures approved decades earlier when satellites made most of the technology obsolete. Some of the old army barracks had been converted to apartments, with officer quarters being quite grand and infantry quarters less so.

Sofia was assigned a studio apartment at the end of a row of twenty townhomes. She knew it was the worst of the units. It looked like more of an afterthought or a chance to squeeze in one more unit.

Yet, she loved it. It was basically four walls with a cutout for a bathroom, but it was *her* four walls that she could retreat to at the end of the day. She had been able to fit a twin-sized bed at the back of the room, where she ate most of her meals and absorbed novels late into the night. She also squeezed in a two-person dining table near the appliances. This was perhaps the one mistake she made in furnishing the place—the sight of the table made her lonely. It begged for Talon to walk through the door and join her. She found she never chose to sit at the table.

Her most precious acquisition was an old thin-screen that she mounted over her bed. Images of the ocean, including waves breaking on the beach, were streamed from cameras mounted on the upper floors of a few well-positioned buildings scattered throughout the complex. The images not only expanded the feel of her small place, but reminded her of a world beyond the compound, a world to which she longed to escape. Still, mistakes and all, Sofia cherished her retreat.

She didn't have friends at her new home. One day she might. It was now July, and she was told she could begin school again in September. Her classmates would be the children of visiting workers. As a renowned technology innovation hub, the Lab attracted highly educated and accomplished people from around the world. Most signed up for a year or two and didn't bother to seek off-campus housing. They were assigned plush condos on-site and were allowed to bring their spouses and children. Sofia had run into some of the children; a few were in her building—none were older than ten, though. She guessed most teens were spending their summers at home with their friends and would only come to this complex once the school year began. For them, it was like being an exchange student. She hoped they would be accepting of her.

Regardless, Sofia didn't know what life would bring for her here. She didn't even know if she would one day be allowed to leave, but she was determined to make the most of being surrounded by these brilliant minds. She was going to learn from them in an effort to better herself.

She was also going to learn all she could about the Fabrication Center and what had become of Talon. She knew the Technology Lab fed into the Fabrication Center, where most of the final products were produced. She had yet to meet anyone who would talk about where the Center was located and what became of the people there. This secrecy deeply troubled her. She couldn't help but think the worst. Nor could she forgive herself or her father for taking the easy way out. She should be at the Center, where she could keep an eye on Talon.

She sighed. She shouldn't have entrusted their fate to others. They should have run.

Sofia collected herself. It didn't help her to feel like a rat in a cage. She knew she couldn't let the technicians' lack of empathy trip her up. Succumbing to their ridicule wouldn't get her one step closer to her goals and, if she wasn't careful, could prove to be an obstacle to her moving forward. While her father's recent actions confused her, her parents, like Talon's, had always taught her to be strong and persevere. Adversity was to be faced and overcome.

She went back to the tech room and approached the door. The LED turned red. She retreated and approached again. The LED glowed red a second time. She had caught the attention of the technicians, who weren't smirking this time around. They looked bewildered and even a bit scared. Determined to gain entry, Sofia backed away and again approached the door. Green light! As the door slid to the side, she stormed in.

The box Sofia had delivered was still resting on the floor a few feet from the technician who had fumbled it earlier. She approached the now-wary technician and stopped before him, then slammed her foot down, crushing the box. She nailed it over and over until the flaps broke open, revealing nothing inside. She looked up, registering the wide eyes staring back at her. She flipped the technician off, turned, and headed out the door, deciding she liked overcoming adversity.

Chapter Thirty-Three

Shadow

July 2 - 8:46 p.m.

He no longer wanted to be 'Shadow' or any other name people wanted to attach to his alter ego. It didn't take much looking back to realize all this secret identity crap had gotten him nowhere. He hadn't shielded his family. He was nowhere close to saving his community or making a better life for disconnects. He had achieved absolutely zero with all his revolutionary dreaming. Quite the opposite, his last mission had wreaked more harm than he felt his soul could bear.

Perched on top of a sand dune with the summer evening fading to twilight, he desperately tried to focus on his reason for being there. It was pointless. The painful memories could never be kept at bay. They haunted him in his dreams and boldly stalked him in broad daylight.

There was no escape as the scenes once again washed over him—lifeless bodies collapsed on the ground, terror-filled faces peering out from the bus windows, and his partner convulsing in some crazed rhythm that matched his own flailing movements. The worst was the sight of his dad taking his last breaths and the scream of rage from his brother as his transport fled the scene.

Wilder lay back on the dune, wishing the sand would creep over his body and claim his "Shadow" persona and all the related memories. With eyes closed tight, he told the universe he was prepared to throw in his life as part of the bargain.

After a few minutes passed, he opened his eyes and focused on reality. Nothing was going to happen. Nor was he ready for such an ending—yet. He might be willing to abandon any aspiration he had of liberating his community from the Program's oppression, but he wasn't willing to desert his brother. He would rescue Talon before he gave up his last breath.

This was no simple commitment. Talon and Espar, his targets for the mission, had vanished. Once he regained mobility after the Taser strike, Wilder had no means of following them. Prior to the mission, Haris had no reason to provide him with information on where they were going, and Haris wouldn't provide information to anyone ever again. Wilder still wasn't sure how his mentor ended up a casualty. Weak heart? With Haris's death, Wilder lost all connection to anyone who might have an interest in making the mission right.

This left him with very few sane options. Contact the police? With the deaths of two of their own, the police had every incentive to piece together what happened. And they had a lot better tools to get the job done. Contacting them would have been his first choice if only the police thought highly of him. No police.

Reach out to his sister? Sage was the rock for their family, and she would make any sacrifice to get Talon back, including her own freedom. Wilder ruled out bringing her into any of his schemes. She would be guilty by association. He wasn't going to take her down with him.

These were Wilder's thoughts as he watched the night descend upon the Tech Lab below. He might not be able to readily locate Talon and Espar, but he knew where Sofia Abreo had landed. Haris had let Wilder know of the strange turn of events. Apparently, Sofia's father had connections. Wilder wasn't eager to approach the police chief for answers, but Sofia was a different story. She had to know strings were pulled, so what else did she know?

He put his night glasses on and resumed studying the complex below. He was going to uncover its weaknesses. He was going to confront Sofia for answers. He was going to find Talon.

Chapter Thirty-Four

Sofia

July 8 – 2:30 p.m.

Sofia was nervous. Dr. Sur was legendary at the Tech Lab. He was the vice president of product development, making him responsible for all product development supporting the current Bee Sting Program. Approaching seventy, no one was quite sure how he was lured out of retirement after years of being a serial entrepreneur in the tech industry.

He had nothing to prove. Yet he was here and he hadn't disappointed. The Lab was churning out products and he was the visionary behind those products. The program initially kicked off with chip-reading portals that looked like modified versions of the original metal detectors used at airports and the early devices positioned at toll bridges and along highways to track commuters. Dr. Sur took it from there and was instrumental in seamlessly integrating chip readers into doorways, vehicles, gates, elevators, windows, and more.

Workers throughout the Lab were immensely proud of him, being quick to point out the Program could never have been successful without keeping the disconnects at bay. Dr. Sur shored up the barriers that kept the law-abiding people safe from those that were otherwise free to kill them.

Sofia mostly bought into their enthusiasm. Although sometimes when their gushing became too great, she reminded them she was a disconnect, while omitting the part about not being able to kill anyone. Still, it was hard not to get caught up in the Dr. Sur mania. Thanks to his many devices, his genius was on display throughout the world.

So why did Sofia find herself standing outside his office? *Damn technicians!* No doubt they complained about her, leading Sofia to meet the legend for all the wrong reasons.

She looked through a glass door into an office that looked more like a lab. There were gadgets littered around the room, and an older gentleman studying a device that looked like a silver ball. He was spinning it on the top of his desk, which, come to think of it, was actually a tech bench. Reassured she had the right office, she knocked on the door.

Dr. Sur grabbed the ball and shifted his focus to her. She gave an awkward wave, certain she looked both stupid and nervous. After what seemed like a minute, Dr. Sur waved her in. She looked at the door and saw no handle, so she pushed, only to find it locked. She looked at the doctor and shrugged her shoulders. He waved her in once again.

Was she missing something? Was his door chip activated? Sofia backed up, waited a few seconds, then approached again and pushed. Nothing. Sofia looked at the good doctor again, only to see him infuriatingly wave her in one more time. Her nervousness began giving way to rage as she was not enjoying this game. Screw it. He was the one who wanted to see her. She turned away from the door and began walking toward the exit, only to hear Dr. Sur call out, "Sorry about that! Please come back."

She turned to see him holding the door open. She hesitated. Dr. Sur read her reluctance and smiled. "Humor me … please."

She walked back, but was in no hurry to enter his office. She had endured enough. Her anger now drove her to ask, "Are you the one who ordered everyone not to assist me in my struggles? Is my torment some game to you?"

Dr. Sur stopped smiling and looked sincerely pained. "Please come in and I will answer that question and more. I think a talk is long overdue. Please." He motioned to the chair across from his desk, but as the door shut behind Sofia, she froze, unnerved by the prospect of being locked in with this stranger.

"Oh, sorry about that. Let me open the door," he said, proceeding to move his arm like he was waving someone in. Sofia saw the door pop open and then caught the doctor staring at the ball. "Odd. This device is supposed to enhance chip signals," he mumbled. "Theoretically, it should have increased your chip's signal strength, enabling your chip to successfully trigger the door release. Instead, it may have distorted your chip's signal further, making you certain to go undetected."

He walked around to his desk chair, already lost in some thought. Or maybe it was just his way. Perhaps he was always distracted by the load of data rattling around in his brilliant mind. Before sitting, he motioned for Sofia to sit. Sofia paused to assess the man before her: the gray, thinning hair and smile lines etched around the corners of his eyes made him seem harmless enough. She took her chair and cautiously watched him follow.

"Did you order everyone to avoid helping me?"

The doctor might not look threatening, but it didn't mean he was a good person. Sofia's experiences to date suggested he was not.

His eyes drifted downward. "I don't think I'm a very good teacher," he began. Then he went quiet. Just when Sofia was beginning to think this was all he had to say, he continued. "You must know that your father had connections and used them as best he could to get you placed in my facility." He looked up to confirm his suspicions.

Sofia nodded, and he resumed, "I'm sure you didn't know I was set to reject the request made on his behalf. I'm not big on politics. People around me are here on their merits. However, before I rejected the request, I did a bit of investigating into your background. Let me just say that your type of chip defect factored in my decision-making, but your rebellious nature ultimately won me over.

"I chose to have you join this team because you have a unique opportunity that comes with your chip and, I hope, the determination to turn your chip problem into an asset. So, to answer your question, yes, I told everyone to leave you to work out your access issues. But no, I didn't ask the technicians to ridicule you when things didn't go well." He grinned broadly. "Your response rather alarmed them, you know. That's the spirit I was hoping to see."

"I'm missing something ... you think being a disconnect is a good thing. How? It's ripped me from family and friends and landed me in this land of asshole technicians. Uh, sorry, but I'm just not understanding how this mess turns into a positive."

Dr. Sur's expression became stern. "Don't misunderstand. I'm not saying you should feel good about your current situation. However, I do believe your defective chip provides an opportunity that you can exploit. For example, my guess is that you still want to track down your friend, Talon Russit. Am I right?"

Sofia was taken aback. "What could my chip possibly have to do with locating Talon?"

"We don't know each other well enough for me to answer that question yet. Let's first get a better idea of what your chip can do."

"Excuse me? My chip can't even get me through a frickin' door."

"Alright, I understand the anger. You do need to channel that a little better, though. Let's do this. You spend the next few days concentrating on getting through 'frickin' doors.' I don't care how you do it but figure out how to get through doors without so many attempts. And, yes, I can monitor the number of attempts you take at each door. If you significantly improve on your success rate, we'll continue this discussion."

"What? Wait. What discussion? I'm not sure what we're even talking about. Why is it important to you that I can access a door like a normal person? How is it important to Talon?"

"I didn't say you needed to access a door like everyone else. I can tell you need some time to think about what we've discussed. Shall we plan to meet again in a week? Would that be enough time for you?" Dr. Sur got up, making it clear the meeting was over.

Sofia so wanted to extend her middle finger in the same salute she gave the technicians. The doctor had not only confirmed that she was a lab rat, but then dismissed her with less thought than one might give such a critter. The only thing that saved him from her exploding in his face was that he had dangled Talon in front of her. Did he know this? Was he completely toying with her? Sofia forced herself out the door before she killed her first lead to Talon.

Chapter Thirty-Five

Sage

July 9 – 10:07 a.m.

Sage was fuming as she stood in the Ridge Crest CID lobby. Her immediate attention was on Rani, who had the current misfortune to be working the front desk. They had run into each other numerous times, both in the office and at work-related gatherings. Sage was impressed. Rani was only a little older, but she already had her career well underway. At the same time, she was easy to approach, never talking down to her. In fact, when Sage tried to pick her brain about career advice, Rani insisted she return the favor, providing a second opinion on office politics. Rani made her feel like an equal.

Today wasn't the day to form a Rani Admiration Society, however. Rani had reluctantly delivered the news that Gabriel was busy and could not break away to meet her. Sage didn't want to make life difficult for the young cop, but this was her third time being put off.

"So Rani, how do you feel about working for someone who won't even make time for the daughter of one of his fallen officers?" she asked, watching Rani look away in shame. "You might let Gabriel know I plan to wait him out this time. And while I'm waiting, I'll let every person who walks into this lobby know who I am, who my father was, and that this is my third attempt to see him. You looked bored when I came in, but I'm betting this turns out to be an exciting day after all."

Rani seemed to brighten up, maybe even holding back a smile. "Serves Gabriel right. I'm tempted not to tell him anything and just join you. But I'm not sure I'm ready to lose my job; I worked hard to get here, so let me walk to his office and share your plans."

Sage didn't have to wait long for Gabriel to arrive, with Rani following closely behind, not even trying to hide her smile this time. "Sage, I'm sorry for being hard to track down. How are you holding up?" Gabriel stopped in front of her and took her hands, giving them a squeeze.

She took her time sizing up the chief. Next to her father, he had been one of the more influential adult figures in her life, almost like another parent. With the loss of her father, she had expected him to worry over her, but now catching the anxiety etched across his face, she wondered if he viewed her as more of a PR nightmare. These dark thoughts helped lend a bite to her tongue. "I could be doing a lot better if I had a bit more support! This isn't what I expected from you, especially with our families having spent so much time together. Aren't we more than good-times acquaintances?"

Gabriel took a step back, raising his hands as if to ward off the blows. "OK, OK, you're right. How do I make things right?"

"I need answers," Sage insisted.

"Right … OK … can we go back to my office? I think Rani has had enough entertainment for the day," Gabriel said, glancing at Rani.

"Not really," Rani said, visibly enjoying her boss getting reprimanded.

"Fine," Sage said as she walked toward the office. "Thanks, Rani. At least you've been supportive."

Neither said a word as she marched to Gabriel's office. She seated herself, not waiting for Gabriel to reach his chair.

"I get it. You're disappointed in me," he began. "Sage, I'm disappointed in myself. I've been avoiding you because I don't have much in the way of results to share with you."

"You don't know how Dad died? Or where my brother is?"

"Not completely," Gabriel said as if to plead for mercy. "Look, you probably don't even want to hear what little I do know."

"Really? Let me be the judge of that."

"Sage, you have a life ahead of you. You don't want to be scarred by this mess."

"That's not for you to decide. This mess is about my brother and my dad, so I expect to be told everything."

"OK, but I can't sugarcoat this." He shook his head, resigning himself to something he did not want to say. "Your dad killed a fellow officer. Jesse."

"What?! He ... *killed* Jesse? He was *stung out*?"

"It looks like it. No idea why. No clue what Jesse was doing at the scene either. We found your dad and Jesse at the scene, and one other body seems to have been dragged away."

Sage told herself not to give into shock. Sadly, she knew her dad would have told her in such a situation to stay strong and command respect. "So how are you going to work out the answers?"

"Honestly, I don't know," Gabriel replied. "Jesse's car should have captured everything that took place. Unfortunately, all recording devices were disabled. We think it was Jesse, but we can't be sure. We scanned the site for DNA, but the only identifiable hits we got were Jesse and Drake."

Gabriel stopped, but Sage could tell he was holding something back. "Go on ..."

"There is a possible approach. I don't like it, but I guess it's better if you hear it from me. According to the Tech Lab guys, we can recover images captured by Drake's chip as he was dying."

"You can do that? How?"

Gabriel was slow to respond, but Sage was determined to wait him out. "The tech guys say that when a person is stung out, a portion of the chip survives intact. My understanding is that it works like a black box on a plane. This surviving portion captures the last thirty seconds of brain activity before and after the host's death is triggered. Everything Drake saw or heard when he died is supposedly in that little black box."

"So what are they waiting for?"

"Well, they need your approval for starters. This type of retrieval is not taken lightly. The CID doesn't have the authority to act on its own in basically desecrating a body and sucking out the mind's experiences. A request must come from an immediate family member."

"Fine. Tell me what I need to sign."

"Sage, this shouldn't be taken lightly. You're pretty upset. Why don't you give it some thought and get back to me? Nothing is going to change by giving it a few more days."

"I'm not waiting. My dad apparently killed someone, and I need to know why, especially with the whole episode being connected to my brother. You said yourself that you're short on answers. If Dad's final experiences can help, then let's do this."

"But what if you don't like what you see? What if your dad wasn't justified in taking a life?"

Anger surged through Sage like a force impossible to control. "What's really bothering you? You've known my dad longer than most. He was a good man. An amazing father. No way you can suspect he was in the wrong here. If you have a real reason for stalling this investigation, tell me!"

The chief's dark-rimmed eyes went wide. "I'm not stalling anything. I just don't want more pain for you," he said, looking genuinely hurt. "Alright, you've made it clear I'm being overly protective. I'll get you the documents to sign and we'll see if we can get some answers."

"OK, good. Thanks," Sage said, worrying she had crossed a line, having practically bullied this man.

Chapter Thirty-Six

Talon

July 12 - 4:51 a.m.

"Run, boy!"

Talon sprang from the ground as the warning rang out. He jockeyed along the building in the moonless night, picking up speed as he heard someone closing behind him. He didn't for a second question who was closing on him or what would happen if he were caught. Instead, he concentrated on churning his legs faster while continuing to probe the wall as he ran.

Initially, he heard footsteps on the hard-packed desert earth. Now he could hear the pursuer huffing just a few feet back. He was losing hope when his fingers brushed the wall and felt it transition to a chain-link fence. He counted his strides—four, five, six. "Gotcha!" yelled his pursuer as Talon felt a hand grasp his shoulder. Talon completed his seventh stride and dove into the chain-link fence, only the fence had abruptly ended. Talon felt a tug on his collar as his would-be assailant tried to hold on, only to shoot past Talon. "Oh fuck! Shit! What the hell!"

The screams echoed behind Talon as he followed the new section of fence that continued from the corner he had abruptly rounded, eager to gain separation from the threat he barely evaded. Perhaps a hundred feet farther along, he walked into some open space and sat down, knowing he was all but invisible in the dark.

The screams hadn't stopped, but now they were directed at Talon, "I know you're out there! I'm hunting you, you little shit! It's just a matter of time! Be scared!"

Scared? Talon didn't need any help with that. He had been at the Fabrication Center for almost two months, which was plenty of time to learn how wrong the place was. Fabrication Center was a deceptive name, indeed quite fabricated. A labor camp for disconnects was much more descriptive.

The compound was separated into four quadrants: one was dedicated to the facility's administration and was fairly unknown to Talon. The remaining three quadrants shared the same layout, with each featuring a large manufacturing building along one wall and residential quarters along the remaining three. The perimeter walls were approximately 150 feet farther out from the buildings and looked to be at least twenty-feet high. Everything was made from a sand-colored stucco that blended perfectly with the barren compound's desert floor. The one exception was the gray chain-link fences that wrapped around substantially all the buildings' perimeters, creating a twenty-five-foot vacant span extending out from the building walls. The purpose of this design didn't make sense to Talon until he spent a few days in his assigned housing.

His building had the same layout as the other eleven residential buildings strung along the quadrant walls. The buildings were two stories with concrete walls and floors. Not a spot of paint inside. Hallways ran the length of both floors. Off each hallway, there were five large barren rooms with twenty-four cots stuffed into each. At the end of the hallways were bathrooms with four toilets along one wall. The toilets had no water but were mounted over holes leading directly to large septic tanks. The entire building lacked running water and had no air conditioning, and each room had only two windows, each three feet square. By some bare minimum of mercy, the windows did open, which allowed temperatures to be maintained below ninety degrees most nights.

The sleeping quarters were designed for anything but rest. Talon first thought that the idea was to make everyone seek the outdoors. Then he began to understand the purpose of the fences. They were positioned along the buildings so that at no time of the year would disconnects be able to reach the shade waiting there. It was mental torture. More important to the sick mind behind this torture, the fences helped drive people into the manufacturing facilities for survival.

The facilities manager, who went by the title 'Warden,' took pride in the fact that he converted his band of outcast disconnects into useful and willing 'workers'. He was known to brag that while no workers were assigned more than five eight-hour shifts a week, most chose to work sixteen-hour days, seven days a week. He left out the fact that the manufacturing buildings in each quadrant were sadistically designed to be the only places of refuge for the more than eight thousand disconnects crammed into the compound. If you wanted to escape the unbearably hot days the Mojave Desert could bring, you headed to work.

If that wasn't enough incentive, then perhaps hunger and thirst would drive you there. You could get water, rice, beans, and occasionally a morsel of meat at the manufacturing building. You could even take a shower twice a week, but if you wanted any of these 'perks', you had to sign up for an eight-hour shift. Everyone routinely signed up for two.

The threats and screams flung at Talon brought him back to the present. The big hulk he had temporarily eluded was known as Feist. He was a twin. Both brothers were considered extremely dangerous, if not completely insane. Feist's brother, Letcher Mercer, was rumored to be locked up somewhere in the compound. Supposedly he was much more cunning and brutal than Feist, so much so that even the warden didn't want him roaming loose. That thought sent a shiver through Talon because he knew too well how much the warden enjoyed the wild frontier he had created outside the building walls.

Two weeks after arriving at the Center, Talon learned that his stay in the residential quarters was over. Wandering across the compound, he fantasized about collapsing into an exhausted sleep. Reaching the building entrance, he approached the screen to the right of the door. He hit the button that would trigger the facial scan and dutifully viewed the screen, waiting for it to flash green.

Instead, the warden's image appeared on the screen with a prerecorded message telling Talon that he no longer had assigned housing. Due to a shortage, he would need to take up residence in the yard. Talon asked what he had done, knowing people were assigned to the yard only as punishment. In response to his plea for an explanation, the message played over again, only this time expanding to warn that anyone entering the residences without permission would be removed by security after all those in the building had been gassed.

This was a favorite tactic of security, who only set foot on the grounds after the workers had been knocked out by a rather vile chemical compound. After being knocked out, people generally woke up thirty minutes to an hour later with nasty headaches. Many were left retching uncontrollably.

Ironically, after the warden's message finished, the screen turned green, signaling he could enter. Perhaps this was another taunt from the warden. Talon wasn't about to risk the wrath of his fellow workers, so he retreated to the yard, hoping he could set things right the next day.

That was many weeks ago, yet he still hadn't been given a chance to speak to the warden—or anyone else, for that matter. He had asked all who would listen, including his production supervisor, how he might arrange to speak with someone about his housing. The few who were sympathetic to his situation explained that there was no way to schedule time with the warden, or with security, unless they chose to approach him. These sympathizers invariably added that they had never heard of anyone his age being placed in the yard. They would only wish him the best and look away, making it clear most didn't expect him to survive.

Well, he had survived. At least until now. Talon routinely worked until 11:00 p.m. when it was cool enough to sleep, then got up at 4:00 a.m. before the other hundred or so in the yard awoke, allowing him to escape into the manufacturing facility. He was exhausted most of the time. However, on the few occasions where he did sleep too long, he was awakened by someone stomping on his back—even, once, by a fist to the face.

Evidently, he had gained a following among those who were slighted by his continual quest to escape the yard. They took it personally or, more likely, as an opportunity to bully someone ill-equipped to fight back. The fist to the face had come from Feist just two weeks ago. Feist was king of the bullies and had finally decided to take his turn at Talon. Talon was jarred awake, and while his head was swimming, he could tell by the light outside he had overslept.

As he prepared for the many blows that were sure to follow, he heard a shout: "Lay off, Feist!" The shadow that was Feist hovered over Talon for what seemed like several minutes, then kicked him in the ribs and disappeared. Talon had a hazy sense of being guided to a chain-link fence, where he was lowered to a seated position. The fence kept him from falling onto his side.

Once he gathered his wits, he realized it was Robert and his friend Blunt. They were well known throughout the yard. Both were large and ripped. However, Robert was not at all an imposing figure. He was kind to everyone and wouldn't think to hurt a soul. It was Blunt that must have scared Feist off. Blunt didn't care for anyone or bother to talk to anyone. He was broad and grim looking. His face, hands, and shoulders looked like he had been in a fight with a barbed wire fence. No one knew why he was friends with Robert, but he was. Since no one wanted trouble with Blunt, no one messed with Robert.

Seeing that Talon was coming to his wits, Robert sat beside him against the fence. "Boy, I think I messed up. Feist isn't going to take it well being forced to back down to anyone. I'm pretty certain I've put a target on your back and maybe even mine." He looked up at Blunt, who stood over them, shaking his head in disgust. "You need to make sure you sleep somewhere different every night and have an escape route plotted out before you close your eyes."

Robert's words had brought a little more clarity to Talon's situation. He was approaching two months at the compound, but he knew it would be a challenge to make it three.

"You're probably right about trouble coming my way. Still, without your help just now, all my troubles might have been buried along with me. At least you've bought me a little more time to find that winning ticket out of here. Thanks."

Robert chuckled, "Boy, I like your thinking. And I sure would like to see someone make it out of here still breathing. Don't give up that dream. Make a plan to stay alive and make a plan to get out." He got to his feet and wandered off.

Still hiding in the dark as Feist continued to blast out threats, Talon remembered taking Robert's advice seriously. At least the part about staying alive. Every night he found a different place to sleep, sometimes in the middle of the yard and sometimes along a building wall or fence. Oddly, every morning when he woke up, he would find Robert and Blunt sleeping nearby. This was a great comfort, though at the same time disturbing. If they could find him without fail, then so could Feist. And Talon sensed Robert was right. Feist was coming for him. So, with this understanding, he had been working on quick escapes.

The cleverest one was the one he laid out tonight. While there weren't any large pieces of glass around, a good number of small pieces could be found among the trash scattered throughout the yard. The biggest piece he found wasn't larger than the tip of his thumb, but that worked. He eventually accumulated a pocketful of crushed glass. He scattered them past the corner of the chain-link fence about five feet out.

Then after a couple of trial runs, where he paced off his strides along the fence, he called it a night.

Now, as he heard Feist screaming his name with menace attached, he knew it had worked too well. Feist was no doubt picking glass out of his feet while he plotted Talon's demise. If Feist had not been committed fervently enough to Talon's destruction before, he would double down on that effort now. He only hoped the rumors were true about Feist being networked, making him an exception to the imprisoned disconnects. If not, Talon was dead.

He was plotting how to sneak past Feist and into the temporary safety of the manufacturing building when he heard Feist's retreating voice. "Remember this night! You know I will. Keep an eye open, boy, 'cuz I'm coming."

The sun was on the rise, but still Talon could barely make out Feist's outline. Was his surrender for the night a bluff? As Feist headed off, he moved incredibly slowly. Unless he was putting on a great performance, Feist was in no condition to run him down.

Emboldened, Talon followed from a distance as Feist made his way back to where the chase had begun. This also brought him back to where Robert and Blunt perched nearby. Robert was the one who had shouted the warning, and both had stuck around to make sure everything turned out alright. Talon realized he had a friend in Robert and perhaps one in Blunt, too. Robert got off the ground with Feist lumbering toward him. Blunt rose as well but, as always, was content to stand in the background.

Tiring of his slow approach, Robert walked out to meet him. "This needs to end, now."

Feist held up his hands in surrender. "I know. You're right." He stepped forward and launched a wicked right to Robert's chin. Robert went down like a sack of potatoes. Feist leered down at him before suddenly collapsing. Watching Blunt come to a stop and hold his gaze on the bodies, Talon knew Robert had cashed in on the only known ticket out of here.

Feist's demise was of no concern to him, but Talon had cost Robert his life.

Chapter Thirty-Seven

Rani

July 15 - 12:18 p.m.

Rani sat across from Sage in a small boutique cafe, thinking hard about the situation she had walked into. She knew why Sage had asked her to lunch: she wanted answers. Did she have answers? Rani had a lot of questions about the department herself. Shit, she'd worked so hard to drag herself up and get her job, but recently, being a cop had not been feeling so good.

Giving her own spin on Rani's silence, Sage finally said, "I get that you aren't comfortable being seen with me."

Rani didn't correct her misperception. Her thoughts merely turned to Sage. She had never been one to seek the spotlight, rather was content to fade in the background, more concerned with keeping her family together. Before she had shown up at the department the other day to confront her boss, Rani would have bet Sage was at home, curled up in a ball. Rani had underestimated her. Sage was what, twenty-one? Just a little younger than herself and yet she was boldly stepping out of the shadows, letting people know she was a force to be reckoned with. Rani liked to think she would step up as well if faced with the same adversity, but she had her doubts. Reining in her wandering thoughts, the bottom line was Rani wanted to help Sage. She just didn't want any pretense that she had all the answers or that she had been asked to lunch for anything other than a good grilling.

Sage continued to misread Rani's quiet reflections. "What I don't get is *why* you're so uncomfortable. When did Ridge Crest CID start worrying about which community members they were seen with? What is happening to our small community?" Sage glared at her, but Rani merely returned the stare as if she would never utter a word, until a smile broke over her face.

"Very dramatic. Our community rests on whether I have lunch with you? Good one!"

"OK, perhaps I am being dramatic," Sage said. "But you have to admit the CID is on edge. I can't get a word out of your boss. He's back to hiding from me. And you didn't exactly seem thrilled to have lunch with me."

"When have I been thrilled to do anything with you?" she asked, not wanting to miss out on the dig.

Sage let out a genuine laugh, and Rani realized it felt good to see the sadness erased from her face, even if only for a fleeting moment, but then Sage leaned in, making it clear her questions couldn't be deflected forever.

"Is it me that's putting everyone on edge? Or is something going on?"

Rani took a good look at the young woman in front of her. Her determination was rousing, and right then, Rani knew whose side she was on. "No, it's not you. I'm not sure what's going on. The chief is getting visits from CID personnel I've never met. Word around the office is they're honchos out of D.C. And he's been making trips down south, but he won't say where.

"He claims he's been given some confidential assignment that's a big deal for the CID and an honor for our department. But he won't share anything further, so no one's feeling great about the assignment or the new people crawling around the department. We're on edge. And I haven't even told you the worst of it."

Rani delayed just long enough to make sure Sage was listening closely. Sage leaned in even more.

"You know that recording you keep asking me to check on with the chief? Pretty sure he received it. I signed for a package from the Tech Lab when he was out. Yesterday, I confronted him. Told him I thought he had the recording. He didn't deny it. But he did remind me how I work for the department and not for you, then pretty much threw me out of his office. So, maybe you were being dramatic, but, yeah, some big shit is going on."

"I ... I need to catch my breath here, try to process half of what you're saying. Can I ask you something off the wall?"

"After my big spill? You bet."

"Why tell me all this? Don't get me wrong, I so appreciate you sharing with me. But you've never opened up before."

"Know why I became a cop?"

"No."

"Maybe I'll tell you more another time, but I can say I didn't join the department to belong to some shitty secret society. When I signed up, I thought I was going to hunt down all the bad guys and make Ridge Crest the best place in the world. Now my boss is telling me I'm not supposed to help people. I'm wondering if this job might be right for me, after all."

Rani watched Sage's eyes go wide with alarm. "No ... you can't! Think about quitting, I mean! Your boss is the one with issues—not you. The department *is* here to serve Ridge Crest."

"Well, thanks for that. Hey, I'm not going to rush any decisions. It's not like I have another job lined up. I'll wait to see whether these times are the new normal."

Sage sized her up. "Alright. Can we agree to talk more about this before you make any decisions?"

"Deal."

"Well, what is the chief up to? He sure does seem to be keeping a lot of secrets these days. Do you know what airport he's flying to when he makes these trips?" Sage asked.

"LAX. He also gets a Mini, so no telling where he goes after he lands."

"Any idea how long he's been making these trips?"

"Less than two months, but he's probably been down there three or four times already."

"And that's where he is now?"

"Mmhm. Are you may be thinking of tracking him down?" Rani asked, toying with the idea of hunting the chief down herself.

"Tempting. No, it would be silly to think I could find him. I'll just have to wait for him to get back. But I'm done letting him hide. We'll be having a talk soon."

Rani had underestimated Sage. Smiling to herself, she mused on her take-charge attitude. "Great. Feel free to slap some sense into him. We could use some leadership from him right now."

"Yeah, and I could use his help. Any idea if he's viewed the recording?"

"No idea. Do you mind telling me what's on it? Maybe something he said was connected but I didn't know it."

"With all you've shared, the least I could do is tell you. Just ... I'm not ready to talk about it yet. Is that alright?"

"Yeah, sure. We all got our shit. And you've sure got a lot you're sorting through right now. We can take things at your pace."

"Maybe next time I'll be ready to."

"Next time," Rani agreed. She had found she liked the idea of another outing with Sage. While their circumstances differed, she and Sage shared a few things when it came to family loss.

Chapter Thirty-Eight

Sofia

July 19 - 7:06 p.m.

Sofia took a new approach to security portals. Previously, she had struggled to be like everyone else, badly wanting to saunter through an entrance with the same confidence and acceptance. No longer. She now took advantage of doors carelessly left open and found opportunities to drift behind someone as they entered a facility. If her presence registered with either a green light or a red light, she counted it as a failure. It meant that Dr. Sur could track her activities, and she wanted nothing to do with his prying eyes.

On the other hand, if her presence didn't register, which was more often than not, she felt free to explore that space, confident she was undetected and offline.

After a week of going offline, Sofia felt pretty good about her newfound freedom. At about 7 p.m. on a Friday, she sidled into the Lab offices as one of the last employees was leaving for the day. She carried an empty package to support the idea of a late-night delivery in the event she was seen.

Passing empty office after empty office, she noted that some of their glass panels were opaque while others were transparent. She had learned that the panels could be switched between clear and opaque, depending on the desired privacy. Fortunately, most of the glass panels were set to allow her prying eyes to explore the contents held within. She wandered through the labs imagining what she might be able to uncover: new products, who developed them, and more importantly, where they were produced. She was pretty certain Talon's location sat at the end of this last mystery. He had been shipped off to the Center, where everyone knew the Tech Lab's inventions became reality.

Growing tired of peering in at displays and papers left out on desks, it occurred to her that she had been playing at being a simple spy long enough. The next stage was to figure out how to access people's desks and discover who held what secrets. The problem she faced was that while most employees didn't bother to lock their doors, she was certain each doorway held a chip reader. She was tempted to enter an office and gamble that she wouldn't be detected, but if she was, she would have a problem.

She might be able to explain that she got confused while delivering packages, but anyone checking her story would notice she had suspiciously slipped into the building undetected.

Her heart was racing so hard with the thought of breaking into an office that she nearly jumped out of her skin when a voice called out.

"Hey, you! What are you doing here?"

Fighting to regain her wits, she slowly turned back to the office she had just passed, resisting every impulse to run. An imposing figure rose from behind a desk. He had a shaggy beard and long, wavy-brown hair tinged with gray. The giant had to be at least six and a half feet and north of 250 pounds. It wasn't all muscle, but close enough. In a feeble effort to present some kind of defense, Sofia raised her package for him to see.

With intense brown eyes that seemed to penetrate her innermost thoughts, the beast sized up the situation and growled, "I could care less about the package you're carrying. Come in here, please."

Too afraid to flee, Sofia walked into the office, and the massive guy pointed to a metal chair.

"Feel free to sit. I have a feeling we're going to be talking for a while. Sofia, isn't it?"

"How do you know me?" she asked.

His face was now consumed by a smile that left him looking far from scary. "Your reputation precedes you. I'm Jonathan. Jonathan Pruitt."

He held out his hand like a gentleman. She shook it, and only then did he allow himself to be seated.

"I'm the chief engineer. You've done a good job of terrorizing my technicians. They consider you wild and unpredictable! So, when I saw a young woman wandering through the halls without receiving any prior alert, the first thing that came to mind was this must be Sofia."

Sofia had started to relax when she realized Jonathan might know she snuck into the building. How? Not wanting to confess to her stealth activities, she decided to play dumb.

"Was I supposed to alert you that I was here?"

"We both know you entered the building undetected. You were hoping your presence would go unnoticed?"

"I ... I, well—"

"Alright," he said, raising a hand. "I'm going to help you be a smarter player in whatever game you're playing. Let me give you a quick overview of our security system. We have chip readers at every building entrance, along the hallways, and at all the office doors. A person entering a building is monitored, including both audio and video recordings, as the readers pick up their journeys through the building. The only places we don't monitor people are in their offices and conference rooms. People are tracked in and out of offices, but no recordings when they're in them. As intrusive as surveillance has become, we've drawn the line at a few safe havens."

"Why don't you just record twenty-four/seven throughout the hallways?" Sofia asked, intent on absorbing every security detail Jonathan wanted to share.

"Some would say cost," Jonathan replied, looking annoyed. "The memory required to store a continual stream from all the buildings throughout the campus would be significantly more than the intermittent recordings triggered by the readers. However ..."

"You don't agree with this," Sofia stated.

Jonathan shook his head. "Very perceptive of you. Yes, cost shouldn't have been the reason for failing to put in a better system. The difference in memory cost wasn't that great. The truth is that this system is left over from when the Fabrication Center and Technology Lab were one facility."

Sofia perked up even more at the mention of the Center.

"The security chief at the time was Alfred Simmons. He took over leadership of the Center when the two organizations split. He now goes by the grand title of 'Warden.'" Jonathan said, rolling his eyes. "Anyway, Simmons was more concerned about saving every dime he could, hoping to direct the savings to his pockets rather than on eliminating possible security threats."

"Why don't you update the system now?" Sofia asked.

"Too costly to modify the system today. And even though the two organizations split long ago, there are a lot of legacy issues from when they were joined." Jonathan smirked. "Including security personnel."

"What do you mean by—?"

"Enough," he said with a raised hand. "I've done enough venting. Let's get back to you roaming undetected in the halls."

"Really?" Sofia hoped that subject could be put behind them.

"Really. Now you have a basic idea of how our system monitors people. And guess what? I happen to have access to that system and receive notices when people pop in after hours. Yet, here you are and you weren't picked up. That leaves me with a few mysteries. First, how did you get through the front door? And let me be clear, Dr. Sur has let me know about your chip. My understanding is that you can pass by readers unnoticed. But that won't open a secure door. Doors only grant access once your chip is read. So how did you get in here?"

Sofia looked up to see that Jonathan's scary face had returned. He wanted an answer and wasn't above intimidating her to get one. She decided to dig in. "I'm not going to get anyone in trouble."

"So, you snuck in when someone was leaving?"

Sofia couldn't hide her surprise and knew it registering on her face was all the confirmation Jonathan would need.

"Thanks. So why are you here, prowling around the hallways? And why didn't you get detected by the hallway readers?"

Choosing to ignore the first question, she said, "I really don't know."

Jonathan studied her. "I think the answer is luck. Had you passed enough readers, your faulty chip would have eventually registered and given you away. Have you been sneaking around any other evenings? How about other buildings? If you have, then all I have to do is access old records linked to your ID and I'll be able to pull up the after-hours recordings."

"Damn," Sofia muttered, realizing how sloppy she'd been.

Grinning at her inadvertent admission, Jonathan waited for more, but Sofia wasn't going to add to the mess she was already in. "Alright. Here's what I need to know—what are you doing roaming around all these buildings late at night?"

Sofia wasn't eager to confess to anyone. She didn't see how it could be helpful. "I can't tell you."

"You can't tell me? Or won't? If you don't tell me, then I'll have to turn this over to security," Jonathan calmly explained.

Sofia looked at him to confirm he knew the extent of the threat he was making. The smirk on his face confirmed he did. Everyone, including newbies, was warned to stay away from security. By 'security,' people meant Chief Hill. The chief was said to be a sadistic psychopath who lived to destroy. Rumor had it that a meeting with Chief Hill was a one-way ticket to the Center. Or worse. Sofia had yet to have the pleasure of meeting him, and she didn't want to start tonight.

"Fine. As you must know, Dr. Sur challenged me to learn how to get access to secure areas. He has an interest in watching me struggle to find my way through this complex, like a rat in a maze ... Being someone's experiment stinks, so I decided to go offline. But I didn't realize I wasn't really offline and that someone like you could tell I was sneaking around. Here I thought I was thumbing my nose at all those who had me trapped in this cage, but now it turns out I was too stupid to realize nothing had changed." She hung her head so Jonathan couldn't see her fighting to hold back tears.

Jonathan waited for her to collect herself, finally saying, "I understand. It can't be fun being here. You didn't choose to have this defective chip. Then you're shipped off to the Tech Lab and find yourself not only in a strange place, but you're a kind of a strange person in a strange place. No one would enjoy being in your shoes."

Sofia felt a tear run down her cheek. As long as she had been here, no one seemed to have a clue about what she was going through. No one seemed to care. Now this big, scary guy had picked up on her tragedy completely. "I have to go," was all she could think to say.

Chapter Thirty-Nine

Wilder

July 21 – 5:21 a.m.

He had been careless when entering the park. He had worked his way to the middle of perhaps a thousand people when one set of eyes turned his way and followed him. He knew he was identified. The person was twenty feet away and making his way through the bodies that separated them. Wilder tried to keep calm as he moved away from his pursuer, but it was starting to unravel.

As if by some unknown signal, awareness of his presence spread through the mass of people like a wave. All eyes began turning his way. He dropped all pretense and dashed through the crowd. Arms reached toward him, bodies moved to encircle him and block his escape.

Panic! Suppress the panic ... If he could only—

Wilder snapped awake, gasping ... ragged breaths coming fast.

Another bad dream. He lay still, trying to regain his bearings. Through the gray light of dawn, he could make out scraggly branches reaching out toward him, and he remembered he was tucked away in a thick stand of brush. The brush had thrived in this site near the creek, partially shaded by the train trestle overhead. His pulse began to slow as he was able to assure himself that unlike in his dream, he was completely alone.

Wilder knew his sleep was haunted by the very fears he had been wrestling with the last several weeks, having made numerous ventures into the heart of Seaside while never forgetting he was a highly sought-after fugitive. He had walked the streets of the town, hung out on restaurant patios, and even visited a dog park, all in search of information. In his experience, it was often the simplest overlooked details that determined the success of an operation. He had been tireless in gathering relevant and irrelevant facts about the Tech Lab in preparation for penetrating its security and contacting Sofia.

The casual style of most Californians made it easy for him to blend with the Seaside residents. He used a cover story that his fiancée had secured a job at the Lab and was expected to start in a couple of weeks. It didn't take long for people to open and spill their knowledge about existing in the shadow of the Lab. Most of the residents either worked there or had close relations with someone who did. He patiently listened to all that people wanted to share, including which events the Lab sponsored, who to reach out to if you had a complaint, and even which complainers to ignore.

Fortunately, people were also quick to share their weirdest experiences, like if you strayed off the roads near the Lab, a drone would immediately be dispatched to track you; if you didn't soon return to the roads, the drone would swoop down close to you. Several people guessed their IDs were being extracted from their NACs.

Wilder also learned that the Lab had a community outreach program in which they opened the gates to locals. It hosted a barbecue in the parking lot and offered guided tours of the campus, although explaining virtually nothing about what the Lab actually did. The next event was to be held on August 8, less than three weeks from now. Perhaps he could make use of this event.

Reviewing his present situation, he decided he was safe. He would spend the morning planning his investigation into Lab security and assessing possible ways to reach Sofia. He dug his backpack out from where he'd buried it under the leaves beneath a bush and took inventory of what he had, most of which had been supplied to him by Haris to assist in his clandestine activities.

Haris … Damn, it was tough that he was gone. It was so hard to feel so alone all the time.

Wilder sighed, but sorting through his belongings was cathartic; it focused him. And it was as good as any method to trigger ideas for possible approaches. He set aside dried packaged foods, smirking at the thought of using them to poison the guards. He had an assortment of explosive devices, one of which could release a flash of blinding light and ear-splitting sound. Another released a gas that would drop anyone within a ten-foot radius, though it only knocked people out for a minute or two. He even had a device that would generate enough heat to melt or burn almost anything it encountered, including most metals.

His drones were equally impressive: a "bee" and a "bird," both devices designed to look like their namesakes from a distance. They were mostly used for capturing images, as they didn't readily transmit data—too easy to be tracked that way. Their ranges were impressive, too, with the bird capable of operating up to two miles away. The bird would flap its mechanical wings as it flew, though really it was propulsion assisted. It also landed on two feet and could hop. Your average person would need to be within thirty feet of the bird and give it more than a glance to realize it wasn't real.

Wilder also had binoculars and a telescope, both of which he used frequently. He located several concealed viewpoints along the bluffs bordering Seaside. While he was not able to view most of the complex that faced away from Seaside and out toward the ocean, he figured he had been able to inspect over half of the outdoor compound.

And he had located Sofia! This was the one bright spot that was currently stopping him from letting this morning drag him under.

He was also fairly certain he knew where she lived. He was able to track her to the door of a building that could only be housing. Not only had she entered the last two evenings, but she later emerged to lounge on the bench located immediately outside the door. The previous night, she appeared to read until the evening light faded before retreating inside.

As best as he could tell, Sofia spent most of her time alone. At this time of year, the complex was not overly crowded and Sofia could readily be seen scurrying from building to building. And he had yet to see her accompanied by anyone.

Wilder wasn't worried about why she was alone. He was finding it difficult to hold much empathy for her, since she had received special treatment to land at the Lab, while his brother had been cast off to the Center. He had few questions as to who pulled the strings, but he did have a lot of questions about why Sofia's father hadn't rescued Talon as well. Last he recalled, Sofia and Talon were inseparable. Soulmates. He was having a hard time reconciling what he knew of Sofia with what she had let happen to her brother.

No. Her being alone didn't tug at his heart. Her being alone merely meant she should be easier to reach, but how? This puzzle was stopping him from getting out from under this funk he couldn't shake.

Would he signal her with some light? No, certainly the whole complex would catch on to that one. Perhaps he could approach her at the upcoming barbecue? Maybe. He was not excited about being on enemy ground—and he would need to evade whatever security accompanied the event. Plus, he wasn't sure a face-to-face meeting would be wise. People change ... she knew he was a disconnect. What was to stop her from turning him in? So, if he wasn't going to approach her in person, then what? Befriend someone and trust them to slip her a note? Not likely. Getting to know someone that well could take months. With Haris gone, he only trusted himself and the equipment Haris left with him—which gave him a crazy thought on how to reach out to Sofia.

Chapter Forty

Talon

July 22 – 2:31 p.m.

What the hell?

Talon watched in amazement as Blunt walked across the production floor toward the exit. The first shift had ended and supposedly everyone was welcome to leave. Almost no one ever did, though, since people were too hungry to miss a meal and hesitant to face the mid-afternoon heat. Blunt was perhaps the one exception. His routines were anything but routine: it was common for him to head outside at midday. The heat meant nothing to him.

Today was different. Rumor was spreading through the factory floors that a special visitor would be touring the facilities today. Some said it was a four-star general. Hopes were high that this would be the catalyst for change. This general had supposedly insisted on touring the facilities, overriding the objections of the warden.

Surely a decorated and accomplished patriot would not stand for citizens being stripped of all rights and forced to live as slaves, especially those who had committed no crimes. One walk through their living quarters should be enough to blow the cover of this operation and bring it to an end. All anyone wanted to talk about was when this general would arrive and whether he would tour their building.

Talon couldn't ever remember such a positive vibe running through the place. Even those who were half-dead, those long past any hope of getting out of the place alive, suddenly had a sparkle in their eyes. Long-forgotten dreams were being rekindled right before him.

So why would Blunt choose this moment to head for the exit? If anyone had a reason to leave, it was Talon. His co-workers—or co-prisoners, if he was being honest—had turned a cold shoulder to him since Robert's death. Robert had looked to protect Talon and paid the price for this generosity. Such acts had left Robert well-liked. Talon, on the other hand, was known to very few and was the face behind Robert's demise. He understood the animosity toward him. He blamed himself as well. He never should have let Robert get involved in helping to solve his problems, but hadn't that always been Talon's way?

Like most kids, he had dreamed of being a superhero. He spent years running around in a cape, wearing a magic ring, and trying desperately to discover his unique superpowers, but his life had turned out to be far short of heroic. Instead, he relied on everyone else.

Was that Sofia's attraction to him? Was she looking for a cause and he was happy to be it? Her intervention with the football team was something he had simply come to expect from her, however embarrassing. Why didn't he ever step up and take charge of his own destiny?

Like his brother had.

Talon's justification for not running had been concern for his parents. He wasn't going to repeat his brother's mistake. Only, this weak excuse got his father killed.

And now Robert had been fatally drawn into his drama.

Sadness filled Talon. He couldn't think of anything worthwhile he had done for anyone. Trapped in this place with everyone and everything stacked against him, he didn't see much chance of changing that outcome.

It was times like this that he forced himself to remember his promise to Sofia. He could not join those who had surrendered all hope of escape, especially today. The odd question forming in the back of his mind was who offered the best chance of escape—the visiting general or Blunt.

Something about Blunt choosing to break from the crowd and head out struck him as Blunt not fitting here. Or maybe it was he didn't plan to fit, as if he might be gone tomorrow. And while Talon had originally been fixated on Blunt's every movement because he desperately wanted to take responsibility for the loss of his friend, he now equally wanted to unravel the mystery of Blunt.

Talon finally took notice of his supervisor, who kept showing up on his workstation display, yelling at him to get his head back into his work. His boss didn't give a damn that his good friend had died mere days ago. He was more worried that his source for process improvements had gone quiet. No question his supervisor had been riding his ability to analyze work processes and had taken complete credit for suggestions he had made. Although his boss was pressing for the next big idea, Talon could hardly care less.

The only thing he really wanted was to settle the argument in his head: Was the crowd right about this general being the ticket out of here, or was Blunt a better gamble?

As Talon watched Blunt disappear, his boss's dark features engulfed the space before him, a hologram emanating from the screen. This was new. His boss was making a big effort to capture his attention. Leaving now would be a slap in the face of his supervisor and his own self-preservation.

Talon headed for the door.

Chapter Forty-One

Sofia

July 22 – 2:33 p.m.

Sofia wasn't surprised when she was invited to meet with Dr. Sur again. It would have been too much to expect Jonathan to keep silent about her break-in. His loyalties would be with his boss, not her. Still, she couldn't help feeling betrayed.

Deciding there was no point wasting time on hurt feelings, she began mulling over what was to come. What would Dr. Sur do? Exile her to the Center? Well, at least she would find Talon that way. Was there anything scarier than the Center, though? She couldn't think of anything.

Which meant she didn't have a lot to fear. Meeting with Dr. Sur shouldn't knock her off her game. He might have plans for her, but she would stay alert for ways to use the doctor in pursuit of her own plans.

Lost in thought, she almost failed to see Dr. Sur waving her in. She sighed as she realized he was again doing that stupid thing with that geeky ball. He was trying to grant her access with absolutely no success. Probably remembering her reaction the last time he made this attempt, he gave up right away and rushed to let her in.

"Jonathan said he made this one specifically for your visit. Evidently, access is not one of the functions he had in mind. Pretty sure you could stand at my door all day and you would never come close to being let in, let alone detected. Anyway, let me apologize again. It's my new tradition for starting off our meetings."

With her nerves settled, and thinking she was beginning to figure out his quirky behavior, she sat down and got to the point. "Am I in trouble? Did I do something wrong?"

"Oh, the Jonathan thing. Is that what you're talking about? Well, should you be in trouble?"

"No."

"Why not?"

"You told me to work on gaining access to secure areas. I think I went above and beyond."

Dr. Sur considered this. "I agree. Though technically you did get caught." When Sofia merely rolled her eyes in response, he asked, "If you don't think you did anything wrong, why are you surprised that I agree with you?"

"Why am I here then?"

"We did agree to meet again. Plus, I wanted to check with you to see if you've had any correspondence regarding Talon."

Sofia's heart immediately started racing. "No ... I–is there something I should know about him? Is Talon trying to contact me?"

"Oh, sorry. No. I just know you were close to him. I was merely trying to be friendly."

Sofia studied the doctor's face, but he simply smiled back at her. Sofia found it difficult to believe Dr. Sur had brought her in for a social visit. "This is the second time you inquired about Talon. Can you tell me what's going on?"

The smile faded. "This isn't the time to be talking about Talon. Please, let's focus on your ability to move about the compound."

"Really? You're confusing me. You bring up Talon and then you go quiet. Why? And why do you even want me sneaking around? What are we doing here?"

Dr. Sur responded by quietly gazing at her with his hands folded on his desk.

Sofia continued, "OK, so you still don't trust me? You still want me to prove myself before you clue me in?"

The man merely raised his eyebrows as if to ask, "What do you think?" He sure knew how to push her buttons.

"Fine. I'll get back out there and prowl around. But nothing's off limits. Who knows? Maybe I'll find I don't need your help."

"Fair enough. Just don't get caught this time."

Rising to escape, she noticed the silver ball resting in the middle of his desk. She snatched it and headed for the door. "Thanks for the present. I won't get caught."

Chapter Forty-Two

General Stafford

July 22 – 2:33 p.m.

The general sat impatiently in his armored transport with his security detail. He had been waiting outside the Fabrication Center's main gate for over fifteen minutes. As the newest member of the Board of Directors, he was determined to tour the facilities ... and neutralize Talon Russit.

He didn't know the exact threat Talon posed to the Program. Quite the opposite, he had confirmed beyond any doubt the Tech Lab had not released his module into the public domain. His plants at the Lab were well placed. Their firm denials addressed his initial fear his module was associated with the recent spike in Ridge Crest disconnects.

Still, the general was unnerved by Russit's mere existence. Something wasn't right. Dajani Haris's interest in Russit, but not Ms. Crashan or Ms. Abreo, was disturbing. Haris was vehemently opposed to the Program yet willing to make a deal with the devil to get control of Russit. Today, the general would learn what made Russit special. Or he would eliminate him.

"Mr. Simmons, I'm done waiting for you to admit me. You knew I was arriving today to inspect your facilities. I strongly suggest you open the gate."

The warden's voice floated out over his armored vehicle's sound system. "Not sure how your visit didn't make it into my calendar, General. I'm trying to see what I can do to accommodate you."

"Really?" The general had very little patience for these games. He looked at the twenty-foot-high main gate before him. Making a quick calculation, he commanded, "Detail, station yourselves outside the vehicle and train your weapons on that gate."

Instantly, five soldiers filed out of the military transport and aimed their missile launchers at the front. The general remained in the vehicle, certain the warden had cameras watching their every move. "Don't take too much time, Mr. Simmons. I plan to let myself in within the next sixty seconds."

This was all for show. The launchers were overkill—the weapons were designed to take out much more than a gate. Firing while a mere twenty yards from the target would take his men out as well. The show was simply a cover because the general wasn't eager to reveal to his adversary the real technical prowess at his disposal.

Still, the general wasn't bluffing about entering. His lightweight armored vehicle could convert to air flight in less than thirty seconds. He would land in the middle of the warden's compound if necessary.

He relished the technical superiority of the military, even though it had not come via accelerated innovation. Rather, civilian innovation, such as the adoption of the flying cars, had all but been extinguished, while military innovation, under the threat of punishment to those sitting at the bottom of the command chain, had labored on. This gave the military an edge against any civilian threat, playing perfectly into the Program's quest to maintain a peaceful society.

Looking at the windshield display, the general was surprised to see thirty seconds remained. Each second that ticked by grated on his nerves. He looked forward to the very near future when his module was deployed and these charades would be put well behind him. He could march his troops through any security portal without even asking permission.

For now, he would practice patience—to a point. With less than fifteen seconds remaining, he emerged from the vehicle, doing his best to portray he was about to give the lethal command.

Not two seconds later, the gate began rolling open. The warden, in his haste, hadn't even made a request that they disarm. Big mistake.

Chapter Forty-Three

Talon

July 22 - 2:35 p.m.

Talon entered the Transition Room, which consisted of white-painted walls lined with metal hooks to hang work smocks. He was disappointed to find the room empty, having missed Blunt. Talon tugged on his smock until the metal snaps released. The room lighting pulsed continuously, which reminded Talon that he was being scanned for any items he might be trying to smuggle from the facility. The pulsing transitioned from soft white to red as a voice rang out. "Please proceed to the Clearing Room." Clearing Room? Talon had no idea what the Clearing Room was, nor where it was, until he noticed the red light flashing above a side door. The door had never registered with him during the countless times he had passed through the Transition Room.

He walked over and stood before the flashing light, holding out hope that it would soon stop. The light continued pulsing, perfectly content performing its one job. Talon's shoulders sagged and he pushed through the door. The walls, ceiling, and floor were pure white. The room didn't have a single piece of furniture or even one blemish to break up the monotony. Talon reluctantly let the door close behind him, knowing it would no longer open. He walked to the center of the room and then slowly turned a full circle, looking for some visual clue that might help him figure out what he was supposed to do. Pretty confident he hadn't missed anything, he called out. "Hello? Am I alone here?" No response. "Hello? Is there a point to me being here?"

"Mr. Russit, why are you in such a hurry?" The female voice emanated from every inch of the room, giving it an eerie omnipresence.

"I finished my shift and was leaving for the day," Talon called back to the ether.

"You don't normally leave after your first shift. Why today?"

"Why not today? Did I do something wrong?" Any last feeling of free will was quickly vanishing. The oppression of this place was suffocating.

"Is this connected to the special guest we're expecting?"

Talon perked up. So there *was* going to be a visitor today! "No. I mean, I thought perhaps the visit was a rumor. Until you just confirmed it. Is it really a general?"

When seconds turned into minutes and no response came, he began to worry he had said too much. Just because everyone on the manufacturing floor heard rumors, that didn't mean that security knew the news had been leaked. Now they did. Feeling queasy, Talon sat on the floor and tried to calm himself. He dropped his head forward, concentrating on regaining a sense of calm.

"Comfortable?"

"Ah, uh, yes." The question startled Talon. It was a new voice.

"Good, perhaps you could help me with a few questions?" The voice was sickly sweet, sending shivers up his spine.

"Ah, sure. If you want." Talon realized his response sounded dumb, but he was concentrating on that voice. He had heard it before.

"Good. Then what can you tell me about today's visitor?"

"Me? Well, nothing." He had it! It was the warden! He remembered the voice from the recording the warden had left for him, banishing him from the residence hall.

"Let me be clearer. What do you know about the general?" the warden asked.

Damn. Talon really had said too much. "I promise I don't know more than I've already said. Some general is supposed to visit this place today. That's it."

"Are you sure that's *all* you know?"

That was all Talon knew, but the question he had been trying to ask for the last several months popped into his head and out of his mouth before he even thought about it. "Do you know that I still don't have a place to sleep?"

"Excuse me?"

Talon realized it was probably not his place to ask the warden questions, but there wasn't a day that went by he didn't chew over the puzzle of why he'd been kicked out into the yard. "Warden, are you aware that I have no place to sleep? I'm still not allowed in the residence halls."

"I see. So, we're bargaining here? Alright, if you tell me something worthwhile, I'll make sure you have a place to sleep. Deal?"

Talon wanted to say that wasn't what he meant, but the words just didn't come so easily. Was he willing to bargain? What would he give up to escape the hard-packed ground and the beatings that often caught up with him in the waking hours?

Taking his silence for consent, the warden continued. "Let's start with an easier question. How did you know about our visitor?"

Talon didn't see any harm in playing along. "The rumor spread throughout the entire shop floor. There's not a person who hasn't heard about it."

"Fine. Fine. But how did the rumor get started? Someone has a connection to my people. I'm not thinking it's you. Takes nerve. But I bet you can give me a name. Maybe you know someone who's been acting suspiciously? Does anyone stick out?"

Blunt! That was the first thought that popped into his head. If there was anyone whose behavior couldn't be explained, it was Blunt, but as quickly as that thought popped into his head, he swatted it away. Talon didn't know anything, other than he was in over his head and about to get someone in trouble to save his own skin. Damn. He was certainly no superhero. Not even a decent human being.

"Well? Any thoughts? Come, come, I have business to attend to."

"Sir, I simply heard bits of conversations as I went about my work. I couldn't pinpoint someone because no one takes the time to speak with me. You must know I'm not exactly popular around here."

"Hmmm. Good point, son. Admittedly, you don't amount to much. Guess the deal's off. As for leaving ... I suggest you head back to your station and make amends for the time you wasted. You can spend time outside when you sleep ... or when you're dead, for all I care."

Long after the warden's voice faded away, Talon didn't move. He worked hard to make sense of what he'd heard. Was this real? Where was the hostility coming from?

He tried to put his fear and anger behind him when he finally left the room. He looked toward the manufacturing door, then at the exit. He walked to the exit and pushed on the release bar. The door swung open. No alarms appeared to be triggered. He took that as a sign it must be all right to go outside, after all.

It was time to learn whether Blunt was his ticket out of here.

Chapter Forty-Four

Talon

July 22 - 3:08 p.m.

The mid-afternoon sun beat down on Talon as he trudged across the hard-packed earth, dressed in Center-issued work boots and dark-blue coveralls designed to absorb heat and further encourage workers to seek out the work facility. He had many miserable hours ahead. Knowing Blunt had to be somewhere in their giant cage, Talon roamed the grounds, scouting from corner to corner. On his second sweep, he backtracked erratically, even circled buildings in case Blunt was playing hide-and-seek with him. Nothing. Blunt had disappeared, and Talon was confused. If Blunt wanted him out of his space, there were many subtle ways of getting the message across, including pounding him into the dirt. Blunt didn't need to hide.

Two hours of slogging around in the 110-degree heat started him on his way to dehydration. He stood at the entrance and tried to think of his options. It only took a moment to realize he had none, since no one was allowed to enter the facility mid-shift. Getting the perks that came with working, such as water, required committing to the entire shift, and leaving after the first shift meant no returning for the second.

Talon bent his head toward the earth, to hide his face from the sun, and plodded over to the buildings across from the manufacturing facility, where a slight breeze was generated from air forcing its way between the residence halls. He rested his head between his knees while his thoughts drifted from surviving the heat to his search for Blunt. Talon had originally sought him out to make things right for Robert's death, all too aware any encounter could end in violence, but now his pursuit was equally driven by the mystery that was Blunt. What was behind his midday activities? How did he disappear? Was he the mole?

Lost in thought, Talon hardly noticed the plume of dust making its way across the complex until it reached the front of the manufacturing building. As the dirt cloud swirled its way back toward the desert floor, three SUVs shimmered into view.

The dust had hardly settled when bodies began streaming out of the vehicles, encircling the SUVs, and taking measure of their surroundings. Talon, squatting three hundred yards off, stood to get a better view. The security detail took notice, with three members advancing toward Talon, spreading out in a line, making it known he was anything but welcome.

Talon took a step back to diffuse the sudden tension, and moments later, a lone figure emerged from the backseat of the middle vehicle. The man stretched to his considerable height and surveyed the yard. Talon caught the glimmer of numerous shiny medals on his dark uniform and knew the rumor must be true. This had to be a general.

Talon had an impulse to sprint toward him with arms frantically waving, hoping, like everyone else, to be rescued.

Before he could act, as if waiting for the general to smoke out any threats, a second person materialized from the same vehicle. This man was much smaller. He wore a dark suit that seemed diminished next to the general's decorated uniform. While Talon couldn't make out his facial features from this distance, he guessed that this must be the warden. It made sense that he'd want to escort the visiting general on this tour.

The warden's head jerked nervously one way and then the other, searching for overlooked threats, until his gaze locked onto Talon. Talon's earlier desire to be noticed vanished. After their prior conversation, he had no wish to be caught in any kind of vulnerable situation, like he was in now, alone in the yard. Could the warden tell it was him? All reason told him no, but he began taking slow steps backward just the same.

The warden's stare abruptly ended when the general, dismissing any possibility of danger, marched toward the front door. Two more from the security detail fell in step behind him. The warden then scurried to catch up as the general disappeared into the building.

Talon stopped his retreat since he really had no place to go. Deciding to wait for the tour to end and see if he could pick up the general's reaction, he had begun pondering whether to move closer when he heard gravel crunching behind him. He peeked over his shoulder to see who was heading his way. Blunt ...

By the time Talon stood to face him, Blunt was just inches in front of him. His steel-gray eyes bulged with anger as Talon braced for the first blow, but Blunt's fists, clenched tight, stayed at his side. "You can't stay here," he grumbled. "Follow me."

Chapter Forty-Five

Sage

July 22 - 4:30 p.m.

The chief continued to be elusive, ignoring Sage's numerous attempts to contact him. Frustrated, she finally released The Hound. "Hound Services" specialized in tracking people down. They had at their disposal every medium to reach out to people on behalf of their clients. They called, zapped, and utilized social media to make their clients' requests known, often embarrassing their targets into responding. They would even make face-to-face contact if they were paid for this premium service.

Sage didn't pay. When Gabriel still failed to respond, she decided to stake out his house herself.

She knew Gabriel was back from his trip. Rani let her know he had returned four days earlier, so catching him at home would be easy. The Abreo house was in a cul-de-sac near the end. Sage parked just inside the entrance to the cul-de-sac. Her car wouldn't be visible until Gabriel turned into the court as it was shielded by giant oak trees characteristic of the groomed quarter-acre lots. She parked at 4:30 p.m., knowing that if the day wasn't too eventful, he would be home within the hour.

Sure enough, it wasn't yet 5:00 when the chief's police vehicle turned the corner. She could see his eyes widen as he passed her. The vehicle didn't go far before it reversed direction. When Gabriel was even with her, they raised their gull-winged doors.

"Hello again," she began. "Do you want to talk here or inside with Avan?"

Gabriel looked unhappy, but he also looked defeated. Sage was making no pretenses. She would be all too pleased to involve Avan.

"Here is fine," he said.

"Why are you hiding from me?" She raised her palm. "No. I don't even care anymore. What I care about is my dad's chip. Do you have it?"

Gabriel hedged, and Sage had a pretty good guess as to why. He had to be sizing up whether she knew he had it. "That would be a 'yes,'" she said.

"I did have it. But it was defective so I sent it back."

"You sent it *back*? Then care to share what you saw?"

"Not really." Gabriel tried for a sincere look. "I worry you couldn't live with what little I could make out."

"You worry? I literally have to corner you to get your attention, and I'm supposed to believe you care? Tell me this since you worry so much: Where is Talon? Being CID and all, I'm sure you know where the Center is. Have you checked on my brother? Is he OK? Is he alive?"

She didn't bother to wipe the tears streaming down her cheeks, but still refused to look away. Instead, she studied Gabriel, trying to see past his mask of sadness, wanting desperately to learn what he was hiding.

Giving up nothing, he finally replied, "I get that I haven't been helpful. You probably aren't going to believe me when I tell you I'm trying."

"True. I do find that hard to believe. If you were trying, you might have made sure Talon was assigned to the Tech Lab, like Sofia. I hear you should be able to visit Sofia soon. Did you know I can't visit Talon?" She hadn't known she could be this mean, but she could no longer stop herself.

Gabriel had no response to her attacks. Sage wiped away tears and sat up because she didn't want to appear weak. "I want the chip, Gabriel. I trust myself to decide if I can handle what's on it. Do you understand me?"

"Yes, but I really did send it back."

"Very well. The chip is a copy, right? The Tech Lab wouldn't release the original, correct?" His silence was confirmation. "So, ask them to program another one."

"I can check. I don't know how this works, but if the chip wasn't the original, it must have been programmed from it. The original could be bad," Gabriel argued.

"Are you going to get me a copy or not? Because I'm ready to drive right up to your house and ask Avan what she thinks. I bet she'd want you to help."

He took a moment to consider his options. "Give me a week," he responded without emotion, triggering his door to lower between them.

As Gabriel rolled away, Sage's anger retreated, and she felt no joy in having secured a commitment from him. She came to the realization she was willing to sacrifice friendships in her quest and, eerily, she wondered if she cared. She knew what she did care about—finding Talon.

Chapter Forty-Six

Talon

July 22 – 5:22 p.m.

Talon wavered, wanting to stick around to learn something about the tour, but with Blunt walking back between the buildings and rounding the corner out of sight, Talon put aside all indecision and set off after him. Catching up, he could not help throwing out questions. "That was the general, right? Why leave? Where are we going?"

Blunt didn't respond. Marching along the perimeter wall toward the corner of the yard, he called over his shoulder. "You do know to stay away from the walls, right?"

This time it was Talon's turn to go quiet. Orientation for this awful place included dire warnings about going near the walls, with newcomers being treated to gruesome stories of careless workers being impaled on mechanical lances.

Walking fast to keep up with Blunt, Talon tried to catch a glimpse of the security detail between the buildings. No luck. Just before they reached the corner, Blunt abruptly stopped and looked past Talon in the direction they had come.

"What's wrong? Is someone following us?"

Blunt ignored his nonstop questions as he walked to the far side of the last building until he could peek around the corner and down the adjoining passageway. Evidently seeing nothing, Blunt positioned himself so he could watch both corridors and signaled for Talon to join him. Talon had never seen Blunt so wary.

Blunt again scanned both corridors, then turned his attention toward Talon. "There's more to the general's visit than the rumors you've heard. Somehow, you're a threat he plans to neutralize ... and the timing might be now."

"You're the mole! The warden was asking me who had connections to his guys. It's you!"

Blunt's steely eyes locked onto Talon, causing him to take a step backward, with the sudden realization Blunt might be a bigger threat than the warden or this general that supposedly had it in for him.

"Are you a disconnect?" Talon squeaked out, afraid he was otherwise dead.

Blunt continued to glare menacingly. "A mole, huh? That's a crazy ass thought. One we'll explore real soon. And you're going to tell me everything you said to the warden. Right now, though, we have bigger problems. I'm guessing when the general doesn't find you in the factory, he's going to come looking. Our only hope is to stay hidden. That means you need to be ready to run. You following me, kid?"

Talon couldn't comprehend anyone sizing him up as a threat. Blunt, on the other hand, was the guy everyone knew to leave alone. Now this character wanted to protect him? Talon was pretty sure Blunt didn't even like him. If he had to pick the one most likely to smash him to pieces, it would be Blunt.

Reality engulfed him like scorching heat from the desert sun: he had been out of his mind to allow himself to be caught alone with Blunt. He had to get away and do so without Blunt becoming unhinged. "Um, so, maybe we should split up? Why make it easy for the bad guys to pick us both off?"

Blunt's cold eyes crinkled at the edges and a wicked grin spread across his face. "Kid, oh, make my life easy. Yes, run away and see who trouble follows."

Talon ignored the sarcasm, deciding to take advantage of Blunt's suggestion to run, but when Talon turned to escape, he caught sight of a vehicle rounding a corner.

"Let's go!" Blunt yelled and shot off down the opposite corridor.

Talon stood frozen as he watched one, two, and then all three security vehicles round the corner, perhaps a quarter of a mile off and gliding toward him.

Blunt paused his mad dash. "You gotta trust me!" he screamed "Damn it, run!"

Caving to the urgency, Talon took after Blunt as they both raced for the far corner of the building, only for the SUVs to whip into view, ending any chance of losing them.

Talon slowed to a jog around the corner, weighed down by the knowledge his failure to react had condemned them both, only to catch sight of a swarm of people spreading throughout the yard. They looked agitated, angry, ready to rip something apart. Blunt didn't hesitate; he ran toward their enraged co-workers, waving his arms and shouting. "Over here!"

The crowd lurched toward them, and Talon, not hesitating this time, made a mad dash forward, joining Blunt as they both plunged into a mass of chaos, putting themselves at the mercy of the angry mob.

Fixated like a single organism, the horde flooded past Blunt and Talon, intent on smothering the security vehicles in their rage. The SUVs didn't waste time, abruptly retreating the way they had come and accelerating away from the onslaught.

Talon bent over with his hand on his knees, gasping for breath.

"We can't rest yet," Blunt said. "We need to get to the facility and have a look inside."

Approaching the building, they found the source of the horde, with people staggering out from within, half-drunk and angry. Blunt moved past them toward the entrance, swimming upstream through the flow of bodies. Security wasn't an issue. No one tried to stop those leaving, even as workers ignored the exit scans and other security protocols.

Talon followed, tracking Blunt back through the Transition Room as they made their way to the large production floor.

Talon tried to make sense of the scene before him. There were several bodies slumped over the workstations and just as many sprawled out across the concrete floor. He feared he was looking at a mass execution before noticing that people were making the rounds from lifeless body to lifeless body, shaking them until they regained consciousness.

"Gassed," Blunt muttered. "This isn't going to go well."

Talon was relieved despite the suffering laid out before him. "Let's help these people get back on their feet."

Talon failed to make it more than two steps before Blunt grabbed his arm. "You don't understand the situation," Blunt whispered. "We need to get out of here. Get some water, then we're leaving."

"Getting gassed sucks, by the way," Blunt explained between huge gulps from the faucet. "When you come to, you feel like throwing up and you usually do."

All of a sudden, the putrid smell of vomit came crashing in on Talon's senses. He gagged.

Blunt ignored him and continued his description. "Your head feels like a mule took a nice kick at it. This combination can fuel tremendous rage. Right now, these people are zeroed in on the retreating tour group and their security detail. But that tour group is long gone. Soon the crowd is going to look for new targets. And guess what?" Blunt was heading to the door. "This crowd is going to realize you and I were missing during this horrible episode and wonder why we were the only two spared."

They followed the last of the stragglers through the Transition Room and into the yard.

Blunt's point had sunk in, and Talon nervously looked around to see if anyone noticed them or was heading in their direction.

"They will make the connection, kid. Some explaining needs to be done. You're going to have to stay out of sight until I can smooth things over, assuming they give me a chance to explain."

"What just happened?" Talon asked. "What are we caught up in?"

Blunt looked into Talon's eyes for a moment and then growled as he walked off, "Just stay out of sight."

And with that, he was gone.

Chapter Forty-Seven

The Warden

July 22 – 6:48 p.m.

---

ontrol. The warden viewed himself as a master of control. He found that all went well when he commanded all that was around him, but right now, as he sat in his office, he was struggling to keep control of his temper. The nerve of the general! The warden didn't care a bit about the shiny little stars sewn on the man's clown outfit. The man was not in charge in the warden's domain. General Stafford was merely a board appointee from the CID. The CID had to have their hands in everything, but in the warden's case, the CID's involvement was symbolic. The CID appointed two members to a five-member board that oversaw the Fabrication Center. The other three appointments were left to the warden, which the warden knew was out of respect for his tremendous leadership during his fifteen-year tenure at the facility. The CID had given him control of the facility, and no puny board member was going to challenge that control.

"Mr. Simmons?"

The warden's focus returned to the general standing across from him at his desk. "Yes, please sit down, General." Control. Control the anger. "I wanted to speak with you before you departed, which I suspect will be soon."

The general merely nodded.

The warden again sized up General Stafford. The general's piercing blue eyes stared back, letting him know he didn't have time to waste.

"Let me get on with this then," the warden began. "I have an issue with you and your security detail trying to run down one of my workers." The warden had offered the general and his security detail the lead vehicle for the trip back to the main office. He had no idea the general would take off after Russit. The warden, seated in the trailing vehicle, was forced to helplessly follow. The lack of control was embarrassing and infuriating. He felt violated.

"Mr. Simmons, I made it clear that my intention in visiting was to tour your facilities and check in on Mr. Russit. Was I not clear?" The general spoke as if instructing a young child, which grated on the warden, renewing his effort to stay calm. "The fact that you did not have Mr. Russit available during the factory tour, as discussed, was a problem that needed to be addressed."

The warden was not buying the story. "I'm curious how you intended to visit with him. You knew we'd be gassing the workers. It simply isn't safe otherwise. So talking during the tour wasn't an option. And your mad chase afterward didn't seem like an effort one makes when planning to have a casual chat. Let's be candid. You intended to kidnap him, which, let me inform you, would not have ended well for you."

The general didn't bother to object to the warden's accusation. He merely raised his eyebrows as if to say, "what took you so long to figure that out?" The arrogance was intolerable!

"General, I think it's time you share your little secrets with me. After all, it is me, not you, that controls Russit's fate at the moment."

The general didn't blink. "I've told you enough. Mr. Russit is a severe threat to the Program ... while alive."

The warden found himself admiring the general's willingness to openly discuss his goals, no matter how disturbing he found them. "Yes, he's still alive. I've searched my soul and found I have an aversion to being stung out. I have, however, taken steps to let nature and even Russit's fellow men do their best, but he doesn't seem to want to die either. Perhaps we could both work on our motivation skills.

You motivate me by telling me about Talon Russit and I will try to better motivate Talon to stop breathing."

The glare from the general sent chills through the warden. He was well on his way to making an enemy of the man. He decided a less sarcastic approach might be better after all, "Look, Stafford ..."

"General."

"What?" The warden didn't understand the interruption.

"You can call me General or General Stafford, but my title is general. I am not a private citizen."

The warden saw the general's arm muscles tense, prepared to spring into action if slighted by the warden's next words. The warden wasn't going to challenge him, not head-on. Nor was he going to give in. He never gave in.

"Interesting," was all he replied, as he made a mental note not to use any names or titles for the man sitting across from him.

"Well, Mr. Simmons, I think we are done," the general stated matter-of-factly. "The board meeting is in three weeks? That should give you enough time. I expect you will have a plan to address this threat, or I will get an order from CID to transfer Mr. Russit into my care. How's that for motivation?" Without looking at the warden, the general was up and out the door, dismissing him like he was a speck of dust.

The general's threat both alarmed the warden and enraged him. He knew he could never let a worker leave the Center. No worker had left since the time the Center spun off from the Lab, giving him full control. His superiors knew that an assignment to the Center was a lifetime sentence. It wasn't an option to set disconnects free, allowing them to wander around unrestrained. Without working NACs, they could slaughter citizens like sheep.

What his superiors often overlooked, and the public definitely did not know, was the conditions of their captivity.

These disconnects had been sent to him because they were unfit for society and had been stripped of basic rights, such as freedom. By the time these wretches arrived at his door, it was the warden's job to determine what was left for them.

He had to weigh his decisions against other responsibilities, such as protecting society as a whole and operating at a reasonable cost. The products the Center manufactured formed the bonds that kept everyone orderly and safe. Chips, readers, displays, and more were all pumped out of his facility. And it wasn't as if he was given an unlimited budget to do this. He had price targets for each item produced, and his ability to meet those targets determined the well-being of the networked employees in his charge.

These real workers still belonged to society. Whether security personnel, production staff, or maintenance crew, they were paid well—very well. Everyone shared in the incentives that were doled out for achieving production goals and cost savings. Of course, the warden was compensated the most, which was important for him and his crew. An effective leader needed to be successful and set the standard by which others might measure success.

This meant he could not be too generous with the disconnects that had been cast off by society. He provided them food, a place to stay, and clothing. They also had control over their work schedule, once they had put in their forty hours. He wasn't responsible for making them happy or successful. Those considerations had been taken away when they had been given a lifetime quarantine from society. He could give them more, but never enough to make them happy. It seemed like a waste to throw resources at an impossible task. Harsh maybe, but no one else had his responsibilities and no one could judge.

Therefore, he had no plans for his disconnects to leave, ever. He would not be able to control who they encountered and to whom they told their stories.

The fury he felt toward the general returned. He fought the impulse to reach out to his security and ask them to detain the pompous man. His security would do it if he asked. The thought of turning the tables on the general and the general realizing he was at the warden's mercy was tempting. He should be taught a lesson in respect, but then what? He couldn't have him killed. Nor could he make him disappear. He would be missed.

Control. The warden admitted to himself that he liked control. All leaders did. He reminded himself that in order to have control, he first had to control himself. With this, he turned his thoughts to Russit. Why was he so important? What did the general fear? The kid was sixteen. He hadn't done anything remarkable since he'd been at the facility. He wasn't even well-liked.

This last thought gave the warden a good idea. The warden smiled to himself as he once again found himself solving everyone's problems and keeping society safe. He was a remarkable leader.

Chapter Forty-Eight

Wilder

July 23 – 6:06 p.m.

His plan was simple. He was impressed with it, actually. In the modern era of technology, he was going back to an archaic means of delivering messages, with a twist. Wilder wrote a note on a small piece of paper. He rolled it up and tied it to the right leg of the bird. He tested the drone to make sure it was still operable. After a few adjustments to the note so it was secure around the leg, Wilder found he could control the drone just fine. Operating the controller, he found the bird tended to pull down and to the right slightly, but with a little practice, he easily compensated for this.

Wilder then set up shop overlooking the Lab, catching glimpses of Sofia through his binoculars, waiting for her to once again be alone. Lying between a few shrubs, his position was well concealed from the facility below and any surveillance device that might pass overhead. He used a scope to measure the distances along the paths Sofia tended to follow and confirmed most were within the bird's range.

A few days passed before conditions looked promising, with Sofia emerging from her unit on a clear evening and settling in on her patio bench to read. People occasionally walked by, but none paid any attention to her, and she didn't make any effort to acknowledge them. Good.

Wilder was more worried about the fog that was creeping in from offshore. Fog was pretty much a daily occurrence in Seaside during July. Mornings would almost always be soaked in gray. The sun might break through in the afternoon and bring some blue skies and welcomed warmth, as had been the case today, but evenings were usually reclaimed by the wall of gray. Wilder figured he had twenty to thirty minutes before the fog chased Sofia indoors.

Wilder looked the bird over one more time. The notepaper he had used was bright red. It wouldn't be good if the wrong person happened to notice a strange bird with a red note tied to its leg, but the risk couldn't be avoided, really: Wilder needed to capture Sofia's attention. He would fly the bird well overhead before spiraling it down for a landing.

He set the bird on top of his backpack. Taking the controller, he took a brief video of the expanse between his position and Sofia's patio. The controller would superimpose the drone's position on clips taken from the video footage, so the operator could locate the drone at any time. He planned to switch to live feed from the camera implanted in the bird's chest once he landed the drone. This camera was small and provided a limited field of view, but should be enough to help him navigate the patio and approach Sofia.

He launched the drone and set it on a course straight down the middle of the footage he had captured. He kept the bird roughly forty feet off the ground. The drone was designed to oscillate a few inches up and down to coincide with the flapping of its wings. Once directly over the center of the patio, Wilder decided to switch to the camera and let the drone land itself. He targeted a position in the center of the patio and pressed the landing button. The bird spiraled downward, making sure to detect any objects that moved into its path. Within a few minutes of the initial launch, the drone safely alighted.

He toggled the camera around until it came across Sofia. It couldn't quite take in the entire bench, nor all of Sofia. He zoomed in on Sofia's face and found she was intently watching the bird. Good.

Now he needed to make sure she noticed the note. Not knowing what to do, he made the bird hop up and down, until he lost Sofia's face as she stood. Refocusing, he found Sofia was still intensely staring at the bird, but now she appeared to be alarmed. Rethinking the situation, he resigned himself to waiting her out, but as time passed, she made no move to approach the drone, and then wisps of fog began obscuring Sofia's image.

This wouldn't do. Sofia was not going to see the note if the bird became immersed in fog, prodding him to hop the drone forward until it was a couple of feet away. The response was immediate. A black tennis shoe accelerated toward the camera, blasting the bird backward and flooding the controller screen with scrambled images until it went dark.

Wilder jumped to his feet to see what the hell had happened. Then he realized he wasn't going to see the bird from that distance and, if anything, he had just exposed himself. He quickly dropped back down to his concealed location, reciting every bit of profanity he could recall. What had that unhinged girl done to his drone?

Chapter Forty-Nine

Sofia

July 23 - 6:32 p.m.

"Shit! Damn! Whoa! OK, what was that?! Alright, don't lose it. And stop talking to yourself." Sofia looked around to see if anyone was watching. Nobody. "Whew. What was that?"

She strained to see in the dimming light. She walked to where her patio merged with a footpath. About ten feet beyond the path, she made out a small object on a manicured lawn. She moved a few feet closer and realized that the strange bird that wanted to attack her was possibly disabled. She summoned more courage, moving forward until she stood over it. It lay motionless on its side, fueling her confidence to bend down and take a close look.

Designed to look like a bird, but not a bird. "OK, guys!" Sofia yelled, spinning around, squinting into the darkness. "You've had your fun! Come get your toy!"

Sofia waited for it to rise. "You don't want it?" She was certain the techies were behind this, but she wasn't going to wait for them to decide their next move. When they didn't immediately respond, she grabbed the bird. "Mine now! Thanks, boys!" she called as she walked back to her unit.

Entering the house, she commanded, "Full light," and the ceiling glowed brightly in every nook in her tiny place. Holding the bird in front of her, the red band around its leg caught her eye. She wanted to check out the mechanical bird because it was impressive in its replication of the real thing, but the item around its leg was just as interesting. It had to be a note. Another prank from the techies? She knew herself enough not to debate whether it was wise to open that note or not—curiosity always won out with her.

In no time she had the note off the leg and unfolded on her dining table.

As she stood reading, her heart began to race. Word after word came at Sofia like waves, tossing her about. After finishing the note, she sat down, then read the note again, even more slowly.

Sofia. I need your help. We sort of know each other. We last met when your mob decided to stink up the CID Programming Center. Impressive work. I stunk for weeks. If you care about Talon, help me find him. I believe he's in trouble. I need to know where the Fabrication Center is. I believe you can't go looking for Talon. I can. Sorry to involve you, but you now must decide whether to work with me or to help capture me. I get that I'm the bad guy in your hometown. Think about the bad things I did—no one got hurt. They weren't much different than your prank. Or maybe a little. I'm trying to say that you have no reason to distrust me. Consider what you lose by helping me compared to what you might lose if you don't. Please give me a chance. I ask that you tell no one about this. Not even your father. You can respond by attaching a note like the one you found and leaving the bird outside tomorrow, 8–10 a.m. – Shadow

The bird. Sofia examined it. Nothing was bent as far as she could tell. She had kicked it really good, though. She had no way of knowing if she busted it up inside. Wait! She was completely caught up with responding before even thinking through whether she should!

She should. Actually, an easy decision. She was deathly worried about Talon and was open to any means to find him. And Shadow was right. He had never harmed anyone as far as she knew. Shadow! She couldn't believe it was the legendary Shadow. If anyone could sneak into a facility to check on Talon, it was him.

Yet, how was he connected to Talon? What was Shadow's motivation for finding him? Equally important, Sofia had to consider what she owed him. Her dad would certainly want him captured. Wasn't that the right thing to do?

The ugly truth was she could hardly ignore the possibility that helping to capture Shadow could go a long way toward earning the trust of those around her. As matters stood, she had no means of giving Shadow Talon's location, no matter what his intent, but winning the trust of Jonathan or even Dr. Sur might get her the answers she wanted. Could she then escape and go after Talon herself?

Sofia had a lot to consider.

Chapter Fifty

Rani

July 24 - 4:56 a.m.

Sleep had hardly come to Rani over the last several nights. She thought about her career and whether it had been a mistake. After all, was she really doing good? That wasn't what kept her awake, though. The thought of Sage fighting her department to learn about her father's death and her brother's well-being really pissed her off. Why was Gabriel ignoring pleas for help? Worse yet, why was he barking at Rani to back off? What was to be gained by leaving Sage alone in the dark?

She tossed and turned in her one-bedroom condo, which she rented because it was close to work, not because it was a cute place to live. On the contrary, it was a dump. She hadn't cared when she rented it six months ago. Her attention had been on the exciting world of law enforcement, into which she had planned to escape.

The life she fled from was full of glitter and disappointment. Her parents had been big on the party scene down in Hollywood. Her mom, a B-movie actress, and her dad, a middle of the road lawyer, had grabbed for the big life by throwing glamorous, drug-induced parties they couldn't afford.

And Rani? She coped with the stress-filled household by playing with drugs as well. All the fun stopped when her parents' bills piled up and their stuff, their cars, and their old home were all repossessed. Still, strange angry people showed up at their new dump of a home. Rani wished she had the power to make them go away, but they kept on coming. And the more these collectors showed up, the more her parents stayed away, until one day she came home from school to find a note in which her parents explained she was better off without them and left her with the promise that they loved her.

Rani was on her own at seventeen. She spent her super senior year in Oakland, couch surfing at her friends' homes, finding ways to score drugs, until she was asked to move on. She miraculously managed to graduate high school, but she had run through her friends and any sympathy their parents might have had for the wasted teen. She spent a few months roaming the streets in a very dark place, wondering if this was the sum of her life. One day, looking to score some ecstasy, she pulled up to a sketch home that she previously never would have dreamed of visiting. She worked up the nerve to knock on the door, and the guy who answered was one of the threatening men who had visited her home. It hit her hard that she shouldn't be supporting these thugs. She should be bringing them down. If she brought them to account, maybe someone like her wouldn't get abandoned, maybe wouldn't end up in the gutter.

She spent the next five years working her way out of the dark place she had crawled into. Getting a job wasn't hard. Renting a one-room place in Santa Clara was more of a struggle. And graduating from JV, then San Jose State in a mere three years was hell. Two years later she was a cop.

She had burst out of the dark and into the light of justice. Right? Well, now she was wondering if she would ever escape the darkness. She was beginning to realize being a cop didn't always mean you took down the bad guys and rescued the good ones. Her chief was doing a damn fine job of hammering that point home. Rani couldn't follow what he was thinking, but he wasn't coming close to doing right by Sage.

At 5 a.m., she rolled out of her twin bed and started getting ready for work. She wasn't giving up. Helping Sage fit perfectly with why she had become a cop, for chrissakes!

Shit. Come what may, she was going to right the wrongs, regardless of policies. If she got fired for being the cop she had set out to be, then she'd wear that badge with honor.

By the time 9:15 rolled around, Rani had done a lot of digging and was ready to reach out to Sage. Sage connected immediately.

"I was two seconds from trying you!"

"Hey. How are you holding up?" Rani asked.

"I've had better times. Much better. Sorry, I mean I'm doing the best I can."

"I get it. I know it's not easy getting out of bed after what you've been through. Ah, shit. Stupid comment. I'm trying to say that you've got a lot to overcome, and I want to help. I'm offering to be there for you."

"Thanks, Rani. I can use a friend these days. I think I'm becoming a horrible person. The day before yesterday, I ripped Gabriel to shreds without any hesitation. I'm viewing him less as a person and more as an obstacle in my hunt for Talon."

Rani wasn't going to defend her boss. "I'm not sure what to think of Gabriel these days. And hey, you're *not* a horrible person. You're a very worried sister. If you did anything less than move heaven and earth to find Talon, *then* you'd be a horrible person. You're doing the right thing, Sage. I mean it."

Rani thought she heard crying, so she gave Sage time. Eventually her voice returned.

"You're a sweetheart. I didn't realize how much I needed to hear a few positive words."

"I meant every word," Rani said. "Now, before I start rambling on, tell me why you were about to call me."

"OK, but are you still good with discussing things that can't be shared with Gabriel?"

"Hey, I'm standing in the department parking lot. What do you think?"

"Seriously, tell me if I ask too much of you." Rani didn't respond, so Sage continued, "So, remember that chip I've been trying to get from Gabriel?"

"Yeah."

"I wasn't ready to tell you before, but it's my dad's NAC."

Once Sage started, she poured everything out. She relayed everything Gabriel told her about the chip's capabilities. She also described her back-and-forth with Gabriel as she tried to get possession of it. She concluded by letting Rani know she wasn't willing to wait on Gabriel any longer.

"Couldn't agree with you more. Even if Gabriel is being truthful, he doesn't seem motivated to help. You got a plan?"

"I'm going to file my own request for Dad's chip. I'm hoping you could point me in the right direction so I can figure out what form I need to submit to the Tech Lab. If you aren't familiar with the form or aren't good with me bypassing Gabriel, I'll drive to their facilities and start knocking on doors until I get what I'm after."

"I bet you would," Rani quipped. "Not to interfere with your crusade, but I'm aware you're trying to get your dad's chip. I'm not going to tell you how bad I am as an employee or what depths I've sunk to, but I did find out about your quest. Then I started wondering why Gabriel needed to be in the middle of your quest to secure the chip."

"Why?"

"Turns out there's widespread concern about NAC personal information leaking out into the public domain. To prevent this, CID tightly controls each NAC. They require all requests and deliveries to be handled by a CID officer. What I'm trying to say is you can't make the request, Sage."

"But ... but—"

"But I can."

Sage's voice faltered as she tried to speak. "Y-you would do that? Won't you get in huge trouble if you got caught?"

"Trouble? Haven't you been listening to me? If Gabriel finds out half of what I've been doing, I'm fired. And shit, you know what? I'm good with that! I need to start doing something that feels right again. Helping you feels right, Sage. And before you object, I don't think I'll be caught anyway. Not soon, leastways. As an officer, I've got all the credentials I need to make such a request, assuming I have your signature. And Gabriel will never catch on that the chip's been delivered to me. He's hardly around these days, and when he is around, he doesn't give a damn what's going on around him. And Sage, we'll know if he tries to get another chip because you'll have to sign that request as well."

"And I won't sign his request."

"You got it," Rani said. "All I need is your signature."

"You're the *best*!"

Hearing that spark of excitement in Sage's voice was the light Rani was chasing.

Chapter Fifty-One

Talon

July 24 – 5:53 a.m.

Staggering across the compound toward the factory entrance, Talon twisted his body to check for pursuit, causing pain to erupt across his side. He could only guess he had a cracked rib, his punishment for sleeping late, when a new face had set upon him, likely trying to score points by beating up the most hated guy in the facility. Unfortunately, the attacker was too new to know that pummeling Talon was nothing special. Pretty routine, actually.

Luckily, the assailant hadn't bothered to pin him down. After being woken to a kick in the side and a glancing blow to the cheek, Talon had kicked out, landing his foot smack in the guy's groin. Talon was woozy as he approached the entrance, dreading that more punishment waited within.

Pushing, bumping, and even elbowing were the normal greetings that awaited Talon. Rumors had spread about the last gassing, with some likely started by the warden and his staff. Everyone was speculating as to how Talon knew to leave the building right before the gassing took place. Many insisted he received preferential treatment from their captors. Others believed his sudden disappearance spooked the visiting party, encouraging them to gas everyone out of an abundance of caution.

Ironically, no one gave a thought to Blunt's disappearance. Nor did they consider the fact that Talon slept in the yard when they measured his special treatment. Their hopes were crushed when the general's visit proved to be a bust, hammering home that their never-ending hell was all they could count on. The anger from that realization had to be directed somewhere and the mob wasn't going to waste time on the general or the warden. That only made them feel powerless. Talon, on the other hand, was accessible. He was an easy target.

The moment he entered the Transition Room, the barrage began. Several antagonists took advantage of the close quarters to give him a bump or a shove. A Neanderthal-like man, replete with a bodybuilder's physique, managed to land a perfectly placed elbow to Talon's injured ribs, causing him to gasp and his knees to buckle. Hunched over, taking quick little breaths, he looked up in time to witness an incredible sight: Espar, who had all but ignored Talon since their arrival, connected with a resounding slap to the back of his assailant's head. The man's head shot forward with the blow, before he collected himself and turned slowly toward Espar with a furious glare. His struggle to hold himself in check was unmistakably conveyed by his ever-expanding eyeballs, while the workers immediately next to the small skirmish stood frozen in terror.

Everyone knew that security was trained to allow a little scrimmaging among men, especially if the target was considered deserving, but they were not to tolerate any abuses of women. In the warden's rules of order and control, everyone understood that any action against a woman was certain to get everyone gassed. Emboldened by this reality, Espar glared back at her adversary.

Silence followed as the rest of the room clued into the standoff and watched, knowing if the guy lost it, they would all be waking up with chemical hangovers. After a few tense moments, the man muttered a slew of curses at Espar and turned away. Espar seemed ready to smack him again, but let it go. With the hostility abated, the room filled with chatter and attention returned to Talon, with the aggression against him reasserting itself—maybe with a little less enthusiasm—until Blunt walked into the room. Then it abruptly stopped.

Bodies quickly distanced themselves from Talon, giving him a wide berth. No one wanted to tangle with Blunt, who had made it known he wouldn't tolerate attacks on Talon. Talon's face turned red. He hated being emasculated.

In a different moment, when he could fill up half his lungs, he needed to tell Blunt to back off. Of course, this was assuming he could actually have a discussion with him. While Blunt seemed to want to protect Talon for some reason, he also wanted nothing to do with him. Over the last three days since the general's visit, Talon had followed Blunt into the yard after the first shift, only to lose Blunt as he disappeared around one building or another. It was like magic. After he lost sight of Blunt, Talon would wander aimlessly around the yard, never picking up a trace of him.

Today, though, was going to be different.

Chapter Fifty-Two

Wilder

July 24 – 7:37 a.m.

Wilder was back at his encampment overlooking the complex well before 8 a.m. He was anxious to find out if Sofia would help, assuming the bird could still fly. His bike was stashed at the bottom of the dune in case she betrayed him. His plan was to get the bird and ride like hell.

This was a pivotal moment for him. He would love to establish a connection with someone who was also focused on his brother. He had been reflecting a lot on his escapades on behalf of his now distant resistance. More than ever, he was thinking his break-ins at UCSC and the Programming Center, plus Haris's willingness to risk everything to rescue Talon, all placed Talon at the heart of the cause.

Wilder couldn't avoid the sting of having been kept in the dark, even about the rescue attempt, until he showed up on the scene to see his own brother in the middle of the action. Part of his disappointment was with himself, though. He should have asked more questions. Haris had been more forthcoming toward the end, offering bits about who they were up against and what they hoped to achieve. Wilder could have pressed for more. Now that resource, and his close friend, was gone.

Now he hoped to establish a new resistance with Sofia's support, but if she betrayed him, he had no plans to surrender. He could never give up. He would still pursue Talon. He would still promote the resistance. Someone had to.

Haris adamantly believed the Program was slowly tearing apart the best aspects of society. Freedom, trust, innovation, and equality were all sacrificed in exchange for the safety the

Bee Sting system offered. Haris often railed that people throughout history had kicked safety to the curb and sacrificed their lives to win the right to be free. Then in a matter of a few years, the individuals and families their forefathers fought to free turned around and surrendered those freedoms without a fight—to feel safe. Wilder had decided that if he could dedicate his life to anything beyond saving his brother, it would be rekindling the fight for freedom. He sure hoped his grand quest didn't end with a whimper. He mustn't be captured.

Before he could succumb to the pressure he was heaping upon himself, Sofia walked out of her unit promptly at 8 a.m. Wilder followed her through his terrestrial viewing scope as she set the bird down in the middle of the patio. He found himself chuckling for the first time in weeks as he watched Sofia back off a few feet and make a shooing motion, as if she were trying to scare the bird into flight. It might have been Sofia pretending it was a real bird in case someone was watching, but she sure looked like she believed the bird, mechanical or not, made up its own mind whether to fly away.

Smiling and encouraged, he set down the scope and picked up the controller. He activated the camera and was instantly rewarded with an image. He adjusted the camera to focus on Sofia. Sure enough, she was now stomping on the ground in addition to frantically waving her hands at the bird. If she hadn't betrayed him, she was going to get them caught with all the attention she was likely bringing to herself! He quickly hopped the bird away from Sofia. So far, so good.

He swiped his finger across the screen in the direction he wanted to launch the bird and was elated to see it flawlessly take flight. He barely watched the drone as it made its way back. He had selected the return function on the controller, instructing the bird to retrace the path it had initially taken. He used the flight time to scan the surrounding areas for anything out of the ordinary. All seemed clear: either he wasn't very good at surveillance or there wasn't anyone tracking him.

Soon the bird landed, a new note attached to its leg. Wilder snatched it, scooted to the bottom of the dune, retrieved his bike, and casually pedaled toward town, certain he had gained Sofia's trust.

Chapter Fifty-Three

Talon

July 24 – 2:21 p.m.

Talon went about his workday, regaining the ability to breathe and waiting for the clock to hit 2:30. He had a relatively peaceful day since his supervisor was pleased with him at the moment. He had recently made some recommendations on rebalancing activities between workstations to speed up reader production. These recommendations were implemented a few days ago, and a few minutes had been shaved from the production cycle, which was a big deal for those in charge. Talon knew it wouldn't be long before his super was looking for the next improvement, but as the shift approached an end, he was grateful for a period of relative calm in his life, however brief.

The shift alarm rang as the displays at the workstations flashed 2:30. Workers abandoned their stations and formed a line to the double doors that led to the break room. Blunt, however, went straight to the Transition Room, with Talon right behind him. Talon was done being discreet.

Entering the room, Talon said to Blunt's back, "I didn't say anything."

Blunt turned, his eyes and nostrils flared. He didn't utter one word as they both raced to get through the room and out the door.

Pouring out into the boiling heat with Blunt stomping ahead of him, Talon tried again. "I didn't say anything about you to the warden. Nothing."

"Stay away from me!" Blunt exploded in response. "You're going to get people hurt. Do you even know the danger you pose?"

Taking in Blunt's anger, Talon finally got it. It wasn't Blunt's job to save him. Talon had been a fool to follow him around like some hero-worshiping child. "You're right. I'm an idiot," Talon said as he turned and walked away.

Later, having settled down between buildings, he set his mind to the task of making another nightfall. The wooziness had returned, telling him he didn't have much left to offer the scorching heat waves that danced in front of him, except perhaps the skin off his bones. With his head resting on his skinny arms, giving him a view of his bruised and bony legs, he knew that thought hit too close to home.

His mind wandered to Sofia, as it often did. Thinking of her was one of the few escapes he had from this place. Perhaps not this time, though. With the promise to return to her slipping further from his grasp, he wondered if that was a bad thing. After all, he had no more to offer her than he could offer the sun above. What little he arrived with had been ground away.

Realizing he was talking himself into surrender, he grew angry. Would he wither away, never having found the strength to stand on his own? He defiantly reminded himself he wasn't finished, only to have his next breath painfully tell him he was close.

Chapter Fifty-Four

Sofia

August 7 – 1:07 p.m.

Sofia's life was suddenly filled with intrigue. In addition to her job, she spent off-hours trading messages with Shadow and prowling the Tech Lab facilities. She still hadn't decided what to do with Shadow. He was determined to convince her to let him help find Talon. As proof of his good intentions, he conveyed his story about the botched attempt to rescue Talon and Espar. He provided details about the deaths and how he was taken out of action. He was pressing her hard to let him make another rescue attempt. He insisted that all he needed was Talon's location and he would take the rest of the effort upon himself.

Sofia wanted to buy into his story. She just wasn't one to believe in masked men and caped crusaders. She responded by pressing him to reveal his identity, certain this would tell her all she needed to know, one way or the other, but they were at an impasse. Undoubtedly, he didn't trust her either. If he had caught wind of her hearing before the board, then she fully understood.

Trying to put these frustrations behind her, she threw herself into the clandestine trade, entering building after building and roaming the hallways without being seen. She worked on identifying retreats, such as a stairwell, utility closet, or even the nearest corner. She worked on casually peeking around corners and rapidly scanning offices and hallways. At the first hint of a person or even movement, she moved back to her retreat. For now, she stayed away from facilities with posted security guards. She also stayed away from individual offices, except for Jonathan's.

Sofia spent a good amount of time tormenting Jonathan and his technicians. She considered it an opportunity to work on her skills in close quarters, but in the case of the technicians, it was also payback. Initially, she left packages on their desks, addressed to them. The stink bomb and blaring siren went off without a hitch.

It didn't take long before the technicians were afraid to open any package. Equally fatal for them was to leave out equipment she could readily move. The next day, the unlucky technician would be an unwitting participant in a treasure hunt. She initially left notes directing them to different locations in their building, eventually expanding hunts to cover numerous facilities she might visit later that night.

Jonathan took it well. He must have figured the payback was deserved. Plus, the technicians were beginning to enjoy the games. Sofia suspected some technicians left things out for the fun of the hunt. There was a connection forming between her and the group. They were swift to jump up and open the door if they saw her coming, sometimes bowing as she entered, feigning to be in the presence of royalty. She trash-talked and good-naturedly tormented them. She kept them on edge, delivering a group of packages and letting them know all were real but one, then watching with delight as they dissected the packages, deciding which were safe, until they got to the final one, and with curiosity too great to ignore, drawing straws to see who had to open the last package. The unfortunate technician trembled as he picked apart the tape with a scalpel. After several minutes, perspiring, he lifted the flap, only to find out it was empty. When Sofia departed a few minutes later, everyone was still entertained recounting their comrade's near meltdown.

Jonathan wasn't safe either. Sofia decided that anytime she caught Jonathan away from his desk, she would steal his chair and stick it in the technicians' room. The third time he had to retrieve his chair in front of the smirking technicians, his competitive nature kicked in. He tried feigning he was headed out to lunch, then doubled back to catch her. After retrieving the chair a couple more times in front of his crew, who were now nearly falling out of their own chairs laughing, he decided to make some serious effort. First, with the help of one of his crew, he rigged a trip wire, which was set to trigger an alarm. Having to retrieve the chair a sixth time, he went full in. He wired a motion detector under his chair, again linked to an alarm. When he returned from lunch to find Sofia proudly standing next to his chair and his technicians doubled over, he just smiled and continued to his office.

A few minutes later, he called down to the tech room and asked that when everyone was done recounting his failures, could they please send Sofia to his office. Sofia didn't waste time making her way to his office, walking through his door, dripping with the thrill of victory.

Jonathan looked victorious, too. "I cheated," he announced as Sofia took a seat. "I recorded footage of my office while I was gone."

Sofia blushed. "I knew the fun had to end sometime," she said, nervous she had taken the game too far.

Jonathan saw her concern and broke out into such an infectious belly laugh that Sofia found herself laughing along with him. "Imagine my surprise to find my own technicians working with you to dismantle my little device! I bet if I checked the rest of the footage, I'd find them helping disable the trip wire, too?"

Sofia only giggled.

"Did they keep tabs on me every time I was coming and going from my office?" Jonathan asked, knowing the answer before he even finished the question, and now they were both cracking up. After a few moments of struggling to regain his composure, realization registered on his face. "You turned my team against me. Impressive! I've underestimated you."

"You're giving me too much credit," Sofia corrected, "It was their idea to get involved more than mine. A chance to put one over on the boss."

"No, you're resourceful. Are you still feeling like a misfit?"

"Sometimes," Sofia said, realizing she had all but forgotten her teenage-girl desire to be like everyone else.

Jonathan went quiet. When he finally did speak, it was clear he hadn't called her in just to reminisce about her recent pranks or pry into her personal space. "Let me switch gears on you. You ready to talk about something serious?"

"Sure, you've got my attention," Sofia said, seeing Jonathan take on the gruff composure he did so well.

"Alright, where to start ...?" Jonathan began.

"What's up? I can take critical feedback," Sofia encouraged, guessing he was worried about offending her.

He looked off in the distance, then returned his attention to her, having made some decision. "Sorry, it's not about you, at least not completely. I've got a few obligations that go along with my job. One is to help keep this compound secure. Let me put it this way—did you know that anything entering or leaving this compound picks up micro-particles? It's something we do by design. Then if enough particles attach to an object, we can get a pretty good transmission from that object and track it wherever it goes."

Jonathan paused to make sure she was following. Sofia was not only following; she was now drowning in fear.

"Skin collects these particles really well," he continued. "One or two passes and we've got our target. Metal, though ... that's much harder. It can take ten or more trips until we get it locked in ..."

Sofia knew she was busted, again. This time for a much more serious offense. She was overflowing with panic. Did they know about Shadow? Had they captured him? Was Jonathan going to call security? Was he goading her? She was dying for him to get to the point, but his technical mind found it important to give her a detailed picture of just how badly she was busted.

"I get it. You got me—"

Jonathan held up his hand, indicating she should stop. "Let me be clear. One of my jobs is to filter data from these particles to identify trends, especially unwanted intrusions. I've been following one item in particular. Right now, I can track it coming into the compound, but I can't follow it much outside our perimeter. As to its destination in the compound? Well, I probably need another data point or two to confirm whether its destination is random ... or not. Assuming I get that confirmation, then I would have no choice but to turn my findings over to security. And we both know that means Chief Hill." Jonathan leaned forward, as if he needed to make sure she was paying attention to his every word. "Any thoughts on whether I'll get this confirmation?"

Sofia wasn't clueless. He was warning her off. That was loud and clear, but his effort was exactly why she decided to turn the conversation around. "Jonathan, do you worry that what we're talking about could be picked up by security?"

He blinked with surprise. "Yes. That's why precautions are taken. Putting Chief Hill aside, I try to respect that most security personnel are here to do their jobs. But when it comes to what I say in my office, I think I have a right to keep it confidential. And while security does make attempts to be part of what goes on in here, I have the advantage of being at the forefront of some pretty interesting technologies, such as that silver ball you're carrying around."

Jonathan's honesty and concern for her sold Sofia. "So, are you ready for me to tell you what's going on?"

Jonathan suddenly looked panicked. "I think I made that clear. No."

Ignoring Jonathan's suggestion, Sofia plowed forward. "Glad you're ready because I need help." She went on to explain about Shadow. She detailed Shadow's activities in

Ridge Crest and even shared their one encounter. Jonathan managed a smile when she mentioned the skunk juice and Shadow bolting out the door. Then Sofia took him through their recent interactions.

After spilling everything to Jonathan, she ended by saying, "I don't know whether to trust Shadow or not. How do I know he's not fabricating a story or twisting it to make him look like a good guy? He certainly wasn't known as a good guy in Ridge Crest. For all I know, if I help Shadow, he might take Talon out."

When Sofia finished laying everything out, Jonathan looked overwhelmed. She waited for Jonathan to process everything, fearing she had overshared.

"That's a big risk you took, telling me everything. I guess I can't be on the fence anymore about whether to help you find Talon. You're never going to give up the search, are you?"

"No," Sofia answered, aware that Jonathan knew the answer and was stalling for time.

"I see ... alright, I'm in. I might be able to learn a thing or two that could help you reach him. I have to say, I don't know a lot about Shadow, other than what you've told me. Let's agree to keep him close but not share too much with him until we can confirm his intentions."

Sofia beamed. For once, she had real hope.

Chapter Fifty-Five

Sage

August 8 – 1:44 p.m.

As she turned onto the road to the Tech Lab, Sage was greeted by a large crowd that blocked the way forward, spilling over into the fields on both sides. Her first thought was that the Lab's annual community outreach event was incredibly popular. As she drew nearer, she heard chanting and saw people carrying signs. She stopped her Mini about fifty yards out, trying to understand what she was facing.

"Magnify windshield," she commanded. The view in front of her was magnified tenfold, allowing her to see individual faces and easily read the signs.

Sage grimaced at how slow she had been to realize this was a protest, especially since Program opposition had been boiling over across the country. It was becoming impossible to look at any news streams without catching something about the latest uprising.

One message read: "BIG GOV UP, FREEDOM DOWN – WE ARE ALL GETTING STUNG!" Another read: "I'M ALIVE, BUT TOO AFRAID TO LIVE." And another: "WHAT HAPPENED TO GIVE ME LIBERTY OR GIVE ME DEATH?!"

A few more signs confirmed what she suspected. The protesters, like countless others across the nation, were caught off guard by the rapid adoption of the Program. They worried over the price paid for whatever limited safety they received, which was hard to gauge since most people, like the stiffs clogging up Ridge Crest's roads, didn't know how the Program worked. Many felt they had lost control of their lives, unsure how to avoid being stung out.

The crowd didn't appear to be unruly. No one was advancing on her ride. At the same time, people weren't clearing a path for her either.

She supported the crowd's cause more than they could know. Her mother's family had migrated to the U.S. a decade before the Program was enacted. They were fortunate. Many of her family's friends, including her mother's closest childhood friend, disappeared as they attempted to reach the U.S. during the early Program trials.

Perhaps due to her dark past, Sage's mom had been content to remain in the background, keep the family running, relying on her husband or anyone else willing to take on any threats to their way of life. Sage had been no different. She had learned her mother's lessons too well. Until now.

She no longer had the luxury of keeping a low profile or waiting on others. Nor the desire. And as much as she longed to join the protest, she couldn't afford to be slowed down by this crowd. She needed to reach Sofia.

Sage's strong feelings for Sofia gave her an idea. "Project message on windows."

"What message would you like to project?"

"Visiting my sister," she replied. Not too great an exaggeration, since Sofia had grown up around her family. With the message illuminated on all windows, including the front and back windshields, she instructed the Mini to move forward slowly. Within ten yards of the crowd's edge, she stopped. "Capture outside noise." Sage wanted to know right away if her message *wasn't* well received.

Her fear proved unfounded. Several nearby protesters stepped forward to read the message, then shouted. "Visiting family! Let her through." The message spread and the crowd parted, offering her passage.

Sage changed the message on the windows to read, "I love your cause!" before continuing on.

Chapter Fifty-Six

Sage

August 8 - 1:54 p.m.

Sage's Mini had barely come to rest in the Lab's visitor lot when Gabriel and Avan walked past. Only the tears streaming down Avan's face, as she tried to hide them against Gabriel's shoulder, stopped her from lunging out of the vehicle and jumping into Gabriel's face.

Since they last spoke, she had a whole new list of reasons to call Gabriel out. The bullshit he had given her about being willing to help retrieve her dad's chip completely unraveled a week earlier when Rani called, barely able to contain her excitement. Turned out Rani had been able to get the replacement chip expedited in a matter of days. To this day, Gabriel had yet to submit a request form.

Equally disturbing was the Lab's response to Rani's expediting request. When a clerk called seeking more information, Rani explained Sage's efforts to view her dad's last moments and the trauma of being sent a defective copy. The clerk assured her the first chip was fine.

The clerk went on to send that same chip by drone and included a 3-D viewer. Rani went out of her way to drop the chip off that night.

Sage wasn't sure she could watch her dad's last moments alone and asked Rani, who she felt was becoming close, to watch it with her. The recording was only about thirty seconds, but it was the most disturbing thirty seconds of Sage's life. It began with her dad making a dash toward his partner, pulling a knife from his belt as he ran. He slammed into Jesse, intent on jarring loose a controller Jesse was holding. Then Jesse rolled over and it became clear he'd fallen on the knife, with the blade penetrating through his rib cage near the heart.

Within seconds Jesse was dead and her dad was following. His last seconds captured Talon running toward him. Rani sat patiently with her, putting her arm around her shoulders as Sage viewed the footage over and over again.

It wasn't until the next day that Sage could think about the video without lapsing into dysfunction. Her sadness hadn't diminished, but she braced herself and forced herself to reflect on nagging concerns. Foremost was Jesse had been prepared to take out Talon and everyone else on the transport, as evidenced by the IEDs revealed in the final footage. Was Talon the target? Jesse obviously knew Talon was there. And what drove Jesse to make such a sacrifice? Or *who* drove him? Gabriel came to mind. He had gone to great lengths to conceal her dad's chip. Sage feared this cover-up meant the assassination attempts weren't over, and Gabriel was at the front of those efforts.

These realizations made it difficult to sit unseen and watch Gabriel walk past, but while her initial concern for Avan gave her pause, Sage realized it would be foolish to approach the chief. Right now, Gabriel thought she was clueless. If he learned otherwise, any plans for Talon's demise might be accelerated. Her heart raced with the unwelcome thought that she could already be too late. She couldn't be sure her little brother was still alive, but she would sense if he wasn't, right? She forced herself to let the fear go because it just couldn't be true. It just couldn't.

Her search for answers had been merely one more reason to visit Sofia. Sage and Sofia were practically sisters. Since the day she learned Sofia was hauled off to the Lab, Sage had been calling, harassing anyone who would answer, demanding to speak with Sofia.

Sage imagined Sofia didn't see her own situation as much better than Talon's. She was essentially imprisoned, largely separated from family and friends. She had to see what she could do to help Sofia cope.

She waited impatiently for the Abreos to retrieve their car and leave the parking lot. It was 2 p.m. The event wasn't over until 5 p.m., and likely Sofia's visits would be cut off then. It was odd that Gabriel and Avan would leave before they had to.

With their car retreating down the road, Sage headed across the parking lot, past the barbecue area, and over to a long row of informational booths, surveying the crowd the whole time for any sign of Sofia. She had no interest in the countless booths dedicated to explaining all the great things the Tech Lab did for the community and the entire planet. Looking past the booths and onto the lawn before what must be the administration building, she spotted a tent with a large banner that read, "Visitor Information." She walked to the tent, where a 3-D avatar greeted her.

"Good day! How can I assist you?"

Sage tried to understand the point of this orange-haired, blue-skinned character in a white tuxedo. "I want to track down someone who works here. I mean, lives here. Can you help me?"

"I will endeavor to do so. Who might that be?"

"Sofia Abreo."

"Abreo ... Sofia. Yes. She is available. May I tell her who—"

An ear-piercing shriek erupted behind Sage, giving her just enough time to turn before Sofia came flying into her arms, nearly knocking her over.

Sage hung on tight, and her tears flowed. How she had missed this girl!

"And there she is," the animation said.

This brought some laughter and Sofia pulled back. "I'm sorry." Then she dove right back into Sage's arms.

Sage hugged her even tighter. "Oh, how I've missed you,"

She pulled away to get a good look at her 'little sister.' She had all the signs of a growth spurt. Not only was she now over

Sage's five feet six, but she was even skinnier than before. "Are you eating?" she asked, suddenly concerned her weight might be due to more than rapid growth.

"Yes, Mom," Sofia responded, sassy.

Her eyes sparkled with joy as she continued to look Sofia over. Same bright blue eyes. Same gorgeous auburn hair, now past her shoulders. She was going to have a few guys following her around. Sage frowned as she remembered she had hoped one of those boys would be her brother.

"Are you OK?" Sofia asked, picking up on her change in mood. "Thoughts of Talon?"

How perceptive Sofia could be. "Sister, don't ever use your good looks. With your brains, that combination would be so unfair! So, do you have some time to spend with me? Could we go somewhere and talk?"

"Please! I had some friends drop by earlier. And my parents. But I was hoping so hard that you would visit." Sofia took her by the hand and led her along a sidewalk.

Sofia had always been sweet, unless pushed to be otherwise, and Sage had caught her sad expression when she mentioned her parents. She decided to let Sofia decide whether she wanted to talk about them.

"Do you care where we go? Do you need to eat anything?" Sofia asked as she steered Sage onto a crushed-granite path that meandered through white stucco buildings and manicured landscaping.

Sofia had been this way as long Sage had known her. How old had Sofia been? Six? She was always leading, this way or that. Sofia knew where she wanted to take Sage, but she was thoughtful enough to make her feel like she had options. Sage loved it. "I'm good, Sofia. Just lead the way, as usual."

The campus was large, and the circuitous path continued for what must have been a quarter-mile when it fed into a large open area ringed by white stucco buildings with old-style adobe roofs. Cypress trees with fragrant lavender plantings covered several acres.

The path snaked through the trees, and Sofia pulled gently on Sage's arm as she urged her to pick up the pace. They soon emerged from the foliage, where their path led to a larger crushed-granite swath that encircled a magnificent sculpture. The display featured a half-scale humpback whale and her calf, sculpted from granite, suspended above large black lava rocks interspersed with sand. The feature was ringed by a bench made from blocks of Carmel stone.

Sage struggled to fully absorb the magnificence of the setting. "Amazing! Are we allowed to get closer?"

"Of course!" Sofia walked across the ground cover. "I forget, you aren't allergic to bees, right?"

Sage hadn't noticed the bees, busily flying from flower to flower. She and Sofia both had on capri-length pants and T-shirts, exposing ankles and arms. "All good," she said, captivated by the floating whales. Drawing nearer to the main feature, the air under the whales looked distorted.

"Fiber optics." Sofia pointed at two columns under the larger whale and a smaller column under the baby. "The light is funneled around support columns using thousands and thousands of fiber strands."

Sage couldn't see the actual columns, but could make out their locations based on the slightly distorted images. "You must come here all the time. This is stunning."

Sofia's mood faltered. "No, only once before. This place makes me sad. But right now, I'm happy." Sofia must have realized Sage wasn't following. "I'll explain later."

As Sage tried to understand what Sofia wasn't telling her, she could see Sofia's lips tighten and a serious look come over her. She braced for what was coming.

"Sage, please don't take this wrong. I'm so thrilled you came to see me, but I'm worried to death about Talon. Do you know how he's doing?"

Sage teared up and instinctively embraced Sofia. She was unable to speak, so overcome with emotion and so grateful to be with someone who cared deeply about her brother. She took Sofia's shoulders and stepped back in order to be face-to-face with her. She shook her head, still too choked up to be sure she could talk.

This time Sofia pulled Sage in for a hug. "I'm so sorry for asking."

Sage eventually let go and sat on one of the stones that formed the bench. Sofia sat beside her. She finally said, "I am so grateful you asked. You can't imagine what your concern means to me. I wish I had positive news, but it's been a challenge to find him."

"I'm going to find him," Sofia blurted out.

"Really?"

"Seriously. There are people at this complex who know where he was sent. One person in particular is going to help me to reach out to him."

Sage tried to smile at the news. Instead, her lips turned down and she found she could no longer make eye contact with Sofia as her thoughts turned to the fear she had yet to face. "Do you know if he's still alive?"

"Oh, Sage," Sofia held her hands, "Yes, he's alive. The people I'm talking about know enough about what happens in the Center to know if he wasn't."

Sage covered her face with her hands, her shoulders shuddered, and tears leaked out between her fingers. She wasn't too late!

"I'm worried we're going to use up all our hugs," Sofia said, leaning in for another embrace.

Sage laughed, not having any control over her raw emotions. Then she heard a whoosh and water cascaded down on them. Sofia stood, laughing, and Sage rose with her, looking about, puzzled. Sofia pointed at the whales, and Sage turned in time to see another blast of water shoot out from the mother's blowhole. Sure enough, they were showered again. Sofia laughed harder and Sage joined her, thankful for some comic relief.

"That's how this ground cover gets watered!" Sofia said. Realizing the watering might not be finished, Sage pulled Sofia's arm and hurried back to the path. They reached it as water burst forth again, this time lightly sprinkling them. "Any other surprises, Sister?" Sage asked, feeling like a cloud had been lifted.

"As a matter of fact, yes. How would you like to meet the person who's going to help find Talon?"

Chapter Fifty-Seven

The Warden

August 9 - 4:38 p.m.

The warden sat at the head of the conference table and took stock of the room one more time. He wasn't looking for anything specific, just trying to find some distraction to help him endure the two-hour grind. He hated board meetings, which were quarterly events as dictated by the Fabrication Center's bylaws.

He detested the room, which he personally designed. No paintings, screens, or electronics, just a conference table and chairs to seat twenty people. The table had an industrial look with a polished bronze top, its matching chairs having minimal padding. The floor was a cream-colored porcelain tile, while the walls were off-white plaster, barren of trim. The room was designed to get people out quickly. He had even resorted at times to turning off the air conditioning to motivate people to finish their business and stop wasting his time.

The room was grating on his every nerve. Perhaps it was the fact that there were only five people meeting, including himself. He tried to focus on his security chief, who was droning on about something.

He had placed the man in charge of the agenda, so again, he had no one to blame but himself. His chief had a bodybuilder physique that was currently stuffed into a blue blazer and khaki pants. With plain features, brown hair, and brown eyes, the head of security didn't offer anything remarkable. The warden wished he'd hired a chief who had some battle scars or other injuries that at least came with a good story. He was desperate for a diversion from the drab room with boring people and his less than inspiring thoughts, when his chief finally got to the exciting part of the show.

"The final agenda item is Letcher Mercer."

The warden felt the energy flow back into his body. He glanced at the other board members—the general, the new board member, and the first shift security supervisor. They were all listening.

"No disrespect, Warden, but when I raised a concern over Letcher, you suggested we discuss it at the board meeting," the chief said, looking to the warden for confirmation he could proceed.

"No offense taken. This is a serious matter that all of us, as leaders of the Center, must consider. Please proceed." Such a brilliant move to ensure the chief would bring this topic before the board.

"Right," the chief began. "For those who aren't familiar with Letcher, he not only has a history of violence toward security but also against his fellow workers. He was deemed such a threat to all those around him that he has been confined to restricted quarters for the last twelve months. Restricted quarters are the equivalent of a series of jail cells," the chief clarified for the new board member.

He again looked at the warden for confirmation that he should continue, clearly smelling something was wrong here. The warden nodded his approval, and the chief had no choice but to go on.

"The warden placed conditions on the confinement whereby every thirty days Mr. Letcher's confinement must be reconfirmed—by the warden. If not reconfirmed, Letcher is to be returned to the working population within a week. Further, he is to be returned to the quadrant from which he was extracted, which is the same quadrant where his brother, Feist Mercer, was stung out. As you know, sir, two days ago that reconfirmation was allowed to lapse."

The chief glanced at the warden yet another time. "Please finish," the warden encouraged, quite pleased by how this was going.

"My concern, as head of security, is that we will not be able to contain the threat that Letcher poses not only to the general worker population but more specifically to Blunt Morgan and Talon Russit. These two were involved in his brother's death, and while they may not have been to blame, Letcher will see it differently. Further, while Blunt may be able to handle himself, Talon Russit is a scrawny teenager who won't have a chance," the chief finished with conviction.

The warden had to constrain himself from clapping. He couldn't have crafted the chief's speech better himself. The general should be impressed with this plan to address the Russit problem, as unwittingly laid out by the head of security. "Chief Gorman, I do understand your concern and admire your extremely cautious approach to Mr. Mercer," he began. "At the same time, after being in what was basically a jail cell for an entire year, I believe Mr. Mercer understands there are consequences for bad behavior. Also, since he is not a disconnect, if he were to kill someone to exact revenge, he would be stung out like his brother. He knows the consequences, which our society has agreed is an effective deterrent to such behavior. If he even maims someone, he now knows he will be back in that cage. I'm pretty sure he doesn't want to end up there again."

The chief, now emboldened, pleaded for common sense. "Sir, everything you say makes sense to a rational person, but Letcher isn't rational and has become a lot less connected to reality since he's been at this facility."

The warden was getting irritated at the man's persistence. "Chief Gorman, do you really want to argue that Mr. Mercer is going to kill someone now, when he has come this far in life without killing anyone?"

The warden's statement couldn't be any stronger warning for the chief to stand down. Both the chief and the warden knew Letcher and his twin, Feist, had teamed up to torture and kill their father at the age of fourteen. They had then gone on to get networked before being exposed, leading the CID to quietly enroll the "networked killers" into the Bee Sting work programs.

Getting the signal the warden demanded unconditional agreement, the chief complied. "No, I would not."

The warden wasn't done. He wanted to make sure if Letcher did harm anyone, as he hoped he would, his superiors couldn't single him out for releasing him. He wanted to use the board for protection. "I don't want to make a mistake here. Chief Gorman has brought up a legitimate concern. As the board of directors, we are tasked with making some difficult judgment calls. This is one we don't want to get wrong. Does anyone want to make a motion for me to extend Mercer's confinement in restricted quarters?"

The warden looked to each person for an answer. The chief shook his head when the warden looked his way. The security supervisor started to raise his hand until he saw the threatening look in the warden's eyes. His hand lowered and he shook his head.

"Not I. I trust the people who work here," the general simply said.

The warden turned his attention to the new board member. If he made a motion to extend, he would get voted down four to one. He had achieved his objective. It really was brilliant. Most importantly, he was certain he wouldn't be stung out, no matter what happened next. The warden had heard stories of people hiring assassins and being stung out themselves. The theory was that the brain made the same connection to using an assassin as using a gun. He wasn't taking any chances in case these stories were true. In this case, he wasn't actually taking action to release Mr. Mercer. He just wasn't taking action to confine him. In essence, he was doing nothing. Refocusing on his new member, who was staring down at the table, the warden prodded him, "Mr. Abreo?"

Gabriel Abreo faced the warden with a distant look in his eyes. He appeared to be giving serious thought to his response. After another moment, his gray eyes cleared and drilled right into the warden. "No," he said, issuing what could only be a death sentence.

Chapter Fifty-Eight

Talon

August 10 – 11:53 p.m.

If anyone was awake at midnight, they might have caught a glimpse of two silhouettes facing off in a violent confrontation. One was much larger than the other. The larger was always moving forward, stalking its adversary. The smaller darted side to side, staying out of corners, continually probing for a means of escape.

Minutes ticked by with the smaller figure nimbly frustrating the pursuer over and over again. The hulking shadow would appear to swallow its prey, only to see the smaller body slip through an unseen opening. This dance went on until the small figure feigned to dart away, then abruptly changed course and slammed into the larger mass. The large body took the impact, lifted the imp, and hurled it to the ground. The massive figure wasted no time moving in for the kill.

"Kid, you have no chance of getting the best of this guy. Right now, Letcher would have a knee in your gut and be pummeling your face. You would be left broken or dead." Blunt held out a hand to help him up.

Talon took it, his head still swimming. This was his fourth session with Blunt since he had been warned to stay away.

When Talon walked away that day, Blunt had stormed back to Talon until his looming presence threatened to stop his heart mid-beat. He didn't dare breathe while Blunt scowled at him, seemingly planning which way he would die.

"This isn't a game! You might have noticed you got a lot of people's attention right now, and that's not only your fellow workers. I've stuck my neck out for you, but if I get linked to you, people might start checking out my background and what

I've been up to. That happens, good people are going to pay the price. Got that?"

Talon had heard nothing further from Blunt until five nights ago when he was hunting for an isolated place to turn in for the night. Blunt had stepped from the shadows, scaring him pretty good, and berated him for being too easy to track down. Rumor was going around that Letcher would soon be released into the yard. Blunt figured Talon was going to be an obsession for this lunatic, and Letcher wouldn't flinch at being stung out.

Talon's first reaction was to downplay the threat. Considering the countless other forces working to end his life, what was one more?

"Look. I realize this place has to be a lot tougher on you than some. And it doesn't help that you have a target on your back from the warden on down to the people you work and live with. You're at a tipping point right now, kid. You're either going to cave or decide to fight like hell. If a sour shit like me feels bad for you, I'm wondering if there're others in your life that might feel a hundred times worse. A dad, mom, siblings, a special friend ...?"

"My mom and brother are long gone. Thanks to me, my dad passed as well."

Blunt took a deep breath. "That's rough, kid. That leaves a ... girl?"

Talon nodded. "Yeah ... and a sister."

"So how would your sister feel about you deserting your girl?"

Talon felt his rage boil and erupt. He rotated his shoulder and slammed his fist into Blunt's skull, rocking Blunt's head to the side before even realizing what he'd done.

Blunt just sat there, grinning. "So, you do have some fight left! Not exactly how I was hoping you would react, but not bad." Then taking a small sack that Talon hadn't realized was slung over his shoulder, Blunt produced a hydro flask and what looked like an energy bar. He stood up, leaving the food by his side. "Eat. Then we begin training. Down the road, I'll share how I got these things and my stupid dreams of survival. But only after you prove to me that you got what it takes, that you got dreams of your own."

With that, the training sessions began. And while Talon was smart enough to know he had little chance of ever leaving this compound alive, he at least wasn't yet ready to throw in the towel.

Chapter Fifty-Nine

Wilder

August 11 - 9:36 a.m.

Wilder was discouraged. The 'open house' event hadn't helped his spirits. He had spent the day looking for any opportunity that he might have used to approach Sofia, but not only was the swollen crowd too much to navigate, Sofia had a constant barrage of visitors.

Seeing his sister make an appearance nearly broke him.

He couldn't keep doing this. He was failing to win Sofia's trust. He had previously been excited when Sofia had confided she was having trouble with the Lab's head of development. She described him as sketchy at best. Wilder responded with information he hoped might be relevant. Haris was convinced there were some unsavory characters in key positions at the Lab. At least one plant was doing the bidding of a power-hungry general, coding some special program for him.

Receiving nothing further from Sofia on the subject, Wilder pressed to keep the communication going. In his latest correspondence, he provided a big reveal on Talon. Wilder had thought long and hard about the chip he stole from UCSC. Shortly after the theft, he had inserted it into a handheld at the Programming Center, as instructed. He assumed the chip contained a virus, which the handheld would upload to the CID network when connected. Now he thought otherwise.

He contemplated Talon's near abduction a thousand times. Haris and Jesse's laser focus on Talon had to add up to something. When the lightbulb finally came on, he felt rather stupid. The fact that the handheld was at the Programming Center should have tipped him off that the more obvious use for the chip was to *download*, not *upload*, a program. Talon's popularity meant he was most likely the recipient of a very special program.

This enlightenment hit Wilder hard. He had unwittingly been an accomplice to an experiment on his own brother, a failed experiment as evidenced by his defective chip, but then why the continued interest in Talon? Could people be so ruthless that they were willing to retrieve the chip from a living soul for further study? The thought made Wilder sick.

He confessed to Sofia that all his escapades resulted in Talon's NAC being programmed with what had to be next-generation software.

Expecting this to be the major reveal that shattered Sofia's barriers, he was crushed when her only response was, "who are you?"

Every message Sofia sent ended with that same question. Only this time, this one question was all she bothered to send. She was done sharing; she didn't believe him and was turning him loose.

Wilder was left with the choice of walking away or going all in to gain her trust. Moving on didn't mean giving up on the mission. He could never give up. He would go back to the redwoods outside of Ridge Crest and desperately plead with the fugitives to join him.

He knew it would be a huge challenge: most outcasts didn't interact closely because more interactions meant better odds someone you knew would be captured and roll over on you. Wilder knew he likely traded information and goods with far too many people, and he was a sucker for anyone who needed a hand, but he hadn't grown close to anyone besides Haris. It was hard to break through people's defenses when breaking through could cost them their freedom—especially amongst a population that savored freedom above all else.

Still, worst case, he would have to try. On the other hand, if his current mission succeeded, he would use it to show the fugitives that they could win. More people were hiding out in the redwoods than the CID imagined. He just had to convince them to fight back rather than retreat.

Ultimately, they would somehow cripple the Program, he dreamed. A rebel group could maybe put a big dent in it by performing surgical strikes.

But he needed to get the momentum going. He needed to get wins and he needed to be able to point toward the initial few willing to join the cause. And that started here. If he rescued Talon, he knew he would join him. He knew the same of Sofia—if only he could get her to give him a chance.

If he was going to ask people around him to come out of the shadows and risk their well-being, plus the safety of their families, then he had to set the example. He prepared a special note. Reading it over, he felt he didn't need to say much more.

"It's time we trust each other. Your friend, Wilder Russit."

Chapter Sixty

Talon

August 12 – 7:40 a.m.

All of the pushing, bumping, and elbowing had stopped. Some people had even taken up saying "hi" or "hello." What Talon could do without was all the wishes of "good luck." While sincere, it drove home the reason many people changed their attitude toward him. Everyone suspected he was a dead man. It was just a matter of time.

Whether starting the workday or returning to the yard after work, Talon knew life was going to be even more hazardous from here on out. Letcher was scheduled to be released tomorrow and his hunt for Talon would begin. Ironically, Talon was worried he might not get the opportunity to face Letcher since his work had also taken a turn for the worst. The production operation was being revamped to introduce a new product called the tracer. It was a chip reader designed especially for law enforcement. Rumor had it that the reader, shaped like a missile launcher, could lock onto a specific chip from over one thousand yards away. If a suspect was networked, that person could instantly be picked out of a crowd or located in a skyscraper. The possibilities were endless.

The tracer appealed to Talon's geeky side. The technology was impressive. At the same time, Talon knew it was irrelevant. He needed to concentrate on producing the new product, as opposed to what it could do. He was one of ten workers chosen to test new factory equipment.

This was not an honor bestowed on ten lucky workers. It was a possible death sentence. None of the equipment had been integrated into an assembly line. Each workstation had multiple tools covering tasks such as metal punching, welding, laser etching, and drilling. The tools had never been set up to coexist before, nor had the stations been connected to create a complete assembly operation.

The conveyors and robots that fed materials to the line and moved assemblies from station to station had previously never been linked together as well. It wasn't just a challenge to have them physically coexist, but every piece of equipment had to be programmed to recognize the other robots, conveyors, and tools operating around it. This operation was designed to rely heavily on artificial intelligence, allowing the equipment to adjust when mistakes were made. The problem was that this production trial was in its infancy and the AI had a lot to learn. This resulted in tools, assemblies, robots, and conveyors crashing into each other, providing countless opportunities for testing crew to get maimed or killed.

The ten-person crew monitored the workstations and all the supporting equipment. The production engineers and supervisors also roamed the line via their avatars. If equipment malfunctioned, the workers were responsible for getting the operation up and running. This could be as simple as rebooting a tool or as complex as writing a few lines of code under the guidance of a software engineer. If the problem was too severe, production would be halted, the workers evacuated, and the engineers sent in to handle matters themselves.

Nothing could be handled remotely. For security purposes, all equipment was connected solely via a local network, with the servers controlling the equipment located on a mezzanine erected over the factory floor, providing a deterrent to hacking and physical sabotage.

Talon could imagine how this operation might have come together smoothly if it had been given more time. Based on the profanity and snide comments from the engineers, the product introduction was being rushed.

Talon suspected that he was one of the factors in the decision to rush this introduction. He was indeed being targeted. Considering recent events, he would be a fool to deny this fact, especially if he wanted any chance of surviving.

This was the fourth day the crew was brought in to run the line, with each day bringing multiple accidents and even a few minor electrical fires.

Talon spotted Espar at the shop floor entrance, taking in the assembly line. He dropped his effort to reboot a laser and went to greet her. She seemed genuinely happy to see him.

"Hey, Espar, are you the latest recruit?" Talon offered his hand in greeting.

She lifted his hand and examined it from every angle before declaring, "You've still got all your fingers. I heard that's an accomplishment here."

He wanted to laugh, but it was too close to the truth. "That's right. How did you get picked for this?"

"You know how it goes. My dear supervisor popped up on my display and told me to get over to the new line."

Talon did know how it went. With little choice but to take on assignments, he was recruited in the same manner. Monday morning, his supervisor told him to go next door for his new work instructions. 'Next door' was walled off from the main production. Passing through a temporary door transported disconnects from an orderly production environment to a chaotic mess that would be an apt setting for a dark comedy based on a world of defective robots, where the laughter was replaced with horror as the workers were maimed and killed.

Knowing that any instruction Espar received from her supervisor wouldn't touch on safety protocol, Talon risked the wrath of management and took time off from his duties to give Espar a rundown on the dangers of the workplace and how to try to avoid them. Before she moved on to her new assignment, she thanked him. "Good luck tomorrow."

Chapter Sixty-One

Rani

August 12 - 9:19 a.m.

Rani rushed across the parking lot, agonizing over being late for her shift. She hadn't been too worried about breaking rules these days. Shit, she had pretty much violated every office policy in helping Sage. Still, that didn't mean she would be a lazy cop. No, she still wanted to be the best she could be for as long as she publicly served. And that meant pulling her weight. She entered the lobby to be greeted by two fellow officers with Tasers drawn and pointed across the front desk at a familiar-looking figure. She could only see his back, but she recognized the long, dirty-blond hair and rushed up beside him. "Whoa, guys! What's going on here?"

Officers Johnson and Simone kept their Tasers lasered in on JT, pointedly ignoring Rani.

"Don't even think of walking out of here," Johnson said.

"I'm not. I merely said I'm not going back there with you," JT stated.

"That's not really your choice. You may not be a disconnect, but you've been known to aid fugitives and we suspect you can lead us to Shadow," Simone said. "So, plan on sticking around, or we'll drop you before you can take a step toward the door."

"I plan to stick around. I'm here to see her," JT replied coolly, nodding his head in Rani's direction.

"That's right. Hey, lower the weapons, yeah? He came at my request." Without even waiting for her colleagues' response, she gave JT a tug to follow her and was off.

Filing into her office behind JT, she shut the door and didn't bother to offer him a seat. "What the hell was that all about? You can't simply drop in here!"

"Why not?"

"Because what they said out there is true. Aiding fugitives places you on the wrong side of the law. I think you know that's not a great place to be."

"If people aren't supposed to stick up for the persecuted, then maybe I'm on the *right* side of the law," he shot back.

Rani realized she had no reason to be arguing with him, what with her own doubts about law enforcement these days. "Yeah, well, you might be right. What can I help you with?"

They both settled into chairs, the situation diffused. "I'm looking for Wilder. Wilder Russit."

Rani hadn't met Wilder, but she knew enough about Ridge Crest and the department to understand a bomb had just been dropped in her office. "Wilder is dead," she said slowly.

"Hardly. Look, understand I'm breaking a confidence with him I vowed never to break. But he disappeared a few weeks ago and I'm worried."

Rani believed JT. Her little experience with him was that he didn't seem to play games, preferring to tell people how things stood. Plus, in the little digging she had done into his background, she knew he had been close to the Russit family. That was a good enough reference for Rani.

"You know that my next conversation is going to be with his sister. She's got to be told," she stated to herself as much as to JT.

"I know. Wilder always thought he was protecting his family. He doesn't have much faith in the Program. He felt there were people who would use his family against him if they knew he was alive. Now with his father's death and Talon's disappearance, he's suffering from the choices he made. Hope he hasn't done anything stupid. With thousands of ways to die out in the woods, the distance between wishing you were dead and being dead can be pretty small."

Shit, Sage didn't deserve to learn her brother had been alive, but then killed himself. Maybe her next call shouldn't be to Sage, after all. Looking at JT's knowing eyes, she suspected he knew that as well. "Lemme dig around," she said. "I've got a few thoughts to follow up on." And she did. She guessed that if Wilder was still alive, he would be hunting down Talon as they spoke. With the best-kept secret being the Fabrication Center's location and the worst kept being the Tech Lab's connection, she had a strong hunch he would have headed that way.

"Alright. I'll be back," JT replied.

"You can't return. Hey, I gave you my number, right? When a girl gives you her number, means you should use it," she said, more than flirting but also trying to keep JT safe.

"Why would I call when seeing you is much better?" he threw back at her.

Rani had met her match. Not wanting to further escalate something that couldn't work in her world, she looked to change the subject. "So, while you're here, what do you think about helping us out with Shadow?"

JT smiled and headed for the door, calling out, "I just did."

The hell?! Another secret she was going to have to swallow. Until he was located, Sage shouldn't suffer the news that her supposedly dead brother was the notorious Shadow.

Chapter Sixty-Two

Talon

August 12 - 2:33 p.m.

The new production line didn't have a second shift. The first shift had ended at 2:30 and the small crew was required to exit through a temporary scanning portal and door. This dumped them into the yard, around the corner from the main entrance. They could then make their way to the main production area, assuming they wanted to work a second shift and be afforded the opportunity to have their first drink of water since the workday began.

Talon got up from his station. He stretched and surveyed the area to confirm everyone had made it through another day. Espar spotted him and headed his way.

"Are you really checking to make sure everyone made it through the shift? You're about to get your brains beat in tomorrow and you're worried about everyone else?"

Talon didn't know how to respond. He was sure she meant to be funny, but the thought of Letcher stalking him didn't allow for any humor. Talon and Espar waited as everyone formed a line at the door, then fell in behind them.

"Sorry about that. Not such a good joke," Espar said.

"Thanks for giving it a try anyway. Can I ask you something personal?"

"Personal ...? Okay."

They trailed the group out the door. Unfazed by the bright light, Talon asked, "Why are you being nice to me?"

"Hmm, not sure. Maybe this place is mean enough without me adding ..." Espar trailed off, staring over Talon's shoulder.

Talon turned to see a shaggy-looking troll with long brown hair and a beard to match close the gap between them.

Letcher! This menacing muscle-bound giant had to be him!

Not even thinking, Talon reached back behind him and pulled the door open. He fled back inside, Espar following close behind.

He turned on her. "What are you doing? Get out of here!" He needed to think of an escape plan, and he certainly didn't want Espar to get in harm's way if he failed.

Espar didn't pay him any attention. Instead, she pushed on the door. It didn't budge. "The door's locked." As if to confirm what she'd said, the door rattled as someone tried to force it open.

Espar and Talon stood, amazed that it wouldn't yield, while the effort to get in grew more frantic. The rattling grew louder, accompanied by swearing, and still nothing gave. The effort ended with a loud bang and a whimper after the troll somehow decided it would be smart to ram a metal door.

With the noise dying away, Espar asked, "What just happened?"

"Letcher tried to break down the door and it held?"

Espar rewarded his worthless response by swatting his shoulder. "I mean, how did you open that door? Why didn't the alarms go off? There are safeguards against people entering from the yard."

Espar had Talon's attention. Was the door shut when he opened it? It was! A cascade of thoughts overtook him. He forced his memory back to the horrible episode in which his dad's partner tried to blow up their transport. In the many, many times he had recounted that day, one of the mysteries had always been how he had accessed the transport's control panel, especially when the security guards were repeatedly locked out. He hadn't done anything they hadn't tried. The difference was that he was given access when they weren't.

His chip-programming day invaded his thoughts as well. Another mystery. He remembered his father insisting they go back into the Programming Center to confront the technicians about his failed programming. He specifically recalled the technicians' stunned faces when his dad pulled open the door and walked in. The security system that protected against general entry had broken down. Was it his own presence that overrode those protections?

"What's going on in that thick head of yours?" Espar demanded. "You know what just happened, don't you?"

"Maybe ..." He needed time. He needed to think through what this meant and who he should share it with. He also wanted to make sure it wasn't something he was making up in his head. "I need time to get my head around this. Would you keep this quiet for now?"

"Of course," Espar assured him. "We need to focus on getting out of here anyway. It's not like this little stunt just eliminated all your enemies."

Chapter Sixty-Three

Sofia

August 12 – 3:21 p.m.

"We have to get him out of there. We received word he's got enemies and they're closing in."

Sofia's head was throbbing. Jonathan had asked to meet her by the whale display, then upon greeting her, explained that many protections against eavesdropping were built into the exhibit, including radio wave transmitters that jammed listening devices. She was having a hard time grasping these precautions, having grown up in a law enforcement family, where there was a general trust in government, but this was the second time this week her trust was being challenged.

Shadow's recent communications had her wondering whether she was extremely naïve or he had been left out on his own too long. She hadn't shared his thoughts with anyone for fear she would be viewed as some conspiracy theorist, but now Shadow wasn't sounding all that crazy. "What do you mean by 'enemies'?" she asked.

"There's no easy way to say this ... I mean there are people that want Talon to disappear forever. Having him killed might be their preferred way of making this happen."

Shadow's claims about Talon's download and the Tech Lab bad guys seemed to fit with people targeting Talon. Before sharing Shadow's words, first she wanted to fully understand the dangers to Talon. "Why Talon? And isn't murder off the table? I mean, isn't the whole Bee Sting system all about preventing murder?"

"That's a couple of tough questions," Jonathan said. "The Program can't completely prevent people from doing horrible things to each other. According to CID statistics, murder rates have been reduced by ninety-five percent, but that's still not zero."

"Zero is pretty much what my generation is buying into. What's the point of the Program if Talon or anyone else can still be extinguished? This is so wrong!"

Jonathan seemed disturbed by these strong emotions, compelling him to explain the complicated choices the Program faced. "Maybe you're right. I imagine we'll get closer to zero with the next iteration of Bee Sting. Or the one after that. But that means buying into monitoring every person on this planet twenty-four/seven because anything less isn't going to completely snuff out murder. Is that a good trade-off? If, as a society, we could give up all freedoms to achieve complete safety, should we do it?"

"No! This system sucks!" Sofia hadn't meant to answer Jonathan's question. It was a gut reaction that slipped out. The system had her imprisoned and it couldn't even protect Talon. Her rose-colored glasses had finally shattered.

A sadness seemed to sweep over Jonathan as he acknowledged her verdict. "I'm not going to argue with you. We all have doubts and we all have to decide where we stand."

"What about Talon? Why him?" Sofia asked, steering them back to what was most important.

Jonathan took his time before replying. "I can't answer that one."

"Because you don't know?"

"I can't talk about what I know or don't know."

"Really?" Sofia asked, not trying to tamp down her anger. "So this is how you help me reach out to Talon?"

"It gets worse. A plan has been put in place to help Talon. I—"

"And no one thought to get my input on this plan?" Sofia interrupted.

"Reaching out to Talon is complicated. The effort will put a lot of people at risk. It was decided the less you know, the better for everyone, especially you."

"Wow. So why are we even talking?"

"I need your help."

Sofia laughed. "Excuse me?"

"If you don't want to help, I understand."

"That's not fair," Sofia said, knowing she had no choice. "What is it you'd want me do?"

"I need you to break into Dr. Sur's office."

"Seriously?"

"You need to steal a chip."

"Why me?"

"You're the only one who can pull this off without leaving a trace. Let me lay it out for you. With the help of the small device you took from Dr. Sur's office, you can enter the building and make it all the way to his office undetected. Knowing you can't access his office without being identified, the door will be left open. The chip you're looking for will be somewhere on his desk in a small, square silver case. Grab it and head out of the building. Make sure you exit unseen behind someone else. Go back to your place and leave the chip on your patio bench, and I'll be along to collect it."

"Sounds like Dr. Sur's in on this. Why not have him grab the chip? Or why don't you bring it out?"

"You're the only one that can take the chip without being identified. Embedded in the chip is a security protocol ensuring the building readers can track it. The theft won't go unnoticed forever, but hopefully long enough for the chip to be on its way."

"You aren't going to tell me what the chip does or how it could help?" Sofia wanted to know.

"I can't. If it brings any comfort, I'll be the one delivering the chip down south."

"When?"

"Tomorrow."

Sofia gasped. "You want me to do this tonight?"

"Yes. I'm afraid we don't have much time."

Sofia went quiet. Jonathan's refusal to share with her stung. She glared at him, furiously, wondering how to turn the tables on the fake friend standing before her. She certainly wasn't going to be sharing Shadow's information with him anytime soon. With that last angry thought, the rebellion ended as she acknowledged to herself she had no leverage.

"You know I'm doing it," she finally admitted.

Chapter Sixty-Four

Talon

August 12 – 3:40 p.m.

Swiveling his head side to side in search of Letcher, Talon hurried across the scorched earth toward the nearest residential building. This was the perfect time to test whether his escape from Letcher amounted to anything. Virtually everyone would be at the factory, choosing to work the second shift for food and water and for refuge from the sweltering sun.

Entering the hall would be his first test. Glancing around to make sure no one was following him, Talon tugged on the door handle. The door swung open without a sound! He had half expected blaring sirens to welcome him.

Hot, stuffy air greeted him instead as he went inside and journeyed along the hall toward the other end of the building. He peered into the rooms he passed, seeing the beds shoved together, thinking he really didn't miss being in these cramped quarters. Minus the beatings, he could be content sleeping on the hard-packed, dusty ground. All he needed was some space and the stars above.

Taking the exit at the far end of the hall, he surveyed the grounds for security personnel and, of course, Letcher. He was just beginning to test his limits. He traveled along the chain-link fence until he reached the gate. He had never given much thought to the locking mechanism that barred entry to the cherished shade beyond. Looking at it closely, it was just a reader embedded into the gate underneath the handle. It didn't look any different than the readers at building entrances. Talon figured that the reader was different only in the fact that it was programmed to allow security and maintenance personnel, as opposed to workers. Not being either security or maintenance, this was the first true test of his capabilities.

He grabbed the metal handle and pulled. It didn't budge. Then laughing at himself, he realized the gate had an old-style mechanical latch as well. He turned the knob, releasing the latch, and pulled again. The gate opened with a screech of rusted metal hinges. He gaped in disbelief. All this time he had looked longingly at life-preserving shade, and it had always been within his reach. Like a small child, he ran through the gate until he was engulfed by cool shadows. He couldn't stay long, but also couldn't ignore the luxury. He practically counted every second he was there until he forced himself to continue with his exploration.

It was time for him to face the ultimate trial. Making his way to the corner of the yard, he stopped well short of a formidable gate, maybe twenty feet tall and equally wide. This was one of two metal gates that offered passage out of their quadrant. The other was located at the opposing corner of the yard.

Talon, like everyone else locked in this death camp, continually fantasized about escaping. Feeding this dream, he had paid attention to every scrap of information concerning the avenues to freedom. Standing before the formidable gate, he thought of what lay beyond. Behind was a corridor. If he headed down the corridor to the right, he would be heading toward the center of the quadrants. Across the corridor sat another gate, which barred entry to the administrative quadrant. The warden resided there. Talon had no plans to visit him. A left down the corridor would take him to the main gate, where freedom lay beyond.

Freedom. The thought tugged at him. This venture had started off as a trial run to test his capabilities. Now, as he sized up the possible escape, any arguments against flight seemed to slip away. He would be leaving in broad daylight, but while guards were located in towers that protruded innocuously above the walls, would they pay much attention to someone walking *out* the main gate? Perhaps.

Talon resolved to make the decision once he laid eyes on the corridor and confirmed what lay beyond. His focus returned to the barrier before him and his thoughts went back to a conversation he had with a production engineer while she remotely tried to walk him through a software fix.

After an hour with no luck, she began grumbling about the unnerving prospect of visiting the facility. In her ever-increasing agitated state, she didn't hold any secrets back from Talon's inquiring mind, explaining that the compound's gates had been designed by some twisted individual, most likely the warden.

Passage entailed approaching the metal barrier until, at about eight feet out, the readers picked up your ID. A loud click would announce the release of a mechanical latch and the gate would then begin rolling off to one side ... assuming your ID had been entered into the gate's control module. Sadistically, at about six feet, if your ID wasn't read, the same click would ring out, releasing the deadly spikes.

Sweat now poured down Talon's face, and it wasn't due to the heat. He looked down both passageways to ensure he was still alone ... no sign of Letcher.

Knowing he was avoiding the inevitable, he began creeping toward the gate. Within ten feet, he stopped to gather the courage to keep moving forward. Being a geek, he dearly wished he knew exactly how his NAC worked. No point going there, though. He reminded himself that his chip had worked on every occasion leading up to this final hurdle and that escape had never been so close.

Now trembling, Talon resumed baby steps toward the gate. Did he really have to get within *eight* feet of the spikes? He would surely know if he were approaching *six* feet, right? He inched forward until he was sure he was no more than nine feet away.

He waved his arms. Remembering it was the chip that would be captured by the reader, he looked around to ensure no one saw his act of sheer stupidity. Thinking less than clearly, he decided to turn around, reasoning that the chip was actually embedded in the back of his neck. Approaching what had to be less than eight feet, Talon had a jolt of fear, thinking no one else had probably been dumb enough to tread backward through the gate. What if this defeated the system?

Talon still had enough of his wits about him to realize he was panicking. He took a few deep breaths and slowly faced the gate. He told himself he had every right to be afraid. He just had to force himself to move forward. Barely able to move his feet, he shuffled forward until he reached what had to be seven feet. It had to be! He was torn between the knowledge that his NAC should have triggered the gate by now and the refusal to admit defeat. Gathering the nerve to move forward one more time, he suddenly heard the scraping of footsteps behind him.

He slowly turned his head to see a massive figure coming into view. Talon almost leapt toward the gate, but he caught himself when he realized the figure was shorter and stockier than Letcher.

Blunt reached out a hand and grabbed Talon's shoulder. "The gate isn't opening, kid," he said while pulling Talon away from sure death. "Is there something you want to tell me?"

Talon couldn't bring himself to respond. He looked longingly at the gate, feeling the need to escape tug at him like an addiction. Blunt kept a grip on his shoulder, perhaps sensing his desire to take one more run at it.

Chapter Sixty-Five

Sofia

August 12 – 10:39 p.m.

Getting into the building had been no problem, thanks to the janitorial crew. Sofia proceeded slowly through the labyrinth of hallways leading to Dr. Sur's office. This was no dress rehearsal. She was dressed in dark, baggy clothing and wore a head covering. Underneath, she wore a lightweight running outfit. If she were spotted, her only hope was to elude capture and shed the dark clothes.

The reflections of herself in the glass-paneled offices made her jump half a dozen times before finally reaching the hallway leading to the doctor's office. Encouragingly, the only light ahead was that seeping out from the offices lining the hallway. It meant the silver trinket she picked up from Dr. Sur was doing its job, keeping the chip readers from picking up her presence and engaging the lights overhead.

Still, this darkness felt different. She peered into it, seeking any sign of the doctor's office. Her vision seemed unnaturally absorbed, leaving her with nothing except a sense that something was lurking there.

Her nerves were getting the best of her. All her late-night sleuthing had done nothing to prepare her for the adrenaline now coursing through her veins. She looked back the way she came, the urge to flee calling to her. Desperate to regain her composure, she clamped her eyelids tight and reached for a familiar image. Soon a pair of unforgettable green eyes came into focus. She could always picture Talon's eyes. She held that image, reminding herself why she had come.

Her heartbeats slowed to a little less than she could expect from an all-out sprint, and she headed into the darkness. As she slowly progressed past panel after panel of glass, some of the panes were pitch-black while others allowed low light to filter out from the screens and other electronics contained within. Her ghost-like reflection disappeared and reappeared, pacing her across the black and clear panels. It shouldn't have bothered her, but it added to the eerie surroundings, causing her to walk faster and faster until she was greeted by her reflection coming at her and she literally jumped. She had reached her destination.

She breathed deeply and gathered her thoughts. The door was to be left unlatched, so entry wasn't a problem. The biggest concern was finding the chip. She peered through the glass door in vain as it was too dark to make out Dr. Sur's desk ... She would have to use her palm light. Once she found the chip, she would extinguish the light and exit in the dark. She took one more deep breath and pushed on the door. It rattled, but didn't budge. She pushed harder with no luck. The latch was engaged.

Then off to her right, she heard a sound come from the adjacent office. Was that a cough? As quietly as she could, she retreated down the hall, ready to break out into an all-out sprint if the office door opened. She remembered Jonathan's warning about not getting caught, deciding that sounded like good advice now. She broke into a jog before remembering the rest of what Jonathan had told her. He was leaving tomorrow to deliver the chip. Whatever the plan, she knew time was running short and the chip was important.

The task before her was looking grim, but Sofia wasn't ready to quit, knowing Talon could already be in serious danger. She crept back to investigate what she'd heard. Approaching the office next to Dr. Sur, she noted it was the only one darkened amongst all the nearby offices. Maneuvering to where she could peak at the door without standing directly in front of it, she could tell something was stenciled there. She strained her eyes to make out the words.

No luck. The darkness was proving to be more an enemy than an ally.

Sofia forced herself to inch closer and closer until she was standing directly in front of the door, where the words came into view: *Chief Hill*. Oh, no!

As the name registered, she also heard a chair squeak, followed by footsteps moving her way. She stared at the door, unable to move. The footfalls advanced, seemingly stopping right before the door. Sofia felt like a child playing hide-and-seek just before the cupboard door is opened. Like a child, she tried to quiet her breath, slowing each breath she took in and let out. Soon, she could hear her breathing getting louder as she struggled for more oxygen. She was almost forced to bolt when the steps retreated, ending with another creak from the chair.

That should have been her cue to move, but she didn't budge. Any movement now would end in a mad dash for the exit. She forced herself to hold her position and think. Chief Hill! Why hadn't she noticed his office before? Probably because she was so focused on the infuriating Dr. Sur.

Fine. Trying to shove thoughts of Chief Hill aside, she considered her options. Retreating was the easiest one. Continuing on might be impossible. What would it take to get into the good doctor's office? From prior meetings with him, she learned —painfully—that absent the silver ball, her chip should be able to get her in. Of course, without it, she would also be identified. She could think of no other way.

Standing in front of the chief's office, she resigned herself to being caught. She would ditch the silver ball, revealing her identity. She would try Dr. Sur's door, and if necessary, she would break the glass. She would get the chip and run for the exit. No stealth. It was a matter of buying enough time to get the chip cleanly away.

With her lousy plan in place, Sofia allowed herself to move. She stepped as lightly as possible, moving off down the hall, away from the doctor's office. She set the silver ball down about twenty feet from his door, judging the distance to be far enough. She then turned to her reflection and gave the thumbs-up. She crept back toward her target office, keeping her eyes on Chief Hill's door, waiting for it to spring open.

Finally reaching the doctor's door, she saw it flash red. Did this mean she couldn't get in or that her chip malfunctioned? She retreated and approached again. Red. She slunk back to her silver trinket, pushing it further away. Turning back toward the doctor's office, she again kept her eyes on the chief's door as she stealthily made her way back to her destination.

She exhaled as she passed his door, only to have the hallway instantly turn bright as day. She inwardly kicked herself for forgetting her presence would trigger the lights. Not knowing what to do, she stumbled forward toward Dr. Sur's door ... It flashed green! She pushed through, triggering the office interior to light up as well.

The chip was sitting plain as day on the corner of the desk. Grabbing it, she ran back to the door, jerked it open, slamming it against the wall. She sprinted past the chief's office, seeing it light up out of the corner of her eye. Barely slowing, she snatched the ball off the ground and raced for the end of the hallway. Could the chief lock down the building? She rounded the corner before she heard the chief begin shouting. Well, she had unquestionably been noticed, but was she seen? She guessed that thought was irrelevant because she was being recorded. She continued her adrenaline-fueled mad dash through the corridors, wondering how far she might make it before being captured.

Reaching the lobby, she was surprised to see the front doors propped open. Making her way across the massive space, she noticed two janitors cleaning the front windows, and she slowed to a fast walk. Then remembering how many ways she was busted, she broke into a jog and waved at them as she hustled out the main entrance. Apparently, they were too shocked to react. That or they didn't care.

She hurried toward her residence, staying off the path, and broke into an all-out run again, trying to distance herself from the building in case the janitors decided they did care. In no time, she reached her patio, where she remembered to put the chip on the bench before stepping inside.

Sofia stood with her back against the door, her heart thumping wildly, and it wasn't from the run. It had been a disaster. She figured she was identified, recorded, and sighted. Not exactly what she planned for her first mission.

Ready or not, the race was underway. She struggled to stop herself from opening the door to watch for Jonathan, desperate for him to arrive before security. Reminding herself that she had drawn enough attention, Sofia let her back slide down the door until she was firmly planted on the ground. Would she hear Jonathan if he made it? She cringed with the realization she would have no problem hearing the shouts to "open up!" when security arrived.

Chapter Sixty-Six

Talon

August 13 - 5:25 a.m.

The sounds of metal rattling against metal brought Talon awake. His mind was as blurry as his vision in the gray light of dawn. Other than his roving eyes, he remained dead still while he tried to orient himself. He soon remembered he was tucked up against the dark recesses of a building, having used his newfound abilities to escape into the sanctuary of the surrounding chain-link fence.

The rattling sound returned, only louder. Talon peered out to where the fence traversed the yard until he spotted the source of the noise. A large silhouette that could only be Letcher stood at the gate, evidently leering into the recesses beyond. Talon pressed himself harder into the wall, hoping it was still too dark to be seen.

The spine-chilling phantom shook the gate, pressed his face up against it, then proceeded to shake it again. Was there another exit? Talon scolded himself for not checking earlier. The gate came under attack again, this time so fiercely that Talon thought it would burst open.

Then all stopped. Talon's heart skipped a beat or two when he couldn't locate Letcher, but then he sighted an apparition moving off into the distance.

Now knowing what it felt like to be the caged bird harassed by the family cat, Talon wasted no time fleeing, deciding it was time to find safety in the manufacturing facility.

He took a circuitous route around several residence halls before emerging from between two buildings to get a peek at the main entrance. In the growing light, he could make out Letcher camped in front of the entry doors. He had suspected this and was relieved to know Letcher's whereabouts. Easing back between the buildings, he circled the perimeter of the yard and re-surfaced at the exit door for the tracer production line.

Walking up to the exit, Talon continually looked about, making sure he was alone. He hesitated, unsure whether his chip would work this time. It was frustrating not knowing how or when his chip might perform. He quickly glanced around one more time, feeling it would be wise to keep his newfound abilities guarded. He then grabbed the handle and swung the door open. When the door shut behind him, he let himself soak in a moment of relief. His reprieves from the deadly pursuit were growing shorter and shorter.

With this in mind, he eyed the entry on the other side of the workspace, where he should be able to sneak into the main manufacturing facility. The next peril before him was to slip into the main production area and snag some food. He grimly made his way to the door, fully aware he had mere days, if not hours, to get out of this place, or this cat-and-mouse chase was going to have a very gruesome ending.

Chapter Sixty-Seven

Sofia

August 13 – 7:02 a.m.

Back pain worked its way into Sofia's dream until she was startled awake. She found herself resting on her side, next to her front door. She strained to get oriented. The light seeping into her unit told her it was morning. She couldn't believe she had fallen asleep. More baffling, she couldn't understand why no one had come for her.

She stood and stretched some of the stiffness out of her back. Looking down, she realized she was still in her dark clothing. She stripped off the outfit and stashed it under her mattress. Dressed in running clothes, she hurried to the bathroom sink and splashed water on her face. She fussed with her hair for a moment, then decided she had bigger worries. She marched over to the front door, prepared herself, and flung it open. She nearly shrieked. Hopping up and down in front of her door was the drone. She couldn't believe Shadow's horrible timing. With her pulse still racing, she forced herself to look up from the bird and over to the bench. The chip was gone! Encouraging, but she needed to be sure.

She grabbed the drone and headed inside. She set the bird aside on the table. Whatever Shadow had to say could wait.

Sofia went for a quick run to get her thoughts straight and to kill time until 8:30 a.m. when Jonathan would typically arrive at work. His failure to show would confirm he was headed south.

After sweating away some of her fears, Sofia headed off to the engineering facilities, where she was soon hurrying through the halls. She gave a peace sign as she passed the technicians. Then she rounded the corner and sighted

Jonathan! He was in his office with a man she didn't recognize.

Instinctively she knew this was not good, but before she could backtrack, Jonathan spotted her and waved her in. Sofia popped her head in the doorway and said, "I don't want to interrupt. I'll catch you later."

"It's alright. The timing's perfect. Let me introduce you to Chief Hill. He's head of security. Chief, this is Sofia Abreo. The chief was asking about you and planned to track you down. Let me save everyone some time and get Sofia a chair." Without waiting for her to object, Jonathan was out the door, flashing his eyes wide at her as he passed. Sofia didn't need the warning. She was already freaked.

Sofia waited near the doorway. The chief did not carry his weight well and craned his neck around to look at her, making it clear he wasn't getting up to greet her, so she forced herself to take the initiative, walked over to him and extended her hand. "Nice to meet you, Chief Hill."

The chief couldn't be bothered to say a word, but he did find it in himself to offer his cold sweaty hand. With pleasantries out of the way, he was content to stare at her with bulging eyes, sending shivers down her spine.

None too soon, Jonathan returned with a chair. He made room on his side of the desk, aware that Mr. Hill was not about to budge.

"Chief Hill was bringing me up to speed on a security breach last night. Apparently, someone broke into Dr. Sur's office and took a very important chip."

Sofia knew this was coming, but still found it difficult to mask the alarm.

Chief Hill assessed her with unblinking eyes, "It's a next-generation chip for the Program. Very important chip." Sofia waited for more, but he merely resumed staring at her. She could only assume he thought his bulging eyes would make her break.

With adrenaline pumping, she let her sarcasm kick in. "Thank you, Chief Hill, for that description. This being my first security briefing, is there anything I should know?"

"Ms. Abreo. I have no intention of briefing you. I—"

"Your late-night deliveries have caught Chief Hill's attention," Jonathan interrupted. "I've let him know I've received a few of these deliveries myself, but he wanted to hear about them directly from you."

"Mr. Pruitt, if you don't mind, I can take it from here. Ms. Abreo, why so much after-hours activity?"

"Package deliveries. Like he said." Sofia pointed at Jonathan. She was extremely confused. He had her on video, her backside flying down the hallway. Yet all he was worried about was her late-night activities?

"Yes, package deliveries," the chief repeated. "Can you tell me why you don't deliver the packages during regular hours?"

Sofia knew she'd have to wing this one on her own. "It's rather personal."

"I don't care."

"Of course you don't. I imagine you know my NAC is defective. Everyone does. It's embarrassing to blunder through crowded office buildings, having to ask for assistance while everyone watches. Some even laugh at me when I can't make it through a simple door. So, yes, I deliver packages at night. The late hours are much better. There aren't as many spectators to pity the broken girl." Her story resonated with enough truth that Sofia even managed to tear up.

Sofia could see satisfaction lurking at the corners of the chief's mouth. The twisted soul seemed to relish the torment she described. "Very well, Ms. Abreo. I'll check out your account of things," he said while laboring to get to his feet. As he walked away, he added, "I expect I'll be following up with both of you real soon."

Jonathan turned to Sofia. "Would you mind getting the door?"

The second the door clicked shut, Sofia asked, "Why didn't he haul me away?"

Jonathan ignored the question. "You should have aborted the mission when something went wrong. Let's take a minute to review the list of things that went wrong. You were detected going into the doctor's office. You—"

"Only because the door was latched. It was supposed to be open!"

"Sometimes plans go wrong," Jonathan continued. "I checked the recordings. One of the janitors noticed the door wasn't latched and fixed it. The point is, you were supposed to abort if the plan went wrong. Instead, you got identified and recorded. Best part was watching you wave to the crew as you fled the building." He let that sink in.

Sofia realized why she hadn't been hauled off yet. If Jonathan knew something about her activities and no one else did, then he had done something. "What did you do? Why am I still free?"

"Same reason I'm being watched. I told you I have access to the security system. I deleted a few detections and recordings last night. I couldn't hide the deletions, but I'm a good enough programmer to cover my tracks."

Then it clicked. Sofia had to force herself not to ask, "How good of a programmer?" Jonathan was the programmer Shadow hinted was in bed with the general! She assumed Jonathan was covering for her in front of Chief Hill. In reality, the charade had been to cover that she had stumbled on Jonathan meeting with the chief. Of course, Jonathan hadn't been hauled away. Nor would she, as long as they didn't figure she had caught onto the fact that she had unwittingly done their bidding. She had stolen a chip from Dr. Sur! What an idiot!

So who had helped her with the theft? Someone had arranged for the chip to be on the desk. Chief Hill! He even remained in his office to make sure all went well. He must have laughed his ass off over the noise she made coming and going. No wonder he walked to the door yet didn't open it. It played to his sadistic appetite to give her a good scare.

And Dr. Sur's locked door made sense. Jonathan knew she would still go forward with the theft. Now, if someone needed to take a fall, she was busted every way possible.

Sofia averted her eyes to her lap, trying to look remorseful, but desperately trying to hide the shock. Jonathan had played her. She must have been an easy target. He was a friend when she had no friends. She stole Dr. Sur's chip!

She needed to get out of here without giving herself away. "I'm sorry, Jonathan. I've put you in jeopardy. Is it just a matter of time before security figures everything out?"

"They know there aren't too many programmers with my skills. But there are a few."

"Did they recover the chip?"

"No," Jonathan replied without enthusiasm. "I have it."

She wanted to ask where. Stealing it back would go a long way to recovering the situation. "Isn't that a good thing?" she instead asked.

"Sofia, I'm the one who's supposed to deliver the chip down south. Security is watching me twenty-four/seven. It's not getting delivered."

"I blew it, I know. But what do we do about Talon? We can't give up on him," she insisted, scrambling to keep up the pretense.

She glanced up to see Jonathan's look was grim. She acknowledged he was a better actor than her. "I'm kind of out of ideas," he said. "Look, this chip had to be delivered down south tonight. That's not happening. Talon's going to have to hang in there until we can come up with another plan."

That was it? He could do a better job of portraying concern for Talon. She was certainly concerned. Jonathan's ruse could be based on a half-truth—the truth being that Talon could really be in danger, but Jonathan wasn't going to help.

Any rescue was up to her. What did Jonathan want with that chip, anyway? If she got her hands on it, could she use it as leverage to rescue Talon? Stealing the chip from Dr. Sur, even if Jonathan had her do the dirty work, meant he had wanted it badly. She would have to give this more thought.

She again peeked at Jonathan to get a read. He was fixated on her. He expected her to push back. Sadly, he knew her well. She would never give up on Talon or leave without a plan, but now, staying wasn't an option. She was starting to sweat, certain he could read her every thought. She had to get out while selling him on her insistence they get back on track.

"I'm not giving up. I'm coming back with a plan," she said lamely, heading for the door. Acting was not her calling. She exited, fully aware Jonathan hadn't been fooled. Chief Hill and his security goons would be coming for her.

Chapter Sixty-Eight

Sofia

August 13 – 10:12 a.m.

ofia fled to her apartment and locked the door, as if that would keep all the world's evil at bay. She was traumatized by the prospect of being dragged out of her little haven, leaving Talon to fend for himself.

She stood in the middle of the room, taking in the studio, deliriously hoping she would stumble on some brilliant solution. Her eyes flitted past her small table, then returned to the mechanical bird resting there. Shadow had been a giant disappointment. Why hadn't he come clean about his identity? What was he hiding? Probably that he was aligned with those trying to take out Talon. Had he been sharing bits of information in an attempt to play her? Was he no better than Jonathan?

Sofia walked over to the table and grabbed the bird. The sight of the note stoked the fury that was smoldering inside. She was sick of being used. It was time to stop being so stupid! She tore the note away from the leg and began ripping it to pieces. Her fury burst into flames as she ravaged the note, turning it into no more than confetti.

Not feeling one bit of relief, her anger turned to tears. Who was she fooling? Blaming Shadow wasn't solving a thing. She couldn't let her fears rule her. She wiped the moisture from her face, put aside the feelings of helplessness, and forced herself to think of actions she could take.

The first thought was to escape. With a little help from her shiny ball, she could engineer her way out of this place. She would escape and go after Talon! Of course, it would help to know where he was.

She had been trying to solve the location riddle for as long as she'd been here. She felt like she was back in elementary school, left out of the secret whispering across all the lips around her. Countless people at this facility knew where the Center was hidden. So far none had chosen to bring her into their confidence. Not even her 'best friend' Jonathan.

Who could she approach? Well, if Jonathan was the bad guy, then didn't it make his victim, the ever-quirky Dr. Sur, someone she could trust? That was ironic, but most likely true. What was that about 'the enemy of your enemy is your friend'? It seemed right, plus she didn't have a lot of options. She also had information about a stolen chip to trade. She probably wouldn't lead with Jonathan's theft because, well, she did play a bit of a role in that effort.

Chapter Sixty-Nine

Talon

August 13 – 11:33 a.m.

The avatar paced back and forth in front of the workstation, spewing every threat known to humankind. Talon brushed off the threats, unable to bring himself to care. Recent events had put matters into perspective. Supervisor's avatar raging away? Annoying. A Neanderthal stalking his every move? Terrifying! The worst was knowing he would have to face that terrifying threat today.

Talon was more confident than drawing his next breath that Letcher Mercer would be lurking outside the exit door when the shift was over. And he had been unable to formulate a plan to avoid the confrontation. He had thought about tricking Letcher by exiting through the main entryway, but to achieve this, he would have to enter the main production area by passing through a locked door with countless witnesses waiting on the other side. His secret would be blown.

He could only guess what the warden would do once alerted. Surely, he would eliminate the sanctuary offered by the chain-link fences? And that move would prove to be child's play compared to the treacherous plans that would follow. No, confronting the boogeyman in broad daylight was better than forfeiting all escape when darkness fell.

He resigned himself to confronting Letcher in mere hours, but he wasn't willing to accept this as the new normal. This malevolent hellhole of a labor camp had already pushed him to the brink of what he could withstand. Talon vowed, one way or another, this would be his final encounter with Letcher.

Chapter Seventy

Sofia

August 13 – 1:03 p.m.

Sofia stared at Chief Hill's office as she crept down the hall. His windows were blacked out, but that could change in a split second. Any sign of life and she would take off. She crept past the chief's office, eyes never leaving his door, when she collided with a pane of glass. Dr. Sur's door opened.

True to their established routine, the doctor immediately started waving at her, only this time to go away.

"I wouldn't barge in if it wasn't important," she said, trying to recover from the unexpected entry.

"Did you get caught again?"

Looking at his desk, where the chip had sat the night before, she said, "No, actually, I didn't, but that's another story."

"Oh, good. Then please sit down and tell me what I can do for you?"

"You can help me save Talon!" she blurted out.

Seeing the doctor's eyes expand till they looked like they might bust his lenses, she gently sat down, telling herself to go more slowly. "I've been corresponding with Shadow. He told me that he stole firmware from UCSC that he placed in a handheld used to program Talon's NAC."

Judging by the blood vessels now etched across the whites of his eyes, she was still moving too quickly. She couldn't help it. She was certain any second he was going to insist she leave.

"Miss Abreo—"

"No. Talon is in real trouble, and I can back this up," she interrupted, "I'm quite certain a powerful general has it in for him and this general has planted key people at this facility to do his bidding. In fact, Shadow has shared some damning details about these traitors with me.

"Miss Abreo, I—"

"And I think Jonathan is the key traitor amongst them. Just last night—"

"Stop! Ms. Abreo! Stop! Jonathan isn't working with the general. Your traitor is me!"

Sofia sat up straight in her chair, then slowly raised to her feet, too stunned to speak and unable to look away from the man before her. He kept his hands folded on his desk, and while he didn't look down in shame, his face sagged like a droopy dog. "You can trust everything Jonathan told you is true," he continued, "Everything. He's an honest man."

Sofia backed up around her chair, still unwilling to take her eyes off him. Then, thinking how she had been prepared to throw Jonathan to the wolves, she wondered if one monster knows not to turn its back on another.

"I'm not an honest man," the doctor carried on as she forced herself to turn toward the door. "You would be wise to believe me now, though. Our conversation has been streaming live to General Stafford. The best we can hope for is that he has other priorities. But he will watch this and when he does, there will be no hiding for either of us. Yet it is Talon who will suffer the most for this."

Sofia felt every last spark snuffing out as she stumbled toward the door.

Chapter Seventy-One

The Warden

August 13 – 1:14 p.m.

The warden knocked and opened the office door. He didn't make it a habit to visit the offices of his underlings, and he certainly didn't need to worry about socially acceptable behavior. He made the rules in his domain.

The numerous handguns and rifles decorating the walls captured his attention. His eyes stopped on what must be an AR-15. He had never held one, but he had read about them. They were quite the killing machine when that type of thing was a part of everyday life. "So, none of these work?" he asked.

"Nope. All the firing pins have been removed," Chief Gorman replied.

"Too bad. One shot could remove a big headache of mine."

"Are you talking about Russit?"

The warden turned to the chief, who was seated at the small conference table. "You figured it out, did you?"

"The fact that you used me?"

The warden's lips turning up was his only response.

"Well, you might want to have a seat. I'm going to show you something you might not find as amusing."

The warden remained standing at the opposite side of the table, making it clear he didn't plan to stay long.

"Very well." Gorman clapped his hands together and a 3-D image of a doorway appeared in the middle of the table. "This is an image from inside the tracer production facility. We're looking at the door that exits into the yard."

"Fascinating," the warden said dryly.

Gorman twirled his index finger above his head and the image came to life, with the door shooting open, two people scrambling through the doorway, and the last one slamming the door shut behind them. Seconds later, they heard another person trying to force their way through the same door.

"In case you're thinking the door is defective and this was a one-time thing, you may want to look at another video taken this very morning."

The warden slowly sank into the chair before him. "Play it."

Chapter Seventy-Two

Sofia

August 13 – 1:31 p.m.

Sofia dashed into her apartment to collect essentials. She didn't have a plan, but she knew she couldn't stay here. As she threw clothes into a bag, she tried to remember exactly what she said and who she had compromised. Dr. Sur was screwed for certain. The general couldn't be pleased with the doctor confessing his ties to him.

Jonathan was in trouble as well. Would the general realize Dr. Sur had cut her off to stop Jonathan from being linked to the chip theft? Regardless, he had been protecting Jonathan and the general would want to know why.

After laying bare the depth of Shadow's knowledge, Sofia was certain the general would double his efforts to capture him. Would he realize Shadow was close by?

She had really done a number on Talon as well. Jonathan had conveyed earlier attempts by the general to capture Talon and possibly kill him. From the general's position as head of program security, he unquestionably viewed Talon as a threat. The general didn't need more reasons to focus on Talon, but she had given them to him anyway.

Was there anyone close to her she hadn't put in jeopardy? Was there any plan she hadn't destroyed?

"Come and get me!" she screamed. She certainly deserved whatever the universe dished out to her, but those around her did not. She had triggered an avalanche that was certain to crush all who had the recent misfortune of encountering her. They would be easy targets for the general, and likely, few would see him coming.

That was it! She would set about alerting everybody. That would be the basis of a new plan. Her plan. Forget delivering the chip. After all, what could a chip do? And who would deliver it? Not Jonathan. Not Shadow. His "I have no name, trust me just the same" pitch wouldn't win anyone over.

She would start by notifying Jonathan, hopefully getting to him before Dr. Sur did. Then she would get a note off to Shadow. No, she had to assume she was watched, which meant launching the bird from inside this prison would not be a good idea. She would escape, then warn Shadow. After that, alert Talon, even though his whereabouts were still beyond her grasp. Better still, she would rescue Talon! She would track down her father and insist he use his connections to find Talon and get him back. Just like that, she had a plan.

Only, it was a crappy plan. She knew she was lying to herself. She should have trusted Jonathan, but alas, she hadn't. She had no hope of carrying her plan out, but looking over at her bed, she at least had something to stop her from crawling under the covers.

Her worthless plan in her head, Sofia started for the door, when she heard her Cube announce a call. "Answer on display," she commanded reflexively. Seconds later an elderly lady with glasses peered into her studio. "Can I help you?" Sofia asked.

The magnified eyes looked Sofia up and down before responding, "No. I think it may be you that needs help. I'm working the front desk and there's a CID officer here to see you."

"Seriously?" Sofia somehow thought she had more time! Now she had no choice but to run. Hoping to buy herself time to get away, she said, "Alright. Give me a moment and I'll be right there."

Then a new face entered the display, saying, "Hurry up. I don't have all day."

Shocked, Sofia ran out the door without saying another word.

Chapter Seventy-Three

Rani

August 13 - 1:45 p.m.

Rani had waited for less than two minutes before she heard rapid footsteps. She turned to see a gangly, but pretty girl launch herself at her, wrapping Rani in her arms.

"Hey. Wow ... how you doing?" Rani asked, completely caught off guard by the fierce hug she was receiving. Rani and Sofia had never been close, with Rani being new to the force and both having little opportunity to connect, but she made no attempt to pull away. The thought of Sofia being exiled from all her loved ones was heartbreaking. A warm embrace was the least she could give.

"Can we go talk somewhere? Private?" Sofia asked.

"Of course," Rani replied and she led them off to the visitor parking, amazed at how quickly Sofia turned an official visit into a cherished visit with a friend. Rani would do her best to be a friend.

They sank into the front seats of her police SUV.

"Engage lockdown mode," Rani commanded.

"Lockdown confirmed," came the reply.

"I hope we don't interfere with any electronics around here, but our conversation should be very private. All signals in and out'll be jammed." She swiveled to face Sofia. "You OK?"

"No," Sofia said, "I've screwed up." She went on to fill Rani in about the dangers Talon faced and the attempts to help. When Sofia got around to talking about how she had botched the plan, Rani struggled to make out the details as Sofia buried her face in her hands and sobbed out most of the words until Rani ended up holding her, wishing she could warn everyone about the general and deliver the chip herself.

She knew that wasn't even remotely possible, though. Not only did she lack the skills for such a mission, but she doubted she could go off-grid to carry out such stealth activities. A missing police officer would attract attention.

Sofia's confession, especially about the dangers Talon faced, forced her to ask, "What do you know about your dad's role in all of this?"

"My dad? My dad's involved?"

"Have you talked to him?"

"No, actually. Not since his visit during the community outreach thing. We had a bit of a falling out."

"Mind telling me about it?"

Rani saw Sofia's eyes widen. "I asked my father to find Talon and make sure he was safe. He said he wasn't here to talk about Talon, and I ended up pleading with him until he screamed at me. He yelled I was never to mention Talon again. I can't remember my father ever being so angry."

"So what did you do?"

"I walked away. My mom tried to come after me but he held her back. I glanced back to see her struggling to break free. It crushed me. I guess I refused to think about it until now. Wait! You don't think he plans to *harm* Talon, do you?"

"I don't know. I just don't know. Like you, I've seen some firsts from your father that I can't explain. He's not himself."

They sat quietly, lost in their thoughts. Rani knew she'd made matters worse for an already distressed Sofia by coming here, looking for information. Maybe her purpose for visiting could wait.

"Are you here to help Talon?" Sofia asked as if reading her thoughts.

"I would like to help, but no, that's not why I came."

"Then why?"

Rani thought back on her conversation with Sage. She sighed, deciding she couldn't live with any more lies. "Shadow. I came to find out if he's contacted you."

"What would make you think Shadow would come looking for me?"

"Because if he couldn't find Talon, he'd probably turn to you."

"I don't understand."

"I need you to keep this confidential. I *mean* it. Can I trust you?"

"Of course!" Sofia blurted.

"OK, right … Well, there's no good way to say this, so … Talon's brother is alive. Shadow is Wilder."

Sofia gasped. "What?! H-how do you know this?"

"JT told me. They live in the same fugitive community."

"JT? What the …?" Sofia shook her head, then suddenly made for the door handle. "What time is it?"

"Wait, I need to … disengage lockdown mode …"

"Disengaged."

"… It's almost two. Why? What's going on?"

"I have a lot to tell you about Shadow—but not now. You might have rescued the mission. Rani, you're the best!" Sofia planted a kiss on her cheek and took off running.

Insanity! Rani reckoned she was normally the one that people had a hard time following, but Sofia had set a new standard. She chuckled, not really sure whether she had accomplished what she had come for.

Chapter Seventy-Four

Talon

August 13 – 2:36 p.m.

"Hang back as we get to the door, will you? I don't want you to be near me when I leave."

"Talon ..."

"Please, Espar. If I know you're out of the way, I can take care of myself better."

"Alright ... I understand. Be careful."

Talon watched the last person in front of them disappear out the door. He couldn't get a good look at what was outside as the door shut automatically, but he knew Letcher would be there. He looked at Espar to confirm she was far enough away, then he turned back to the door and kicked it open. A mangy-looking brute abruptly stepped back to avoid the swinging door, and Talon made as if to shoot out the opening.

Letcher turned to cut off Talon's escape, only for Talon to spring in the other direction, pushing on Letcher's turned shoulder to keep him off balance as he skirted past. He had just escaped the troll's orbit when Espar came flying out the door behind him, crashing straight into the beast. Letcher barely stumbled. Getting a good grip on Espar, he sent her tumbling until she lay sprawled out in front of the gathering crowd.

Talon hardly registered the crowd before darting back into harm's way. He caught Letcher turning toward him and landed a punch in the solar plexus, then let his momentum carry him past. Except this time Letcher managed to stick a foot out, spilling Talon to the desert floor. Then, quicker than a big man should be able to move, Letcher was on top of him.

Talon tried to cover up, but the punches started landing, first knocking the wind out of him and then connecting with his skull until his ears were ringing. He was fighting to remain conscious, certain he was dead if he didn't, when Letcher suddenly tumbled off him. Rolling onto his side, Talon witnessed something he had no right to expect: one man after another lunged at Letcher, determined to take him down. Letcher sent them flying like a grizzly bear swatting away a pack of dogs, but the men didn't give up, and they soon had the big man squirming on the ground, screaming with rage.

Talon tried to clear his head and join the battle, but getting to his knees proved challenging enough until a pair of massive hands clutched him from behind and easily placed him on his feet. Wobbling to keep his balance, Talon found Blunt angrily assessing him. "You'll live, kid. Now get out of here."

Talon looked around for Espar. "The girl's fine, kid. Get," Blunt said, giving him a nudge and sending him stumbling off.

The shimmering heat waves left Talon disoriented as he hunted for a place to recover, with each step becoming harder than the last until he crumpled to the ground. He started to rise, but sat back down. Now might be the time to call it quits, he figured. Sure, Letcher might be out of the game today, but he would be back tomorrow. And the day after that. There wasn't any place to go. The best he could hope for was to delay a fate that would inevitably catch up to him. He wasn't one to give up easily, but he was tired, beat up, and feeling the grind of losing battle after battle for months on end. He was ready to lie down and surrender if that would gain him a much-needed break from the continual struggle.

Then he thought of another time he was on the end of a losing fight and the person who was there to pick him up. Sofia ... she would be so angry with him!

Was she even safe at this moment? For all he knew, she was faced with a similar struggle to survive.

Talon heaved himself off the ground, ashamed he had thought of quitting. He staggered between buildings on the way to the perimeter wall, telling himself he would make it for Sofia.

***

A splash of water to the face brought Talon awake. He looked up to see a hulking mass standing between him and the night sky.

Out of the corner of his eye, he could see the buildings to each side of him, letting him know he hadn't made it to the wall. So much for making it for Sofia.

"Kid, are you looking to get killed?"

Blunt!

Talon sat up, trying to understand what had happened. It was growing dark. He must have passed out. "Did you splash water on me?"

"Want some?" Blunt asked, waving a hydro flask in front of him.

Talon took the flask and drank greedily from it until he had an urge to throw up.

"Easy, kid."

Talon watched as Blunt's eyes examined him. He tried to sit up a little straighter but quickly slumped back down.

"You've weathered a lot more than anyone thought possible. Have you noticed you've got a bit of a fan club growing around you? And what you did for Espar back there was pretty decent of you."

Surprised by these words, Talon found the strength to proudly sit up straight.

"The problem is I don't think you've yet committed to saving yourself."

Blunt was wrong, but Talon didn't see the point in arguing, especially with his head still swimming.

Blunt looked him over a bit more, shaking his head. "Well, kid. Get some rest. I've got you. I got a feeling tomorrow is going to be a big day for you."

Talon understood Blunt was trying to offer more words of encouragement, but he grinned at how prophetic those words would prove to be. He had reached his limit. He could see his co-workers helping him keep Letcher at bay for a day or two, but then what? As he lay down and his eyes began forcing their way closed, Talon told himself that tomorrow, no matter the consequences, he would find a way out of this place ... he just hoped he'd make it out alive.

Chapter Seventy-Five

Sofia

August 13 - 2:43 p.m.

Sofia had scrambled to send off a note to Wilder and now she was on her way to what she considered her "sad place." Jonathan had agreed to meet, leading her to believe Dr. Sur had yet to speak with him. She promised herself to come clean about the trouble she had unleashed, even though this would not help her cause. It was the right thing to do before she set about convincing Jonathan to send the chip down south with Wilder.

The feel-good moment she got from making the right decision lasted about two seconds, which was the time it took to clear the trees and see Jonathan and Dr. Sur sitting at the edge of the display. She stopped. This was not good.

She took a few steps back into the trees, buying herself time to observe. They looked relaxed, certainly not adversarial. Did this mean they were in league with each other? It didn't take long for Jonathan and Dr. Sur to see her hanging back. They began wandering over, flooding her senses with the need to take flight. She fought against this impulse, stepping out toward them instead.

"You know why this display makes me sad?"

"Yes, I think so," Dr. Sur replied.

"You do?"

"I think it's because you can't make the display work and it reminds you that your chip is defective."

Sofia was astounded. Dr. Sur was dead right. The water coming out of the spout was triggered by the presence of people, but only those who could be detected. The mother whale randomly spouted water every ten to twenty minutes when people were within range. This was a playful part of the display that was anything but fun for Sofia. The display had been added to Sofia's list of things that weren't right with her world. "I didn't think you would guess that ... ever."

"Ironically, I helped design the display, and I can't make it work either," Dr. Sur said with a melancholy smile.

"I don't get it."

"Sofia, I'm a disconnect. My chip didn't program ... most likely due to my age."

Sofia was really confused. "Then why are you allowed to leave this place?"

"I'm not. Security would stop me if I tried. I don't even have input on security personnel. Chief Hill was recommended by Mr. Simmons, who likes to keep a close eye on me. Mr. Simmons even had the perimeter security system reinforced with sensors and cameras to make sure I didn't try to mask my chip and slip out. I'm effectively a prisoner."

"Then why do you head up research and development for the Program?" Sofia asked, feeling completely off balance.

"Let's step over by this tree," Jonathan said.

"Good point. No need to get soaked," Sofia acknowledged.

When they were under the foliage behind the circular path, Jonathan corrected her. "It's for security. Where we're standing is out of sight of any of the buildings. I think I already told you the exhibit will block any attempts to listen in on our conversation. We should be good."

"Thanks, Jonathan. Sometimes I forget," Dr. Sur said. "Sofia, I don't want to come across as making excuses for my behavior. Allowing General Stafford to tap into private conversations is inexcusably selfish. Bottom line, the general threatened to ship me off to the Center. I chose to come out of retirement and do his bidding to save my own skin. It's terrible, I know—I've caused so much harm."

Jonathan jumped to his defense. "That's not completely accurate. You initially came out of retirement for the wrong reasons, true. Except you came clean with me early on. Then we both decided to try to turn the tables. If you hadn't cooperated to some extent, he would have simply replaced you with a more willing agent. Better to see if we could slow the general's efforts and glean insights into his ambitions."

Things began to fall into place for Sofia. "That's why you acted so odd every time we met. You couldn't just come out and say things like, 'Sofia, take the silver ball.'" She saw the doctor in a whole new light. "And the reason for having me train to sneak around? It couldn't have been to steal the chip."

"No, you're right. It was for show. I wanted the general, who arranged to have you located here, to think I was turning you into a good soldier that might one day serve his cause. I had no idea it would prove useful to *us*."

Sofia felt used, indignant even, until she remembered all she had done to those around her. She turned to Jonathan. "I owe you a big apology. Did Dr. Sur fill you in?"

"He did," Jonathan admitted.

"Then you can't think much of me."

"I'm disappointed, yes. I consider us friends, and I expect friends to have some trust in me."

"We're ... friends? Oh, I know I have issues, but don't give up on me ..." Sofia pleaded.

"I won't pretend all is good, but I'm not giving up on you either. Let's agree to revisit this later, OK? Right now, I think it would be a good time to tell us why you wanted to meet."

"I guess so," Sofia said, struggling to put aside the open wounds. "I'm hoping it's not too late to go forward with your plan."

"The plan to send the chip down south? What did you have in mind?"

"We use Shadow!"

"Shadow? We don't even know who he is!" Jonathan exclaimed.

"I do. And I want to tell you who he is because I'm extremely confident you'll trust him. But first, I need to make sure he'll be safe. I think you can respect my renewed commitment to watch after my friends," Sofia said, smiling sheepishly.

"Which means?" Jonathan prodded.

"Which means we need to share. You need to know about Shadow. I need to know what we would be getting him into."

Jonathan looked at Dr. Sur, who chuckled. "You said she was sharp. I think she's driving a fair bargain."

"So where do we start?" Sofia asked.

"Would it be alright if we start with Shadow?" Dr. Sur asked. "We need to know if we can move forward."

"Understood. No one's looking to turn him in for his past antics, right?"

Dr. Sur knew the question was directed at him. "I've heard a bit about his exploits. He'll get no trouble from me."

Sofia was surprised how quickly she could go from having no trust to absolute trust in Dr. Sur. "Very well. Shadow is Talon's brother—Wilder Russit."

"Well, damn. How long have you been holding that back?" Jonathan asked.

"Learned about it today."

"Who from?"

"A Ridge Crest officer."

"Sounds like a source we can trust," Jonathan said. "I'm sold."

"I'm on board," Dr. Sur chimed in. "Tell us what you want to know."

Chapter Seventy-Six

Sofia

August 13 - 2:58 p.m.

She wanted to know everything. The big question was where to start. "How is delivering this chip going to help?" Sofia asked. "What's it do?"

"Here's the simple answer: in the right host, it will program Talon's NAC," Dr. Sur responded.

"I thought Talon's chip was already programmed?"

"It was. Talon was given an advanced program."

This didn't make sense to Sofia. "The program doesn't work. It didn't even register. And even if it did work, he's done, right? His NAC can't be programmed again."

Jonathan saw her frustration building and shifted his attention to Dr. Sur. "Maybe it would be best to give the whole story on Talon's chip ... and Sofia's."

"*My* chip?"

"Yes, well," Dr. Sur began. "Sofia, forget what you've learned about NACs for a moment. Not all are created equal. Yes, over the last twenty years, the chips and their software have been stable. And to win public trust, everyone can count on chips being inserted at birth and programming to take place prior to age sixteen. No programming after that. But behind the scenes it's different. The chips and their software are constantly changing. New features are tested all the time."

"New features ... OK. Like what?"

"I'll come to that in a moment."

"Right, and you do all this where?" she asked, looking off into the horizon.

"I don't do this. Our facilities handle some new readers and other supporting infrastructure. Maybe even a software module or two," he added. "Most of the leading-edge R&D happens elsewhere."

"So, you have help. You aren't going to tell me who or where they work, are you?"

"No. It's not that we don't trust you. But just like Jonathan tried to protect you earlier by keeping you in the dark about this mission, there are many others that must be protected from General Stafford. Not to scare you, but I don't know what the general is willing to do to get information in the event he captures you."

That was ... alarming. "Right ... OK ... not to get too far off track, but I imagine the general has thousands that work for him. Shouldn't we have already been bagged, tagged, and bundled up somewhere for him to um, torture?"

"Fortunately, it doesn't work that way. He likes to keep a low profile. Making visible people disappear isn't so easy. Even if he's viewed this morning's conversation, he'll take his time putting together plans. You and I aren't going anywhere, and Jonathan is still largely unknown, but ..."

"But what?"

"We can't say the same for Wilder and Talon," Jonathan said. "Wilder's isolation makes him a lot easier to target. We'll make sure he's well warned before we set him on his way. Talon, we know is at risk. No question the general already has plans underway for him. Multiple plans. I'm not sure if he'll move up their timing, but the outcome is most likely sealed."

Sofia thought to ask what he meant by 'sealed,' but with a shiver creeping up her spine, she decided against it. She looked off to the distance again, thinking she needed to stay focused on getting the immediate mission underway. "So, our NACs ..."

"Yes, the NACs. Your Ridge Crest community, or at least some in your town, has been part of an experiment," Dr. Sur picked up. "*Unauthorized* and *unknown* to all but a few, the experiment was carried out by some of those involved in the initial development of the Program."

"They feared the Program might one day be used against the public it was designed to serve," Jonathan added.

"Right," Dr. Sur said. "Their solution was to give people the ability to continually alter their programming to overcome any schemes to enslave the masses. This is the reason you, Talon, and Espar Crashan have reprogrammable NACs."

"Programmable? So ... are you saying my chip can be fixed?"

Jonathan shook his head. "Unfortunately, no. We believe you and Espar have a defect unique to this experimental batch of chips."

"I get the feeling you both know what that defect is," Sofia said, again looking off toward the horizon.

"Yes. The chips embedded in everyone are designed to communicate at a specific UHF frequency. They are powered up when a reader broadcasts to them," Dr. Sur explained. "Your chip most likely had a production flaw where the built-in antenna was damaged. It's inefficient at picking up the broadcasting frequency. This means that if you have a weak reader broadcasting a signal, such as in the whale exhibit, it won't be able to power on your chip and identify you. The readers used in the building tend to be stronger, which enables them to intermittently power up your chip. Am I making any sense?"

"I think so. So, does the silver ball affect my NAC's antenna?"

Dr. Sur looked at Jonathan and raised his eyebrows. "Very sharp. The ball detunes your antenna, making it even harder for it to communicate with readers."

Another quick glance into the distance. "Got it," Sofia stated before a much more pressing concern dawned on her. "How big is this defect? Will a lot of my friends be suffering this?"

"I don't know for certain, but I doubt it. I'm not privileged to how many of these chips are out there or if they're even contained within Ridge Crest. The good news is I've been monitoring your town's programming and no new disconnects have surfaced."

Sofia was relieved. "Thanks for that." Sofia looked at Jonathan, who was beginning to pace back and forth. "One more question. What exactly will this program do for Talon?"

"They are some additional enhancements designed to help him escape. Hopefully."

"We really should be going," Jonathan said. "How do we find Wilder?"

Sofia looked up at the sky. "In a few seconds you're going to have your answer. Please don't be angry with me."

As if on cue, a bird swooped down, landing before them. It began hopping up and down. "No, Sofia! You didn't," Jonathan exclaimed as he rushed over and grabbed it.

"I was desperate. I didn't know how much time we had. The note will have his location," she explained. Then steering the conversation away from her latest maneuver, she asked, "Who's going to meet him?"

Jonathan stuffed the drone under his shirt. "I'll be delivering the chip to Wilder, along with instructions."

"And you'll warn him about the position I put him in?"

"The position *we* put him in," Dr. Sur corrected.

"What about security? After last night's circus, they have to be watching you closely."

"I can shake security for a few hours. This, however ..." Jonathan said, looking grimly down at his bulging shirt. "This might be a bigger problem."

Chapter Seventy-Seven

Wilder

August 13 – 3:42 p.m.

Wilder watched the great bear of a man lumber up the dune to where he stood partially shrouded by wisps of fog. Like the marine layer blowing in, Wilder's initial elation at gaining Sofia's trust was being dampened by the distrust spreading over him. Sofia had not been forthcoming about her co-workers, leaving him with little knowledge about the large guy closing in, other than he worked for the Program.

Reaching the wind-scoured top of the dune, the bearded giant reached into his coat, triggering Wilder to assume a defensive position.

"Sorry," the big man said. He smiled. "I brought a peace offering." He extended his hand, revealing the bird.

This offering went a long way toward calming his nerves. Jonathan cautioned him not to fly his bird into the complex again, explaining he would do his best to wipe out any record of its recent flight, but the drone was glowing red hot with their security systems.

He took the warning as another reason to be shed of this place. "Sounds like I should be getting underway. Are we ready to dig into my assignment? And did you arrange transportation?"

"Yes, right," Jonathan replied, visibly forcing himself to change gears. "You're going to be taking my motorbike. I will want it back."

Wilder smirked, ready to make some quip, when Jonathan produced a handheld reader from his coat, saying, "And I'm going to need to read your NAC ID."

"Wait up, big guy! That's not happening!" Wilder exclaimed. This was not the comfort he was seeking. Quite the opposite. No fugitive was eager to share personal information. Certainly not your one-of-a-kind ID. And absolutely not with a Program official.

"Right, right, right. Sorry again. Very insensitive of me. Let's go through the mission and come back to that." Jonathan went on to explain where and when Wilder would enter the compound, where he would drop off the chip, and where he would pick up a special piece of equipment, a tracer. Jonathan even explained how the tracer worked, though Wilder only half listened, still worrying over the suggestion he reveal his ID.

Jonathan then got to the meat of what mattered: how the chip could give Talon the tools to escape and how the tracer could enable him to track Talon, in case all else failed and Wilder felt compelled to go in after his brother.

Getting Talon out was the dream Jonathan was selling him and what brought Jonathan back to his initial demand.

"None of this is possible if you can't get in the Fabrication Center compound, and you're not getting in without giving up your ID. Your ID has to be entered into the controllers that manage the gates."

Wilder was sold on getting into the Center, but not on giving up his ID. "I'm pretty resourceful at finding my way into places," he pointed out. "I'm not so sure using my ID is a must."

Jonathan didn't argue. "Fair enough. Let me tell you what you're up against." He went on to explain the pressure-sensitive mats, the gas chemicals, and the spikes that launched from the walls and gates.

In the end, Wilder surrendered his ID.

Thinking the worst was behind him and eager to be on his way, Wilder was not pleased with Jonathan's parting words.

"Watch your back. The general will be sending Program agents after you. Never question whether people are coming. They will be. It's merely a question of when and where."

Chapter Seventy-Eight

Sofia

August 13 - 6:08 p.m.

"Mom? Why aren't you answering me? Where's Dad?" She had been trying to reach her parents since shortly after her disturbing meeting with Rani. It was late in the evening before her mother finally connected.

Avan slowly turned to face her daughter. She lowered her hands, revealing cheeks streaked with makeup and eyes puffy from tears and lack of sleep. "I'm so sorry."

"Sorry for what, Mama?" Sofia feared the worst.

"Your dad is gone, honey. I don't think he's coming back."

"What? What do mean *gone*?! What happened? Where's he gone to?"

"I don't know. I only know he's not coming back because he told me over and over that I had to tell you he loves you and he's so sorry for the mess he's made." Her mom turned away and her head again fell forward, the sobs returning as the screen went dark.

"Mom? Mama!" Sofia cried out, knowing her mother had disconnected.

Sofia stood in the middle of her room, looking at the blank screen over her bed, almost afraid to think of what might be next. She threw herself down on the unmade bed and drew the covers over her head.

What felt like only seconds later, she clawed herself awake, trying to escape her suffocating dreams. Images of Talon and Wilder being buried alive in some barren place came flooding back. She tried to remind herself that it had only been a dream, but it felt like a warning. With the early morning glow doing little to chase the shadows from the corners of her tiny hovel, she slipped on her running clothes to escape the walls that were closing in. As she entered the walking path and broke into a run, she felt her anxieties keeping pace. It didn't matter if she was asleep or awake, inside or outside, running or standing still, she couldn't find shelter from the problems cascading down upon her.

She finally let reality sink in. It was time to do something. She had supported Jonathan and Dr. Sur's effort. She had every belief Wilder would go toe to toe with the Program if that's what it took to save his brother, but that didn't mean nothing more needed to be done. Sofia saw no reason she should wait for the general to come for her when she could escape and join the fight. Maybe even find and turn her father.

Ready to take action, she set out to find Jonathan and enlist his support.

Chapter Seventy-Nine

Wilder

August 13 – 11:48 p.m.

Brussels sprouts. Rotting, overheated Brussels sprouts. Wilder sat in the pitch-black, cramped quarters trying in vain to ward off the relentless attack on his senses. The fact that he had discovered the source of the attack was no help whatsoever. He had too many memories of gagging down the horrible vegetable when he was a child and his parents thought it was good practice to eat everything on your plate. In the case of sprouts, his parents agreed they were incredibly healthy for growing children, that he would develop a taste for them in time. Sitting in this foul-smelling hot box, Wilder thought his parents couldn't have been more wrong.

The absurd thought of finding another means of escape was beginning to weigh on his mind when a rumble and an abrupt jolt of the compartment told him the time for second-guessing had passed. The delivery truck was departing the Center. He grasped the tracer he had been given, making sure it didn't rattle against the truck bed as the storage compartment bounced and shook every which way.

With the truck getting underway, Wilder realized in disbelief that this assignment had so far been one of his easier ones. The most difficult part had been the initial preparations with Jonathan. Nothing had prepared him to have a Program official ask him to read his chip.

Everything had gone smoothly from there. Using side roads, he had flown the motorbike across the terrain, reaching the Center before 11:30 p.m., when trucks were let in to deliver supplies. It seemed they wanted the compound to have a low profile, preferring deliveries be made after dark.

Darkness had always suited him fine.

Security for the administrative quadrant had been lax. It helped that his ID had been added to the access list, but he had sensed overconfidence, perhaps borne from having the fortress stand secure for so long. He had hitched a ride on the undercarriage of a delivery truck, then made his way to a storage building, where he left the chip and picked up the prototype tracer that had been left for him.

The horrid smell brought him back to the present. He estimated he was well away from the Center by now. At least as far as his nose was going to allow him to go. Fortunately, the old delivery truck was piloted by a driver. Scrambling back to the roll-up door, Wilder released the safety latch and pulled. The door slid up a foot with ease. Perfect. He slammed it back down with a loud bang. When a few seconds ticked by with no reaction, Wilder opened and slammed the door again. A few more times and the truck began to slow.

Opening the door one last time, he seized the tracer and jumped.

Ouch! He had underestimated the speed, causing him to tumble before gaining his feet. Still, no broken bones. And the tracer was intact. He sprinted into the desert night, making it a few hundred yards before looking back at the road.

The truck had stopped. He found his night glasses in his utility bag and slid them on, catching the driver climbing down from the back of the trailer. He proceeded to roll the door closed and latch it, without further investigation, before climbing back into the cab. The old truck was soon rumbling down the road.

Relieved, Wilder wandered off farther into the desert to find a place to rest. Tomorrow he would scout the perimeter of the Center. Looking over the tracer one more time, he decided he would tackle it as well. Jonathan assured him it could be programmed to lock onto Talon, assuming Wilder could get close enough.

Spreading out a ground cover, he lay on his back and tucked his arms behind his head, gazing up at the countless stars. It had become a routine for him to find comfort when he could. Life as a fugitive was often overwhelming. He learned to cope by appreciating opportunities like this to slow things down.

Tomorrow would come soon enough, and it was shaping up to be a challenge. Being so near Talon, it was hard to stay back from that edge where he threw all caution aside. Just one hiccup in their plans and he knew he wouldn't be able to stop himself from going in after Talon.

Chapter Eighty

Sofia

August 14 – 8:29 a.m.

"Good morning," Jonathan said, entering his office, where Sofia was already seated. "Seems my invite was rather timely. You must have something you want to see me about as well."

"How did you know that?" Sofia asked, surprised by his observation.

"I left you a message to stop by. I didn't say when. Yet here you are at 8:30. Oh, and look at that, your legs won't stop bouncing." Jonathan laughed as she tried to restrain all movement. "Go ahead. You go first."

"No, well, OK. You need to help me get out of this place."

Jonathan only appeared mildly caught off guard. "That's quite the request. So, you're planning on going after Talon?"

"First, I'm going to try to find my dad."

"Hmmm. And the effort we have underway isn't doing it for you?"

"I don't see why more can't be done."

Jonathan sat back in his chair, taking his time to think the request through. Sofia knew to wait. "I will admit I wouldn't mind having you out of the way while I deal with the latest messes. It could be a win for both of us."

His words hurt. Sure, she was the one choosing to leave, but she expected him to miss her a little bit—not be relieved by the thought. "What messes?"

"You don't want to know."

"Now I really *do* want to know."

"Very well. Chief Hill is planning to take a good portion of his security force and go south in the next couple of days. I think he's going after Wilder."

"Damn. How did this come about?"

"The security team locked onto Wilder's drone. I went into our system to delete the latest flight data and found someone had already viewed everything. Worse, the drone had accumulated enough particles that it was pretty lit up. The good news is that I can tell Wilder successfully made it in and out of the Center to deliver the chip; the bad news is so can everyone else. Anytime he has the drone on him and he's near the facility, he's fair game."

Sofia sighed, incredulous that things could get even worse. "Have you warned Wilder?"

"Can't. He doesn't have a Cube. He wouldn't accept one for fear of being tracked."

"What about if he's in range of the network?"

"I can see him, but that's about it. The network is designed to block all communications with disconnects. But trust me, I'm trying to devise a way around that. And I'm also trying to cover up any connection that drone made to you, me, and the doctor."

"Oh, no! Jonathan, I'm so sorry. I didn't stop to think I might be putting Chief Hill on your tail."

"I know." His attempt at a smile turned into a grimace. "To be young and full of ideas. I admire that ... and your big heart."

"Uggh. What a disaster. First the general, now security. If I were you, I couldn't get rid of me fast enough." Somedays she wondered why she got out of bed. Embarrassed, she discarded the idea of asking Jonathan to help her dig a hole she could crawl into. "Help me get out of here and I promise not to bother you again. And I'll try my best to set a few things right, starting with my dad."

"That's not happening."

"No?"

"Sofia, I would feel responsible for you. Life as a fugitive isn't easy. Plus, you're part of our team now. You can't abandon us the minute you face adversity."

Sofia nodded her understanding. She understood, but didn't agree ... a very important difference. She thought of her silver ball and wondered if she could get far on foot.

Showing once again he knew how her mind worked, Jonathan said, "I'm not going to ask you to turn over your detuner. It's up to you to decide if you're ready to trust more than yourself."

Chapter Eighty-One

Rani

August 14 - 8:29 a.m.

Another quiet morning at Ridge Crest CID. A few junior officers hung about the office, but everyone of inspiration was gone. Drake's absence would always be missed. In a weird way, so would Jesse's. No one knew until the end that he had gone over the rails. The D.C. bigwigs wouldn't be missed. They departed when the public lost interest and internal affairs moved on to the next sensation. Even her boss had gone AWOL. Not a word from him in days.

The chief's absence got under Rani's skin. What was he up to? Was he off being a hero for the department, as he often professed? Or was he out there somewhere doing evil? She knew she should let it go; she also knew she couldn't. Her job had to have meaning, which meant she needed to know her department was a champion for good. She couldn't look the other way knowing her boss might be the reason Jesse went off the rails or he might be part of the lethal force bearing down on Talon.

It didn't take long for Rani to drift into Gabriel's office. Drift might be the wrong description since the door had been locked. Fortunately, Gabriel had added her to his portal's list of permitted IDs. He had also given her access to his calendar since he wanted her to be able to schedule the staff meetings and other administrative duties. Nothing like being the most junior officer. Pulling up the calendar, she held her breath, hoping he had yet to pass this privilege on to the new hires.

Nope! She was in. Gabriel would soon know she was in his calendar. He would also know she had gone into his office to access it, since he didn't keep his calendar on the network. She never understood why he was so worried about network security, yet freely gave access to her and others. Anyway, she would worry about a cover story later.

"Hi, Rani!" came a call that had her nearly popping out of her skin. Simone poked her head inside the office. "What're you doing?"

Rani realized she just didn't care. "Checking to see what the boss is up to. Do you know?"

"Not a clue," Simone said, stepping around the desk to look over Rani's shoulder.

"Do you really want to be sleuthing around in your boss's office?" Rani asked, momentarily forgetting about the calendar.

"The door was open, and I didn't access his display. I don't know about you, but I'm good."

"You realize you don't have to be the one to unlock his door for the boss to know you were in here."

"Got it. See you later. If the chief asks, I was checking to see what you were doing in his office," she said and headed out the door.

Rani returned her attention to the calendar. Immediately, she was struck by the fact that there was only one entry for all of August. The chief had always been a slave to his calendar and routinely made multiple entries for each day.

Enlarging the calendar, the lone entry read "Board Meeting." It was slated for 1 p.m. on August 16. Two days from now.

"Board Meeting" sounded legitimate. She had no reason to dig further. After all, Gabriel could be watching her every move at this point. Not only her movements within the office but her every probe inside his calendar. She should end it here.

But she wouldn't. Why only one entry? She pointed at the event and snapped her fingers. Might as well go out in style. The response was immediate—and soul crushing. The event notes read "End Tal."

End Tal ...? End *Talon*?

The hell?! It made no sense and yet too much sense. What was once unimaginable was now totally believable.

Rani knew what she needed to do next.

Chapter Eighty-Two

Wilder

August 14 – 10:21 a.m.

The flat, barren desert didn't offer a lot of places to hide. Jonathan told Wilder he had to get within a few hundred yards of Talon's quadrant to make sure the tracer could lock onto him. What Jonathan didn't say was that there wasn't a shrub or a hill within half a mile of the perimeter wall. Plus, there were guard towers that encompassed the complex. The complex perimeter consisted of four walls, each approximately one mile long. Each corner had towers barely protruding above the twenty-foot walls. Between the corner towers, each wall held two additional towers. Twelve towers in total, spaced about a third of a mile apart. It seemed like a big separation, but guards looking out across the flat land below probably wouldn't miss a kangaroo rat approaching within a mile of the place. And if this wasn't enough eyes on the perimeter, Wilder periodically spotted motorcycles taking a spin around the outer walls.

Even worse, drones could be deployed at the whim of the guards. According to Jonathan's sources, there was no outrunning them and their range was essentially limitless. The saving grace was the guards were deathly afraid of using them due to the danger of launching projectiles about the size of bullets that would transmit a video of everything surrounding their flight paths. These "vision bullets" had spectacular capabilities. They were designed to penetrate camouflage mesh, capture 360-degree images, and operate in low-light settings, but they could be nasty: if they hit someone in the wrong place, they could kill. Guards were unwilling to tie their lives to these flying gadgets, fearful they could wind up being stung out.

Still, Wilder wouldn't press his luck with these drones. Nor did he want to mess with the pressure mats surrounding the complex. The perimeter was retrofitted with a special mat, buried eighteen inches under the ground and extending one hundred feet from the wall, designed to identify anything over seventy-five pounds that sported a chip. With the exception of small children and the local wildlife, almost everything fit into that category. Wilder knew he did.

Thinking of all these threats, including the guards, he knew it would be wise to wait for darkness before exploring what he could pick up with his tracer. Of course, knowing what was wise and doing what was wise didn't always go hand in hand. He had no intention of passively observing Talon, hoping he miraculously discovered something about his chip that would lead him to escape; he needed to find a way into the complex, and since picking up subtle details could be the key to success, daylight offered the best scouting.

He circled the perimeter, noting each wall had a gate like the main entry, located about midway between the corners. Further, none of the towers came within 250 yards of these gates. He had expected gate security to be intense. It was not. The workers couldn't scale the high walls and the outside world had no reason to be more than mildly interested in what was going on at the facility. It was, essentially, hiding in plain sight, and he might never have noticed the guard towers were built into the perimeter if not for Jonathan being privy to this information.

Wilder was left surveying the land before him, a safe mile from the complex, wondering how he could extract Talon from the compound. The entry points didn't look promising. He knew the main gate didn't provide direct access to Talon's quadrant, and he doubted the other gates would be more productive, since he hadn't seen any traffic in or out. Thoughts of the outer walls left him queasy. Even if he could scale twenty feet, Jonathan had warned him about the spikes.

He guessed his explosive devices could blow a large hole in one of the walls. Still, this would leave him with the problem of finding Talon and getting away. Security would close in on them long before they could reach his motorcycle and escape.

Wilder reached into his bag of goodies for his field glasses to inspect the desert lands. It didn't take long to discern there were a few crevices that could get him within a couple hundred yards of the complex. One had an outcrop that might also shield him from view. Moving closer was a big gamble. The safe bet was to wait until nightfall. It was also a luxury Wilder didn't have. No one knew when Talon's time would be up.

Chapter Eighty-Three

Talon

August 14 - 1:11 p.m.

A light hanging from the middle of the shop floor began flashing red, signaling it was time to switch workstations. The supervisors insisted the crew cycle from work center to work center to ensure everyone could operate each station and that the stations could be powered down and powered up without glitches. If your station had any issues under your watch, you put your thumb down and waited for the next person to make their way over to you.

The supervisors didn't like this delay. Their avatars were out in full force, screaming and threatening to gas the workers. The crew, quickly bonding over the adversity, didn't flinch. They kept to the routine, quite willing to endure the wrath rather than needlessly risking their lives.

This was the fifth day of operations, and failures were rapidly declining, tremendously accelerating the transition between work centers. Talon waited for the operator behind him to look his way. He flashed a thumbs-up, letting him know everything was good, then turned toward his next station. Henrick, a senior technician, flashed the thumbs-down.

Approaching the station, Talon noted that his co-worker was on edge. Strange. Talon might have expected this from most of the crew, but not Henrick, in his thirties and older than anyone else on the crew. While he wasn't a physically imposing figure, with a wiry build that didn't extend much over five and a half feet tall, his self-assuredness made a big impression on everyone. When all went off the rails in this place, Henrick could be counted on to maintain a calm demeanor. Until this moment. Henrick was visibly sweating while he clenched and unclenched his fists, looking anything but calm.

"I don't know what you want to do, but I'm not sure you should power up the station," he said, regarding the work center as if it were possessed. The station he feared was the paint oven, which consumed tremendous amounts of power as it baked the protective coating in place for all the tracer shell components.

"It seems to be glitching during power-up. When I flipped the switch, the contraption didn't do anything. Then just as I was ready to reset it, the station surged to life."

"Did you report it?" Talon asked.

"I did. So did everyone before me. The supervisors don't care. They say they'll have someone check it out after the shift. Oddly enough, the engineers aren't worried either. Never seen them ignore a power-up glitch. Something's not right here."

Talon had to stop himself from laughing. Nothing had been right about this place since the day he arrived. Whether it was the warden kicking him to the yard, Feist trying to pound him into small pieces, or Letcher trying to finish the work, nothing made sense here.

He could refuse to power up the station, which would get everyone gassed, then probably thrown out into the yard, where he could be nursed back to health by Letcher. Or he could power up the station, hoping it blew up so this whole nightmare would be over.

"Thanks for letting me know. Believe it or not, this is the least of my problems."

Henrick must have thought of Letcher as well, as he was suddenly awkward. "Oh, yeah, right. You sure?"

"I'm sure."

"Well then, good luck," was all Henrick could say as he shuffled off.

Despite the confidence he tried to project, Talon was extremely nervous. A possible glitch at power-up left any sane person on edge. While everything had surge protectors and breakers designed to prevent an overload, the nature of a prototype manufacturing line was that these safeguards failed, like everything else.

Talon stood in the middle of his station, looking anew at the layout. Off to the side of the hardback chair was the entrance to the oven. A two-inch-thick heat-resistant glass panel shielded him from the oven's heat. He was certain it wouldn't shield him from an explosion.

Talon looked over at the work centers adjacent to him, perhaps fifty feet away. Henrick peered back, making no attempt to mask his concern. With the amount of power feeding into the oven, Talon hoped the guy was beyond the blast radius. Henrick continued to stare, making Talon realize he needed to move. He gave the technician a thumbs-up and slid into the ill-fated chair. With his weight being detected, all he needed to do was say a couple of magic words to get the things underway. "Station on," Talon finally whispered.

Nothing happened. The conveyor didn't move. The oven LED, which should be signaling a heat ramp up, didn't turn green. And the station display remained black.

"Station on," Talon repeated louder. Crickets …

He began counting to himself, which he often did when he was nervous. If he reached a hundred, he would move away from the station. This secret pact with himself was the only way he could find the nerve to stay. At twenty-five, he decided he would only wait until he reached seventy-five. When he reached forty, he figured sixty would do. At the count of fifty … damn it! He launched himself out of his chair.

His vision went slate black as bright-white letters spelling "PROGRAMMING COMPLETE" invaded the darkness. He fell back into his chair; certain he was having a stroke.

Slowly his surroundings returned, and the letters faded as the station sprang to life. He stood up, looking around, struggling to process what had happened. Everyone appeared focused on their stations, oblivious to his plight.

After a few minutes of standing in place, questioning his sanity, an avatar blinked to life in front of him. A very angry-looking man with twitchy eyes barked at him, "Are you bored, Mr. Russit?"

Before Talon could answer, the lettering returned, this time only superimposed across his field of vision: "SHUTDOWN SUPERVISOR AVATAR?"

Ignoring his supervisor's question, Talon replied, "Yes," and the avatar vanished!

Talon, ever the geek, had read about chip implants restoring vision by stimulating the visual cortex. Was his NAC capable of doing the same?

Within seconds the avatar blinked back to life, with his enraged boss saying, "did you say 'yes'? Am I boring you now?"

At the same time, the lettering reappeared: "SHUTDOWN SUPERVISOR AVATAR?"

His anxiety spiked even further. He had two sets of questions coming his way and if he wasn't careful, a very pissed-off super might be provoked into gassing everyone in sight.

"Well?" the avatar demanded.

"No!"

The lettering disappeared but was quickly replaced: "ASSUME SUPERVISOR IDENTITY?"

This was too good to pass up. Relegating his supervisor to background noise, he enthusiastically answered "Yes" at the same time his boss's latest angry question hit home—"Are you messing with me?"

Oh shit! His supervisor had no way of knowing his answer wasn't intended for his ears. Talon stood frozen in place, looking at the avatar, waiting for all hell to break loose. Only the avatar didn't move or make a peep. Talon barely breathed, having no intention of breaking their standoff, that was until he noticed the previously twitchy eyes patiently fixed on him. Unable to resist, Talon waved his hand in front of the avatar, only to watch as the avatar mimicked his movement. Intrigued, he stuck out his tongue ... the avatar did the same.

Unbelievable! He had hijacked his super's avatar! The celebration by his inner nerd was cut short when he detected a strange, sickly smell and crashed to the ground.

Chapter Eighty-Four

Wilder

August 14 – 1:33 p.m.

Move! Come on, move!

Wilder was hunkered down behind a small rock formation, less than two hundred yards from the Center's outer wall. He glared at the tracer screen, waiting for the blinking red dot to move just a fraction in any direction along the screen. He had been confident just ten minutes ago that he had connected to Talon. Now he wasn't so sure.

Desperate to see if he had screwed something up, Wilder hit the "off" icon on the tracer screen and popped open a small cover on the back of the display, exposing the main chip. Jonathan specifically programmed this chip to lock onto Talon's ID, an ID he obtained by configuring a station to search for the one Neuro-Activated Chip that repelled all efforts to engage. Jonathan had warned him it would be hard to stay locked on to Talon since his NAC was programmed to avoid detection. That turned out to be a major understatement.

It had taken him over two hours to get anything to show up on the display. When he finally did, he ended up with a blinking dot that wasn't moving. The dot wasn't supposed to be blinking: a solid red dot for Talon, a green dot for anyone else. Nothing had been said about a blinking dot. And if it was somehow Talon and he was still alive, shouldn't the dot be moving?

Confirming the tracer chip was properly installed, Wilder tapped the tracer display, causing it to power back up. He pointed in the general direction of the quadrant and within seconds, the blinking dot returned. He felt a small tinge of relief, believing that the tracer had learned to locate Talon's

NAC. He further suspected the blinking was a result of the tracer struggling to stay locked onto a NAC that was fighting to disengage.

The comfort Wilder was trying to attain remained out of reach because the blinking red dot refused to move. Jonathan had embedded an overlay of the Center into the tracer program. The dot was positioned inside what was clearly a building—he just didn't know which one. The display was supposed to have a navigation guide for the complex, which would undoubtedly have labeled each building. He was pretty sure he needed to activate it, but blanked on that part of the training. Out of desperation, he flipped through every screen. Nothing. Maybe voice commands?

"Tracer, activate navigation guide," he whispered. The screen was instantly populated with words and colored zones that brought clarity to Talon's position. This was both exciting and sobering: his brother's life hung in the balance, and Wilder was one screw-up from tipping things into the abyss. He examined the display, trying to regain his composure.

Damn it! If only that blinking dot would *move*.

Chapter Eighty-Five

Talon

August 14 – 1:45 p.m.

The metal grate that made up the underside of the mezzanine blinked in and out of view as Talon lay on his back, struggling to regain consciousness.

Gas ... pure retaliation for what his supervisor deemed as disrespectful behavior.

Talon took his time sizing up his situation. He felt the back of his head, where he had a sizable knot. No bleeding, though. His vision was clearing ... he could now fully see the mezzanine above, where the servers were situated. He raised himself to a sitting position and, surprisingly, didn't throw up. His stomach felt only slightly queasy. Craning his neck this way and that to see how the rest of the group was fairing, it appeared that almost everyone was moving about.

Spotting Espar getting to her feet two stations over, he stood and wobbled over to her. "Hey, are you OK?"

"Gassed, right? Yeah, surprisingly, I'm doing good. How long were we out?"

Eyeing her station's display, he was surprised to see the shift wasn't even over yet. "Looks like only fifteen minutes. Strange ... we should have been out for at least thirty."

"We didn't get a full dose; I think I know why," Henrick said as he came walking up. "You both alright?"

"Yes, why do you think we were spared?" Espar asked.

"When they walled off this area for the tracer production, I don't think they took the time to separate the gas delivery piping. Just by luck, I bet we have fewer delivery points over here."

"But that means the main production facility was gassed as well," Talon pointed out, suddenly feeling extremely guilty.

Even though he hadn't tried to mess with his boss, he reminded himself he had been the trigger.

He felt compelled to confess, but he had no way of explaining what had happened. Did he imagine the letters? He wasn't sure what to think, acknowledging that strange visions normally weren't a good thing. Yet, he didn't feel mentally off, and he was pretty sure he had actually taken over his boss's avatar, but really? How?

"Are you sure you're good?" Henrick asked, waving his hand in Talon's face. Then turning to Espar, he said, "Keep an eye on him. I'm going to check on the rest of the gang."

The second he walked off, Espar nudged Talon's shoulder. "What's going on in that thick skull of yours? Did this have something to do with you? Maybe more of the strange shit from the other day?"

"Maybe. Maybe worse," Talon replied. "Let's go check on everyone in production."

Espar nodded and began walking toward the exit.

"No. Let's try the other door," Talon called to her, pointing to the door behind them, situated in the wall that divided the tracer production from the main manufacturing floor.

"Really? It's locked from this side. Are you going to try some of your magic on it?"

Talon didn't know what to say. He hoped he would be able to do more than unlock the door. With some trepidation, he admitted to himself that he hoped the messages would reappear. "Sure, let's try some magic."

He led the way between the stations until they came to the corridor skirting along the back wall. He found himself stopping, looking for words to invade his vision, until Espar pushed him in the back.

"Don't be afraid. Let's go try your shit out."

Talon began walking slowly, still looking for words where none should be, while trying not to look like an idiot or a coward. When he reached the door, he stopped again. Nothing. He was growing more worried he had imagined everything.

"Go on. Do your thing," Espar encouraged.

He reached out hesitantly, then gave the door a push. It sprang open.

"So live! That's stuff I ain't ever seen before!" Espar called out behind him.

Her infectious excitement was cut short as the devastating scene beyond came into focus. Bodies were everywhere, littered across the concrete floors. Talon wished it were merely a scene in an apocalyptic movie, but these were people Talon and Espar knew.

"They got the full dose," Espar whispered, as if afraid of waking them.

Talon ran to the nearest person, a co-worker sprawled on the floor. "Could we hurt her if we try to wake her?"

Espar hovered over the body with her ear close to the woman's face. "She's breathing. Let's check a few more to confirm they're alive, but let's not wake them. No telling how long until the chemicals run their course."

They spent the next few minutes rushing from body to body, checking their breathing, until people began moaning and stirring to life. Talon and Espar did their best to assist those who were recovering, making sure their co-workers hadn't bumped their heads or suffered serious injury. No one asked how Talon and Espar had come to be there, too disoriented to think much about what was going on around them and driven solely by the need to get fresh air.

Making their way through the Transition Room, Espar tugged on Talon's arm. "Let me go out first to check if big and ugly is out there."

"Oh, right," Talon answered, somewhat embarrassed that a girl had to make sure he was safe. He chided himself for being embarrassed as she opened the door and poked her head out. Espar would be safe—Letcher had no interest in roughing her up.

"All clear. Let me bring the first people out before you make an appearance. We should let our crowd recover; they'll provide some protection."

"Espar, no, thank you though." Foolish or not, Talon had his limits. He didn't want to hide behind others forever. "What I'd really appreciate is if you could help these people get back on their feet while I check a few things out."

"Talon, really?" She knew he meant to probe some of the security measures. "It's bad enough that Letcher's out there, but what if security catches you?"

He opened the door and assisted one of his co-workers into the yard. Espar followed right behind, providing her arm to another. Neither co-worker seemed to pay attention to the conversation, so eager were they to get outside; they barely made it out before they began retching. This was going to be rough.

"I've got to go," Talon said, grimacing over the task he left her with.

"You owe me. Grab some food and water before you head off."

"Gotcha," he said, wondering when Espar had become such a good friend.

Chapter Eighty-Six

Talon

August 14 - 7:17 p.m.

Talon had spent hours wandering in and out of residence halls and their perimeter fencing. With every hall he accessed and gate he opened, he grew more frustrated and increasingly concerned he had been delusional earlier. His meandering even brought him back to his original place of residence, where he expected to have the warden's face pop up on the display, warning him of dire consequences should he go further. Nothing. And no words traced across his field of vision.

Desperate, he returned to his nemesis, the gate leading to the main entrance corridor. He began preparing himself for the nervous breakdown that inevitably came with approaching the spike-launching monstrosity, when he sighted Blunt rounding the far corner of the nearest building. The guy strolled toward Talon as if he didn't have a care in the world.

"Looking to kill yourself again?" Blunt called out.

"I try not to think about that possibility," Talon replied, walking over to meet him.

"Are you ready to tell me what's going on?"

Talon was and he wasn't. He certainly wasn't going to tell Blunt that he was trying to get secret messages to appear before his eyes. They headed down the back wall, rounded the corner between two buildings, and settled against the chain-link fence next to one of the gates. The shade stretched to within a mere couple of feet of them. Talon realized Blunt had positioned them so they could easily spot Letcher coming at them from either side, as well as catch any breeze amplified by the natural tunnel created by the adjacent buildings.

"You know, I could do one better," Talon started. "I could get us through that gate and back into that shade. We could be out of the sun and well out of Letcher's reach."

Blunt chuckled. "That would make you the most popular person in this joint."

So be it. Talon got up and walked over to the gate.

Blunt sprang to his feet. "Whoa! Wait, kid! You serious?"

"Absolutely."

"So, this gate's broken?"

"No," Talon said as he made to turn the latch.

"Wait! Wait! Let's sit back down here," Blunt growled. "If you're going to go through that gate, broken or otherwise, it's not going to be in broad daylight."

Talon didn't bother telling him he had spent the last few hours doing just that, certain anyone not too sick to stand would be working the second shift. Even Letcher. Instead, he sat down next to Blunt and filled him on the last few days, only leaving out the messages floating around in his head.

Blunt, to his credit, half believed him. Whether it all mattered that much to him was hard to tell. Everything about Blunt was hard to tell.

"Let me ask you this," Blunt said. "Can you get me to the warden's office?"

Talon thought about the ominous, impenetrable gate. "No."

"How about the perimeter gates? Do you think you could open them?"

"No. Well, not so far," Talon said, not wanting to disappoint Blunt.

"Hmmm. So, you're limited to halls and the surrounding fences?"

"Yeah," Talon said, completely deflated. He knew Blunt would love to see the doors to this place opened wide and everyone able to escape. Even if only Talon could make it out,

Blunt would be an extremely happy man. Any person making it out would provide hope for all the rest.

"Well, kid, there might be more to it than we think," Blunt said graciously. He went on to tell him to keep a low profile. Then he suggested Talon use his newfound abilities to sleep inside one of the gated areas. This didn't sound like something someone did while keeping a low profile, but he figured Blunt wanted to see him in action.

He set out for the residence hall all the way across the yard. He was done with the main gate. Besides, Blunt had pointed out that fleeing through the front entrance would not end well, considering most of the traffic funneled through there. It was dark when they reached the residence. A quick look around confirmed no one was out and about. Locating the entry for the fenced area, they stopped before it.

"You know," Talon said, "I'm pretty sure my NAC shields my presence, but I have no idea if it'll shield yours."

"Good point," Blunt acknowledged and stepped back.

"That wasn't my point. I think we should see if your presence sets off an alarm."

Blunt looked at Talon, then at the gate. "Let's try that one tomorrow, kid."

Talon suppressed a smirk. He was pretty sure Blunt doubted his chip could do much of anything, much less mask either of their identities. Playing into Blunt's fears, he pushed on the gate, not bothering to turn the latch. Doing his best to look confused, he pushed on the gate harder, with no results. Scratching his head, he glanced at Blunt. Blunt stepped in closer, confident Talon had overstated his talents. Talon took that moment to turn the latch.

"Oh! This might work."

With a dramatic shove, the gate swung open, spurring a startled Blunt to jump back. Talon stepped through the gate and shut it quickly, laughing as he went. Blunt, realizing he'd been taken, came after Talon, only to have it sink in that he couldn't reach him.

"Clever, kid," Blunt said with a grin. "You'll be safe from Letcher there. We'll talk tomorrow," he said, receding into the dark. "After I exact my revenge."

Talon was pretty sure he was joking. With a sinking feeling, he reminded himself that he never knew with Blunt.

He wandered over to the shadowed walls, where he planned to rest for a few hours. He would give Blunt and everyone else in the compound time to settle in, not forgetting for a second that this was going be his last night in the place.

Chapter Eighty-Seven

Rani

August 14 - 10:08 p.m.

Night had settled in, and Rani felt like a criminal as she pulled into the parking lot. Well, wasn't she? She had come so far from what she thought it meant to serve her community.

She parked her car at the far end of the lot, where the lights failed to reach. While she waited in the dark, she reminded herself that it wasn't too late to simply drive away. And Talon would probably end up dead. She felt some relief at the thought she could still be saved from herself if no one liked her plan, but, again, Talon would be as good as dead.

This debate raged on while she waited, suddenly wondering if she was being stood up. That would be odd, but possible. This shady meetup probably wasn't fully appreciated by her intended contact, who was already under surveillance.

A rap on the passenger window startled her. A bit unnerved, she released the gull-wing door, and out of the shadows, a body slipped into the seat across from her.

"Why the Mini?" Sofia asked.

"This is far from police business."

"Then how'd you get in here at this hour?"

She sheepishly flashed Sofia her badge. "I strong-armed my way in. Hey, I'm not saying I'm experienced with this spy shit."

"Ok, so what is this 'shit' you're talking about?"

"Do you think you were followed? I can't lock down our conversation."

"No. That's why I was late." Sofia added nothing, making it clear it was time for Rani to spill.

"Alright. Fine. Be patient with me. I've got an idea, just not sure it's a good one."

"Take your time. You certainly know how to pique my interest."

"Wait. Before I completely ruin my career, tell me about Wilder. You pretty much lost it when you found out he was Shadow."

"And that Wilder was alive! Incredible! Short story, he was sent down south after Talon. But now the security goons from this place are on his tail. Worse, he has no idea they're coming."

Sofia proceeded to fill in the rest of the details, and Rani ran through a list of ways to contact Wilder before admitting to herself that he was about to be blindsided. Her plan was no longer feeling completely inappropriate; rather, merely law breaking with the simple twist of exploiting a minor.

With nothing left to lose, she came clean. "Look, I want to kidnap you. Or break you out. Whatever you want to call it."

A huge smile came over Sofia's face. "It's about time!"

"Excuse me?"

"Absolutely! You're my hero! I was prepared to beg you to sneak me out of here so that I can go after my father!"

"Jeez, now I'm scared. I was going to ask you to find your father and talk some sense into him. Now I'm wondering where to look for the sane voice that's going to talk us down from this shitty plan."

"Don't look to me for sanity," Sofia giggled. "When do we leave?"

"Not now! I expected it to take some time to talk you into this. Besides, I can't get you out in this vehicle. There's no locking it down."

"You really aren't very good at this," Sofia said. "I can get out undetected. The problem is I would be betraying a couple of people who truly believe in me." Sofia seemed to reflect on that thought before adding, "Sadly, I have no idea why they do."

Chapter Eighty-Eight

The Warden

August 14 - 10:24 p.m.

The live feeds from cameras throughout the facility were amassed on a giant display that bisected the warden's office. The images were currently arranged in a four-by-eight matrix, with four stacked from the floor to the twelve-foot ceiling, while eight side-by-side feeds spanned thirty feet from wall to wall. The warden reviewed the images, which were gathered from the manufacturing floor, the administration hallways, and the front gate, among other areas of interest.

No feeds from the yard streamed on his display. The warden smirked, knowing no recording devices of any kind were allowed out there. The yard was his wild west, and he had no interest in the public ever catching a glimpse of the banished and their outdoor living conditions. Nor did he want the world to see how his worst employee issues were resolved.

Other than the main gate, the warden was also adamant about keeping all electronic eyes off the perimeter gates and the passageways behind them. Who and what was ferried in and out of his complex was his business. He didn't want to give his employees any means to blackmail him. If anything, that was his department.

Truth be told, if he was going to be candid with himself, he had very little interest in any of the images that were now flashing across his display. In fact, the display just made his office feel smaller and less grand.

The warden only tolerated the images as a means of separating himself from what waited on the other side. He dreaded having to deal with what waited, but deal with it he must. Accepting the reality, he looked down at the console before him.

He loved his console. He was an old-fashioned guy. The console was designed with dials and buttons that allowed him to operate the giant display and manipulate critical safety features around the complex, including the gas plumbed to every structure. Not only could he release chemicals into the manufacturing facility, he could also release gas throughout his entire administration building if he wanted to.

At the moment, though, he wasn't planning to knock anyone out. Instead, he was hunting for that one little button that would discontinue the feeds to his display. He reluctantly admitted to himself that he probably had too many buttons and knobs, making his search near impossible. Following a few more unfruitful seconds, he decided to rely on voice control.

"Clear display," he called out in surrender. Instantly, the feeds stopped and the display became virtually transparent, as if it were a glass pane. In this case, the inch-thick glass pane was practically indestructible, which was important, considering he was barely able to stop himself from flinching when the display cleared, revealing the very perturbed-looking man standing there.

"Welcome, Mr. Mercer. I apologize for dragging you in here at this late hour," he said, knowing he deliberately waited until after 10 p.m. to have this meeting, ensuring all prying eyes had long cleared out of the building.

"Nice big empty space here, Mr. Warden," Letcher growled, spreading out his arms to emphasize his point. "Since you must get a thrill from making others wait, maybe you could make an effort to fit a single chair in here."

Sizing up the gruesome being standing before him, he thought better of making Letcher mad. The tattoos scrawled across his body and face looked like two snakes crawling up his arms, with their heads trying to emerge from just below his eye sockets. More hideous were the many piercings arcing across his forehead and traveling down his nose. They formed some kind of ... The warden gave up. He was not that creative.

If this all wasn't bad enough, he couldn't help noticing that either Letcher had developed a rash or his piercings were inflamed, no doubt a result of his complete disregard for hygiene. The deranged, shaggy guy standing in front of him wasn't one to piss off, despite the protective barrier between them. "I don't often entertain visitors in my office," the warden said, doing his best to respond without emotion. "Don't worry, you won't be here long," he couldn't help but add, wondering if his disdain would go unnoticed.

Letcher took a step closer to the glass, leering down at the warden.

The warden decided a chair would be a nice touch after all. "You do know I could gas you, right?"

Letcher allowed a crooked grin to belie his usual demeanor, acknowledging what they both knew—the warden was frightened. "What do you want with me, Mr. Warden?" Letcher drawled, losing interest in this game.

"Good. Let's get right to it." He clasped his hands together to stop them from shaking. "In two days a very important meeting is going to be held. I won't waste your time with the details. The bottom line is that Talon will be taken away from us at that meeting. He'll be gone for good. Your chance to say goodbye to him will be lost forever."

"Not going to lie, Mr. Warden. That wouldn't sit with me."

"It's not my decision. Alas. He's to be turned over shortly after 1 p.m. on Thursday. If you're going to say your goodbyes, I strongly recommend you do so soon."

"Maybe you could tell me where to find him?"

The warden didn't know. He only knew Talon had not shown up for the second shift, meaning he was somewhere in the yard. "Look outdoors, and be careful not to let him flee inside. He can breach secured doors."

"Thought so. But why's he still here?"

"Ahhh. That hurts. Don't you all want to stay?" the warden asked. Then dropping the pretense, he added, "Gates are different. No one gets through the gates without being on a very select list. Trust me, he's not on it."

"You sure?" Letcher asked, smooshing his face up against the glass separating them.

A few seconds passed before the warden realized his mouth was open and he hadn't said a word. "Of course, I'm sure!" he blurted out.

Letcher smiled before slowly running his tongue up and down the barrier. "If you say so," he said and walked out.

The warden released his hands and stretched them in front of him. They were trembling worse than before. He bowed his head until his forehead touched the desk, closed his eyes, and tried to convince himself that he had nothing to fear. Not Letcher. Not the general. And not being stung out.

It was no use; his fears only grew. He wished he knew more about how the Program worked. Had he crossed the line? He told himself he would be quite happy if Talon merely ended up maimed. He didn't need Talon to be killed. Nor had he asked anyone to kill him. That should be enough, right? He hated not knowing. He absolutely did not want his life tied to Talon's right now.

Chapter Eighty-Nine

Talon

August 14 – 11:13 p.m.

Talon had enough sense to heed Blunt's warning. He was done with the main gate, but he wasn't done with getting out. He sensed it was a matter of hours before Letcher caught up with him or the warden unleashed an even more devastating plan to eradicate him. With the walls closing in, it was growing difficult to breathe. His time to live or die was right now.

He set out toward the nearby perimeter wall, which he planned to follow to the seldom-used secondary quadrant gate and begin his journey to freedom. As he made his way, he worried over making the messages reappear before his eyes. Surely this was the key to assuming an identity, perhaps his supervisor's, and gaining access through the gate. Once through, he merely had to traverse a short distance to the exterior gate, where he would perform his magic one more time.

A darkness cast by the twenty-foot-high perimeter wall brought him to a stop. Peering into the unlit passage before him, Talon watched a shadow morph from the wall, forming into something evil and advanced toward him. Talon shot back the way he had come. He knew he might be a bit uncoordinated, but he had never been slow. He sprinted around the corner of the residence hall, not daring to look back. Nor did he need to as the footfalls behind him kept pace. Evidently, Letcher was fast like his brother!

As they sped past the building, the beast not slowing, tendrils of panic writhed inside Talon, his lungs desperate for air. A roar gave him a jolt of adrenaline, sending him scampering past another building and taking a second left.

Halfway to the perimeter wall, he chanced a glance back to see Letcher just rounding the corner into view. Good. He had gained some much-needed separation.

Talon slowed as he turned down the corridor leading to the corner gate, sizing up what lay ahead. He had an idea how to get out and he was taking the exit now. If he was wrong, he was dead.

Knowing death also ran behind him and afraid to chance another peek, he picked up his pace as he approached the gate and its lethal spikes, all the while praying words would reappear before his eyes. At thirty feet out, nothing penetrated his field of vision. At twenty feet, his anxiety surged. He was alarmed as he rocketed past fifteen. At ten, he dove to the ground, screaming. "Assume supervisor's identity!" A loud click rang out and he flattened himself to the ground, looking to minimize the impact of the spikes.

The anticipation of being impaled was interrupted by the sound of something moving across the hard-packed earth. He opened his eyes to the gate rolling open, exposing the corridor beyond. Emboldened, he looked back to see Letcher standing a mere twenty yards away, mouth agape.

Keeping eye contact with Letcher, Talon rose slowly to his feet as if not to awaken the big man from his stupor, but Letcher blinked hard, visibly resetting his brain, and launched himself in Talon's direction. Talon sprang through the opening and dashed for the exterior gate. Realizing he had no time to make it out, he reversed direction and scrambled to make his way back past the open gate, only for Letcher to fly through, delivering a glancing blow to Talon's hip.

The impact was enough to send him tumbling to the ground, but he had the wits to roll to his feet, while Letcher's momentum carried him past. Talon sprinted toward the heart of the facility, with no plan other than to stay one step ahead of the destructive force raging behind him.

Chapter Ninety

Wilder

August 14 – 11:17 p.m.

Wrapped in his mummy sleeping bag, with only his head sticking out, Wilder was ready to call it a night. The desert air had turned surprisingly cold, the ground was hard, and the day had been long. It had been a productive day, though. Talon was alive and possibly uncovering abilities that could very well save his life. Wilder was feeling pretty good about himself as well. He had the tracer down. He even succeeded in configuring it so it beeped when Talon moved, which allowed him to point the tracer in the general direction of the complex and let it do all the work. Tracking Talon had grown a lot easier over the course of just one day.

With Talon having apparently settled in for the night, Wilder had positioned himself over a quarter of a mile back from the complex, the farthest he could imagine from the main gate traffic and well beyond the motorcycle patrols. He was out of tracking range for Talon, but would move back in range well before the sun rose.

It had truly been a full day, but sleep came slowly. He couldn't help worrying over how the next few days or even tomorrow would play out. Was he going to need to extract Talon? Could he? Or would Talon be able to get out on his own? So many questions were running through his head that he had to fight his way to sleep, which is why when his bedside alarm went off, he didn't bother to snooze it. He just slept on. It wasn't until something deep in his dreams recalled he was far from any bed that he fought his way awake. He recognized the beeping for what it was and groggily wondered what Talon could be up to now. And how could he be in range?

He scooted over to get a look at the tracer's display, still refusing to give up the comfort of the sleeping bag. He strained to focus his sleepy eyes on the blinking dot and its environment. When everything finally came into view, Wilder couldn't dislodge himself from his bag fast enough. Getting to his feet, then regaining his senses and squatting, he grabbed the tracer to look closely at the screen to make sure he was not mistaken. His mouth dropped open as he watched Talon make his way down the corridor toward the back gate. Coming his way!

While he rifled through his backpack to find his night-vision glasses, a list of questions took form in his head. Would Talon try to go out through the gate? Or would he notice there was a pedestrian door? Was he aware of the pressure-sensitive mat? How much did he know about the guards in the towers or those on patrol?

Wilder had a bad feeling as Talon advanced toward the exit. He was willing to bet anything Talon had no script, that he was flying blind.

Sheer dread got him on his feet and running toward the back exit. He ran bent over as he put his glasses in place. Then, realizing he was still a quarter-mile away, he abandoned all attempts at stealth and prayed the darkness would cover his near full-out sprint.

Chapter Ninety-One

Talon

August 14 – 11:21 p.m.

Talon struggled to do more than walk as he eyed his approach to the back gate. He guessed he had run nearly two miles, a feat that had once been an effortless endeavor, but the labor camp had taken its toll, making eating, sleeping, moving, and pretty much every aspect of everyday life a challenge. Running was now a big deal.

No more than a dozen yards from the gate, he stopped and looked back from where he'd come. Letcher was nowhere in sight. Talon had lost sight of him when he took the turn at the intersection of the two main corridors and headed toward the back gate.

This sparked a moment of hope that the chase was over, only to have Letcher round into sight. Christ, the guy was too evil to stop!

Turning back to the exit before him, Talon noticed the pedestrian door several feet off to the right. The metal door looked substantial with holes that did nothing to mask the death waiting behind them. Nevertheless, it appeared to be the lesser of evils. Exiting through the smaller doorway would hopefully draw less attention.

The problem was grasping what less attention bought him. He had no idea what lay beyond. Were there guards, dogs, weaponized drones? He peered back down the corridor to find Letcher had broken into a trot, possibly believing his prey was trapped.

Time to find out. Talon stepped forward with more confidence, quickly approaching within eight feet of the door. Not able to resist his inner nerd, he pressed forward the thought, "Assume supervisor's identity." With a clank, a mechanical latch was released, and the door sprang outward.

My god! The chip *was* tied to his thoughts!

He wasted no time slipping out the door and closing it behind him, not wanting to know how close the boogeyman had come to reaching him. He pressed himself against the fortress wall, looking out to what lay beyond. He could see virtually nothing. If capture or even dismemberment waited for him, he had no idea what form it would take.

Finding no advantage in keeping the darkness waiting, he used the light of a waxing moon to make out what he hoped was an outcropping and shot off toward it.

The rock formation was much further than he thought, but his burning lungs soon became the least of his worries. The farther he scrambled across the desert floor, the more he became convinced there was a growing herd of demons on his tail. This fear propelled him to the outcropping and around the corner, where he was thrown to the ground. He lashed out with fury. Forgetting all he had learned, he kicked, scratched, and tried to bite his attackers but remained pinned.

"Really, Tal? What do you call this?"

Talon recognized the voice, but struggled to make the connection. Then he began to cry.

The arms that held him pinned to the ground pulled him up and into an embrace.

"I'm sorry, Tal. You have no idea how sorry."

Chapter Ninety-Two

Sofia

August 14 – 11:21 p.m.

Sofia didn't need Jonathan or Dr. Sur to explain that what she was about to do was wrong. They had armed her with the little silver field disrupter to help her shield herself from detection. Jonathan's recent decision to let her keep the disrupter was him doubling down on his trust. He wanted her to know he had complete faith in her, but now she would betray him. She could reason her actions away with his refusal to let her go after her father, instead suggesting a diversion, maybe sneaking Dr. Sur out. Jonathan argued that even if they were unsuccessful, Mr. Hill and his force would come flying back. The general might get distracted as well, not wanting to lose his prized possession.

This wasn't good enough. Sofia needed to turn her father. With him on her side she felt they could stop any threat. He was her dad, after all, but there was no justifying her actions. She had been a terrible team player. Now she would be worse.

She saw no reason to go easy on herself. She also so no reason to turn around. With the world closing in on Talon, she was at least going to neutralize her father. If she could do more to help the cause, she would, but she could do nothing from inside her cage.

Crammed into the back storage compartment of the Mini, she listened to the muffled voices as Rani said her farewells on her way out past the guard shack. A minute or two down the road, Rani pulled over so Sofia could join her.

"Where to?" she asked while climbing in.

"I need to turn in my badge. Then it looks like I'm taking you down south."

Chapter Ninety-Three

Talon

August 15 – 12:16 a.m.

Talon stared at his brother as he laid out his plans. Very little sank in; he was preoccupied with convincing himself this was real. His initial reaction had been an overwhelming sense of joy ... and anger. Their dad died still tormented by the loss of a son. It never should have been that way.

Wilder, to his credit, felt the same. His biggest fear had been the ones he loved would be harmed in a ruthless effort to capture him. This fear had blinded him to the suffering his faked death had inflicted.

Talon made sure he brought clarity to that suffering. He spared no details in conveying their father's relentless hunt for him and their sister's daily struggles to get out of bed. He recounted every tear they shed, throwing in a few of his own. He could only bring himself to stop when he noticed drops cascading down his brother's face.

Now he found himself looking on like a little boy idolizing his hero. He forced himself to tune back in, trying to make sense of his brother's excited pitch.

"Look, I know I'm making it sound easier than it will be, but breaking Sofia out will be nothing compared to your escape. And once you're both free, you can share your stories. From everything I've gathered, there are people at the Center, the Lab, and even UCSC ready to revolt against the Program. They simply need proof the Program isn't invincible. You two can be that proof!

"And before you weigh in," Wilder continued, "I want to be up-front. We'd mostly be doing this for the fugitives. They live in complete fear. They struggle through each day without hope. And while I don't think they put much stock in me, that's OK. We still owe it to them to be human, to recognize their suffering and not walk away. If you help me, Tal, life for them could change."

Everything Wilder said made tremendous sense. It completely resonated with Talon, bringing him to say, "I can't help you."

"You what? You can't help me?"

"Not yet anyway. Everything you said fits with my community. The people in there," Talon said, pointing in the general direction of the Center. "I can't walk away. I'm going back in."

"You can't be serious!" Wilder stood over him as he sat with his back resting against the outcropping.

"I'm sorry. All those people have gone through the same shit I have. Maybe worse. I can't just leave." This conviction left Talon feeling stronger than he could remember. The fatigue that came with his relentless concern for self-preservation lifted. He might fail, but he could live with that.

Still hoping to persuade Talon, Wilder asked, "What about Sofia?"

Talon considered this for a moment. "I think about her all the time. And I may very well be breaking a promise to her. If I don't make it out, let her know she wouldn't have liked the person who would have returned to her, having abandoned these people."

Wilder attempted to control his feelings. "Alright, rather than knocking our heads together, let's take a second to think this through."

"Sure, fire away." He knew Wilder's suggestion was an excuse to interrogate him.

"Do you even have a plan?" Wilder started.

"Nope. None. But I know a guy with a rough plan and a lot of connections. Hopefully I can fit in somewhere."

"Do you know what this guy's plan is?"

"No." He held his palm up to let Wilder know he wasn't finished. "You have to understand I didn't really have a lot to offer until today, but my breakout might change everything. I have to find out."

Talon could tell his explanation wasn't good enough. To Wilder's credit, he was doing his best to hold back his exasperation.

"So, you don't have a plan but you have someone who is working on one and he might share it with you. Right?" Wilder asked rhetorically, not doing such a good job of holding back his exasperation, after all. "You do know that a lot of people in there are looking to end you, including the warden? I'm pretty sure your adversaries never expected you to last this long. This means every day you wake up you can bet there's a new plan in place to make sure that doesn't happen again. You better be damn clear on what you're up against!"

Shaking his head, Talon said, "I can't tell you how many days I've woken up certain I wasn't going to make it. I've just now come to accept that risk. And Wild, if I run, that risk won't go away. I'll be hunted no matter where I go. And that goes for everyone around me. I think you know the feeling, right?"

Wilder looked him over. Finally, he relented. "I do ... fine, but I'll be waiting for you out here."

Talon got up and embraced Wilder. "I know." Almost as an afterthought, he added, "I like the idea of having my big brother watching out for me."

"Good. Be safe. Oh, and did you know there's a pressure mat under the ground that runs along the wall?" Reading his surprise, he added, "No idea, huh? Well, it should have triggered an alarm or maybe just a few floodlights. Any idea why nothing happened?"

"Nope, but I'm learning as I go," Talon said, walking off toward the wall.

Chapter Ninety-Four

Sofia

August 15 – 12:23 a.m.

A dark figure skirted the parking lot, drifting from tree to tree. Its destination was clear, but its intent was not, as the silhouette made its way to the building. Fortunately, the thief, assailant, or whatever this creature might be, had no idea one of the cars in the parking lot was occupied.

Sofia weighed her options as she watched the figure edge closer, reaching the side of the police department building and fading from view. She was tempted to get out and head straight for the entrance. Would the assailant stop her? Perhaps that shouldn't be her biggest worry. Anyone working the late shift would be sure to recognize her, bringing a shit cyclone down on Rani.

Still undecided, she watched the emergence of a hooded torso, only to have it sink back into the darkness. Apparently, the assailant was keeping watch over the entrance. Rani would be making her return any minute now and had no clue what awaited her.

Knowing that the second she opened the gull-wing door, the Mini was going to light up, she threw away all thoughts of stealth. She sprang from the door and headed for the entrance, staying slightly off to the side, away from the assailant and out of sight of the front desk.

She advanced boldly, in plain view of the intruder, until nearing the entrance, where she slipped behind some shrubs. She could barely contain her nervous laughter as she caught sight of a torso peering around the corner, retreating, then peering out again. The assailant had no clue what to make of her. He wasn't deterred, though. Sofia spent the next several minutes watching his hood flicker in and out of sight.

Engrossed in the mystery of the hooded menace, she was surprised when the front door clanged open. She waited for Rani to pass and then scrambled after her, careful not to expose herself to the front desk. Looking across the lot, she saw that the assailant mirroring her movement was also closing in.

"Pssst, Rani! Rani!" she hissed.

Rani's head jerked her way, but to her credit, with eyes wide, she kept walking. Sofia pointed to the now rapidly closing assailant, now a mere thirty feet away. Rani's head swiveled, but she kept walking, just a bit faster.

Before either of them could converge on her, Rani made her way beyond the Mini and into the trees. She stopped a few feet inside the shadows and turned.

"JT, this is Sofia. Sofia, I think you know JT. You two are gonna be the death of me!"

Chapter Ninety-Five

The Warden

August 15 - 11:14 a.m.

The warden stood in the administration quadrant, worrying over his plans one last time. He had been too hands-off with previous attempts to deal with Russit. Letcher's latest excuse was ridiculous—"Talon fled into the desert." Did Letcher think he was stupid? It was a quick exercise to confirm Talon had checked into work this morning. And even the warden was realistic enough to know that no worker would ever voluntarily return to this place.

All this mess would end tomorrow. He walked toward the small adobe guard shack in the corner of the yard. It was positioned to monitor all traffic going in and out of the quadrant's lone gate. As he approached, his security chief stepped out.

"Warden. Should we talk inside where it's cooler?"

The warden could see a guard inside the shack. "No, Chief, we need to discuss a few matters in private. I thought we'd go over exactly how Mr. Russit will be escorted to the board meeting tomorrow."

Gorman's eyebrows raised a little. "Sure, boss. Seems straightforward. What do you want to discuss?"

"Mr. Russit will be the guest of honor at the meeting, and he'll need to be retrieved from his quadrant. So, let's start there."

"Right. We'll be looking to get him shortly after 1 p.m. He'll be working on the tracer production line. We'll gas the facility and one of my men will retrieve him. Nothing special."

"That's where you're wrong," the warden said with satisfaction. He really was a better planner than most. "You can't have him show up to the meeting drugged and vomiting.

Instead, have his super order him outside at the threat of gassing the entire facility. He'll go. Two of your men can escort him from there."

"Yes, sir."

"The two you choose must be trusted to do anything required, including nothing. Do you understand?"

The chief nodded, beginning to understand. "Yes, sir."

"Good. The same goes for whoever is working the shack tomorrow. We need them to follow instructions without questions asked."

"I understand, sir."

"And no one comes in the front gate."

"There's usually no traffic through the front gate at that time anyway."

"I want the front entrance sealed. Can I count on you to make that happen?" he asked, removing any doubt about his intentions.

"Of course, sir," Chief Gorman responded slowly. "It's just ... I don't exactly understand why you're going out of your way to have Russit alert for the meeting if he's never going to make it there."

The warden rolled his eyes, reminding himself that most people struggled to keep up with him. After all, very few could think on his level. "Chief, do we not have every intention of delivering Mr. Russit safely to the meeting? I would certainly hope that if anything went wrong, no one investigating the matter would have reason to believe we had other intentions. Does that make sense to you?"

"It does, sir. I misunderstood your intentions," Chief Gorman replied, playing along.

"That's better. Now, let's talk about what each person will be expected to do so we can be sure that something goes wrong—very wrong."

Chapter Ninety-Six

Sofia

August 15 - 11:33 a.m.

Sofia had to remind herself how thrilled she had been to see JT the night before. She was anything but thrilled now. They had spent the night in Rani's cramped apartment, waiting for the inevitable knock on the door. It was simply a matter of time before the connection was made between Sofia's disappearance and Rani's visit to the Lab. Someone would be dropping by to question Rani. Most likely it would be one of Rani's fellow officers, or *ex*-fellow officers. Regardless, they needed to get on the road.

Instead, they were stuck waiting for Rani's return. She had insisted on updating Sage in person. It was going to be an emotional rollercoaster learning both brothers were alive but in great peril.

She alternated between feeling bad she couldn't sneak out to see Sage and relief she wouldn't be there, especially when Rani shared the latest about her father. That drove home how badly they needed to go. It was late morning and time was running out.

Making matters worse, Rani had been gone for hours and JT had spent most of it trying to convince her to visit the fugitive community with him. He called it a recruiting mission. He wanted her to convey Wilder and Talon's dire situation. He was convinced Sofia could be the difference in rallying the troops. She was convinced it was a waste of time. In the little correspondence she had with Wilder, she had learned the fugitives were reluctant to help, and that was doubly so when it came to the notorious Shadow.

"Wilder is wrong," JT said as if reading her thoughts. "He thinks his neighbors ... his community don't care. They do.

They know Wilder is the first to help anyone in need. And Shadow, he may scare them, but he's their hero. He gives them hope against oppression. If they truly believe he needs help, whether Shadow or Wilder, they'll come running."

"Then tell them," Sofia said. "I know it's been a long time and people often grow up differently than you remember them. I'm not the team player you seem to think I am. Believe me on that one. Your people don't need to hear from someone who would rather go it alone." She was damn certain the biggest threat to Talon was her dad, but she knew she could handle her father. She also intended to warn Wilder before Lab security arrived, but time was running out. "I'm going after my father. I can't go on this wild goose chase with you. I'm sorry if you remember me differently."

"No. You're *exactly* as I remember. You never trusted anyone but yourself. What're the chances of finding your father? Are you going to flag him down outside the Center? You won't even find Wilder. You've got the inside knowledge that will ring true to my people. Instead, you're going to get Rani hurt. You're going to make her pay for trusting you."

Sofia knew the truth when she heard it. It hurt, but she would be a better person another day. Right now, it was about Talon, and she was going to save him. Wilder too.

The door opened and Rani burst through, followed by Sage. Sage gave them both emphatic hugs. "Rani's told me everything. I'm not letting you out of my sight. And we're going to get my brothers!"

"You know it! Let's go!" Sofia said, then added. "Oh! And JT isn't going."

"She's right. I can't." Turning back to her, he said, "I get how they put their trust in you, Sofia. It's just funny you can't put the same trust in others."

Chapter Ninety-Seven

Talon

August 15 - 11:53 p.m.

———————————————————————————

"I'm telling you, I walked right out of this place last night!"

"And yet here you are. It doesn't make sense. Why would you return?"

"You know why, Blunt. To help you guys get everyone out of here!" Talon was losing patience. He was also running out of time. Right now, he was reluctantly following his two companions to the corner of the quadrant where he had made his great escape the night before. They were demanding a repeat performance. "Guys, you've both seen me trespass into secure areas. Blunt, wasn't the gate enough for you?"

"No, kid, we have a lot at risk here. I told you our plans get underway tomorrow. If you want to even be a thought in our plans, then we need to be a hundred-percent certain about you." Blunt picked up the pace. "You should be happy we're taking precious minutes out of our preparations."

Talon sighed. He considered the second man walking in front of him. The idea that his mentor, Henrick, was here was still raw. No one seemed to want to tell him anything unless they had absolutely no choice. How long had he known Henrick? Not once had he brought Talon into his confidence.

"Henrick," Talon called, trying to get him to slow down and listen.

"A little quieter," Henrick reminded him. He pointed up toward the dark sky. "It's night. It's late. All indications are that we are trying not to be noticed." Henrick flashed him a smile, letting him know he was ribbing him.

Talon dashed forward to catch up. "Sorry, it's just that you've seen me breach security as well. You watched me escape Letcher through a locked door. What's left to prove?"

Henrick stopped. They were toward the back of the residence halls. The gate was around the corner. "There's more to this than confirming you can make it out. We need to know if your chip can mask us as well. Have you tested for that?"

"No," he replied in defeat.

"Then, lad, let's be done with this … unless you have something more you want to tell."

Blunt had circled back, catching Henrick's last comments. "Spit it out, kid. Something's not right."

"My brother's out there," Talon said.

"What?" Blunt and Henrick asked at once.

"It's not what you think. I haven't been hiding anything. I didn't even know he was alive until last night. I was on my own, looking to escape, when he used one of our tracers to intercept me …" He trailed off to nothing, realizing the more he revealed, the more unbelievable he sounded. Both quietly studied him, and he felt he had no choice but to continue. "He's out there now, tracking me. By now, he's probably locked on to you two as well." Damn, he needed to end this. "The point is, we're about to put him in danger. He'll expose himself in an effort to intercept us."

Blunt and Henrick looked at each other as if to make sure the other one had heard the same lunatic rantings. Blunt finally put their doubts into words, "Are you sure this is all real? Because I remember being your age. I kind of liked to make things a little grander than they were. I mean, your brother's outside with a tracer?"

"I may be young and dumb … even dumb enough to try to take a swipe or two at you and Letcher, but have you known me to exaggerate?"

Blunt only took a second to respond. "Alright then. We need to go meet him."

"Didn't you listen to me? The part about putting him at risk?"

"We heard you," Blunt said, looking at Henrick. Henrick nodded his silent consent. "We have a little pull of our own. Security won't be watching this gate or anywhere along the wall. You're the only risk we'll be taking. Let's find out what you can do."

Chapter Ninety-Eight

Talon

August 16 - 12:13 a.m.

If anyone had cared to observe, three shadows erupted from the depths of the massive adobe walls and shot across the moonlit sand until they disappeared behind the nearest rock formation. Huffing and puffing, the three sat listening between gasps for any sounds of pursuit. After minutes passed and their lungs returned, Blunt seemed almost giddy.

"No sirens! Nothing. So glad no one was watching. Or listening. We were anything but discreet. Don't know about you two, but I nearly face-planted a time or two."

Henrick was just as excited. "Thought for sure when we hit the mat outside the walls it would be over. Jeez, Talon, you did it! Your NAC worked!"

"That it did, kid!" Blunt agreed, craning his head to take a good look around them. "So, where's your brother? You said he'd intercept us."

"I'm right here." Wilder stepped into view. "Hey, Tal," he said as Talon got up and embraced him.

"Still can't believe you're real. No struggles getting here this time?"

"None. Tracked you to the gate and just knew, here he goes again! I was here long before you even made it out." He turned his attention to the other two, who stood to greet him. Sticking out his hand, he started the introductions. "I'm Wilder."

Henrick and Blunt introduced themselves and exchanged pleasantries. Or at least Henrick made an effort. Blunt returned to his distant, intimidating demeanor. Talon was beginning to understand that Blunt's first instincts were distrust.

Talon was eager to finally learn about the well-guarded plans for the mass rescue. He knew Blunt had been formulating an escape for months, if not years. "So, I think it's time to talk plans and how Wilder and I can help, right?"

Henrick looked at Blunt. Blunt looked back, clearly not eager to take the lead.

"Go ahead," Henrick said.

"Alright," Blunt said, looking back and forth between Wilder and Talon. "We don't know where you fit in. Actually, the old plans were a little rough. We kind of just storm the place. Lots of fighting and chaos. Hopefully, we get control of the warden's office and kind of open all gates. Then we run like hell."

Talon and Wilder stared at Blunt, incredulous. Talon was coming to grips with the fact that Blunt had stopped talking. It wasn't a joke. No hint of humor followed the description.

"That's the plan?" Talon asked.

Henrick cleared his throat, obviously uncomfortable leaving the explanation there. "OK, well, Blunt is being a little short. A lot of thought has been given to this. And, yes, it does rely on a lot of brute force. Our options had always been rather limited." Henrick glanced at Blunt to see if he wanted to add anything, but Blunt merely looked away. "What Blunt doesn't seem to want to admit is that your NAC changes everything."

Wilder and Talon's initial shock gave way to intrigue.

"Why don't you lay out what you want to do," Wilder said. "And we'll see how we can help."

"Alright. So, the big push is to break into the warden's office and buy me some time there. Keeping this short, in a former life, I used to build the control panels the warden used, which are fairly old. When they were designed, someone had the less-than-clever idea of providing secure and non-secure panels. The secure version involved popping in a chip."

Talon couldn't help but ask, "Did anyone really buy the panels without the security feature? And why a chip? That's a lot more work than downloading software."

"It was all marketing. No one expected customers to buy the non-secure versions. The head of marketing schemed to make more money by having all the customers pay for an upgrade. And the reason for the chip was our marketing guru felt people would pay more for an IC than a simple download."

"Seriously?" Wilder couldn't believe it either.

"It was a long time ago. And the marketing guy was fired," Henrick said, bringing that distraction to a close. "The point is, I can remove that chip. Then I can open the gates and disable the gas. Then everyone runs like hell!"

Wilder was nodding as if he could see the plan coming together. "Sounds like you're a little short on plans to get you into the warden's office and getting people safely away once the gates are open. I assume you haven't finalized how to keep security away from your operation either." Wilder's instant transition into planning mode reminded Talon that his brother had a lot of experience with these undertakings.

Blunt had been sizing up Wilder. "You're right. Let's start with getting Henrick into the warden's office. We may have that covered thanks to Talon." He went on to explain there was a 1 p.m. board meeting at which Talon was to be turned over to the general. Blunt assumed the warden would underrate Talon, only having one or two guards escort him. Blunt and Henrick would be waiting in the corridor between quadrants and overtake the guards. The rest would be up to Talon. They figured he could get them access all the way into the warden's office. "Is everyone good with this part of the plan?"

Talon had doubts about strolling through the quadrant and up to the warden's office, but it was Wilder who voiced the concern. "You don't expect to encounter security or other personnel who might sound the alarm?"

"That's the beauty of the warden," said Blunt. "Nonessential personnel will be sent home. He'll only want trusted people in the building, and he doesn't trust many, if anyone. If we have a few people to avoid, we can handle it. There's a guard station that might have a person or two on duty. If so, anyone coming through the gate won't be viewed as a threat, giving us the advantage we need to neutralize them."

"That doesn't sound like much of a security presence. He doesn't worry about anyone breaching the building?" Wilder asked.

"He's quite smug about the cage he's built for his disconnects. In his mind, if we were going to find a way out of our cage, it would have happened a long time ago."

"How about the board members?"

A wicked look came over Blunt's face. "That's where I come in. Henrick will have as much time as he needs in the warden's office."

"Gotcha. And what if security comes rushing to the rescue?" Wilder asked, testing to make sure the plan didn't have any holes.

"We're hoping you might help with security," Henrick said. "Do you think you could keep their attention somehow? We want to be sure they're up on the walls or outside the complex. We can't have anyone prowling around the quadrant and certainly not near the admin building itself. We figure if they're up on the walls, they'll be too slow to respond if the alarm is sounded."

Wilder nodded. "The challenge is to keep their attention, but not have them so concerned that they put the place on lockdown or send an alert up the chain of command, correct?

What do you think if I ride up on my motorbike and then do a lap or two around the complex? Not real close. I'd try to play it like I'm an extreme rider that came across the building and wanted to get a look."

"I like it," Blunt said. "Even if they were suspicious, they probably wouldn't want to be called out for overreacting, especially if you don't come in too close."

Talon figured they had the break-in well in hand. "So, what about the workers? Gates are open. How do we get them out?"

Blunt and Henrick looked at each other. "This is where things get tough," Blunt admitted. "We can't get everyone out. Plus, not everyone's going to want to go. Think about it. Everyone who leaves this place will be a fugitive. Most will be rounded up and sent back here ... or to someplace worse."

Wilder knew well what they were talking about. "Tal, it's not a fun life. Being a fugitive isn't for everyone."

This wasn't what Talon expected or wanted to hear. "What about those who want to take the chance?"

"The second you get me into the warden's office," Henrick said, "you head to the manufacturing facility. Most everyone should be there. Spread the word and try to get everyone enlisted in the cause. Have people reach out to the other quadrants too. We need to be prepared to overpower security by sheer numbers and get access to all the vehicles we can. The main parking is behind the administration quadrant. We should expect to find a couple of transports, maybe thirty-plus Minis and perhaps a dozen trucks and other work vehicles. We need them all. You may have to access each one yourself. Load up as many as you can. Wilder, you might have thoughts on where to go?"

"It won't be easy, but I do, yes."

"Thousands will be left behind!" Talon objected.

"Yes," Blunt agreed, "You got a better idea, kid? Think of it this way, a lot of attention will be brought on this place. It wasn't meant to be a slave camp. You can bet the warden won't be in charge anymore. With this place exposed, it'll get reformed. The disconnects that stay behind will have better lives."

Talon said no more, deciding he needed to give more thought to whether he could do the most good helping those trying to get away or staying behind with the ones who couldn't or wouldn't go.

"Guys. I'm not sure I can get you in the warden's office," Talon said, suddenly realizing he would need the warden's ID.

"We've got that one covered," Blunt replied. "The warden has a nasty habit of keeping his door wide open when he's in the conference room. Lazy bastard must figure he's right down the hall."

"How do you know this?" Wilder asked.

Blunt looked almost embarrassed. "Sorry, guys. Not my secret to tell."

Chapter Ninety-Nine

The Warden

August 16 - 12:59 p.m.

"Mr. Abreo, please feel free to join us at this end of the table," the warden spoke across the conference room. Gabriel hovered at the far end of the table, away from the warden and the other board members.

"I would, but I feel a touch of the flu coming on. No sense in getting everyone sick." Gabriel said, taking a seat near the door.

True, Gabriel was looking pretty run down. The warden decided he liked Gabriel, especially since he seemed to share the same disregard for Talon, but without pushing his own agenda to control him. It dawned on him that he probably could have worked a deal with Gabriel to fix his Talon problem, but no matter, that was already in the works.

The general interrupted his thinking, "Are you ready to begin, Mr. Simmons?"

Why not? If the general was impatient now, wait until Talon didn't show! "Yes, let's get this going." As Chief Gorman went through the motion of calling the meeting to order, the warden decided this was one board meeting he wanted to lengthen. He was going to savor this.

He looked at Stafford. "You called this special board meeting. There's only one agenda item. Why don't you get us started?"

"I appreciate that," the general replied, appearing surprised at how readily the warden was cooperating.

The warden chided himself for being so compliant. No doubt his behavior would be reviewed during the inevitable investigation that would follow.

The general pulled an envelope from his coat pocket and handed it to Chief Gorman. "This is for your records," he said. Then he reached into his briefcase and pulled out a stack of papers. "Like the warden, I can be notoriously old school. So, I also made paper copies for each of you. This is an order from CID, signed by Commissioner Benson, requiring that Mr. Talon Russit be immediately turned over to my custody. All of you are witnesses to this change of custody. Any questions?"

The warden made a show of looking over the document, trying to project concern. He was struggling. Everyone knew this document was coming. What they didn't know was that Russit was not, which left him feeling smug. Still, he did his best to hide his feelings and play out his role. After what he thought was enough time, he looked up from his studious review.

"I agree that this order grants you custody of Mr. Russit. At the same time, for the record, I believe the transfer of custody is unwise. If Mr. Russit is in any way a threat to society, then his uneventful stay here has demonstrated this is the perfect place to neutralize that threat."

The general looked at the warden, bored. "Anything else you want to add to your speech?"

The warden felt his 'speech' was quite good, if not sincere. He thought about glaring at the general for effect but couldn't muster the anger. He was *so* looking forward to seeing the man's expression when he realized that Talon Russit had eluded his grasp. He looked at his chief of security. "Chief Gorman, please arrange to have Mr. Russit detained and escorted to this conference room. Now."

Chapter One Hundred

Talon

August 16 – 1:25 p.m.

Talon was sweating as he crossed the quadrant. His perspiring had nothing to do with the early afternoon sun. He glanced side to side, trying to size up the two guards trailing slightly behind. It was hard to believe that in a minute or two, he would be looking to take them out. He had never done anything like this, and best he could tell, his escorts were at least ten years his senior and outweighed him by more than thirty pounds each.

With no warning, something smacked the back of his left hamstring and he tumbled to the ground, scraping his hands over the sandy gravel. He groaned as he rolled over, looking up to find one of the guards holding up a baton and grinning with malice. "Keep your eyes straight ahead. You make me nervous when you keep looking at me."

"Me, too," the other guard said with a chuckle. Then he lifted his baton and took a good swing at Talon's calf, delivering another jolt of pain. "Get up, boy! And keep moving. You scare us when you look all angry and tough."

Talon scrambled backward and up to his feet. He limped forward as fast as he could, both legs aching like he'd been shocked with a cattle prod. He kept well in front of them and now looked forward to a chance to return the favor, but as they turned onto the corridor leading directly to the gate, his escorts increased their pace and raised their batons. That's when he realized they were herding him straight into the gate, hoping he would thrust himself into the spikes.

With less than thirty yards to go, Talon broke into a trot until he stopped slightly out of range from where he expected to trigger the sensor. He turned as the guards advanced, wanting to be sure they were close enough. The guards approached cautiously. He wasn't sure what they'd been told, but was pretty sure they believed they wouldn't be stung out if he impaled himself, so he waited for them with his hands raised in surrender. "Aren't you going to give me a shove, guys?"

They stopped within a few feet of him. The guard on his left feinted like he was going to push him, and Talon obliged them by taking a step back. The evil that had spread across their faces gave way to shock as the gate began to roll open. Before they could react, Talon sprinted for the opening. There wasn't much room to spare as he shot through the gap. A guard came through not far behind him, only to be clotheslined by Blunt. The second guard caught the action as he came through, and when Henrick stepped forward to take a swing, the guard blocked it with his left forearm and carried through with a right straight to Henrick's temple. Henrick dropped like a sack of potatoes.

When Henrick went down, Talon didn't wait for Blunt. He stepped right in on the guard, prompting the guard to take a roundhouse swing. Talon slipped under the swing and delivered a neat, powerful uppercut to his gut, just as Blunt had taught him. With the guard doubling over, Talon jerked his knee up violently to connect with the guard's nose. He felt the guard's nose crunch as he fell backward in a bloody mess.

Talon turned to see Blunt smirking at him. "I told you training wasn't a waste of time."

Blunt took duct tape from a pocket and went about binding and gagging the guards while Talon checked on Henrick. Henrick already had a goose egg-sized lump on his temple, and he wasn't responding to prodding.

"What do we do?"

Blunt checked him out. "He should be fine, but he's not going to be helpful here on out. Let's keep going."

"You're joking! He's the only one that knows the control panel. We're done without him."

"Get ahold of yourself, kid. We're not finished. We'll figure it out. We've got to."

Talon saw the confidence Blunt possessed and decided he had no choice but to put his faith in them getting it done.

"You ready?" Blunt asked. When Talon nodded, Blunt pointed at the gate across the corridor. "Lead the way."

Talon took one more look at Henrick sprawled out on his back—no way was he coming along. He crossed to the gate and was greeted with the familiar click of the barrier opening.

Blunt whispered a reminder. "We walk steadily, kid—not rushed—to the guard shack as if we're expected there."

Once the gate opened enough for both, they headed out, side by side. Talon concentrated on walking forward and not letting the terror show in his eyes. Halfway to the guard station, the door opened, and an awfully big brute stepped out to meet them. Letcher!

Letcher's crooked grin, breaking through his heavily tattooed face, gave him a demented look. "You two! What could be better?"

Blunt didn't take his eyes off Letcher. "Go!" he told Talon.

Talon didn't feel like running from a fight, so he made to stand his ground.

As Letcher advanced, Blunt spat at Talon, "Kid, stop thinking of yourself! I'll give you a head start, but it's all you now." He shoved Talon back and stepped out to meet Letcher.

Talon stumbled before breaking into a run toward the administration building. As he ran, he tried to picture the map that Henrick had produced, showing where the warden's office was located. Christ, how did it come to this? All Talon could think was that if he were everyone's last chance, then they were screwed.

Chapter One Hundred and One

Wilder

August 16 - 1:30 p.m.

Wilder let the motorcycle drift to a stop. He slowly raised the tracer to his shoulder and aimed it at the corner guard tower. Every movement was careful and deliberate. Resting a quarter of a mile out from the backside of the complex, he wanted to attract attention without posing a threat. It was a fine line. This was his second time around the complex and he hoped to see results. After a few seconds, a dot registered on his display. "Not bad," he muttered to himself, swiveling the tracer until it was aimed at the next nearest tower. "Better!" he exclaimed as the tracer captured two NACs. Both towers were empty when he'd made his first pass. He latched the tracer to the back of the bike and continued his trek across the rocky terrain. He eyed the gate as he passed, making his way to the next couple of towers.

This effort continued until he completed his second lap. Letting the bike come to a rest, well away from the front entrance, he debated whether he should make a third lap. His second lap confirmed he had security's attention since every tower was now occupied. He could only hope he was capturing security's attention without kicking them into a high-alert status. That thought decided it. A third lap might be pushing his luck. He looked at the gate and out past the corners of the front wall. No movement. Good.

His old mentor, Dajani Haris, had no tolerance for complacency, prompting Wilder to shift his focus to the desert behind him. Gazing out on the barren expanse, he reminded himself that a thousand people could be concealed out there. The many rock formations and arroyos offered cover where he'd once thought there was none. He let his eyes sweep back and forth across the empty land, scanning farther and farther out. Then out of the corner of his eye, he caught a flash of light.

He looked straight out and to the right, where he thought he'd seen it. Minutes passed before he made out a cloud of dust rising from the desert floor. He considered the possibility that it was a vehicle moving along the road, then discarded the thought. The road didn't wander out in that direction. In the brief time he took to consider what was out there, he was sure he could now identify two trails heading his way.

He grabbed the tracer and pointed it. Dots appeared on the screen, then disappeared. Whoever was out there was at the edge of the tracer's range and advancing, but with its help, he could make out three distinct people, then four, five, six.

Damn it! Trouble was coming! He stowed the tracer, chiding himself for having forgotten Jonathan's warning.

His first instinct was to flee into the desert, but he immediately put the thought aside. The key was to allow them to close in on him, then run. He had to draw off whoever was approaching and buy his team inside more time.

Chapter One Hundred and Two

The Warden

August 16 – 1:42 p.m.

The charade was grinding on in silence. The warden was no longer savoring every moment. The only conversation was the schoolgirl-type whispering between his two security officers. No bonds had been made between board members, and everyone was tired of staring at their hands or at the blank walls. The general finally broke the silence.

"This is taking more time than I would have expected, Mr. Simmons. I'd appreciate it if you'd check on the delay."

"No need for impatience. Mr. Russit has to be retrieved from the other side of the complex. Give it a few more minutes." It was important that the warden portray absolute confidence that Russit would be arriving soon. He then got the idea of continually glancing down the hallway as if he expected Russit to appear at any second. He continued this pretense, worried about overdoing it, until he actually did catch sight of him! Russit stared into the conference room as he crept along the hallway.

In shock, the warden could only stare back as Russit stopped at his office door.

The other members noticed the warden's astonished look and turned to see what had captured his attention. Russit froze for a second, then disappeared into his office. Seconds passed as the group registered what they had witnessed, then the warden stood, pointing to his office, and yelled at his security officers. "Get him!"

Before they were halfway out of their chairs, the door slammed shut. Gabriel stood in front of it, with a grim expression that told everyone he didn't think the meeting was over.

Chapter One Hundred and Three

Talon

August 16 – 1:46 p.m.

Talon swung the solid metal door shut behind him and raced over to the desk in search of the notorious control panel. Seeing a sizable slot in the desktop, he didn't hesitate to push the large black button embedded next to it.

He was rewarded with metal grinding on metal as the panel rose up through the slot. He counted to eight while waiting for the panel to rise, turn, and lower itself onto the desk. He pushed the notion that he was out of time to the back of his mind.

Jeez! Over a hundred buttons, switches, and knobs sat before him. His eyes sifted through a dozen columns, zeroing in on the one labeled "Gates." Ten switches descended this column, marked with names such as "North Exit," "South Exit, and "Admin Quad." Not seeing one switch to open all gates, he flipped all of them to "open."

"Commands queued," a synthesized voice responded.

This was not what he expected. "Execute commands," Talon demanded.

"Invalid authorization," returned the voice.

"Hell, knew we were screwed," Talon muttered to himself, realizing he could get all the commands he wanted ready to go; he just couldn't execute them. Only the warden could, and that wasn't going to happen.

Then Talon remembered the strange episode with his supervisor. On a hunch, he looked over at the door and called out, "open door."

"Invalid authorization."

"OK, maybe all is not lost," Talon told himself.

Remembering he needed to disable the chemicals, he located the column labeled "Gas." A series of buttons were marked "Quad 1 Mfg.," "Quad 1 Res.," "Security," and so on. His hand hovered over the buttons as he hunted for the shut-off. Then hearing angry voices heading his way, he took a chance and pressed one.

"Command queued," came the reply.

The squabbling drew nearer, stopping before the door.

Talon looked over. The fate of thousands was about to be decided in seconds.

Through all the turmoil, he heard the warden command, "Open door!"

A message flashed before Talon's eyes "GRANT MANAGER ACCESS?"

Knowing he had to take the chance, Talon mouthed to himself, "Yes."

The door immediately slammed open, and a security guard raced through.

"ASSUME MANAGER ID?"

With a bald, muscled man bearing down on him, Talon yelled, "Yes! Execute commands!" while turning just in time to get obliterated.

"Commands executed," he heard through the blows raining down on him.

He was doing his best to cover up when a gunshot rang out, abruptly bringing everything to a stop.

"Get the fuck off him, idiot," a voice growled.

Talon looked up to see a furious general aiming a real gun at Talon's attacker. Who had guns anymore? Would he really fire? As if to answer him, the general addressed the assailant. "You really don't want to test me. Get your ass off my property."

The security guard complied, and the gun tracked the officer all the way to the door, where he joined the dumbstruck warden. The general then shifted his gun to Talon.

"Up!" he commanded. "We're heading out. Move it!"

Chapter One Hundred and Four

General Stafford

August 16 – 2:01 p.m.

The general took stock of all before him. Barren sandy soil extended in all directions, nearly blending with the surrounding adobe walls. The only interruptions were a small storage building in one corner and a guard shack situated before an open gate in the other. He stood with his gun casually pointed at Talon.

Discounting the youngster next to him, the closest threat was the fifteen or so men gathered at the other end of the building. Oddly, they stood in the shade with no apparent urgency to cut him off or approach. The only expression of interest in his prisoner came from a stocky, scar-faced man, who yelled out, "how you doing, kid?"

The general poked his gun in Talon's side and answered for him. "It's hot. He's got a gun trained on him. He's had better days. We were thinking of leaving."

"Please," the man replied, sweeping his hand out toward the gate.

Heading out across the quadrant, they soon found the small group of workers following behind. Then upon reaching halfway, people began streaming out of the gate and into the yard.

The general anticipated this possibility and quickly herded Talon toward the spike-infested wall. The wall would provide a front he wouldn't have to defend.

Standing with his back to the wall and Talon at his side, the general knew better than to panic. He began sifting through the possible means by which he could coerce the crowd into submission. Coming up with no ideal options, he was pleased to see the warden and his two security officers scrambling across the yard.

"General! General! Hold up!" the warden yelled out.

As they drew closer, the crowd pulled back to give them passage, all too happy to have them contained as well. The warden and his entourage stopped several yards away, with the warden poking his head out between the shoulders of his men.

"General, let's not do anything rash. The perimeter is locked down and will only open on my command." Then lowering his voice, he said, "Now, it just so happens, I have a security detail stationed outside the front gate."

After scanning the crowd again, the general rested his eyes back on the warden. "Tell me about this detail."

"They're from the Tech Lab. All loyal to me. Backup in case something went wrong."

"I see," the general said, fully understanding their true purpose. The warden had been planning his own kidnapping. "What are you proposing?"

The warden wasn't ready to move out from behind his men. "I thought we might discuss how to deal with the crowd and then work out some arrangement regarding our boy here."

"I'm open to a plan," the general said. "One of your men?" he added, pointing behind the warden.

The warden turned to see a security guard running their way. Relaxing, he stepped out from behind his officers and strolled toward Talon and the general. "Yes, Stafford. I think we'll shortly have things under control."

The security officer approached the crowd without fear, stopping before the stocky, scar-faced man. "What mess have you dragged us into now?" he asked.

Looking at their matching builds and blond hair, the resemblance was obvious. Brothers!

The general turned his focus to the warden standing next to him. "This obviously shakes my confidence in your security. Do you have anyone coming who's loyal?"

"Of course!" The warden snapped, looking nervously toward the towers.

"Security isn't coming anytime soon," the newcomer said. "I just got back from the wall. They've been knocked out. Gassed. All of 'em."

"It worked," Talon mumbled in disbelief.

The general turned his attention to Talon, aiming a gun at his thigh. "Do you have something you would like to tell us, son?"

Talon didn't see the harm. "I saw the button on the warden's control panel labeled 'Security.' I thought the warden wouldn't possibly think of gassing his own men. But I pushed it anyway. Now we know."

"I guess it's time for a new plan," the general said, grabbing the warden's collar and flinging him backward. The crowd gasped as the warden, eyes wide as the moon, stumbled toward the wall.

Spikes sprang out in response, skewering him, unnaturally suspending his body above the ground like an insect in a bug collection. As his bulging eyes gazed out at them, unseeing, the crowd stared back with morbid curiosity. He was soon fighting for that one last breath, which wouldn't come. Instead, his lifeless head dropped to his chest, and the crowd zeroed in on the general, wondering how long it would be between the warden's last breath and that of his nemesis.

The general gazed back and allowed a smile to spread across his face.

"Now you understand!" he called out, loud enough for the silent masses to hear. "You are faced with no ordinary citizen. I'm a goddam four-star general! A *very special* general." He paused to make sure his captive audience listened closely.

"Here's how this works. I'm taking Mr. Russit out of here. Don't make me make examples of anyone else."

Chapter One Hundred and Five

Talon

August 16 – 2:25 p.m.

An intensifying murmur rose from the crowd. Blunt took a step forward.

"No, Blunt! Stay back! Everyone stay back!" Talon yelled.

Blunt grudgingly conceded and stepped back into the crowd.

"Wise decision," the general said. "Here's what we're going to do ..." He motioned to direct the crowd into the middle of the quadrant, clearing the path to the main gate. "Thank you. As a reward for your cooperation, you will get to witness something quite special. Mr. Russit is about to magically walk us out a locked gate." With that, he guided Talon into the corridor.

A brief reconnaissance of the passageway confirmed no one was in sight. His assailant prodded him with his gun.

"Let's go meet the security detail. Mr. Simmons never knew they liked working for me more than him."

Talon expected the general to lag behind him, especially when they drew near the sickening spikes. Instead, he walked right alongside as if they were taking a stroll. Stopping just short of where the lances might be triggered, he flashed a sinister smile.

"You're going to learn that I know a lot about you. Shall we?" He motioned for Talon to proceed and matched him step for step until they heard a reassuring click.

The gate rolled open, revealing a security force much bigger than Talon had imagined. A good many were standing a mere twenty feet away; countless others hung back amongst hundreds of vehicles. Both men took in the spectacle before them.

"Not what I expected. You?" his captor asked.

Talon couldn't help but let his jaw hang open, as he struggled to grasp who these people were. Definitely not security.

"I'll take that as a no. Unfortunately, I don't think they've had the good fortune of my earlier demonstration. I guess I'll need to educate them as well."

From the crowd, Wilder stepped forward. "Looks like you have a gun."

"Two, actually," the general said, pulling another one from his waistband and pointing it at Wilder.

"Handy," Wilder said casually, making a sweeping motion with his arm to direct attention to the crowd. "Guess how many they have?"

Rifle barrels appeared from windows and over the tops of truck cabs. "That's right," Wilder continued, "hundreds. And the people behind the guns are fugitives. And I'm pretty sure the vast majority are disconnects. I know I am." Wilder now had a pistol aimed at the general's midsection.

"Who are you?" the general asked, clearly trying to size-up this latest turn of events.

"Nobody important," Wilder replied. "You don't know me, and I don't know you. What's important is that you're threatening one of ours and that's not OK. Lucky you, though. Because we don't care about you, we're going to give you a chance to drop your guns and head out."

The general started to speak, but Wilder cut him off. "This isn't a discussion." He raised his voice for all to hear. "Five, four, three ..."

"Wilder!" Talon screamed, ending the countdown.

The general repositioned his gun a mere inch from Talon's temple, making it clear Talon had his attention.

Talon's mind flashed back to the deaths of his father and his friend Robert. Too many had tragically stepped in harm's way for him. Now Wilder was looking to do the same. This time Talon was determined to keep the spotlight trained on himself. "Shoot him!" he yelled, turning his back and starting to walk, knowing he probably wouldn't complete a single step.

Waiting for the "click" and the crash of his skull, Talon heard two thuds. He slowly turned to find raging eyes locked on him and empty hands stretched toward the sky.

Chapter One Hundred and Six

Sofia

August 16 – 2:34 p.m.

The sun beat down, and the few gusts of wind spat sand in their faces, but no one complained. The world had been righted, if only for a moment. Sofia, Talon, Sage, Wilder, Rani, and JT found themselves all in one place. Sage inspected her little brothers, worrying over their lost weight and every bump and bruise. She nearly squeezed them to death just the same.

Sofia snuck in her own hugs and did her best to hide her tears when she took stock of the scars, welts, and other traumas that spoke of the abuse Talon had endured. Her natural reaction was to lash out at the culprits behind this atrocity, but the weaselly warden had already met his righteous death and the arrogant general had been allowed to flee into the desert, where Sofia could only hope Mother Nature judged him harshly. This left her dad.

She caught sight of her father emerging from the facility. He took a few steps toward her group, only to stop when he saw her. She could see he had his share of lumps and lacerations, but that didn't stop Sofia from glaring at him without mercy, daring him to approach.

He hesitated, then averted his eyes as if not seeing her, and slunk away, hugging the wall to avoid the crowds. She was torn as she wanted to run after him, demanding an explanation. Except his decision to flee made it clear her father had no redeeming story to tell. She was left watching his every step until he rounded the corner, out of sight, while Talon grabbed her and held her to stop her from breaking.

Fugitives and Center workers scrambled around, unified in a shared mission to subdue the guards before they recovered.

Others rounded up those workers who wanted to leave. The Russit group had earned a break from the heroics and left the coordination to Blunt, Henrick, and a number of others willing to address the challenges at hand.

Tears were shed during their brief time catching up, heroics too.

JT spoke glowingly of how Sofia lit a fire under the fugitives. The crowd was frothing when she revealed the security goons' cowardly plans to ambush 'Shadow.' It also didn't hurt that Sofia had hinted a large-scale government sweep of the forests was soon to be underway. Everyone was eager to clear out and rescue their hero.

Wilder denied he was anyone's hero, yet still looked rather like a boy whose wish had come true. Sofia wanted none of the credit. She made sure everyone knew she was almost too stupid to listen to JT.

Diverting the attention away from herself, she pointed out the only ones dumber than her were the Lab's security guys. The small force had ridden into the fugitive ranks, expecting the five-hundred strong to scatter. Last Sofia knew, the goons had been tied up and stashed in some crevice.

Through it all, Talon remained relatively quiet, even with everyone clamoring for his story. Rumors of his heroics were already swirling. His fellow mates passed by, shouting out to him and clapping him on the back. Talon was appreciative, but had nothing to add. When pressed about his silence, he explained he had spent almost every day thinking about himself and his survival. The last couple of days had been all about everyone else. He wanted to keep it that way.

The brief reunion ended when Espar ran up, requesting Talon's help. Blunt and his brother needed the back gate unlocked.

The timing couldn't be soon enough because at any moment the lid might be blown off the Center. It would only take one employee showing up for work or a supplier making a delivery to notice something was wrong.

The vehicles were overflowing with people, even though only perhaps a thousand of the roughly eight thousand workers were choosing to flee. The rest weren't ready to lead a life on the run and were prepared to pin their hopes on the next iteration of the Center, believing change was inevitable. She hoped they were right. True, the Center was going to be under the national spotlight and a lot of leaders were going to have to answer for the activities that had gone on there.

Soon, the evacuation was complete and the next phase of the rescue mission was underway. The plan was for the vehicles to scatter across the desert until they came to one of the many networks of backroads that would provide passage to the redwood forests. Some would likely be caught along the way, but most would get through. Promises were made that, upon their return, they would form a united resistance and end the abduction of their neighbors. Vows were even made to rescue those who didn't make it back safely.

Sofia didn't know these people well enough to judge whether the promises exchanged were sincere or simply everyone being caught up in the moment. She suspected Wilder did, though, and from the smile that wouldn't leave his face, Sofia felt a surge of hope.

Chapter One Hundred and Seven

Talon

August 24 – 6:12 p.m.

They ditched their mountain bikes about a thousand feet below, making the trek up to the top of Loma Prieta as the sun was casting its final shadows on the landscape. Wilder had stopped at the edge of the brush, below the rocky terrain leading up to the peak.

"It's been a long day getting here," Talon said. "Do you think we could turn in for the night?"

Wilder ignored Talon's whining. "Stay here. I'm going to look around."

Talon didn't argue. He thought it was almost comical that Wilder felt the need to make sure all was safe before allowing him to go further. Perhaps Wilder didn't want to acknowledge the many hardships he had faced at the Center. He didn't mind, though. It was great to be with Wilder again and back in the Santa Cruz Mountains. He hoped it was a long time before he ever set foot in another desert.

Wilder returned fifteen minutes later. "No one's around. Let's head up."

Talon diligently clambered up the rocks and gravel right behind him. At the top, Wilder held back and waved him forward.

It took very little time to understand why Wilder had brought him here. In the waning light, Talon could make out a chain-link fence about fifty yards away that cordoned off a construction site. He could see a newly poured, large concrete pad. He also saw heavy equipment scattered around the site, including an enormous crane. The crane's purpose was clear. A huge metal structure shaped like a pyramid had been assembled and laid on its side.

Talon returned to Wilder. "I get it. Have you seen any more of these sites?"

"The same construction is underway at the tops of Mount Umunhum and Mount Thayer. I'm guessing they're underway on other peaks as well. My biggest fear is that they're probably being erected across the entire nation."

"I've heard rumors about this, but it's still hard to comprehend it's real! These cell towers, combined with satellites already in place will allow the Program to track people no matter where they are, in the most remote locations, and even in their homes.

"Networked or not, no one will escape detection. If you're networked, the Program will know what you're doing and who you're with every second of the day. If you're not networked, I bet they'll still be able to identify you through your NAC ID, similar to how mine was picked up on the assembly line. Fugitives will be rounded up by the thousands!"

"Pretty ugly picture there, Tal. I agree this is bad shit. Still, you might be underrating the fugitives. My bet is there are quite a few cells like ours throughout the country. We know Blunt has his clan in Colorado. The advantage all of us have is that we're not networked. Well, you are ... somehow—

"Anyway, most of us fugitives aren't bound to the Program. If the Program wants to stir up a hornet's nest or two, they'll send people after our camps, where thousands of armed people aren't afraid to shoot."

"I get it, Wild. There's some hope there. On the other hand, do you have any idea if the general is one of a kind? If not, that's going to be a problem, because I'm fairly certain they have access to better weapons than we do."

Chapter One Hundred and Eight

Sofia

August 27 - 7:05 p.m.

Talon and Sofia sat perched on Eagle Rock, enjoying a late-August evening and each other's company. The outcrop towered over the redwoods, providing a panoramic view of the majestic forest below and the Monterey Bay beyond.

"You know this is illegal, right?" Talon asked.

"Trespassing on deserted government land in the middle of nowhere?"

"Exactly. You're always getting us into trouble," Talon teased.

"Based on the messes you've been getting into, you've graduated from my class," she said, cherishing the banter. They fell into silence, appreciating time together that they no longer took for granted. "I missed this," she said.

"Getting us into trouble?" Talon quipped.

"Not letting it go, are you?" Sofia's voice was still strong, though softer now than when they were in high school. "It's a mystery why you and the rest of our posse went along with my dumb ideas. I was always pursuing my schemes with little regard for the consequences."

"You're serious?" Talon studied her. "You were a little wild, but we were all having fun."

"I was reckless. I'm glad you didn't see me at the Lab when it was no longer fun and games. I put everyone at risk, including your brother. I was full of myself."

"Wow. That must hurt, beating yourself up like that," he said, playfully bumping her shoulder. "Sofia, you're destined to lead. You let others contribute ... most of the time. At least you listen before doing whatever you want," he needled, then looked at her with sincerity. "You'll figure it out. Any posse would be lucky to have you."

"I do wish I could see life through your eyes," she said. With their banter fading, Sofia decided to tackle the discussion they were avoiding. "What are you going to do, Talon? Are you going to make a home in these mountains?"

Talon put his arm around her and pulled her close. "I want to spend some time with Wild and sneak in a visit or two with Sage. I badly want to make long-term plans with the people I care about." He looked at her intensely, causing her to blush. "But Sofia, I've caught the attention of some powerful people. If I stick around, people I care about are going to get hurt."

Sofia's heart raced. "Talon, you'll hurt people worse if you leave. Think of how you felt when you lost Wilder."

"Yes, and now I understand why Wilder did what he thought he had to do." He paused, and Sofia waited for him to find the words to tell her what she did not want to hear. "Blunt wants me to join him and his group. Now that the fugitives have brought down the Center, we need to realize what that means. They never thought to strike back against the Program before, but now they're thinking differently. There's talk of forming a *nationwide* resistance, and Blunt thinks I could help. He's made contact with someone who knows about my chip, and as Blunt says, 'I might not be entirely worthless.' You probably can't tell, but that's high praise, coming from him."

"I'm missing the humor, Talon."

"I know, sorry. But look, the Center ground into me exactly how wrong the Program can be. I *have* to help."

Sofia sat quietly for a while. She felt she knew Talon better than he knew himself. No matter the odds against him, he always moved forward. And if someone knocked him down, he got up. If he had a chance to help people, even in dangerous circumstances, he was going to take the risk, no matter how small the chance of coming out on top. The reality was tough to deal with, but she had known it all along. She was going to lose Talon.

She looked up to see his face close to hers, his eyes trying to read her expressions as he waited for her to share her thoughts. She closed the distance and pressed her lips against his. She took her time, enjoying the sensation, wondering why they hadn't done this before. She pulled back and saw Talon's surprised expression. He clearly didn't see that coming.

"… or I could completely change my mind," he said.

Sofia laughed, though it hurt. He made her so happy and sad all at once. "I knew you were going to go. So, I'm leaving, too. I'm going back to the Lab."

"Are you joking? You just escaped from that place! I'm pretty sure they're not going to go easy on you."

"What will they do? Lock me in the mailroom? I have to make things right with a few people. Things may be difficult for a while, but working from inside might be the best way to do my part against this Program."

Warming up to her idea, Talon said, "at least I'll know where to find you."

Sofia thought Talon could be the biggest idiot at times. "That works for *you*. How will I find *you*, Talon?"

Talon opened his mouth to respond, then wisely closed it.

Sofia contemplated the expanse of land and sea in the distance, trying to accept what lay ahead. She needed to face the truth; the future held no guarantees, and that lack of control was frightening.

Eventually, she turned to Talon. Yes, she was going to lose him, but she wasn't going to give him up. She locked onto his dark green eyes. "Come back to me, Talon."

Talon leaned in for another kiss, whispering, "I promise."

END

Thanks
for Reading

Thank you for procuring and reading this book. We hope you enjoyed it.

Remember *Fifty Shades of Grey*? 'Twas good ol' word of mouth that spread the word for that. It's *you*, the *readers*, that are the lifeblood of publishing. Honest reviews encourage readers to check out and buy books, and sales enable writers to write the stories you read ... Simple!

So, if you did enjoy the story, please consider letting others know, won't you? A brief review—even just a line or two—& rating on your bookseller site and/or on Goodreads can mean so much to authors and independent publishers.

Bookseller site: *scan here*

Goodreads: *scan here*

Author Bio

Happily married for 35 years and watched after by two wonderful children, Cullen Scott (pen name) has a BSME and an MBA from Santa Clara University. His expertise spans biotech, satellites, mainframes, RFID, and fiber optics, and he is a listed inventor for several patents in the field of Radio Frequency Identification. Cullen has been published in numerous technical magazines and journals. The *Deep Sting Series* is his first creative publication. "Along with having fun, I'm looking to test the limits of what future worlds might look like and what readers might believe."

Find out more about Cullen at https://cullenscottbooks.com/

Also Available from
PAPILLON DU PÈRE PUBLISHING

DUSTLANDS

by

Carla Rehse

A near-future environmental thriller

"A quick-witted, timely thriller with
impeccably balanced heart and grit."

– Lilla Glass, author of *The Reel of Rhysia* series

Attention all citizens. Texas is now an independent nation. Remain calm. Jobs will be allotted. Resources will be allocated.

There're worse things than sleeping in a locked cellar ... Some jerk breaking down the door, determined to do unholy things to my sisters and me; burying said jerk after I blow a hole through him. So, yeah, there're worse things.

Forty years after a mega-drought has wrought devastation, the USA is divided between the drought-plagued west and the flooded east. With jobs in Texas scarcer than a dust-free day, nineteen-year-old Analee Cooper struggles to keep her younger sisters alive through her less-than-petty thieving, until a right-wing militia takeover of Texas separates her from them. But hope is at hand when Analee is plucked to work with CLIMA-INNOVA, a shadowy organization that needs her survival and thieving skills for a last shot at attaining plans and equipment that might yet save some of the US. Still, stealing back into Texas, acquiring the crucial items, and getting her sisters out won't be easy. With Texas on lockdown and under martial control, Analee's testing times are just beginning ...

Carla Rehse's novel explores loyalty and ties against a backdrop of global warming and drought. "Especially with all the wildfires igniting in so many countries, I wanted to create something environmentally relevant, to make people think about where the planet is headed," Carla says. "But this is still a story about people: about family, love, what brings us together—about the lengths we'll go to protect those we love. And I get to ask to the question, how many bad things can you do before you're no longer good?"

**Citizens, remain calm ... Texas is now an independent nation ...
Jobs will be allotted ... Resources will be allocated ...**

Grab a sample / grab a copy in **paperback** and **e-book**

books2read.com/Dustlands

or *scan here*

Cover design

Papillon du Père Publishing

www.papillon-du-pere.com

@PapillonPere

Copyediting

Jay Allchin

@ the Editing-Store.com

www.editing-store.com

www.ingramcontent.com/pod-product-compliance
Lightning Source LLC
Chambersburg PA
CBHW050957180726
48291CB00006B/1860